THE BETTE
OF REGINAL

BY THE SAME AUTHOR:

THE ITINERANT LODGER

OSTRICH COUNTRY

A PIECE OF THE SKY IS MISSING

THE DEATH OF REGINALD PERRIN

THE RETURN OF REGINALD PERRIN

THE BETTER WORLD
OF REGINALD PERRIN

by

DAVID NOBBS

LONDON
VICTOR GOLLANCZ LTD
1978

First published October 1978
Second impression December 1978

ISBN 0 575 02540 9

To my mother

Printed in Great Britain by
West Central Printing Co. Ltd, Haverhill, Suffolk

CONTENTS

I

The Plan

HE AWOKE SUDDENLY, and for a few moments he didn't know who he was.

Then he remembered.

He was Reginald Iolanthe Perrin and he was fifty years of age.

Beside him his lovely wife Elizabeth was sleeping peacefully.

It took him a few moments longer to realise *where* he was.

He was in room number two at the George Hotel in Netherton St Ambrose in the county of Dorset. The pale light of a late October morning was filtering through the bright yellow patterned curtains on to the bright green patterned wallpaper and the bright red patterned carpet.

On a small round table by the window stood the wherewithal for making tea and coffee.

Soon hotels would expect you to print your own morning newspaper.

He closed his eyes, but the decor faded only slowly.

Suddenly he sat bolt upright. He wasn't Reginald Iolanthe Perrin at all. He was Arthur Isambard Gossamer, and it was the lovely Jennifer Gossamer who was sleeping so peacefully beside him.

It was still late in the month of October, and he was still fifty years of age.

Three days ago they had left their old clothes on the pebbles of Chesil Bank and set off in disguise towards a new life.

Wait a minute. He was Reginald Iolanthe Perrin, former senior sales executive at Sunshine Desserts. He had caught the eight-sixteen every weekday morning for twenty-five years. He had given the best years of his life to puddings. How had he come to be wandering the world disguised as Arthur Isambard Gossamer?

7

Perhaps it was all a dream.

Perhaps he was a dream.

He stepped out of bed carefully, not wishing to wake his wife, whether she was called Elizabeth or Jennifer, whether she was part of a dream or not. He tiptoed across the room, and drew back the curtains gently. There was nothing there. Just a white wall of absolute blankness.

'Oh my God,' he said.

'What is it?' said his wife sleepily.

'There's nothing. There's nothing outside the window at all.'

'It's fog, you fool. They forecast it.'

A double-decker bus edged slowly past the hotel, its outline faintly visible in the thick autumn fog, the passengers wraiths. A wave of relief swept over Reggie.

'We really do exist,' he said.

'We can go where we like and be whoever we like,' said Reggie as they finished their breakfast alone in the autumnal dining room.

'The world is our oyster, as C.J. would say,' said Elizabeth.

'Yes, I'm afraid he probably would,' said Reggie.

He smiled at the memory of his former boss, who had also left his clothes on Chesil Bank and set off for a new life, dressed as a tramp. Reggie wondered how he was faring on this raw October morning.

There was silence save for the hissing of the gas fire and the crunching of toast by middle-aged teeth. There were hunting scenes on their table mats.

'We're free from the grinding wheels of commerce. We're free to shake off the bonds of an acquisitive society,' said Reggie.

'Yes.'

Reggie's coffee spilt over the scarlet coat of the Master of Foxhounds. He rubbed it around the mat, spreading the thin grey liquid over man and hound alike.

He gave a curious half-smile. For a moment he looked like the Mona Lisa's brother.

'Let's go home,' he said. 'Let's become Mr and Mrs Perrin again. We'll sell the house. We'll sell Grot. We'll sell the shops, the prime sites, the juggernauts. Then, when we're rich, we'll really be free to shake off the bonds of an acquisitive society.'

The sun shone out of a cloudless early December sky. The Mediterranean was deep blue. Seven cats lurked, waiting for crumbs.

They were breakfasting on the terrace of their hotel in Crete. They had sold the house in Coleridge Close. They had sold Grot. They had sold the prime sites, the juggernauts. They had set off on a world tour. Even allowing for the depredations of Capital Gains Tax, they were rich.

Below them a ragged olive grove fell stonily towards a tiny private beach. Across the bay, the stern masculine mountains wrapped their secrets firmly to their dark breasts.

The tea came in tea-bags which you made in the cup. The instant coffee came in individual sachets.

The cats waited.

Reggie sighed.

'Happy?' said Elizabeth.

'Wonderfully happy,' said Reggie, tugging at the lid of his individual jar of apricot jam.

'I'm glad,' said Elizabeth.

'I'm glad you're glad,' said Reggie. 'It makes me very happy, darling, to know that you're glad I'm happy.'

'I'm glad,' said Elizabeth.

An old woman dressed in black rode her donkey through the olive grove. Behind her trailed a mangy goat. She did not look at the gleaming white hotel. Nor did the mangy goat.

Reggie removed the tea-bag from his cup and placed the sodden lump in his saucer. It oozed a thick acrid liquid. When he lifted his cup, drops spilt on his fawn holiday trousers and his buff short-sleeved holiday shirt.

'Yes,' he said. 'This is sheer bliss.'

He sighed.

The cats waited.

'If you're so happy, why do you keep sighing?' said Elizabeth.

'Sheer bliss isn't enough,' he said.

*　　*　　*

9

'Did you mean what you said yesterday?' said Elizabeth.

Reggie sipped his beer slowly. They were sitting on the terrace of the tourist pavilion at Phaestos.

'That sheer bliss isn't enough?' he said. 'Oh yes.'

Below them, the fertile Messara Plain stretched to the foot of Mount Dhikti and the Lasithi Range.

They were weary after exploring the remains of the Minoan palaces.

'Is it guilt?' said Elizabeth.

'I expect so,' said Reggie glumly. 'It usually is. Guilt, the curse of the middleclasses.'

Far away, cow bells jingled.

A robin hopped on to a nearby table.

More than fifteen hundred years before Christ, the unique, intricate and artistically joyous civilisation of the Minoans had flourished here. Now, far overhead, a plane laid a thin vapour trail across the clear blue sky, like planes the world over.

'Summers in England, winters in Crete and Gozo, it isn't for me,' said Reggie.

Eighteen French tourists with blue guide books and painful feet invaded the winter peace of the tourist pavilion.

'There must be something that it's absolutely right for me to do next,' said Reggie.

The French tourists sat noisily all about them. They had bought oranges and postcards.

Far above, two vultures waited.

For what?

The French tourists sucked their oranges.

The cow bells tinkled.

A scooter roared briefly, then spluttered into silence.

'It's simply this,' said Reggie. 'I'm just an ordinary bloke, old Goofy Perrin from Ruttingstagg College. I'm no different from anyone else who walked out on his job, faked suicide, started a new life, returned home in disguise and remarried his wife, opened a shop selling goods that were guaranteed useless, to his amazement succeeded, walked out again, faked another suicide and started another new life.'

'But no one else has done that,' said Elizabeth.

10

'Exactly,' said Reggie. 'So there must have been some purpose behind it.'

The bones of ten red mullet were eloquent evidence of their greed. In the wine bottle only a few drips of retsina remained. In the salad bowl, one piece of cucumber floated bravely in the succulent dark-green olive oil of Greece.

Elizabeth smiled at Reggie.

Reggie smiled at Elizabeth.

'This is the life,' said Elizabeth.

'That's just it,' said Reggie. 'It isn't the life at all.'

He clasped Elizabeth's right hand, firmly yet tenderly.

'I want a home again,' he said.

She smiled at him.

'Oh so do I,' she said.

'Then I can start on my plans,' said Reggie.

A spontaneous outbreak of singing began. They smiled and clapped.

When they had entered the restaurant, they had bought twenty plates, to break when the spontaneous singing began. They broke them now. The plates were English. The Cretans found that they broke more easily than other plates, and imported them in bulk.

'There are still some things we British do best,' mouthed Reggie across the hubbub.

Elizabeth grinned.

The singing and dancing and breaking of plates ended as suddenly as they had begun.

'What plans?' said Elizabeth.

'I don't know,' said Reggie.

On their first day back in London Reggie discovered what their plans were.

They were staying in a hotel, tourists in their own town. It was eleven days before Christmas and tawdry angels hung listlessly over the Oxford Street crowds. Elizabeth had gone to buy shoes. It was an afternoon of raw mist and intermittent drizzle, eminently suited to the purchase of footwear.

11

It was three minutes to two when Reggie entered the bank where the fateful revelation was to come to him.

There were queues of equal length at the windows of Mr F. R. Bostock and Miss J. A. Purves. Reggie didn't join the queue of Miss J. A. Purves, who was moderately attractive. Looking at the breasts of bank clerks was a thing of the past, and so he chose the queue of Mr F. R. Bostock, who was moderately unattractive.

Rarely can virtue have been so instantly rewarded. At that very moment Miss J. A. Purves closed her window and set off, did Reggie but know it, to have a late lunch with her friend from the Halifax Building Society, Mr E. D. Renfrew (withdrawals).

A large, florid man moved angrily over from Miss Purves's window and stood in front of Reggie.

The man behind Reggie, a small, leathery man with a spectacularly broken nose, leant forward and prodded the florid man in the back.

The florid man turned and glared at Reggie.

'What's the big idea?' he said.

'It wasn't me,' said Reggie.

'This man was 'ere before you,' said the small, leathery man with the broken nose.

'I have been waiting twenty minutes,' said the florid man, with the careful enunciation that follows a large liquid lunch, 'and I'm in a tearing hurry.'

'Listen mush, that man was before you,' said the broken nose.

'Thank you, but it's quite all right,' said Reggie, turning towards him.

'What did you say?' said the large, florid man slowly.

'I said, "Thank you, but it's quite all right",' said Reggie, whirling round to face him.

'Not you. Him,' said the florid man, pointing dismissively at the leathery man.

'I said, "That man was before you",' said the leathery man.

'Nobody orders me around,' said the florid man.

'What did you say?' said the broken nose.

'It honestly is quite all right,' said Reggie, turning first to

12

one, then the other, smiling desperately. 'I'm in no particular hurry.'

'I said, "Nobody orders me around",' said the florid man. 'So kindly mind your own business.'

The queue shuffled forward towards Mr F. R. Bostock's window, but the argument continued.

'Ah, but it is my business, innit?' said the broken nose. 'This gentleman 'ere 'as waited just as long as what you have, and then, lo and behold, you barge in in front of him, you great fat pig.'

'Please, it's all right,' said Reggie. 'It's raining outside, so why hurry?'

'What did you say?' said the florid man with icy anger.

Reggie swung round to face him.

'I said, "It's raining outside, so why hurry?"' he said.

'Not you. You keep out of this,' said the florid man.

'Next,' said Mr F. R. Bostock, who now had an empty window.

'Thank you for standing up for me,' said Reggie to the broken nose. 'I'm very grateful, but let's forget it.'

'I won't bleeding well forget it,' said the broken nose. 'If you won't stand up for yourself, I will.'

'You called me a fat pig,' said the large, florid man.

'Come on, come on, who's next?' said Mr F. R. Bostock.

'I do not like being called a fat pig and I'll ask you to kindly keep your hideous broken nose out of my business,' said the large man, who was growing steadily more florid.

The small man, who had no comparable chance of growing steadily more leathery, grabbed hold of Reggie and used him as a screen against the florid man.

'Oh, it's aspersions on my wonky hooter now, is it?' he said, prodding the florid man with Reggie. 'It's down to personal abuse, is it? Well sod off, you fat drunken pig.'

'You started it. You called me a fat pig,' said the florid man, prodding Reggie to emphasise his point.

'You are a fat pig,' said the broken nose, thumping Reggie's back.

'Please,' said Reggie, shaking himself clear of the two men.

'Will somebody come and get served?' said Mr F. R. Bostock.

13

'If you're in a tearing hurry, do go ahead,' said Reggie to the florid man.

'I'm not in such a hurry that I'll allow a pipsqueak short-house with a nose as bent as West End Lane to call me a fat drunken pig and then accuse me of using personal insults,' said the florid man.

'You did,' said the broken nose. 'A broken nose, that's a personal disability, allied to your squints and your 'are-lips. Being a fat drunken pig, that's your bleeding character, innit? That's having too many double brandies down the bleeding golf club.'

'Please, gentlemen,' said Reggie.

'Sling your hook, you,' said the broken nose. 'My quarrel's with alcoholics anonymous here.'

'Come outside and repeat that,' said the florid man.

'With pleasure,' said the broken nose.

Reggie, who had been feeling more and more like a United Nations Peace Keeping Force, suddenly stopped whirling dizzily about. He smiled broadly.

'Thank you, gentlemen,' he said.

He shook them both warmly by the hand.

'Thank you once again,' he said.

They stared at him in astonishment, their quarrel momentarily forgotten.

'Please!' pleaded Mr F. R. Bostock. 'Will somebody come and get served?'

'Shut up,' said Reggie.

He walked briskly out of the bank. He knew now what he had to do.

He hummed gaily as he walked through the Oxford Street drizzle towards the shoe shop.

Then he remembered that he'd forgotten to draw out any money.

He returned to the bank and joined the back of Mr F. R. Bostock's queue.

Reggie and Elizabeth just had time for a corned beef sandwich and a drink before closing time. The big-eared landlord opined that the weather was bad for trade. It was the worst pre-Christmas trade since he'd moved from the Plough at Didcot.

They sat in the corner by the grimy window. Elizabeth showed Reggie her new shoes. In vain. He was far, far away, in the land of his plans. But how could he tell Elizabeth? How could he persuade her to spend the rest of her life in the way he wanted? Not here. Not in this inhospitable hostelry. Tonight, in an intimate restaurant, over the last of an excellent burgundy.

'You aren't listening to a word I say,' said Elizabeth.

'Sorry,' he said. 'I was thinking. What were you saying?'

'It doesn't matter.'

'Darling, I'm not one of those male chauvinist pigs who think that the conversation of women consists largely of idle chitter-chatter. I'm sure it was well worth hearing and I'd like to hear it. Now, what did you say?'

'I said these corned beef sandwiches aren't too bad.'

'Oh. No, they aren't, are they? Not too bad at all. Well, mine isn't anyway. I can't speak for yours. But if mine's nice, it's hardly likely that yours will be repulsive. Especially as you say it isn't.'

It was three o'clock. The landlord opened both doors wide. Raw, damp air poured in.

'What's wrong?' said Elizabeth.

'I've had an idea,' said Reggie. 'This isn't the time to tell you about it.'

It was one minute past three. The landlord switched the Xpelair fans on. Cold air blew down their necks.

'When is the time?' said Elizabeth.

'Tonight, after a good dinner,' said Reggie.

'That sounds ominous,' said Elizabeth. 'Am I going to be so hostile to it?'

'No, of course not.'

'Tell me now, then.'

Reggie swallowed nervously.

'In the bank just now there was an argument,' he said. 'I started to think about all the unnecessary hatred and anger and violence in the world.'

'Come on you lot, haven't you got homes to go to? What do you think it is? Christmas?' yelled the landlord.

15

'Thank you, landlord,' Reggie called out. 'An apt intervention!'

'Well, go on,' said Elizabeth. 'What was your idea?'

Reggie swallowed again.

'I intend to set up a community, where middle-aged, middle-class people like us can learn to live in love and faith and trust,' he said.

'I think that's a marvellous idea,' said Elizabeth.

'People will be able to come for any length of time they like,' said Reggie over the aforementioned burgundy, at the end of an excellent dinner in Soho. 'They'll be able to use it as a commune where they can live in peace and happiness, or as a therapy centre where our staff can help them to find the love and goodness that lurks inside them.'

Their brandies arrived.

'Where will it be?' said Elizabeth.

'Cheers,' said Reggie.

'Cheers. It could be anywhere, I suppose.'

'Absolutely.'

'An old country house. An island. The Welsh hills. Anywhere.'

Reggie stretched his hand out under the table, and patted Elizabeth's knee affectionately. She had taken the idea of the community better than he had dared to hope, but this was going to be a bitter pill for her to swallow.

'I'm sorry, old girl,' he said. 'But I want to live in an ordinary suburban house in an ordinary suburban street.'

'Thank God for that,' said Elizabeth. 'So do I.'

II

The Recruitment

IT DIDN'T TAKE Reggie and Elizabeth long to realise that Number Twenty-One, Oslo Avenue, Botchley, was the ideal setting in which to begin their immense task. It was, in the eloquent words of Messrs Blunstone, Forrest and Stringer, a spacious detached residence of unusual desirability even for this exceptionally select area of Botchley.

'Listen to this, darling,' said Reggie as they entered the hall. ' "Accustomed as we are to inspecting three or four properties a day, we were, nevertheless, very greatly surprised on entering this residence to find such an astonishing sense of space, particularly within the Principal Reception Room, the Added Conservatory, the Master Bedroom and the Kitchen Area." '

'Do you have to read from that thing?' said Elizabeth. 'Can't we just look at it for ourselves?'

They walked briskly through the Genuine Hall, pausing only to observe the timbered wainscoting and double-doored integrated cloaks hanging cupboard, and entered the Principal Reception Room.

'My word,' said Reggie, 'this room affords an unrivalled view over the terraced gardens, fringed by a verdant screen of trees that endows the said gardens with a sense of peacefulness which bestows the final accolade on this exceptionally characterful property.'

'Reggie!' said Elizabeth.

They admired the integrated double-glazed windows, noted the modern power circuitry with four conveniently-sited power access points, and were impressed by the handsome integrated brick fireplace.

Then they entered the Dining Room.

'Stap me!' said Reggie. 'More modern power circuitry, and if this isn't an intimate yet surprisingly spacious setting for

17

formal and informal dining, I'm the Queen of Sheba's surprisingly spacious left tit.'

'Reggie! Please!' said Elizabeth. 'I thought you were excited about buying the house.'

'I am,' said Reggie. 'Almost as excited as Messrs Blunstone, Forrest and Stringer.'

They paused briefly to admire the low-level Royal Venton suite and integrated wash-basin in the spacious Separate Downstairs W.C., the amply-proportioned Study, the splendid Added Conservatory, and the exceptionally commodious kitchen with its Scandinavian-style traditional English fully-integrated natural pine and chrome storage units and work surfaces.

Then they went upstairs to the Master Bedroom.

'Here we find the same impression of spacious living as is afforded throughout the ground floor,' said Reggie. 'This handsome room enjoys integrated double-glazing with sliding units, and it is patently obvious that the unusually tasteful decorations are in absolutely pristine order, affording an elegant background to Scandinavian or traditional English sex activities both anal and oral with fully integrated manking about and doing exceptionally spacious naughty things.'

'It doesn't say that,' said Elizabeth.

'Of course it doesn't.'

They laughed. Their lips met. A feeling of happiness and tenderness ran through them. For all they cared, the double-doored fully-integrated floor-to-ceiling wardrobe units might not have existed.

It was approaching the end of January, and the weather was unseasonably mild. Fruit farmers felt the balmy winds morosely and worried about spring frosts. The going at Market Rasen and Plumpton was 'good to firm'.

Reggie and Elizabeth took up residence in a relatively cheap hotel in one of the less fashionable parts of Hendon while they waited to move to Botchley.

'We must husband our resources. I want to pay my staff good salaries,' Reggie explained over their tagliatelle bolognese in one of the best Italian restaurants in Hendon.

'What sort of staff are you looking for?' asked Elizabeth.

'People who are intelligent, mature, kind and trustworthy,' said Reggie.

'How will you find them?' said Elizabeth.

'Personal contacts,' said Reggie. 'Leave all that to me.'

'And me?' said Elizabeth. 'Where do I come in?'

Reggie poured a little more of the rough carafe wine into Elizabeth's glass. It was a placatory gesture.

'I want you to be secretary,' he said. 'It's a very important job. Taking bookings, allocating rooms, handling correspondence. A highly responsible post.'

Their escalopes and chips arrived. On top of each escalope there were three capers and half an inch of anchovy fillet. They each had fifteen chips.

'I've always thought of the secretaries of institutions as cool, hard, efficient, grey-haired, sexless,' said Elizabeth.

'You'll be the exception that proves the rule,' said Reggie.

'You mean I'm not efficient?' said Elizabeth.

'No!' said Reggie hastily.

She laughed. Both the other customers turned to look. The proprietor beamed.

'I'm teasing you, darling,' said Elizabeth.

'Teasing?' said Reggie.

'I'd love to be secretary,' she said.

Reggie's recruitment of his first intelligent, mature, kind and trustworthy member of staff had been concluded.

He popped a caper into his mouth.

The recruitment of the second intelligent, mature, kind and trustworthy member of staff took longer.

It was C.J.

Reggie's former boss at Sunshine Desserts lived at Blancmange Cottage, Godalming. Reggie phoned him from the only unvandalised phone box in Hendon. It was outside the cemetery. Mrs C.J. answered.

'I haven't seen him since October,' she said. 'I understood he was last seen dressed as a tramp.'

'Yes. You mean he . . . he hasn't been . . . he's still . . . good God!'

19

'Yes. I had a letter from him at Christmas. Shall I read it to you?'

'Please.'

'Hang on.'

Light rain fell. A pale, harassed woman came out of the cemetery and stood anxiously outside the phone box. She looked at her wrist although she had no watch. Reggie shrugged. The pips went. He inserted 10p. The woman opened the door.

'I won't be long,' he said.

'But you aren't talking,' she said.

'The person on the other end has gone to fetch something,' said Reggie.

'Only I'm ringing my friend, and she goes out.'

'I won't be long,' said Reggie.

'Only she's not well.'

'I'm very sorry.'

'No, but it's her leg, you see.'

'I'm sorry about her leg, but what can I do?'

'She's not well, you see,' said the woman.

The woman closed the door and waited impatiently. The pips went. Reggie inserted 10p. The woman made an angry gesture and set off down the road.

'Hello,' said Mrs C.J. 'Are you still there?'

'Yes,' said Reggie.

'Sorry to keep you. He says: "Dear Mrs C.J. This is to wish you a happy Christmas. I wish I could send you something, but times are hard. I make a bit working the cinema queues. I haven't much to say. Least said, soonest forgotten. With love, C.J."'

'I see. Good . . . er . . . Good God!'

'Yes.'

'Have you tried to find him?'

'No.'

'Did you have a happy Christmas?'

'Wonderful. I spent it with my friends in Luxembourg.'

When Reggie rang off, the harassed woman started to walk back towards the phone box.

A smooth young man got out of a taxi and stepped into the phone box just before she could reach it.

For four days Reggie trudged round the West End cinema queues. The buskers were most varied, but all had one thing in common. They weren't C.J.

On the fifth day, his travels took him to a fringe cinema in North London. A few earnest young people were waiting to see a double bill of *avant-garde* West German films. One of them was called *L* and the other one was called *The Amazing Social, Sexual and Political Awakening of the Elderly Widow Blumenthal*. The *avant-garde* youngsters appeared to be mean, impecunious, and sound judges of music. None of them put any money in the cloth cap of the middle-aged man who was strumming his banjo so insensitively, and singing, stiffly and very flat, the following unusual words:

Love and marriage,
Love and marriage,
They go together like a horse and carriage.
Dad was told by mother:
I didn't get where I am today without knowing that you can't have one without the other.

'It's good to see you, Reggie,' said C.J., when they were settled in the Lord Palmerston round the corner.

'Really?' said Reggie.

'Of course,' said C.J., downing his whisky rapidly. 'You know what they say. Absence is better than a cure.'

'Prevention makes the heart grow fonder,' said Reggie.

'In a nutshell Reggie,' said C.J. 'Same again?'

'I'll get them.'

'Please!' said C.J. 'It's my round. A few people have been kind enough to reward my efforts with some pennies, enough to buy a whisky and a half of Guinness anyway.'

Reggie smiled as he watched C.J. at the bar, trying to look dignified in his beggar's rags. A woman with large holes in her tights thought he was smiling at her, and he stopped smiling rapidly.

'Cheers,' said Reggie on C.J.'s return.

'Bottoms up,' said C.J.

Reggie's lips felt carefully through the froth to the cool, dark, smooth beer below.

'So, you've stuck at being a tramp, then?' he said.

'When I do a thing, I do it thoroughly,' said C.J. 'I see it through.'

'You certainly do, C.J.'

C.J. glanced round the drab, run-down pub as if he feared that the three Irish labourers standing at the bar might be C.I.A. agents.

'I've had enough, Reggie,' he said quietly. 'Busking isn't really my bag.'

'I imagine not, C.J.'

Reggie took a long sip of his Guinness. He laid the glass down and looked C.J. straight in the eye.

'I want to offer you a job,' he said.

'What is it this time? Another mad idea like Grot? More humiliations for your old boss? More farting chairs?'

'Grot was a success, C.J., and you had a good job. But even that will be as nothing compared to your future work.'

A young man won the jackpot on the fruit machine.

Reggie described the community that he was going to form.

'Where will it be? Some sunny off-shore island?' asked C.J. hopefully.

'Twenty-one, Oslo Avenue, Botchley.'

'Oh.'

The barman came over to their table. He seemed angry.

'You gave me the wrong money,' he told C.J. scornfully. 'You gave me thirty-five pee, three pesetas, two pfennigs and a shirt button.'

C.J. managed to find the correct money, and handed it to the barman.

'You want to be careful of these types,' the barman warned Reggie.

'Thank you, I will,' said Reggie.

C.J. pocketed the pesetas, the pfennigs and the shirt button.

'Mean bloody unwashed long-haired louts,' he grumbled.

'That's not the way you should talk about them, if you're joining my community,' said Reggie.

'Oh. How should I talk about them if I'm joining your community?'

'Fascinating, somewhat misguided, rather immature, socially confused, excessively serious but potentially highly creative and absolutely delightful mean bloody unwashed long-haired louts,' said Reggie.

He bought another round, the better to further his persuasion of C.J.

'What sort of job do you have in mind for me?' said C.J.

'I'm not sure yet,' said Reggie. 'But I promise you it'll be worthy of your talents. Come and give it a try. After all, the proof of the pudding is caviar to the general.'

'That's true,' said C.J. 'That's very true. I'm not sure if it's my line of country, though.'

'You'll have board and lodging and a salary of eight thousand pounds a year.'

'On the other hand, no doubt I could soon adjust to it,' said C.J.

They shook hands, and Reggie bought another round.

'When I've got my staff together,' he said, 'there'll be a period of training.'

'Training, Reggie?'

'We'll all have to learn how to be nice.'

'Oh.'

C.J. gazed morosely at his whisky.

'I didn't get where I am today by being nice,' he said.

'You'll get used to it,' said Reggie. 'Once you are nice, you'll find that it's really quite nice being nice.'

'This free board and lodging, Reggie, where will that be?'

'Erm . . . with us.'

'With you? Ah!'

'There won't be room for everyone actually in the house,' said Reggie. 'Some of you'll have to live under . . . er . . . canvas.'

C.J.'s hand shook slightly as he lifted the whisky to his lips.

'Under canvas? You mean . . . in a tent?'

'Yes.'

'Good God.'

'Yes.'

23

'Eight thousand pounds?'

'Yes.'

'Not that I'd mind, Reggie. It's Mrs C.J. She's a different kettle of fish.'

'She certainly is,' said Reggie. 'And you feel that she might be a different kettle of fish out of water?'

'Exactly. By no stretch of the imagination can Mrs C.J. be described as a frontierswoman.'

'No.'

'She's wedded to her creature comforts, Reggie.'

The eyes of the two men met.

'I seem to recall that she has friends in Luxembourg,' said Reggie.

'Yes. Delightful people.'

'Luxembourg *is* delightful.'

'Absolutely delightful.'

'All the charms of European civilisation in microcosm.'

'Well put, Reggie.'

Reggie smiled faintly.

'Perhaps it would be a rather nice gesture if you were to sacrifice your marital pleasures and let her stay in Luxembourg for a while,' he said.

'What an excellent idea, Reggie. Just for a few months till we get things straight. You're on. Consider me recruited.'

'You're the first person I've come to,' said Reggie.

'Ah!'

'Start at the top.'

'Quite! Thank you, Reggie.'

'After Everest, the Mendips.'

'Absolutely. What? Not quite with you, Reggie.'

'Perfectly simple,' said Reggie, 'If I can make you nice, I can make anybody nice.'

The next intelligent, mature, kind and trustworthy recruit to be signed up by Reggie was Doc Morrissey.

It wasn't difficult to trace the ageing ex-medico of Sunshine Desserts. Reggie soon discovered that he had installed himself in a bed-sitter in Southall.

The bed-sitter turned out to be above a shop that sold Indian spices, next door to a launderette. Asian women of indeterminate age and inaccessible beauty were setting off with Tesco carrier bags from houses that had been built for Brentford supporters and old women who liked a bottle of stout before the pubs filled up on a Saturday morning.

Over the road the Gaumont, designed for films with Richard Todd in them, had gaudy posters for a double bill of romances from the sub-continent.

Beside Doc Morrissey's door there were three bells. Above each bell, untidily secured with sellotape, there was a name. The names were Patel, Mankad and Morrissey. Reggie rang Doc Morrissey's bell.

The air was full of the scents of cumin, garam masala and Persil.

There was no reply. He tried the bell marked Patel. Mr Patel had a chubby face and told Reggie that he would probably find the Professor in the park.

The park was small and bleak. The grass was thin and patchy. The backs of the surrounding houses were shabby and blackened. Grot's erstwhile Head of Forward Planning was sitting on a bench, feeding crumbs of poppadum to sceptical starlings.

'Reggie!' he said, a smile of heart-warming delight spreading across his weatherbeaten face.

'Morning, Professor,' said Reggie.

Doc Morrissey gave an abashed grin.

'It goes down well in these parts,' he said. 'I've set myself up as an English teacher.'

'How's it going?' said Reggie, sitting beside him on the bench.

'Extremely well.'

'How many pupils have you got?'

'These are early days, Reggie.'

'How many pupils?'

'One. I'm not unhappy here, Reggie. I suppose that since I'm one of nature's exiles, I'm better off where it's natural for a white man to feel an exile.'

It was the middle of February. The weather was still quite

mild, but a keen wind was sending occasional reminders about loneliness gusting across the park.

'Old age must be rather depressing for a doctor,' said Reggie. 'Knowing exactly what's happening to your body.'

'Yes it must,' said Doc Morrissey.

He flexed the fingers of both hands.

'Why are you doing that?' said Reggie.

'Preventing the onset of arthritis in the joints.'

The starlings, their glorious plumage dulled by the city grime, had deserted Doc Morrissey and were exploring the lifeless ground around a derelict swing.

Two crows and a blackbird joined them.

'Even the birds are black here,' said Doc Morrissey.

'Are you depressed?' said Reggie.

'No. No. Southall's a million laughs. And I find a certain consolation, Reggie, in the knowledge that by being the worst doctor in England I have saved somebody else from that ignominy. No man's life is entirely pointless.'

'Oh good,' said Reggie. 'I'm glad you're not depressed.'

He trailed his arm over the back of the bench and turned to face Doc Morrissey.

'This is no chance meeting,' he said. 'I've come to offer you a job.'

Doc Morrissey gawped.

'Again?' he said.

Reggie explained about the community and its aims.

'It sounds marvellous,' said Doc Morrissey excitedly. 'What sort of role do you have in mind for me?'

'A medical role,' said Reggie.

'Oh. Isn't there anything else I could do?'

'A different branch of medicine, though. You'll be our psychologist.'

'Oh!'

'It's your undiscovered metier, Doc.'

'It is?'

'Psychology is your nettle and I'm confident that you'll grasp it.'

'You are?'

26

'You will have a salary of . . . five thousand pounds, plus board and lodging.'

They went to the pub to celebrate. They drank pints of bitter and ate gala pie with brinjal pickle.

'I'm no expert, you know,' said Doc Morrissey.

'The experts have had their chance,' said Reggie. 'They have failed. It's precisely your lack of expertise that excites me.'

'Oh.'

On the nineteenth of February, Reggie and Elizabeth moved into Number Twenty-one, Oslo Avenue, Botchley.

Vans brought the furniture that Elizabeth had chosen from the great furniture emporia of London Town.

Men came to connect up the gas and electricity.

The neighbours offered them cups of tea. These olive branches were not spurned.

The houses of the neighbours were smaller than Number Twenty-one. They only had three bedrooms.

The neighbours at Number Twenty-three were Mr and Mrs Penfold.

The neighbours at Number Nineteen were Mr and Mrs Hollies.

Mrs Penfold talked little and seemed neurotically shy. Her tea was too weak.

Mrs Hollies talked a great deal and seemed obsessively extrovert. Her tea was too strong.

The exceptionally mild weather continued. The snowdrops were on the rampage in front gardens. The crocuses were swelling expectantly and sticky buds were forming on the trees.

Mrs Hollies had never known anything like it. But then we didn't get the seasons like we used to. Everything had gone absolutely haywire. Mrs Hollies blamed the aeroplanes. People could scoff, but it stood to reason that all those great big things up there disturbing the atmosphere must make everything go haywire.

The views of Mrs Penfold on the subject were a closed book.

That evening Reggie and Elizabeth explored their neighbourhood. They walked down Oslo Avenue, past pleasant detached residences, several of which had mock-Tudor beams and bay windows. They turned right into Bonn Close. The timing devices of the street lamps were on the blink, and the lights were pale pink and feeble. Bonn Close brought them to the High Street.

They visited the Botchley Arms, where Reggie had two bottles of diabetic lager while his partner opted for two medium sherries.

They walked down Botchley High Street, past supermarkets, shoe shops, betting shops and dress shops, past the George and Dragon, until they came to a parade set back from the High Street. Here there were three restaurants—the New Bengal, the Golden Jasmine House, and the Oven D'Or. They dined at the Oven D'Or. They were the only diners.

Before returning home they sampled the delights of the George and Dragon. It was run by a small man with a large wife and an even larger mother. The locals called it the George and Two Dragons.

Their route home took them along Nairobi Drive, and round Lisbon Crescent to the other end of Oslo Avenue. A right turn brought them back to their new home. They stood by the garden gate and looked at the placid, commonplace frontage of their surprisingly spacious dwelling. Soon it would be bursting with life and love and hope.

A light rain began to fall. Reggie lifted Elizabeth up and staggered in over the threshold.

The work of recruitment continued. The targets were Reggie's old colleagues at Sunshine Desserts and Grot. He felt about them as he felt about his ageing pyjamas. They might not fit, they might be somewhat torn in vital places and permanently stained in other vital places, but a man felt comfortable with them.

He called next at the flat occupied by Tony Webster and his wife Joan. It was in the Lower Mortlake Road. It was ten fifteen on a Saturday morning. Reggie was disappointed to find that his former secretary was out. In fact he only just caught Tony. He was sporting a brown suit and matching suitcase, and carried a lightweight topcoat over his arm.

'Sorry. Were you just going out?' said Reggie.

'Business trip. Frankfurt. Off to hit the fatherland, score a few exports. I'll get a later flight. No sweat,' said Tony. 'Come in. Great to see you.'

The flat bore evidence of both opulence and poverty. There was a threadbare carpet and a heavy, stained three-piece suite. There was also a colour television set, a cocktail trolley and expensive stereo equipment.

'Joan at work?' Reggie asked, installing himself in one of the heavy armchairs.

'Yeah. She does one Saturday in three. I don't want her to work, but you know what women are.'

'Things are going well, are they?' said Reggie.

'Fantastic. Great. Knock-out.'

'I came here with a proposition,' said Reggie. 'But there doesn't seem much point in putting it as you're doing so well.'

'Well, pretty well. This is Success City, Arizona. But I've always been interested in your ideas, Reggie.'

Reggie described the community and offered Tony and Joan jobs.

'Knock-out,' said Tony. 'Absolute knock-out. We'll let you know.'

When Reggie left, Tony set off with him. The suitcase came open on the stairs and his central-heating brochures cascaded into the hall.

'O.K.,' said Tony. 'Frankfurt doesn't exist. But this central heating job's a knock-out. No basic, but fantastic commission.'

That afternoon Reggie invited himself to tea with David and Prue Harris-Jones.

They had a flat in a new block in Reading. Already the paint on the outside was peeling and the walls on the inside were cracking. Their fourteen-month-old boy was Reggie's godson. His name was Reggie. David and Prue greeted Reggie with something approaching adoration. Young Reggie greeted him with something approaching an attack of wind.

David said that he was very happy with the building society, and Reading was much maligned. When Reggie offered them jobs, however, their response was unequivocal.

'Super,' they said.

Later, over his second slice of sponge cake, David Harris-Jones did venture a cautious criticism.

'You know what I think of you, Reggie,' he said. 'I look up to you.'

'Oh dear, oh dear,' said Reggie.

'Well exactly,' said David Harris-Jones. 'I look up to you as the sort of person who doesn't expect or want people to look up to him.'

'I agree,' said Prue.

'Well, thank you,' said Reggie.

'I mean the community idea is super,' said David Harris-Jones. 'But I don't think Prue or I would be happy if you were ... how can I put it? ... well, not exactly a cult figure, but ... er ... not exactly sort of too big for your ... but sort of ... er ...'

'Thank you for speaking so frankly,' said Reggie. 'If you mean that I'm in danger of becoming self-important, please don't worry. The community's the thing. I'll just be the shadowy catalyst that enables it to function.'

'Super,' said David and Prue Harris-Jones.

'What are you going to call it?' said Prue, crossing her attractive but sensible legs.

'Perrins,' said Reggie.

'Super,' said David and Prue Harris-Jones.

Steady rain was falling as Reggie drove home from Reading. The lights in Lisbon Crescent were out, and the February night was very dark. As he turned into Oslo Avenue, he found himself following the single-decker bus, the W288, which ran through these quiet streets to places with deliciously dull names, gloriously ordinary Coxwell, exquisitely prosaic Spraundon.

This was his world.

When he entered the living room, he felt as if he had been there for a thousand years. The phone was ringing. It was Tony.

'We'll take the job,' he said. 'No sweat.'

'Reggie?'' said Elizabeth next afternoon, as they were about to wash up the Sunday dinner things in the deceptively commodious kitchen.

30

'Yes?'

'What's happening about staff? You haven't told me a thing.'

'We agreed that the recruiting would be my responsibility and the furniture would be yours,' he said.

'Well I haven't kept the furniture secret,' said Elizabeth.

'That is rather different,' he said. 'I mean, we couldn't sit on it if you did.'

He donned the real ale apron and began to stack the dishes in the integrated sink with double drainers. He arranged the dishes in a pyramid so that the water would pour over them like a fountain.

'Is there some reason why you don't want to tell me about the staff?' said Elizabeth, wrapping the remains of the meal in the *Botchley and Spraundon Press* (*Incorporating The Coxwell Gazette*).

'Of course not, darling.'

He turned on the hot water. It gushed on to a dessert spoon and sprayed out all over the floor. He moved the spoon hurriedly, and added a few squirts of extra-strength washing-up liquid.

'I've engaged six excellent people,' he said.

'Who?' she asked. 'I know their names won't mean much, but I'd like to know.'

'Er ... one or two of the names may mean something. C.J., for instance.'

'C.J.?'

'Yes.'

'You've appointed C.J.?'

'Yes. He won't be on top of us all the time, darling. He'll probably spend quite a lot of his time in his ... er ... in his tent.'

There was a pause. Reggie lost his dishmop.

'In his what?' said Elizabeth.

'He's going to live under canvas,' said Reggie. 'Mrs C.J. won't be with him. She's no frontierswoman.'

'Reggie, where is this tent of C.J.'s going to be?' said Elizabeth.

'Damn, I've broken a cup,' said Reggie.

He hunted for the remains of the cup in the sud-filled bowl, for, like many a good man before him, he had sadly under-estimated the power of the extra-strength washing-up liquid.

During his hunt he found the dishmop. Life is often like that. In hunting for one thing, we find another.

'Where is this tent going to be?' repeated Elizabeth. 'Near here?'

'Er . . . quite near.'

'How near?'

'Er . . . not in the front garden.'

'Are you trying to tell me that C.J. is going to live in a tent in the back garden?' said Elizabeth.

'Right at the back of the back garden,' said Reggie. 'Miles from the house, really.'

'What will he do about food? Open tins of pemmican down by the compost heap?'

'I thought he'd . . . er . . . have some of his meals with us.'

'Which meals?'

'Er . . . breakfast, lunch and dinner.'

'So we live together, the three of us. That sounds dangerous,' she said.

'Good heavens, no. *Ménages-à-trois*, Bermuda triangles, that would be dangerous. No, they'll all live here.'

'All?'

'All the staff.'

'So I'm expected to share my house with total strangers?' said Elizabeth.

'They . . . er . . . they won't be strangers.'

'What will they be?'

'Well . . . people like Doc Morrissey, Tony and Joan, David and Prue.'

'All the old mob?'

'They've proved their worth, darling. Look what they did for Grot.'

'And what about our daughter? Hasn't she proved her worth?'

'Linda and Tom too. I was going to ask them next. And Jimmy.'

'It's going to get a bit crowded, isn't it?'

'That's the whole point of a community,' said Reggie. 'There's not much point in having a community if nobody's there.'

'Am I expected to cook for them?'

'We'll employ a cook darling.'

Reggie advanced towards her. Suds dripped from his green washing-up gloves.

'I'm sorry,' he said. 'I should have told you everything. I just didn't know how you'd take it.'

'I think it's all very exciting,' said Elizabeth.

After they had finished the washing up, they had their coffee in the living room. The chairs and settee that Elizabeth had chosen had comfort as their main objective, while not neglecting the aesthetic element. Three pictures of bygone Botchley adorned the walls. The smokeless fuel burned placidly. They sat on the settee, and Elizabeth nestled her head against Reggie's chest.

'Did you really mean that?' said Reggie. 'Do you really think it's all very exciting?'

'After Grot, I'll never doubt your judgement again,' said Elizabeth.

It was cosy in the living room in the fading half-light. Reggie put his arm round Elizabeth.

'We're going to have to learn different values,' he said. 'We're going to have to forget that an Englishman's home is his castle. From now on, our home is everyone else's castle.'

The front door bell rang.

'Damn damn damn,' he said. 'Who the hell is that?'

He smiled ruefully.

It was his son-in-law Tom.

'Oh, it's you. Come in,' said Reggie.

'I haven't come at an unfortunate time, have I, Reggie?' said Tom.

'Every time you visit us, Tom, it's ... absolutely delightful. Wot, no prune wine?'

Tom had brought some of his usual appurtenances—his beard, his briar pipe—but none of his home-made wine.

'I haven't had the heart to make any lately,' he admitted. 'You'll have to forgo it.'

'Oh, what a shame.'

They went into the living room.

33

'This room is surprisingly spacious,' said Tom, after he had kissed his mother-in-law.

'Once an estate agent, always an estate agent,' said Reggie.

Elizabeth went to make some coffee for Tom who plonked himself down on the settee. His legs stretched out in front of him till they seemed to fill the room.

'How are things with you, Reggie?' he asked.

'Not bad, Tom. I smiled ruefully just before you came. First time I can recall actually smiling ruefully. I've read about it, of course. Always wanted to do it.'

'I'm not smiling ruefully,' said Tom.

'No.'

'I'm looking lugubrious.'

'Yes.'

'Even when I'm wildly excited I look lugubrious, so it's difficult for people to tell when I actually am lugubrious.'

'You've got no lugubriosity in reserve.'

'Exactly.'

Tom relit his pipe.

'Do you remember what a success I was with my adverts for Grot?' he said.

'I certainly do.'

'I was known as the McGonegall of Admass.'

'Well, you may find this difficult to believe, but I've been unable to get another job in advertising.'

'You amaze me. So, it's back to the estate agent's boards, is it?'

Tom relit his pipe before replying.

'I couldn't go back to that,' he said. 'I've burnt my boats.'

'Burnt your boats, Tom?'

Tom stood up, as if he felt that it would relieve the burden of his folly.

'When I left, Norris asked me if I'd continue to write my witty house ads. I said . . .' Tom shuddered at the memory. 'I said: "You can stick your house ads up your fully-integrated exceptionally spacious arse unit." '

Reggie laughed.

'Yes.'

34

'Very good,' he said. 'I'm surpri . . . no, I'm not. Why should I be?'

'He's told every estate agent from Bristol to Burnham-on-Crouch.'

'They'll have forgotten.'

'Estate agents never forget. They're the elephants of the professional world.'

Tom sat down again, and managed to achieve the impossible by looking even more lugubrious than he had before.

'I popped in at a party last night, at the show house on that new estate at High Wycombe,' he said. 'I was snubbed. Even Harrison, of Harrison, Harrison and Harrison, cold-shouldered me. I wouldn't have been surprised if it had been Harrison or Harrison. They're bastards. But Harrison! He was my friend.'

He relit his pipe.

'I've got bitten by the crafts bug,' he said. 'Thatching, basket-weaving, coopering. I can't seem to get a foot in, though. I can't get any work, Reggie. We're in trouble.'

'I'm sorry, Tom.'

Tom shifted nervously in his seat.

'I've never asked for charity, Reggie,' he began.

'I'm glad to hear it,' said Reggie.

'I'm not a charity person.'

'Oh good. That is a relief.'

'I don't like having something for nothing.'

'Oh good. For one awful moment there I thought you were going to ask me for help. I misjudged you, Tom. Can you forgive me?'

Tom looked at Reggie in hurt puzzlement.

'I should have known better,' said Reggie. 'I always thought that our daughter had married a real man.'

'Oh. Thank you, Reggie.'

'A man with pride.'

'Oh. Thank you, Reggie.'

They sat in silence for a few moments. Tom looked acutely miserable.

'I'm also glad you didn't ask for charity, because you don't need it,' said Reggie.

He explained his project, offered Tom and Linda jobs, agreed

35

salaries, and suggested that they sell their house, but not through Harrison, Harrison and Harrison.

Elizabeth brought them coffee, switched on the light, and drew the curtains on the gathering mists of night.

The front door bell rang again. Early indications were that it was coping splendidly with its role in the smooth running of the household. It was Linda, and she was angry. She swept past her father's affectionate embrace and confronted Tom.

'You bastard!' she said.

Tom stood up slowly.

'Hello, darling,' he said. 'How did you get here?'

'I borrowed the Perrymans' car. You did it, didn't you? You bastard!'

'Linda!' said Elizabeth.

'To what do I owe the repetition of this unmerited description?' said Tom.

'Oh shut up,' said Linda. 'You did it, didn't you?'

'I can't answer you and shut up,' said Tom.

'Oh shut up,' said Linda. 'Well, did you or didn't you?'

Reggie put a fatherly arm on Linda's shoulder.

'What is it?' he said.

'He came to you and begged,' she said. 'I asked him not to. He promised. I can't stand people abasing themselves and begging. I went down on one knee and cried: "Tom, please, if you love me, don't abase yourself. Don't beg." He promised.'

'You've got it all wrong, Linda,' said Reggie. 'Come on. Sit down and discuss this sensibly. There's all this splendid new furniture just waiting to be sat on. Pity to waste it.'

They all sat down except Linda.

'What have I got wrong?' she demanded.

'Tom didn't beg,' said Reggie. 'He obviously took your words to heart, because he rushed all the way over here to tell me... now, what was his exact phrase? ... Yes... "I'm not a charity person".'

'That's right,' said Tom.

'And I offered him a job,' said Reggie.

He squeezed up towards Tom, making room for Linda to sit on the other end of the settee.

He put his arm round her shoulder and explained about the

36

project and the jobs he had offered them and how he wanted them to come and live at 'Perrins'. When he had finished Linda burst into tears.

'It's not as bad an idea as all that is it?' said Reggie.

Everyone played their part in cheering Linda up. She blew her nose, Elizabeth poured her a brandy, Reggie squeezed her affectionately, and Tom remained silent.

Reggie's squeeze meant: 'We love you so much. You're all we've got now that our son is lost to us.'

They had last heard from Mark almost three years ago, after he had been kidnapped by guerrillas while presenting *The Reluctant Debutante* to an audience of Angolan mercenaries. They had drifted into silence about him. His absence was a constant presence which they never acknowledged. Reggie hoped that Linda would understand his squeeze.

'Well,' he said. 'What do you think of my idea?'

'I learnt my lesson over Grot,' said Linda. 'I'm never going to criticise your ideas again.'

A car horn began to blare outside.

"What's that rudely disturbing the calm of our suburban Sunday?' said Reggie.

Linda leapt up.

'Oh my God,' she said. 'I left Adam and Jocasta in the car.'

She rushed outside.

Tom relit his pipe.

'Oh my God,' said Reggie. 'Adam and Jocasta will be living with us as well.'

Reggie felt a lurking sadness that his friends, relatives and colleagues weren't meeting with more success in their various lives.

Surely somebody would stand out against him and his purse? It didn't seem likely. Only Major James Gordonstoun Anderson remained.

Since Elizabeth's elder brother had been made redundant by the Queen's Own Berkshire Light Infantry on the grounds of age in his forty-sixth year, success had not courted him assiduously. He had been divorced from his first wife, Sheila. His marriage to his second wife Lettice had failed to survive his non-arrival at the church. His secret right-wing army had collapsed when his colleague, Clive 'Lofty' Anstruther, had vamoosed with all the funds and weapons. His brief career as Head of Creative Thinking at Grot had ended when the organisation had been disbanded.

An enquiry at his old bed-sitter revealed that he had moved to a house near Woburn Sands. It was called 'Rorke's Drift'.

What could Jimmy be doing in the Woburn area? Army recruiting officer for Milton Keynes? Chief Giraffe Buyer for the Duke of Bedford?

There were pools of water at the roadside, after the overnight rain. Heavy yellow clouds hung low over Dunstable Downs, and it was still very mild for March.

'Rorke's Drift' turned out to be a small, unprepossessing modern bungalow that stood like a tiny corner of some seaside suburb in a clearing surrounded by fine woods. It was deserted. No smoke rose from its rustic chimney. A brief ray of sunshine lit up the clearing, then died away.

A large woman marched fiercely along a track that led out of the woods past the bungalow. She was towing a reluctant and severely over-stretched chihuahua.

'Looking for the colonel?' she barked, perhaps because she knew that the little dog was too exhausted to do so.

"The ... er ... yes.'

'He's out. At work.'

'Ah! Do you ... er ... do you happen to know where he works?'

'Sorry. Can't oblige. Come on, Rastus. Chop chop.'

She led the exhausted chihuahua remorselessly towards fresh pastures. Trees against which it would have loved to cock its little legs were glimpsed like pretty villages from an express train.

At equal speed from the opposite direction came a mild and tiny woman being pulled by a huge Alsatian.

'Looking for the colonel?' she managed to gasp.

'Yes.'

'Narkworth Narrow Boats. Outskirts of Wolverton.'

And then she was gone.

Reggie was happy to leave this strange place. There was

38

more than an air of *Grimm's Fairy Tales* about the silent woods, the nasty bungalow in the little clearing, and the women with their wildly unsuitable pets. What grotesque pair would arrive next? A dwarf, pulled along by a lion? A giant, exercising his field mouse?

The clouds were breaking up rapidly. The sun gleamed on the puddles.

Reggie found Narkworth Narrow Boats without difficulty. It was situated on a long straight stretch of the Grand Union Canal. He parked in a heavily rutted car-park and picked his way gingerly between the puddles into a small yard surrounded by workshops and store-rooms. A smart sign-board carried the simple legend 'Reception'. It pointed to a newly-painted single-storey building.

Jimmy sat at the desk, almost hidden behind a huge pot of flowers. His face broke into a delighted smile.

'Reggie!'

They shook hands. Jimmy's handshake was a barometer of his circumstances and now it had the unrestrained vigour of his palmiest days.

'Nice to see you, Colonel,' said Reggie.

'Nice to see ... ah! Yes. You've ... er ... you've met some of my neighbours. A harmless deception, Reggie. Practically a colonel. Should have been, by rights.'

Reggie sat down, and faced Jimmy round the edge of the flowers.

'Running this show,' said Jimmy. 'Excellent set-up. Landed on my feet.'

'I half thought you might be running another secret army,' said Reggie.

'No fear. Once bitten, twice shy. Bastard took the lot.'

'Clive "Lofty" Anstruther?'

'Lofty by name and Lofty by nature,' said Jimmy mysteriously. 'If I ever run into him. . . .'

What he would do was evidently beyond expression in mere words.

He led Reggie on a tour of inspection, while Reggie described his community persuasively.

'It's a kind of army,' he said. 'An army of peace. Fighting

together, living together, messing together. Living under canvas. Think of the camaraderie, Jimmy.'

Jimmy stood in the yard, thinking of the cameraderie.

Then he shook his head.

'Two months ago, jumped at the chance,' he said. "Good set-up here, though. Leisure explosion. Canals booming.'

'Good. Good. Is there a Narkworth, incidentally?'

'Cock-up on the marital front. Kraut wife.'

Jimmy had never forgiven the Germans for losing the war before he was old enough to fight.

'Sold out, dirt cheap, fresh start, sad story,' said Jimmy.

The sun was beaming now from a cloudless sky.

'Care for a spin?' said Jimmy.

All along the canal there were bollards, and fifteen narrow boats of various lengths were tied up. They were all painted green and yellow. In some of them, renovation was in progress beneath waterproof sheeting.

Jimmy chose a full-length seventy-foot converted butty boat, and they chugged slowly up the cut. Little blue notices abounded by the towpath. They carried messages such as 'Shops. 700 yards', 'Next Water Point, 950 yards', thus ensuring that those who came to get back to nature were reassured that it had been thoroughly tamed in their absence.

Cows stopped chewing the cud to watch their slow progress. They disturbed a heron, which flapped with lazy indignation ahead of them.

'How do you turn round? said Reggie.

'Winding hole two pounds up the cut,' said Jimmy.

'Pardon?'

'There's a widened bit after we've been through two locks.'

'Ah!'

'Good life,' said Jimmy. 'Only one bugbear.'

'What?'

'Johnny woman.'

'You've got woman trouble?'

'Yes.'

'What's the trouble?'

'No women.'

'Ah!'

'Renewed vigour. Indian summer. Bugbear, no Indians.'

'What about the doggy ladies near your cottage?'

'Odd chat,' said Jimmy. 'Time of day. Haven't clicked.'

He negotiated a sharp bend with skill. Ahead was a pretty canal bridge.

'Should have married Lettice,' he continued. 'Poor cow.'

A black and white Friesian lowed morosely.

'Not you,' said Jimmy. 'Nice woman, Lettice. Fly in ointment, bloody ugly.'

'She isn't that ugly,' said Reggie.

'Yes, she is. Got her photo, pride of place, bedroom. Felt I owed it to her.'

They ducked as the boat chugged peacefully under the mellow brick bridge. On the other side there was an old farmhouse. Lawns swept down to splendid willows at the water's edge. Muscovy ducks paddled listlessly in a reedy backwater. Reggie stood up again, but Jimmy remained in his bent position.

'Reggie?' he said, in a low voice.

Reggie bent down to hear.

'Yes?'

'Something I want to confess.'

'Fire away.'

'Started to do something. Something I've never done before.'

'For goodness' sake, Jimmy, what?'

Jimmy lowered his voice still further, as if he feared that a passing sedge-warbler might hear. Little did he know that the sedge-warblers were far away, wintering in warmer climes.

'Self-abuse,' he whispered hoarsely.

'Well for goodness' sake,' said Reggie. 'At your age that's a cause for congratulations, not remorse.'

'Never done it before,' said Jimmy. 'Not in regimental tradition.'

'I should hope not, overtly,' said Reggie. 'I don't know, though. It's quite a thought. The new recruit up the North West Frontier. "One thing you should know, Hargreaves. Friday night is wanking night. And Hargreaves, you can't sit there. That's Portnoy's chair. Oh, and a word of advice. Don't have the liver." '

41

'Not with you,' said Jimmy.

'Literary allusion,' said Reggie.

'Ah! Literature. Closed book to me, I'm afraid.'

'I really can't see why masturbation should be frowned upon by a nation that's so keen on do-it-yourself,' said Reggie.

'Thing is . . .' began Jimmy.

But Reggie was never to learn what the thing was, because at that moment, with both men bent below the level of the engine casing and unable to see ahead, the narrow monster ploughed straight into the bank.

They walked forward over the long roof, and stepped off on to the towpath. The boat was firmly wedged in the bank, and there was damage to the bows.

'Damn!' said Jimmy. 'Cock-up on the bows front.'

They pulled and heaved. They heaved and pulled. All to no avail.

A Jensen pulled up by the bridge and two men in gumboots and cavalry twill walked along the towpath.

'Having trouble, brigadier?' said one.

'Er . . . yes.'

With three men shoving and Jimmy throwing the engine into full reverse, they managed to shift the boat.

'Thanks,' said Jimmy.

'No trouble,' said the first man.

'Regards to Beamish,' said the other.

Jimmy picked Reggie up at the next bridge, and they chugged on towards the winding hole.

'Brigadier?' said Reggie.

'Might have been eventually, if I hadn't been flung out.'

'Beamish?'

'My partner. Tim 'Curly' Beamish. Wish you could meet him. Sound fellow. Salt of earth. Top drawer.'

Reggie's next quest was for a chef. He placed adverts in the catering papers.

He received replies from George Crutchwell of Staines, Mario Lombardi of Perugia, and Kenny McBlane from Partick.

He invited all three to 'Perrins' for interviews.

George Crutchwell spoke with great confidence in an irritat-

42

ingly flat voice. He was unemployed—'resting', he called it—but had wide experience. He was reluctant to give a reference, but eventually named the Ritz.

Mario Lombardi was good-looking and smiled a lot. He assured Reggie that Botchley was more beautiful than Perugia, and told him that they didn't have houses like Twenty-one, Oslo Avenue in Umbria. He gave a reference willingly.

Kenny McBlane might have been good-looking if it hadn't been for his spots, and didn't smile at all. Reggie had no idea what he said because his Scottish accent was so broad. He gave a reference willingly, writing it down to ensure that there was no misunderstanding.

Reggie soon received the three references.

The Ritz had never heard of George Crutchwell and Reggie crossed his name off the list.

Mario Lombardi's reference was excellent. If praise for his culinary skills was fulsome, the lauding of his character was scarcely less so. He sounded like a cross between Escoffier and St Francis of Assisi.

Kenny McBlane's reference was a minor masterpiece of the oblique. It didn't actually state that he was a bad cook, and it didn't actually say anything specifically adverse about his character. It just left you to deduce the worst.

Reggie showed Elizabeth the two references.

'Which do you think?' he asked.

'It's obvious,' said Elizabeth. 'Lombardi.'

'I'd say it was obviously McBlane,' said Reggie. 'Lombardi's employers want to get rid of him. McBlane's want to keep him.'

He appointed the thirty-three-year-old Scot.

The remainder of March was a time of preparation.

Tom and Linda sold their house, and made arrangements for Adam and Jocasta to go to school in Botchley. Adam was seven now, and Jocasta six. They had decided not to have any more children, as they weren't ecological irresponsibility people.

David and Prue Harris-Jones sold their flat in Reading.

Tony and Joan sold their flat and had a ceremonial burning of three thousand central heating brochures.

Doc Morrissey borrowed every book on psychology that

43

Southall library possessed. He read them both avidly, long into the cumin-scented night.

C.J. returned to Blancmange Cottage, Godalming. He told Mrs C.J. of his new job, and suggested that it might be better, for the time being, if she were to visit her friends in Luxembourg. He was surprised by the speed with which she acceded to this proposition.

Elizabeth bought three tents.

March gave way to April, and the mild winter proved to have a sharp sting in its tail.

The great day approached.

McBlane arrived three days before the others. Reggie had booked him in at the Botchley Arms. He was dark, tense and slim, with a hint of suppressed power. His spots had got worse and there were three boil plasters on his neck.

He spent much of the first day examining his equipment. He also examined the kitchen and the range of utensils that Elizabeth had provided.

Reggie and Elizabeth dined at the Oven D'Or. They were the only diners. They felt too nervous to do justice to their meal.

They were worried about McBlane. If the eating arrangements were a fiasco, morale would slump.

On the second day, McBlane stocked up his commodious deep freeze, his spacious fridge, his ample herb and spice racks.

When he had gone back to the Botchley Arms for an evening of hard drinking, Elizabeth examined his purchases. They were varied, sensible and interesting.

Reggie and Elizabeth dined at the New Bengal Restaurant. They were the only diners. They felt too nervous to do justice to their food.

On the third day their doubts about McBlane were swept away on a wave of glorious cooking smells.

Reggie went into the kitchen towards the end of the morning.

'Is everything all right, McBlane?' he asked.

McBlane's reply sounded to Reggie like 'Ee goon awfa' muckle frae gang doon ee puir wee scrogglers ye thwink.'

'Sorry,' said Reggie. 'Not ... er ... not quite with you.'

44

'Ee goon awfa' muckle frae gang doon ee puir wee scrogglers ye thwink.'

'Ah. Jolly good. Carry on, McBlane.'

That evening, Reggie and Elizabeth dined at the Golden Jasmine House. They were the only diners. They felt too nervous to do justice to their food.

The day of the staff's arival dawned. The sun was warm between the scudding clouds. In his letter of instructions Reggie had asked them to be there by noon. C.J. arrived at ten fifty-eight.

'You're the first to arrive,' said Reggie, ushering him into the living room.

'I didn't get where I am today without being the first to arrive,' said C.J.

'We'll erect the tents this afternoon.'

'Ah. Yes. The tents. Splendid.'

Elizabeth entered with a tray of coffee. C.J. leapt up.

'My dear Elizabeth. Splendid,' he said.

He kissed her on the hand.

'You grow more beautiful as you grow ... er ... as you grow more beautiful,' he said.

Elizabeth's eyes were cool as she met C.J.'s gaze.

'Coffee, C.J.?' she asked.

'Thank you.'

'I'm community secretary,' she said. 'Anything you need, indent for it with me please.'

'Ah ... er ... quite,' said C.J.

He sat on the settee. Elizabeth chose the furthest armchair and pulled her skirt down over her knees.

There was an awkward pause.

'Well!' said C.J. 'Well well well!'

'Quite,' said Reggie.

'Exactly. I'm looking forward to getting to know the other staff,' said C.J.

'You'll know some of them already,' said Reggie.

'Really? Good Lord.'

Doc Morrissey arrived next. He looked astonished to see C.J.

'Well well well!' he said.

'Precisely,' said C.J. 'How are you, are you well?'

45

'Pretty well,' said Doc Morrissey. 'I seem to have picked up a touch of arthritis in the joints of my hands. My doctor puts it down to over-exercise.'

'You mustn't believe all the doctors say, Doc,' said Reggie.

Elizabeth smiled radiantly at Doc Morrissey as she handed him his coffee. He sat beside C.J. on the settee.

At eleven twenty-seven David and Prue Harris-Jones arrived. Young Reggie was sleeping peacefully in his carry-cot. They seemed astonished to see C.J. and Doc Morrissey.

'Well well well!' they said.

'Exactly' said C.J. and Doc Morrissey.

'I hope you aren't alarmed to see your old friends,' said Reggie.

'No. Super,' said David and Prue Harris-Jones.

At eleven forty-nine Tom and Linda arrived. Tom carried a bottle wrapped in tissue paper.

'Well well well,' he said, when he saw the others.

Everybody laughed.

'Why are you laughing?' said Tom.

'That's what everyone said,' said Reggie.

'I see. I'm unoriginal. Good,' said Tom.

'Oh Tom,' said Linda.

'Well, I'm sorry, but I just can't see anything riotously funny in the fact that I said "Well well well",' said Tom.

Tom sat in the remaining armchair, leaving Linda to squat on the pouffe. Elizabeth poured coffee busily.

'We're putting up our tents this afternoon,' C.J. told Doc Morrissey.

'Tents. Ah. Jolly good," said Doc Morrissey.

A heavy shower spattered fiercely against the french windows.

'I forgot this,' said Tom, handing Reggie a bottle. 'It's the last bottle of my prune wine.'

'Thank you, Tom,' said Reggie. 'We must keep it for a really suitable occasion. I know. My funeral.'

Everybody except Tom laughed.

'Sorry, Tom,' said Reggie. 'It was just a little joke.'

'I've said it before and I'll say it again,' said Tom. 'I'm not a joke person.'

'No,' said Linda.

46

The doorbell rang again. It was Tony and Joan.

Tom turned towards them expectantly, hoping that Tony would say 'Well well well!'

'The whole gang!' said Tony. 'You crafty sod, Reggie. Knock-out.'

Lunch was a triumph. It consisted of vichyssoise, boeuf bourguignonne and zabaglione.

After lunch, Elizabeth thanked McBlane profusely.

'I thanked him profusely,' she told Reggie.

'Was he pleased?'

'I don't know. There was a sentence in the middle that I thought I understood, but I must have got it wrong.'

'What was it?' said Reggie.

'It sounded like "Bloody foreign muck".'

They spent the afternoon settling into their living quarters.

'I hope you don't mind Adam and Jocasta sharing a room,' said Reggie.

'We insist on it,' said Linda. 'We don't want to give them a thing about sex.'

'Premature sexual segregation promotes incalculable emotional introversion,' said Tom.

The rain held off, and it wasn't too difficult to erect the tents on the back lawn.

The tents were erected by C.J., Doc Morrissey and Tony.

Joan walked across the lawn. She looked displeased.

'Tony?' she said.

'Yeah?' said Tony, who was bent over a recalcitrant rod.

'Who are these tents for?'

'C.J., Doc Morrissey and us.'

'Us?'

'Yes.'

'Stand up, Tony. I can't talk to you like that.'

'I can't stand up or the tent'll collapse,' said Tony.

'Let it collapse.'

'What?'

'You never told me we were going to live in a tent.'

'Didn't I? I thought I did.'

47

At last Tony was free to stand up.

'Easy,' he said. 'No sweat.'

'Tony?'

'Yeah?'

'Why didn't you tell me we were going to live in a tent?'

'You didn't ask.'

'Tony?'

'Yeah?'

'I am not living in a tent.'

'Oh come on, Joany. It'll be fun. A summer under canvas. Knock-out.'

Reggie approached them across the lawn.

'What's the trouble?' he said.

'Joan refuses to sleep in a tent,' said Tony.

'I'll get double pneumonia,' said Joan.

'Rubbish,' said Tony. 'It'll be Health City, Arizona. Anyway, you're as tough as old boots.'

'Lovely,' said Joan. 'What a delicate, feminine compliment.'

Behind them, C.J. stood back and surveyed his completed tent with ill-concealed pride.

'It'll be lovely in a tent, Joan,' said Reggie. 'I wish I could sleep in one.'

'Why don't you, then?' said Joan.

'I'd like to,' said Reggie. 'But I'm head of this community. It wouldn't look right. It's only till the clients arrive, Joan. I'll buy other houses then, and as soon as I do, you'll be the first to move. I promise.'

Joan gave in reluctantly.

Behind them, Doc Morrissey stood back and surveyed his completed tent with ill-concealed pride.

It collapsed.

Later that afternoon, Reggie held a staff meeting.

His purpose was to allocate duties and responsibilities.

They assembled in a wide circle around the living room, which no longer looked quite so surprisingly spacious.

Outside, through the french windows, the three white tents gleamed in the April sun.

Reggie stood with his back to the fireplace.

'A lot of work here will be communal,' he said. 'We'll have group sessions, the first of which will be tomorrow morning at nine. But you'll also have individual roles to play and during your training you will familiarise yourselves with these, with other members of staff taking the place of clients. I will hold a watching brief, and Elizabeth, as you know, is secretary.'

Elizabeth smiled in acknowledgement.

'Doc Morrissey will naturally be our psychologist.'

Doc Morrissey smiled in acknowledgement.

'Tom, equally naturally, will be responsible for sport.'

'Sport?'

'Sport.'

'I know nothing about sport, Reggie.'

'That's all right. Doc Morrissey knows nothing about psychology.'

Everyone laughed.

'Just a minute,' said Doc Morrissey. 'I'll have you know I've been swotting it up like billyo.'

'Have you really?' said Reggie. 'That is bad news. No, Tom, it's sport for you.'

'But I'm just not a sport person,' said Tom.

'It's true,' said Linda. 'He doesn't know one end of a cricket racket from the other.'

'They're bats. I know that much,' said Tom.

'It was a joke,' said Linda.

'Ah, well, there you are,' said Tom. 'I've said it before and I'll say it again. I'm not a joke person. Seriously though, Reggie, I was hoping to do something with old English crafts. I've been rather bitten by the crafts' bug. Thatching, basket-weaving, that sort of thing. I'd prefer it if the popular Saturday evening TV programme was called "Craft of the Day", and its Sunday equivalent was...' Tom paused roguishly '..."The Big Thatch".'

One or two people smiled.

'You see,' said Tom. 'When I do make a joke you don't take any notice.'

C.J. laughed abruptly.

'Just got it,' he said. ' "The Big Thatch". Well done, Tom.

I didn't get where I am today without recognising a rib-tickling play on words when I hear it.'

'No, Tom,' said Reggie. 'Sport it is. We have to be unconventional, if we're to free our sport from competition and aggression, so your pathetic ignorance is just what I want.'

'Oh. Well, thanks, Reggie.'

Reggie smiled at Joan, who was sitting on the pouffe.

'You'll be responsible for music,' he said.

Tony snorted.

'Why do you snort?' said Joan, whipping round to glare at him.

'You're tone deaf,' said Tony.

'Thank you,' said Joan. 'You really know how to make a woman feel good.'

'Tony, you'll be responsible for culture,' said Reggie.

It was Joan's turn to snort.

'Culture?' said Tony.

'Culture.'

'Culture. Fine. With you. No sweat,' said Tony. 'I'll really hit culture.'

'Prue,' said Reggie, turning towards the hard chair where Prue sat, slightly out of the circle. 'You'll be responsible for crafts. Thatching, basket-weaving, that sort of thing. Excellent therapy.'

'Super,' said Prue.

'I must say, Reggie, I think that's a bit thick,' said Tom.

'Need you for sport. Sorry,' said Reggie. 'C.J., your work will be work.'

'I don't follow you, Reggie,' said C.J.

'Nobody understands the problems of man's relationship with his work better than you.'

'Thank you, Reggie.'

'You've caused so many of them.'

'Thank you, Reggie.'

'A lot of the people who come to "Perrins" will be unhappy in their work. You'll simulate work situations and help them overcome their problems. Linda, you'll deal with art. Painting, drawing, etcetera.'

'Must I?' said Linda.

50

'And finally David,' said Reggie.

David Harris-Jones smiled nervously.

'You'll deal with sex,' said Reggie.

David Harris-Jones fainted.

'Art's dreary,' said Linda. 'Can't I have sex?'

'Not while you're married to me,' said Tom.

Dinner consisted of pâté, grilled trout, and trifle.

It was excellent.

Dark uncompromising night descended upon Number Twenty-one, Oslo Avenue, Botchley.

Dark uncompromising night descended upon the back garden of Number Twenty-one, Oslo Avenue, Botchley.

Dark uncompromising night descended upon the three tents lined up at the bottom of the lawn in the back garden of Number Twenty-one, Oslo Avenue.

A Tilley lamp shone on C.J. as he lay in his sleeping bag, looking up at the narrowing angle at the top of his tent.

He was thinking.

He had decided to write a book about Reggie Perrin's community.

He had never written a book before, but there was a first time for everything.

He began to write.

'A Tilley lamp shone on me,' he wrote, 'as I lay in my sleeping bag, looking up at the narrowing angle at the top of my tent.'

I was thinking.

I had decided to write a book about Reggie Perrin's community.

I had never written a book before, but there was a first time for everything.

I began to write.'

What an unimaginative way of starting a book.

'What an unimaginative way of starting a book,' wrote C.J. 'I ripped up the paper and hurled it to the far corner of the tent.'

*   *   *

51

In the other two tents, the lamps were already out. Doc Morrissey was trying to sleep, and Tony was trying to persuade Joan to make love.

The aims were different, the failures equal.

Tom was sitting on the bed, in his underpants. The wallpaper was floral.

'Come to bed,' said Linda.

Tom began to put on his pyjamas.

'Don't put your pyjamas on,' said Linda.

'They said it might be pretty cold later on,' said Tom. 'Minus two by dawn in sheltered inland areas.'

He clambered into bed and kissed Linda on the cheek.

'Night, Squelchypoos,' he said.

'Tom! Please don't call me Squelchypoos, Tom.'

'Well, come on, tell me what you do want me to call you.'

'A proper term of endearment, Tom.'

'Such as?'

'Well, Cuddlypuddles.'

'"Cuddlypuddles is as bad as Squelchypoos.'

'To you it is. To me it isn't.'

Tom propped himself up on his left elbow, the better to assume mastery of the conversation.

'I'm sorry, Linda,' he said. 'But for the life of me I can't distinguish any great difference between Squelchypoos and Cuddlypuddles.'

'Oh stop being pompous, Tom.'

Tom abandoned mastery and plumped for being hurt. This involved lying on his back and staring fixedly at the ceiling.

'I can't help being pompous, Linda,' he said. 'I drew the ticket marked pomposity in the lottery of life. I'm a pomposity person.'

'That's another thing, Tom.'

'What?'

'Do try and stop saying "I'm a whatsit person" all the time.'

'I never say "I'm a whatsit person".'

'You just said ' I'm a pomposity person".'

'I've never said "I'm a whatsit person".'

Linda turned angrily on her side, facing away from Tom.

'You know what I mean,' she said. 'Whatever it is we're talking about, you say "I'm not a whatever it is person".'

'It's just a phrase I'm going through, Linda. I can't help it. It's like C.J. can't help saying "I didn't get where I am today". I just don't happen to be an "I didn't get where I am today" person. I'm an "I'm a whatever it is person" person.'

'Oh, Tom, for God's sake. We're supposed to be setting up an ideal society here.'

'Perhaps I'm just not an ideal society person, Cuddlypuddles.'

'It's been an excellent first day,' whispered Reggie.

Oslo Avenue lay draped in the thick velvet of suburban sleep, eerie, timeless, endless.

Reggie began to stroke Elizabeth's stomach.

'No,' she said, stiffening.

'Stop stiffening,' he said. 'Leave that to me.'

'People will hear,' she whispered.

'They're far too busy,' he whispered.

He put his ear to the wall.

'Reggie, don't,' she whispered. 'That's disgraceful. It's intruding on people's privacy. Can you hear anything?'

'David Harris-Jones just whispered "No. People will hear" ' he whispered.

And he laughed silently, joyously.

III

The Training

IN THE MORNING the temperature was close to freezing point. Joan curled up in her sleeping bag and pretended to be asleep.

'Come on,' said Tony. 'Lovely fresh morning. Knock-out. Let's go and hit some breakfast.'

Joan groaned.

'Oh come on, darling,' said Tony. 'Let's get this show on the road and score some fried eggs.'

He crawled inelegantly out of the tent. A heavy dew lay on the lawn and rose bushes. The sky was a diffident blue.

C.J. was returning from the house after performing his ablutions. He was wearing a purple dressing gown over his trousers and vest and carried a large pudding basin. Neatly folded over the edge of the basin was a matching purple face flannel. Among the toilet requisites in the basin were a luxuriant badger-hair shaving brush, a cut-throat razor and a strop.

'Only just up?' said C.J. 'You've missed the best part of the morning. The early bird gets first use of the lavatory.'

Reggie came over the patio towards the lawn, rubbing his hands.

'Morning,' he said. 'Everybody up? That's the ticket. Lovely fresh morning.'

'I.e. perishing,' said Tony.

At that moment three things happened simultaneously. Mr Penfold looked over the hedge from Number Twenty-three, a tiny double-decker bus, hurled from the children's bedroom, struck Reggie's shins, and Doc Morrissey's tent collapsed.

Mr Penfold closed his eyes, as if he hoped that when he opened them again it would all be gone. Doctor Daines had warned him that there might be side-effects from giving up smoking. Perhaps this whole scene was simply a side-effect.

He opened his eyes. The scene was still there. A child was bawling in an upstairs room, and Doc Morrissey was moaning inside the collapsed tent. Mr Penfold met Reggie's eyes.

'It's a sharp one, isn't it?' he said, and fled.

Reggie joined C.J. and Tony outside Doc Morrissey's tent. 'Are you all right, Doc?' he called out.

'I can't move,' groaned Doc Morrissey. 'I've broken my back.'

It was nine o'clock. Time for the group meeting to begin.

Reggie sat in his study, looking out on to the pebble-dash wall of Number Twenty-three.

In his lap sat Snodgrass, the newly-acquired community cat. She wriggled uneasily.

'It's time for my great project to begin, Snodgrass,' said Reggie, tickling her throat gently. 'But I shall enter slightly late, in order to impress.'

Snodgrass averted her eyes haughtily, in order to impress.

'Is it too ridiculous for words, Snodgrass?' said Reggie. 'Should I go in there and say "Sorry. It's all been a mistake. Go home."?'

Snodgrass made no reply.

'I can't, can I?' said Reggie. 'They've sold their homes. They've given up their jobs. I'm committed.'

Snodgrass miaowed.

'You're wrong Snodgrass,' said Reggie. 'It isn't ridiculous. It will work. We aren't going to be sod worshippers in Dorset or mushroom sniffers in the Welsh hills. We aren't going to pray to goats or sacrifice betel nuts. We aren't going to live in teepees and become the lost tribe of Llandrindod Wells. I'm not going to shave my hair off and chant mantras in Droitwich High Street. I'm not going to become the Maharishi of Forfar or the Guru of Ilfracombe. It's going to be an ordinary place, where ordinary, unheroic, middle-class, middle-aged people can come. It's going to be a success. I'm going to make another fortune.'

He lowered Snodgrass gently to the floor.

He smoothed his hair and straightened his tie. He might have

55

been setting off for the office, not starting an experiment in community living.

He entered the living room.

There was nobody there.

It was almost ten o'clock before the chaos of that first morning was sorted out and the staff were assembled in the pleasant suburban room.

The only absentee was C.J. It was still the school holidays, and, as luck would have it, he had drawn first blood at looking after the children.

Reggie stood in front of the fireplace and looked grimly at his watch.

'It's nine fifty-eight,' he said. 'Not an auspicious start. Now, who'll set the ball rolling?'

He sat between Prue and Tom on the settee, and looked round expectantly.

'Come on,' he said. 'We've wasted enough time already. You're supposed to discuss your problems openly, criticise each other frankly, and so learn to express yourselves and realise your potential more fully. So come on, let's be having you.'

He looked round the room imploringly.

'All right,' he said. 'Let's try a different approach. Why are you all late? Doc?'

He glanced hopefully at his psychologist.

'My tent fell down,' said Doc Morrissey.

'How is the tent now?'

'I find myself suffering from a feeling of deep insecurity in my tent,' said Doc Morrissey, who seemed to have made a remarkable recovery from his broken back. 'I just toss that into the maelstrom of speculation.'

'Ah!' said Reggie. 'Now that is just the kind of thing these meetings are for. Well done, Doc. We're off. We're on our way. The project is launched.'

He looked round the room, embracing them all in his smile of encouragement.

'Has anyone got any ideas why Doc Morrissey should feel insecure in his tent?' he asked.

'Yes,' said Tony. 'The bloody thing keeps falling down.'

Reggie looked pained.

'Isn't that a bit facile?' he said.

'I spoke of a deeper insecurity than that,' said Doc Morrissey. 'As I lie on my back, in my tent, in a tactile me-to-ground situation, I feel a strong sense of the natural world, the earth, beneath me, and the fragile structure of civilisation, the tent, above me, and I realise, I sense, the fragility of our domination over the world of nature around us. And it gives me a real sense of pain.'

'Cobblers,' said Tony.

'Yes, I do have a bit of pain in the cobblers as well. It's the dew, I think. Incipient arthritis of the testicles.'

'Well, that was splendid, Doc,' said Reggie. 'You see, you've taken to psychology like a duck to water. Excellent. So that's why you were late. Anyone else got any interesting reasons why they were late?'

'Because I didn't get up,' said Joan.

'Ah!' said Reggie. 'But why didn't you get up?'

'Because I was in a tent.'

'Yes. I think maybe we could move on from the subject of tents now,' said Reggie.

'Tony'll soon be wanting to,' said Joan. 'He isn't going to get his end away while we're under canvas.'

'Joan!' said Tony, giving her leg a sharp kick.

'Tony!' said Reggie. 'Don't kick Joan.'

'Well what a thing to say. Honestly. Crudesville, Arizona,' said Tony.

'I won't miss it much. You're not all that fantastic at it, anyway,' said Joan.

'Joan, please!' said Tony.

'I think this is going a bit far, Joan,' said Reggie.

'I thought we were supposed to criticise each other frankly,' said Joan, bending down and examining her leg.

'We *are* supposed to criticise each other frankly,' said Reggie, 'but frankly I think you're criticising Tony too frankly. Not that he should have kicked you.'

'Excuse me a moment,' put in Elizabeth, leaning forward in her armchair. 'Aren't we going to be teaching very largely by example?'

57

'That's right,' said Reggie. 'Example from above.'

'Well then, should you give aggressive orders like "Don't kick Joan"?'

'Well, I mean to say . . .'

'Surely it's wrong to counter aggression with aggression, if aggression is wrong?'

'We're quibbling now,' said Reggie.

'Mother-in-law's right,' said Tom. 'It should be a democratically arrived at decision whether Tom should have kicked Joan.'

'I suppose I should have said . . . er . . . er . . . has anyone any idea what I should have said?'

' "Tony, do you think it's in your best interests to kick Joan?" ' said Prue. ' "Might it not lead to her kicking you in retaliation?" '

'Good,' said Reggie, patting the top of her sensible head affectionately. 'Very good.'

' "Tony, don't you think that if you kick Joan you might bruise her legs and render those exquisite long slender limbs a little less pleasant to plant little hot kisses on?" ' suggested Doc Morrissey.

Joan gave him a cool look.

'Just a suggestion,' he said. 'What we psychologists call the appeal to self-interest.'

'Right,' said Reggie. 'Well, if we can now leave the question of Joan's legs and move on . . .'

C.J. burst in. There were lumps of plasticine on his face. He shook his trousers angrily. A green frog dropped to the floor.

'I've had enough,' he thundered. 'I didn't get where I am today by having green frogs dropped down my crutch.'

'Had enough already?' said Reggie. 'You're going to need a bit more perseverance than that if you're to succeed in the great work for which I have enrolled you. You're getting the perfect training with those kids. There isn't a person in this room who wouldn't willingly exchange places with you, but there you are, you picked the plum. Linda, where are you going?'

Linda, who was sidling towards the door, stopped.

'I was going to see if the children were O.K.,' she said.

'Please. Please. Faith and trust. I'm sure that if C.J. has the

58

backing of our trust and faith, he will go in there and start earning his salary.'

C.J. scowled.

'But what'll I do?' he said.

'What about trying simple argument?' said Reggie. 'What about saying, "I say, Adam, old fruit, do you really think Kermit wants to have a trip down my crutch. It's frightfully dark inside trousers, you know".'

'Yes,' said C.J. 'But what'll I do after that?'

'Why not tell them a story?' said Reggie.

C.J. looked as near to panic as Reggie had ever seen him.

'Oh, all right,' he said. "But I don't intend to make a habit of looking after the children.'

'Their behaviour will get much better once we adults set them a consistent example,' said Reggie.

'H'm!'

C.J. left the room with a wistful glance at the comparative safety of the group meeting.

'I see,' said Tom. 'So we haven't been bringing the children up properly. Is that the insinuation?'

'There was no insinuation whatsoever,' said Reggie. 'But the fact that you insinuate that there was suggests that you feel guilty. Maybe we can examine this feeling without interruption.'

C.J. burst in once more.

'Reggie's wet himself,' he announced.

'Then change him,' said Reggie irritably.

Prue fetched a nappy and safety pins, and handed them to C.J. He received them as if they were a grenade and its pin.

'I fold them by the kite method,' said Prue.

'The . . . er . . . ah!' said C.J. 'I . . . er . . . I've never actually changed a nappy before.'

'There's a first time for everything,' said Reggie.

'That's true,' said C.J., grudgingly admitting the force of Reggie's remark.

'In changing the nappy you'll help to change yourself,' said Doc Morrissey. 'Try and look on it as a wonderful journey of self-discovery.'

C.J. smiled faintly at Doc Morrissey.

'Your turn for the wonderful journey of self-discovery will come,' he said, and he closed the door behind him.

'Right,' said Reggie. 'It is now ten twenty-six and we've still hardly got started. This emphasises the importance of starting punctually at nine. It's not good enough and it won't happen again.'

He glared fiercely at them.

'Excuse me,' said David Harris-Jones. 'I may be quite wrong, but ... er ... if you're the example that we're to follow, isn't it wrong that you should give orders and ... er ... virtually ... as it were ... threaten us. I mean maybe I'm wrong and it isn't wrong. But I think I'm right and it is wrong.'

He looked anxiously at Prue. She smiled reassuringly.

'Super,' she said.

'David has a good point,' said Reggie. 'I'd like to rephrase what I said. We should have started at nine, but we didn't and that is ... er ... absolutely splendid because obviously you didn't want to start at nine, but I would suggest that it would be even more absolutely splendid in future if you did want to start at nine.'

'Too early,' said Joan.

They decided to decide democratically what time their group sessions would start and end. They decided to have a vote on it. Then they debated democratically what form the vote should take. Then they voted on what form the vote should take. Then they voted.

The consensus of opinion was that they should begin at nine thirty and break for lunch at twelve thirty. By that time it was twelve thirty. They broke for lunch.

'It's been an excellent first morning,' said Reggie.

Life at Number Twenty-one, Oslo Avenue, Botchley, began to settle into a pattern.

Twice a week they held group meetings. Once a week they held a meeting to discuss their group meetings.

The rest of the time they discussed their problems with Doc Morrissey and their sex lives with David Harris-Jones, wove baskets with Prue, painted with Linda, sang with Joan, sported

60

with Tom, were cultural with Tony, and entered into simulated work situations with C.J.

At first some of these activities were not very successful, while others were worse.

At the third group meeting they decided to set up a rota system for doing the various household activities like dusting, hoovering, helping McBlane and answering the door.

At the fourth group meeting Doc Morrissey suggested that each day they should select a different word, and try to live in accordance with it. He explained that this would be an excellent form of self-discipline and would help to weld them into a corporate entity.

They each chose ten words. The hundred words were put into a hat. Each evening the hat was shuffled, and the next day's word was drawn by a member of the staff.

The member of the staff who would choose the word was chosen out of another hat.

The scheme began on May the second. The word was Courtesy, and it was Tom's turn to answer the door.

'Good morning, Jimmy,' he said. 'Wonderful to see you. What an unexpected pleasure. What a bonus.'

Jimmy stared at him in amazement.

'Courtesy's our word of the day,' said Tom.

'Oh, I see. That explains it,' said Jimmy. 'Jolly good. Like to see Reggie privately. Personal. My car. Case nothing comes of it.'

Reggie went outside and sat in Jimmy's rusty old Ford. There were two dents in the off-side.

All the street lights were on due to a failure in the timing devices.

'This army of yours going well?' said Jimmy, when they were settled inside the car.

'Very well indeed,' said Reggie, nodding to the milkman, who was returning to the depot on his float.

'Offer of a job still open?'

'Well, yes,' said Reggie, surprised.

'On beam ends.'

'But, Jimmy. The narrow boats.'

'Sold out, Reggie. Cut losses. Kaput.'

61

Jimmy was tapping the steering wheel nervously.

'Let down,' he mumbled.

'Tim "Curly" Beamish?'

Jimmy nodded miserably.

'His share of money. Stolen,' he said. 'Ran up debts. Casanova Club, Wolverton. Copacabana Club, Bletchley. Paradise Lost, Milton Keynes. Women. Gambling. Paid for equipment with dud cheques. Our name mud from Daventry to Hemel Hempstead. Clive "Lofty" Anstruther all over again. Bastard!'

Jimmy sank his head in misery and the horn shattered the stillness of the domestic morning.

'What the hell is that noise?' he said.

'You're leaning on the horn,' said Reggie.

Jimmy sat up hastily.

'Funny thing. Wasn't working earlier,' he said.

He switched the ignition off. He seemed marginally cheered by the revival of his horn.

'Don't expect you'll have me now,' he said.

'Of course I'll have you,' said Reggie. 'You did sterling work for Grot. I have no doubt you'll do sterling work here.'

'What as?' said Jimmy.

'Leader of expeditionary forces,' said Reggie. 'Helping old ladies across road, clearing litter, whatever you like. A sort of commando unit of good works.'

'Thanks Reggie,' said Jimmy. 'Kiss you if we were French.'

'Thank God we aren't, then,' said Reggie.

'Yes. Postman might think we were bum-boys.'

They got out of the car, and Jimmy locked up carefully.

'Cock-up on the judgement of men front,' he said. 'Always choose the wrong chap. My Freudian heel.'

'Achilles heel.'

'You see. Wrong chap again. Useless. No wonder army made me personnel officer.'

Next day, a fourth tent appeared on the lawn.

On the following day, the word of the day was Quietude. The peace was shattered at seven o'clock when Jimmy emerged from his tent and blew 'Come to the cookhouse door, boys' on his bugle. Reggie took him quietly to one side before breakfast. They sat in the study, looking out over the pebble-dashed side wall of Number Twenty-three.

'Jimmy, today's word is quietude,' whispered Reggie.

'Damn,' whispered Jimmy. 'Slipped my mind. Get the picture. No bugle till tomorrow.'

'When I said I was running a sort of army,' whispered Reggie, 'I didn't mean it literally.'

'Very literal cove,' whispered Jimmy. 'Leave imagination to you brain boxes.'

'I was using a figure of speech,' whispered Reggie.

'Ah! Figures of speech not my line. Not many metaphors in Queen's Own Berkshire Light Infantry. Hyperbole exception rather than rule in B.F.P.O. thirty-three.'

'No doubt you see what I'm driving at,' whispered Reggie.

'Never see what people are driving at, Reggie.'

'Ah! What I'm driving at is this, Jimmy. I don't think that blowing "Come to the cookhouse door, boys" on your bugle is quite our style.'

'I see.'

'Besides, what will the neighbours say?'

'Ah! Admit it. Forgot the neighbours. Great boon of army life, no neighbours. "Guns one to eight, fire!" "Excuse me, sir?" "Yes, Smudger, what is it?" "Won't we wake the neighbours, sir?" "Good God, so we will. Cancel the firing. We'll have some cocoa instead. Good thinking, Smudger." Doesn't happen. World might be different if it did. Thought?'

'It certainly is, Jimmy.'

But neighbours there assuredly were in Oslo Avenue, Botchley, and shortly after breakfast on the Saturday morning they made their presence felt. The weather was showery.

Mr Penfold, from Number Twenty-three, was the first to arrive. Prue, whose turn it was for answering the door, ushered him into the living room. He had a small head and stick-out ears.

'I'd like to have a word with you if I may, Mr Perrin,' he said.

'Certainly,' said Reggie. 'Would you like coffee? My wife makes excellent coffee.'

Doc Morrissey served coffee and biscuits. When he had gone Mr Penfold said, 'Er . . . excuse me, but this place is a little unusual, and unusual things are really quite usual these days. So . . . er . . . well. . . .'

He swallowed hard.

'That wasn't your wife, was it?' he said.

Reggie laughed heartily.

'No,' he said. 'That was my Doc Morrissey. We share all duties in our community.'

'Community?'

'Yes.'

'Ah. I really must . . . er . . . lovely coffee . . . I really must put my foot down. Well, it isn't really me. It's Mrs Penfold.'

'You really must put Mrs Penfold's foot down.'

Mr Penfold sat perched on the edge of his chair, taking his coffee in tiny sips.

'After all, Oslo Avenue isn't the King's Road, Chelsea,' he averred.

'It isn't the Reeperbahn in Hamburg,' agreed Reggie.

'I'm glad you see it my way,' said Mr Penfold.

'It isn't the red light district of Amsterdam either.'

'Precisely.'

'It's a pity, isn't it?'

Careful, Reggie. You need these people on your side.

Mr Penfold leant forward so far that he almost toppled off the chair.

'Not to me, it isn't,' he said. 'Mrs Penfold is not a well woman, Mr Perrin. I'm afraid that all this . . .'

'All this, Mr Penfold?'

Mr Penfold waved his arms, including the french windows, the three pictures of bygone Botchley and the standard lamp in the environmental outrage that was being perpetrated on him.

The doorbell rang again, and Prue ushered in Mrs Hollies, from Number Nineteen.

Doc Morrissey produced an extra cup, and Mrs Hollies' verdict on the coffee reinforced that of Mr Penfold.

'Don't worry. That's not his wife,' said Mr Penfold, when Doc Morrissey had gone.

'What?' said Mrs Hollies.

'That man who served coffee. He's not Mr Perrin's wife.'

Mrs Hollies looked at Mr Penfold in astonishment.

'Do we owe the pleasure of your visit to any particular purpose?' Reggie enquired pleasantly.

'It's Mr Hollies,' said Mrs Hollies. 'Mr Hollies has to take things very easily. The slightest disturbance to his routine, and Mr Hollies goes completely haywire. It's his work. These are perilous times in the world of sawdust.'

'Sawdust?' said Reggie.

'Mr Hollies is in the sawdust supply industry,' said Mrs Hollies.

'What exactly does that mean?' asked Reggie.

'He supplies sawdust.'

'I see.'

'To butchers, bars, zoos, furriers, circuses.'

'Where sawdust is needed,' said Reggie, 'there is Mr Hollies.'

'Exactly.'

'Do I deduce that things aren't good in the world of sawdust?' said Mr Penfold.

'Not what they were, but then, what is?' said Mrs Hollies.

'You can say that again,' said Mr Penfold.

Mrs Hollies spurned the invitation. Instead, she said: 'In and out like the tide. Up and down like Tower Bridge. These biscuits are delicious. Where do you get them?'

'Finefare,' said C.J., passing through with the hoover.

There were pretty blue flowers round the edge of C.J.'s pinny.

'They share everything here,' explained Mr Penfold.

'Some share more than others,' said C.J. darkly, and with that ominous thrust he departed.

'I must admit that I came round to ... er ... to enquire what exactly is going on here,' said Mrs Hollies. 'I don't mind myself, an Englishman's home is his castle, but it's Mr Hollies's nerves.'

'What exactly are you complaining about?' said Reggie politely.

'Tents in the garden,' said Mrs Hollies. 'It isn't natural.'

'Babies crying at all hours. Comings and goings,' said Mr Penfold.

'Goings and comings,' said Mrs Hollies.

65

'That's the same complaint twice,' said Reggie. 'One man's coming is another man's going.'

'No, it isn't,' said Mr Penfold.

'Just testing,' said Reggie.

Careful, Reggie.

'Anything else?' said Reggie.

'Cars parked outside the house,' said Mr Penfold. 'You probably think that's petty, but it's Mrs Penfold.'

'Mr Hollies is the same,' said Mrs Hollies. 'Me, you could park juggernauts outside.'

'As far as I'm concerned,' said Mr Penfold, 'you could have a line of pantechnicons stretching from Beirut Crescent to Buenos Aires Rise.'

'But it's Mr Hollies,' said Mrs Hollies. 'Mr Hollies is very jealous of his front view. Cars parked in front of our house, they prey on his mind.'

'Mrs Penfold's exactly the same,' said Mr Penfold. 'Cars parked in front of our verge, they're a red rag to a bull.'

'It's the number of people you have here,' said Mrs Hollies. 'It's the uncertainty.'

'I mean, this is a residential street, let's face it,' said Mr Penfold.

'It's wondering what you're up to, with the tents and the bugle and that,' said Mrs Hollies.

Reggie stood up.

'I'm in a position to set your minds at rest,' he said. 'First, the bugle. I can give you a unilateral assurance that there will be no more bugling.'

'Oh well. You can't say fairer than that,' said Mr Penfold.

'So far as it goes,' said Mrs Hollies. 'But what about everything else?'

'Secondly, everything else. You are privileged to live next to an amazing and historic development. In this road, hitherto barely known in Botchley, let alone in the great wen beyond, you are going to see the formation of an ideal society.'

'A utopia, you mean?' said Mr Penfold.

'I suppose you could call it that,' said Reggie.

'If you wanted a utopia, you'd have done better to take one

of those big houses in Rio De Janeiro Lane,' said Mr Penfold. 'They've got forecourt parking, you see.'

'The people here at present are my staff,' explained Reggie. 'They're in the middle of their training, learning how . . .'

Tom burst in from the direction of the kitchen. He had a bucket of water and a chamois leather.

'C.J. has accused me of not pulling my weight,' he said. 'Either he goes or I do. Oh, I'm sorry. I didn't know you had visitors.'

'Tom, these are our neighbours, Mr Penfold and Mrs Hollies. This is Tom, our sports wizard,' said Reggie.

Tom fixed Mrs Hollies with an intense gaze.

'Anyone who knows anything about me knows that I'm just not a not pulling my weight person,' he told her.

'Where was I?' said Reggie, sitting down again after Tom's departure. 'Oh yes. These people are in the middle of training, learning how to be happy, generous, perfect people.'

Mrs Hollies produced a thinly-veiled sneer.

'I know what you're thinking,' said Reggie. 'Well, yes. We all have a long way to go. That's what makes it fascinating. Who'd bother to climb Everest if it was flat?'

'Mrs Penfold and I,' said Mr Penfold. 'It'd be just about our mark.'

'People will flock to this place, as soon as it's open to the public,' said Reggie. 'Casualties of our over-complicated society will seek help in their hundreds.'

Mr Penfold and Mrs Hollies turned pale.

'I hope I've set your minds at rest,' said Reggie.

The next day was Sunday. It rained on and off. There was only play in one John Player League cricket match. The word of the day was Knowledge.

Reggie sat in his study, reading an encyclopedia. The door handle slowly turned. It was Jocasta, bringing him a cup of coffee. Not all of it had spilled in the saucer.

He thanked her gravely.

'Adam's got a willy and I've got a hole,' she said.

'What a satisfactory arrangement,' said Reggie.

'I wouldn't want a willy.'

'Quite right.'

'Has C.J. got a willy?'

'Yes.'

'Have you seen it?'

'No.'

Reggie tipped the spilt coffee back into his cup.

'How d'you know he's got a willy if you haven't seen it?'

'The balance of probabilities.'

'Has he got a hole?'

'No.'

'Liar. He's got one in his bum.'

Reggie sipped the coffee. It was lukewarm.

'Mankind, Jocasta, is distinguished from the lower orders by his capacity to conceptualise about abstract matters of ethical, moral, aesthetic, scientific and mathematical concern,' he said. 'I know you're only six, but I think you ought to be turning your mind to slightly higher questions than you are at present.'

'Does C.J. sit down when he does his wee-wees?'

That evening Reggie told Tom and Linda about Jocasta's thirst for knowledge. Tom looked glum.

'Her failure is a mirror of our failure,' he said.

'Your failure is a mirror of my failure,' said Reggie.

On Monday it rained all day. There was no play in the Schweppes County Championship or the Rothmans Tennis. The word of the day was Innovation.

Tom called on Reggie in his study. He was wearing a blue tracksuit and carried an orange football.

'I've got an innovation,' he said.

'Fire away,' said Reggie.

Tom sprawled in an upright chair that might have been designed specifically to prevent sprawling.

'Football,' he said.

'It's been done before,' said Reggie.

'With a difference,' persisted Tom. 'Football with no aggro, no fouls, no tension, no violence.'

'What's the secret?' said Reggie.

'No opposition,' said Tom.

'Pardon?'

'You asked me to be unconventional. This is unconventional. We have eleven members of staff. The perfect team. Only nobody plays against us. We use skill, passing, team-work, and tactics. It's pure football, Reggie.'

'Interesting,' said Reggie.

'I've been in touch with Botchley Albion,' said Tom. 'They play in the Isthmian League. They can rent us some costumes, for a consideration. We don't want to look ridiculous.'

Tuesday dawned cloudy but dry. The word of the day was Connect.

It was C.J.'s turn to be analysed by Doc Morrissey. The chaise-longue, purchased at the Botchley Antique Boutique, seemed out of place in Doc Morrissey's tent.

'Lie down on the couch,' he told C.J.

C.J. clambered on to the chaise-longue with bad grace.

Doc Morrissey lay back on his sleeping bag.

'A little word association,' he said. 'Both of us making random connections. Sex.'

'Table tennis,' said C.J.

'Why?'

'Random.'

'When I say random, I mean that you're to let subconscious logical associations replace your conscious logical associations. Let's start again. Sex.'

'Table tennis.'

'Oh for goodness' sake, C.J.'

'In my palmier days,' said C.J., 'I had relations with a table tennis player in Hong Kong. She had a very unusual grip.'

'What happened?'

'She beat me twenty-one–seventeen, twenty-one–twelve, twenty-one–nine. Then she took me home and I beat her. She seemed to enjoy that sort of thing. Very disturbing. So did I. Even more disturbing.'

'Why did you say it was a random association, then?'

'I was lying.'

Doc Morrissey sighed.

'You're on this project, C.J.,' he said. 'You might as well take it seriously.'

'Oh very well.'

C.J. stared at the cool white roof of Doc Morrissey's tent. He could feel his mind going blank.

'Table tennis,' said Doc Morrissey.

'Sex.'

'Girl.'

'Dance.'

'Gooseberry.'

'Raspberry.'

'Fool.'

'Jimmy.'

'Army.'

'Resistance.'

'Underground.'

'Rush-hour.'

'Red buses.'

'Moscow.'

'St Petersburg.'

'Dostoievsky.'

'Idiot.'

'Jimmy.'

'Very interesting,' said Doc Morrissey when they had finished. 'Why do you associate Jimmy with fool and idiot?'

'He is a fool and an idiot.'

'People can't help what they are,' said Doc Morrissey. 'Their behaviour is conditioned by many things. You should say, "The many environmental and hereditary influences to which I have been subjected lead me to believe Jimmy is an idiot".'

'He is an idiot.'

'All right. The many environmental and hereditary influences to which I have been subjected lead me to believe that the many environmental and hereditary influences to which Jimmy has been subjected have made him an idiot.'

C.J. clambered stiffly off the couch.

'Is that all?' he said.

'No,' said Doc Morrissey. 'Many other factors influence our

behaviour. The state of the planets. Our biorhythmic cycle. The weather.'

'The many environmental and hereditary influences to which I have been subjected, allied to my low biorhythmic cycle, the relationship of Pluto to Uranus, the fact that it's pissing down in Rangoon and that my auntie was jilted by a tobacconist from Wrexham lead me to believe that you're talking a load of balls.' said C.J.

Wednesday dawned dry but cloudy. The word of the day was Bananas. For the best part of an hour, they struggled to think bananas, talk bananas and be bananas.

Then they gave it up.

Thursday began brightly but fell off fast. The word of the day was Bananas.

They examined the slips that remained in the hat, and found that eight more carried the legend 'Bananas'. They never found out who had chosen bananas for all their ten words.

They abandoned having a word of the day after that. Doc Morrissey explained that it was stifling individual responses and preventing a steady emotional development.

Friday was extremely cold for May. Severiano Ballasteros shot a five under par sixty-six to win the Tampax Invitation Classic by three strokes.

In the evening Reggie put a little plan into action.

McBlane's excellent dinner was already but a memory. Little Reggie was asleep. Adam and Jocasta were watching Kojak. Reggie and Elizabeth waited for their guests in the living room. Four guests were invited. But only Mr Penfold and Mrs Hollies arrived. Their loved ones were indisposed.

They accepted small medium sherries.

'I have great news for you,' said Reggie. 'I've decided that you were right. This is not a suitable environment for our project. We're selling up.'

Mrs Hollies and Mr Penfold tried not to show their relief. They accepted more sherry with pleasure and praised the decor with sudden enthusiasm.

71

'The would-be purchaser is calling round shortly,' said Reggie. 'You'll be able to meet him.'

Quite soon the doorbell rang.

'This may be him now,' said Reggie.

Elizabeth answered the door. Mr Penfold and Mrs Hollies stood up expectantly. Elizabeth returned with Tony, who was heavily blacked up.

'Ah, there you are, Winston,' said Reggie.

'Here ah is, man,' said Tony.

'This is Mr Winston Baldwin Gladstone Vincent Fredericks,' said Reggie.

Tony flashed his carefully whitened teeth, and extended a blackened hand. He was worried lest the boot-polish came off —unnecessarily. Neither Mr Penfold nor Mrs Hollies seemed over-anxious to shake his hand.

'I don't think my new neighbours dig me, man,' said Tony. 'Because I'm a black man, man. Sure is a sad thing. I was really looking forward to scoring some curried goat barbecues with them this summer.'

On Tuesday afternoon Tom led his team out for their football match versus nobody. A 'For Sale' board was being stuck in the soft earth outside Number Nineteen.

The eleven members of staff turned left, past the 'For Sale' board in the garden of Number Twenty-three. They looked self-conscious and sheepish in their Botchley Albion strip. Varicose veins and white legs abounded.

They turned right into Washington Road, Doc Morrissey behind Joan, gazing at her legs.

'Yellow and purple suits you,' whispered Jimmy to Linda. 'Legs as top-hole as ever.'

They turned left into Addis Ababa Avenue.

'I'm playing a four-three-three line-up,' Tom confided to Reggie.

The line-up was C.J.; David Harris-Jones, Elizabeth, Tom and Prue; Tony, Reggie and Linda; Doc Morrissey, Jimmy and Joan.

As they were not all in the full bloom of youth and fitness, they only played twenty minutes each way. It began to rain at half time.

It proved rather boring playing with no oppponents and they had the rain and wind against them in the second half. Even so, the result was something of a disappointment.

'We should have won by far more than four-one,' said Tom as they walked wearily back down Addis Ababa Avenue, hair flattened by the rain, legs reddened by exertion. 'We frittered away our early advantage.'

Next day, a West Indian who bore a striking resemblance to Tom was shown round Number Twenty-three.

The following day another dusky-hued gentleman examined the bijou charms of Number Nineteen. He sounded more like a Southern gentleman than a West Indian.

'You sure has a might fine residence here, ma'am,' he told Mrs Hollies. 'Ah didn't get where ah is today without recognising a mighty fine residence when ah sees it, no sirree ma'am ah didn't.'

Two days later, 'For Sale' Boards went up outside Numbers Twenty-five and Seventeen.

By the end of June, the community had bought Numbers Seventeen, Nineteen, Twenty-three and Twenty-five.

The tents had gone.

Alterations were in progress in all the houses. Kitchens, dining rooms and living rooms were converted into bedrooms.

C.J., Doc Morrissey, David Harris-Jones and Jimmy became house wardens. McBlane moved reluctantly into Number Twenty-one.

The weather was changeable and temperate. It was a year without seasons.

The evenings began to draw in. The training intensified. Jimmy tried to persuade Linda to let him paint her in the nude. She refused.

'Come to my room,' he said.

'I can't, Jimmy. We're supposed to be nice, perfect human beings.'

Jimmy buried his head in her lap.

73

'Come and do nice perfect things in my room,' he said.

Linda stroked his greying, receding hair gently.

'That's all over, Uncle Jimmy,' she said.

'Absolutely. Should never have started,' said Jimmy. 'Just for ten minutes.'

'No!'

'Quite right. Glad you said "no". Best thing. Some time next week, perhaps.'

'No, Jimmy. Never again.'

'Absolutely right. Bang on. Like to paint you in nude, though.'

The opening day was fixed for August the fifteenth. Soon there was only a fortnight to go. Reggie placed an advert in several newspapers and journals. It read:

'Does your personality depress you?

Has life failed you?

Do you hate when you'd like to love?

Are you aggressive?

Are you over-anxious?

Are you over-competitive?

Are you over eighteen?

Then come to PERRINS for PEACE, GOOD LIVING and CARE.

STAY as LONG as you LIKE.

PAY ONLY what YOU think it was WORTH.

Apply 21, Oslo Avenue, Botchley.'

Behaviour improved all round. Reggie Harris-Jones hadn't cried for fifteen days and sometimes Adam and Jocasta went for several hours without doing anything beastly.

Only one week remained before the opening day.

Excitement was at fever pitch, dampened only by the fact that there wasn't one single booking.

Reggie began his final assessment interviews with his staff.

First he saw his psychologist.

Doc Morrissey leant forward and banged Reggie's desk so hard that the knob fell off one of the drawers.

74

'I have an awareness explosion, Reggie,' he said. 'A sensory tornado. An auto-catalystical understanding of my complete orgasm.'

'Don't you mean organism?'

'Possibly, Reggie. Rather a lot of terms, you know. Can't remember them all. Anyway, the point is, my visual, tactile and acoustic lives are amazingly enhanced. You know what that's called, don't you?'

'No.'

'Extrasensory perception, Reggie.'

He banged the desk, and the knob came off again.

'We seem to have a bit of desk castration here,' said Reggie, replacing the knob.

'You know what's done all this for me, Reggie? Confidence.'

Doc Morrissey raised his hand to bang it down again. Reggie removed the knob.

The Websters also expressed themselves delighted with their progress. Joan was enjoying the musical training, even though the staff weren't a musical lot, and Tony was really into culture. Shakespeare was the kiddie, and old Ibsen was a knock-out, for a Norwegian. Tony reckoned they could have been really commercial if they weren't so famous.

'We haven't had a row for three days,' said Joan.

'That's not very long,' said Reggie.

'Well, we like a good argument,' said Tony.

'I don't,' said Joan.

'You don't want to be like those bloody Harris-Joneses, do you?'

'What's wrong with the Harris-Joneses?' said Reggie.

'They always agree about everything,' said Tony.

'I think that's rather nice,' said Joan.

'Well, I don't,' said Tony. 'I'd hate to be married to somebody who always agreed with me.'

'I disagree,' said Joan.

Tony kissed her affectionately on the cheek.

On the Tuesday, a day marred by thunder and the non-arrival

75

of any bookings, it was the turn of the Harris-Joneses to have their assessment interviews.

David Harris-Jones was wearing sandals, fawn trousers and a yellow sweater.

Prue was wearing sandals, fawn trousers and a yellow sweater.

They sat very close together and held hands.

'How are you getting along?' said Reggie.

'Super,' they said.

'It has been suggested that you spend so much time thinking alike that you hardly exist as separate entities any more,' said Reggie.

'I don't think that's fair,' they said.

'Oh, sorry. After you,' they added.

They laughed. Reggie smiled.

A peal of thunder rumbled around Botchley.

'You answer, David,' said Reggie. 'Why don't you think it's fair?'

'Well, I think our marriage is happy because we agree about so much,' he said.

'I agree,' said Prue. 'I think it would be pointless to have to find things to disagree about in order to prove that you could agree to disagree.'

'I agree,' said David. 'Anyway, we sometimes disagree.'

A flash of forked lightning illuminated the room.

'I mean, when we first discussed which side of the bed we like to sleep on, we both said the right side,' said David.

'That was agreeing,' said Prue.

'I disagree,' said David. 'I think it was disagreeing. Because we couldn't both sleep on the right side. To agree would have been to disagree about our favourite side, so that we'd have slept on different sides. As we in fact do, by agreement.'

'Well, it does seem as if, so far as you are concerned, everything's going amazingly satisfactorily,' said Reggie.

'I agree,' they said.

On Wednesday there was great excitement. A Mr C. R. Babba-combe wished to visit the community.

His travel instructions were sent, and he was advised to arrive between three and six on Sunday. The floodgates were open.

It was Elizabeth's turn to have her assessment interview.

'I can't assess you,' said Reggie. 'Give us a kiss.'

'Sexy beast,' said Elizabeth.

Reggie went over to her chair, sat on her lap and kissed her. He kissed her again, harder. The chair tipped over backwards and they fell to the floor.

'I love you,' he said.

'I love you too,' she said.

Reggie kissed her. Neither of them heard the tentative knock on the study door.

Nor did they see Jimmy come in.

'Sorry,' he said. 'Haven't seen anything. Best thing, slope straight out, say nothing.'

Reggie and Elizabeth disentangled themselves, and stood up, dishevelled and embarrassed.

'What did you say?' said Reggie.

'I said, "Haven't seen anything. Best thing, slope straight out, say nothing".'

'Ah!'

'Sorry. Didn't mean it to come out out loud.'

'That's all right,' said Reggie. 'Elizabeth was just having her final assessment interview.'

'Ah!'

'Sorry to barge in,' said Jimmy awkwardly, when Elizabeth had gone. 'Didn't mean to catch you . . .'

'In flagrante delicto.'

'Is it? Ah! Never mind. Want to ask a favour, Reggie. Go AWOL, Friday lunch,' said Jimmy, pacing nervously up and down.

'Stop marching, Jimmy.'

'Oh. Sorry. Nerves.'

Jimmy sat down stiffly.

'Remember a girl called Lettice?' he said.

'Of course. We talked about her on the canal.'

'Built like a Sherman tank.'

'I wouldn't say that exactly,' said Reggie. 'More a Centurion.'

'Not turning up at church like that,' said Jimmy. 'Being here, niceness everywhere. Realised pretty rotten thing to do to a girl. Want to do the decent thing.'

'The decent thing, Jimmy?'

'Marry her.'

Reggie began to pace around the room, then remembered that he had told Jimmy not to, and sat down again.

'Remember the cove I told you about on the canal?' said Jimmy.

'Tim "Curly" Beamish?'

'No. Self-abuse. Images spring to mind. Erotic. A.T.S. parades, Kim Novak, that sort of caper. Yesterday morning, Reggie, I . . .'

'Self-abuse?'

'Yes. Dear old Lettice sprang to mind, Reggie.'

'And this image proved . . . er . . . not unconducive to . . . er . . .?'

'Enemy position stormed and taken, Reggie, no casualties. With me?'

'Yes.'

'Anyway, long story short, rang her people, posed as insurance agent, white lie, wheedled address, gave her tinkle, public phone, George and Two Dragons, back bar: "Lettice? Jimmy here. Remember our wedding? Rotten show. Sorry and all that. Suppose dinner's out of the question?" Surprise, surprise, by no means. Now. Here's the rub. Friday night, Lettice, Greek Islands, month, on tod. Only time free, short notice, Friday lunch." '

'And you want to get your claim in before she goes?'

'In nutshell, Reggie. Strike while iron's hot.'

'Faint heart never won Sherman tank. Of course you can go, Jimmy.'

On Thursday, there were no more applications to join the community.

The floodgates had not opened.

Reggie held his final assessment with Tom and Linda.

They seemed happier than he could ever remember seeing them.

'Tom did a wonderfully nice thing last night,' said Linda.

'Congratulations,' said Reggie.

'I found a whole bottle of my sprout wine that we'd over-looked,' said Tom.

'Oh, I see.'

'I drank the whole lot myself, Reggie.'

'Well done.'

Reggie also held his final assessment interview with C.J.

C.J. seemed happier than he could ever remember seeing him.

It was one of the few warm days of that dreadful summer, so they walked through the quiet streets of Botchley.

C.J. clasped his hands behind his back and took long strides.

'This beats orgies into a cocked hat,' he said.

'You're settling in now, are you?' said Reggie.

'In the early days,' said C.J., 'I felt like leaving.'

'You did terrible things, C.J. That helping old women across roads expedition of Jimmy's. Terrible.'

'I helped her across the arterial road.'

'You helped her halfway across, C.J.'

Their walk had taken them into Rio De Janeiro Lane, known in Botchley as Millionaire's Row. Here there were many-gabled Mock-Tudor fantasies. Here the nobs hung out.

'Then I realised that you have me by the short and goolies,' said C.J.

'Curlies.'

'What?'

'The expression is "curlies".'

'All right then. I thought, "He has me by the curlies and goolies. I'll make the best of it.'

'Well . . . good.'

'I've done two unselfish things, Reggie,' said C.J. 'I laughed at one of Tom's jokes, and I've told Mrs C.J. to stay six more months in Luxembourg.'

'Well done,' said Reggie.

On Friday there were again no applicants, and Reggie felt a twinge of fear.

Jimmy felt more than a twinge as he walked towards his rendezvous in Notting Hill Gate.

The weather was fine and sunny.

Good stick, Lettice, he thought. Looks aren't everything. Looks fade.

But does ugliness?

No miracle. Still ugly. Not horrendous, though. No means as bad as feared. On credit side, not horrendous.

'Hello, Lettice,' in odd-sounding voice.

'Hello, Jimmy.'

Presence of traffic overwhelming, strangely far away yet absurdly near.

'Right. Wop nosh party fall in.'

No! Control nerves. No military jargon.

They walked to the La Sorrentina in silence, handed in their coats as in a dream, found themselves sitting with drinks in their hands and a large menu at which they stared without seeing.

The tables were too close together but as yet the restaurant was empty.

'Well!' said Jimmy.

'Yes.'

'Well, well!'

'Yes.'

More silence.

'About wedding,' said Jimmy. 'Sorry. Cock-up.'

'Please!'

'Sorry. Greek islands, then?'

'Absolutely.'

'Blue sea. Dazzling white houses. Olive groves. Music. Wine. Informal. Joyous. Spot-on.'

'You've been there?'

'No.'

The waiter loomed.

'Bit rusty on my Itie nosh,' said Jimmy, smiling at him. 'Ravioli. Those are the envelope wallahs, aren't they? Lasagne? Aren't they those long flat green Johnnies?'

'Lasagne verde, sir. Excellent.'

'Ah! Well then! There we are.'

Soon they had ordered. The wine arrived, and Jimmy talked about Reggie's project until the arrival of the lasagne verde.

'M'm,' he said. 'Excellent. Theory. Bad soldier, good cook.

Your average Frenchie, magnificent coq au vin, come the hostilities, buggers off to Vichy. Ities, tanks with four gears, all reverse. Pasta magnifico. English, spotted dick and watery greens. Fights till he drops. Reason. Nothing to live for. Waffling. Evading issue. Nerves.'

Lettice smiled.

'Please don't be nervous,' she said. 'The wedding's forgotten.'

She shovelled a forkful of pasta into her mouth.

'Marry me,' said Jimmy.

Lettice stared at him in open-mouthed astonishment. Then she remembered that her mouth was full of lasagne and she hastily stared at him in closed-mouthed astonishment.

'Mean it,' said Jimmy, clasping her hand under the table. 'Thoroughly good stick.'

Two middle-aged women entered. They were on a shopping spree. They had the reckless air of women who have already spent too much and now see no obstacle to spending far too much.

Although there was plenty of room, the waiter put them at the table next to Lettice and Jimmy.

It is rare for the English to live with such intensity that they are unaware of the table next to them, but Jimmy and Lettice were unaware of it now. The result was a great treat for the two shoppers.

'Thank you for calling me a thoroughly good stick,' said Lettice. 'That's one of the nicest things anyone's ever said of me. But you don't want to stare at my ugly mug every morning.'

'I do,' said Jimmy. 'I do.'

The implications of his remark flashed transparently across his honest face.

'Not that your mug's ugly,' he added hastily.

Lettice smiled, and took another mouthful of lasagne. Immediately she wanted to talk. She ploughed through the mouthful as hastily as she could, but it resisted, as mouthfuls are wont to do at such moments.

'Shall I tell you the story of my life?' she said, and the two shoppers nodded involuntarily. 'As a girl I was big and gawky. I felt extremely visible. I became shy. Later I learnt, painfully, to seem less shy, although I was just as shy really. I was

81

emotionally frustrated. I ate too much, in compensation. I became larger still. Now I drink too much in compensation as well. Soon I'll look haggard as well as large. You don't want to marry me.'

'Nonsense,' said Jimmy stoutly. 'Won't pretend you're a raging beauty. No Kim Novak. Got something that's worth all the Kim Novaks in the world, though. Character. A beauty? All right, maybe not. A damned handsome woman? Yes, every time.'

Suddenly, oblivious of the watching shoppers, he began to cry.

'Lonely,' he said. 'So bloody lonely.'

Lettice stared at him in horror.

'Jimmy, don't cry. Don't cry, my darling.'

She lent him a hankie and he blew a trumpet voluntary.

She held his hand under the table.

'I hate to see men cry,' she said.

It seemed that in this respect her views differed from those of the lady shoppers.

'Marry me,' he said.

'I'm middle-aged and ugly,' said Lettice. 'And my name is Lettice. If I was a character in a novel, I'd be a figure of fun.'

'Horsewhip the author personally if you were,' said Jimmy. 'Bastards. Read some. E. M. Forster? Wouldn't give him house room. Virginia Woolf? Some drivel about a lighthouse. Wouldn't have lasted long in my regiment, I can tell you. No, Lettice, nobody's a figure of fun, in my book. You least of all.'

'I couldn't bear it if . . . if . . .'

'If I didn't turn up at church again? No fear of that. Jilted at altar twice? Not on. Marry me, Lettice.'

'Oh yes,' said Lettice. 'Yes, please.'

'Duck, sir?' said the waiter.

Jimmy stared at his duck with uncomprehending astonishment. He felt as if he had ordered it a thousand years ago.

Jimmy and Lettice lingered. They had brandies after the meal.

The two shoppers left the restaurant before them. When they got out into the bright sunshine, one of the women sighed deeply.

'I know just what you mean,' said the other. 'When I get home tonight, Ted won't believe a word of it.'

'Ronald won't even listen.'

On Saturday there was one letter in the mail. It informed them that a new restaurant was to open in War Memorial Parade. It was called the Thermopylae Kebab House. They could have twenty-five per cent off a bill for two on presenting the enclosed voucher. No voucher was enclosed.

The study of Number Twenty-one had been transformed into the secretary's office. On the walls, Elizabeth had pinned several sheets of paper. They revealed the full nature of the accommodation that was available.

There were eight bedrooms, four kitchens, four dining rooms and two living rooms as bedrooms for guests. Seven of these had been fitted out as double rooms, so there was accommodation for twenty-five guests.

Reggie had worried that it wouldn't be sufficient.

At the moment it was sufficient.

There was only one name on the charts: Mr C. R. Babbacombe.

'Oh my God,' said Reggie. 'What have we done?'

'You felt like this at the beginning of Grot,' said Elizabeth. 'And look where that ended up.'

'Yes, but what's Mr C. R. Babbacombe going to think when he finds he's got to face the lot of us on his own?'

It began to rain. The two-day summer was over.

Reggie's expression brightened.

'Perhaps he won't turn up,' he said.

The Early Days

BUT MR C . R . BABBACOMBE did turn up. He arrived, small, neat, shy, shiny and eager at twenty-five past three on Sunday afternoon.

'Hello. I hope I'm not the first,' he said in a thin, metallic voice.

'You're certainly in good time,' said Reggie.

He led Mr Babbacombe to Number Twenty-three, where he would have the room next to the Harris-Joneses.

David Harris-Jones opened the door.

'Oh. Ah. You must be Mr . . . er . . .'

'Babbacombe,' said Mr Babbacombe. 'Must be difficult for you to remember all our names.'

'Er . . . yes,' said Reggie.

'Yes, well . . . er . . . come in and I'll show you to your . . . er . . .' said David Harris-Jones.

He led the way up the narrow stairs.

'. . . room,' he said, when everyone had forgotten that he still had a sentence to finish.

'Pardon?' said Reggie.

'I said I'd . . . er . . . show Mr Babbacombe to his . . . er . . .'

'Oh I see,' said Reggie.

'. . . room,' said David Harris-Jones. 'I was just finishing my . . . er . . .'

'Sentence,' said Reggie.

'. . . that I'd started earlier,' said David Harris-Jones.

Mr Babbacombe looked from one to the other with some alarm.

On the door of his room a card announced 'Mr C. R. Babbacombe'.

David opened the door, and they entered. There was a single

84

bed, an armchair, a hard chair, a small desk, a gas fire and a print of Botchley War Memorial.

'I can't wait to meet all the others,' said Mr Babbacombe.

'Ah. Yes. The others,' said Reggie.

Mr Babbacombe went over to the window, which afforded a fine view over the spacious garden. It was chock-a-block with flowers, of wildly clashing colours, all about one foot six high. It had been Mr Penfold's pride and joy.

The sky was leaden.

'I'm an undertaker,' said Mr Babbacombe.

'Ah!' said Reggie.

'How ... er ... interesting,' said David Harris-Jones.

'But then you know that. It sticks out a mile, doesn't it?' said Mr Babbacombe.

'Good lord, no,' said Reggie. 'Does it, David?'

'Certainly not,' said David Harris-Jones.

'My face bears the stigmata of my profession,' said Mr Babbacombe, sitting on the pink coverlet and testing the bed-springs gingerly. 'My clothes are permeated with the stench of decay.'

'No, they're very nice,' said Reggie.

'I'm an outcast, a pariah. That's why I'm looking forward to this ... er ... course.'

'To meet the others?'

'Yes.'

Reggie looked at David Harris-Jones helplessly.

'Among the other ... er ... what do you call us? Patients?' said Mr Babbacombe.

'Good heavens, no,' said Reggie. 'Guests.'

'Among the other guests I hope to be accepted as an equal,' said Mr Babbacombe.

David Harris-Jones looked helplessly at Reggie.

Mr Babbacombe released the clasp of his suitcase decisively. His packing was orderly and spare. He had two-tone pyjamas.

'I'm afraid I have a disappointment for you,' said Reggie.

'Oh?'

'Yes. You ... er ... you won't be meeting the others ... yet. We'd like to give you some solitude to ... er ...'

85

'Get in the right frame of ... er ...' said David Harris-Jones.

'... mind,' said Reggie.

'I see,' said Mr Babbacombe. 'I don't meet the others until dinner, is that it?'

'You'll ... er ... dine alone in your room tonight,' said Reggie.

'Oh.'

'This will enable you to prepare yourself mentally and physically for tomorrow when you ... er ...'

'Meet the others.'

'Broadly speaking, yes. You'll have a group meeting at nine thirty.'

Reggie called an emergency meeting of the staff and explained the situation. It was decided that the only solution was for five members of the staff to pretend to be guests. The names of the staff were put into the hat, except for Reggie's.

'As head of the project I cannot take part, however much I might want to,' he explained.

The five names drawn were David Harris-Jones, Elizabeth Perrin, C.J., Joan Webster and Doc Morrissey.

They spent the evening preparing their roles for the next day's deception.

Mr Babbacombe spent the evening lingering over an excellent but lonely dinner and getting himself into the right mental and physical state for meeting them.

In the morning Mr Babbacombe's breakfast was brought to his room. Then, in a trance-like state of expectation, he drifted along Oslo Avenue, under the grey August sky, to Number Twenty-five.

Jimmy opened the door and led him into the living room. It was even more surprisingly spacious than the living room of Number Twenty-one. There were no french windows. Three pictures of bygone Botchley adorned the walls. Twelve assorted chairs stood in two semi-circles of six, facing each other.

Mr Babbacombe didn't know in which semi-circle to sit, so he remained standing, looking out over the banal garden with unseeing eyes.

C.J. arrived next.

'Lucas is the name,' he said, in a thin metallic voice.

'Babbacombe,' said Mr Babbacombe, and C.J. realised with

horror that his assumed voice was identical to Mr Babbacombe's real one.

'I feared I might be alone,' said C.J.

'I have the impression there are quite a few of us,' said Mr Babbacombe.

'Oh good,' said C.J. 'One swallow doesn't make a summer.'

'That's true,' said Mr Babbacombe.

'I wonder which chairs we sit in,' said C.J. 'Let's plump for these.'

'Righty ho,' said Mr Babbacombe.

No sooner had they sat, in the chairs facing the handsome brick fireplace, than they had to stand to greet Joan and Elizabeth. Doc Morrissey arrived next, then the staff entered *en masse*, and finally David Harris-Jones sidled into the end seat. He had suddenly realised that Mr Babbacombe knew him, and he'd made frantic efforts to disguise himself as the road manager of a pop group. These efforts were not an unqualified success.

Reggie stood up. Beside him were Linda, Tom, Tony, Jimmy and Prue.

'Good morning,' he said. 'Now the idea of these group sessions is that we all get together to help each other. We, the staff, help you, and you, the guests, help each other, bringing up your problems, and discussing them among yourselves.'

He smiled at Mr Babbacombe, Doc Morrissey, C.J., Elizabeth, Joan and David.

'And you, the guests, can help us,' said Reggie. 'By the end, if the meeting's gone well, it'll be hard to tell who are the staff and who are the guests. Huh huh. Now, I'll call upon the Doc to say a few words. Doc?'

Doc Morrissey stood up.

'Thank you,' he said.

Oh my God, thought Reggie, I forgot Doc was one of the guests. He glared desperately at Doc Morrissey.

'Oh, I'm sorry,' said Doc Morrissey. 'I've just remembered. I'm not the Doc.'

He sat down.

Reggie fixed his glare on Tom.

'Doc?' he said.

Tom seemed to be miles away, but Jimmy stood up.

'Sorry, miles away, brown study,' he said. 'I'm the Doc. Word of advice. If you fancy the local bints, keep well away. Go for a long hike instead. Cold shower every morning, and Bob's your uncle. Carry on.'

He sat down.

'Good advice there from the Doc,' said Reggie. 'Now if any of you have any problems, any neuroses, any phobias, anything, however little, however large, do please tell us about it. Now, who'll get the ball rolling?'

He sat down.

Doc Morrissey stood up.

'I think I'd better explain why I stood up just then,' he said. 'I'm prey to the delusion that I'm a member of the medical profession. It's embarrassing. People say, "Is there a doctor in the house?" "I'm a doctor," I cry. I leap up. "I'm a doctor. Make way. Make way," I cry. I get to the scene of the disaster, they all say, "Thank God you've come, Doc," and I say, "I've just remembered I'm not a doctor. Sorry".'

Doc Morrissey sat down.

'Fascinating.' said Reggie. 'Any comments, Doc?'

Doc Morrissey stood up.

'Not really,' he said.

Reggie glared at him.

'Sorry,' said Doc Morrissey. 'You see. There I go again.'

He sat down and wiped his brow.

Jimmy stood up.

'Just remembered. I'm the Doc,' he said. 'Sorry. Memory's a bit dicey lately. Touch of . . . er . . .'

'Amnesia?' suggested Reggie.

'Yes. Bit tired this morning. Cock-up on the kipping front. Fascinating tale of yours, Doc.'

'Why do you call him Doc if he isn't the Doc?' said Mr Babbacombe.

'Ah!' said Reggie. 'Yes. Er . . . why do you call him Doc, if he isn't the Doc, and of course he isn't the Doc, Doc?'

'Er . . . er . . .' suggested Jimmy.

'I don't want to put words into your mouth,' said Reggie.

'Please do,' said Jimmy.

'You're thinking that if you tell our deluded friend here that he isn't the Doc, he feels rebuffed, but if you pretend he is the Doc, he has the opportunity to deny it himself, he is a part of his own cure, he feels rewarded. Well done, Doc.'

'Took the words out of my mouth,' said Jimmy.

He sat down.

C.J. stood up.

'I can't make friends,' he said, in his assumed voice. 'I'm just waiting for the day when I need the services of the undertakers, that fine body of men.'

'You know, don't you?' said Mr Babbacombe.

'No, I don't,' said C.J. 'Know what?'

'It sticks out a mile.'

'No, it doesn't,' said C.J.

'Since you all know already, I may as well tell you. I'm an undertaker. Surprise, surprise.'

'Good heavens, are you really?' said C.J. 'Well, well, bless my soul.'

'Come off it. Anyone can tell an undertaker from everyone else,' said Mr Babbacombe in his thin, metallic voice.

'Nonsense,' said C.J. in his thin, metallic voice. 'I didn't get where I am today by telling undertakers from everyone else.'

'When I first saw you yesterday, Mr Babbacombe,' said Reggie, 'I thought, "That man's a research chemist, or I'm a Dutchman".'

'I'd got you down for a civil engineer,' put in Linda.

'Any other problems anyone would like to raise?' said Reggie, wiping his brow. 'Mrs Naylor, how about you?'

Joan and Elizabeth hesitated. Both thought the other one wasn't going to speak. Both said, 'Not at the moment, thank you.'

'Ah! You're both called Naylor. Are you related?' said Reggie.

'No,' said Joan.

'Yes,' said Elizabeth.

'This is interesting,' said Reggie. 'There seems to be some doubt about the matter. I'll ask you again. Are you related?'

'No,' said Elizabeth.

'Yes,' said Joan.

'I think I understand,' said Reggie desperately. 'Mrs Naylor denied being related to Mrs Naylor because she's ashamed of her. Mrs Naylor, realising this, tried to protect Mrs Naylor by pretending not to be a relative, but Mrs Naylor had by this time decided to acknowledge her. Am I right, Mrs Naylor?'

'Brilliant,' said Joan and Elizabeth.

'It's what I'm here for,' said Reggie. 'Why are you ashamed of Mrs Naylor, Mrs Naylor?'

'She ... er ...' said Joan.

'I drink,' said Elizabeth.

'She drinks,' said Joan.

David Harris-Jones decided that it was time for him to come to the rescue.

Now Reggie remembered that Mr Babbacombe had met David.

'I'm a roadie for a super pop group,' continued David Harris-Jones, standing with his face averted from Mr Babbacombe. 'I'm sorry to turn away from you like this. I guess I just can't face you face to face. I guess I can't face myself, know what I mean? I have to make trips, all over the country, one night stands, and on these trips I ... er ... I make trips, know what I mean? I mean am I into acid? Am I? Well, I'll tell you. I am. Like you finish a gig, back to some chick's pad, a real super laid-back scene, man. Know what I mean? But what are you, identity crisis wise? Nobody. A bum. I'm fed up with being into music, man. I'm fed up with being into acid. I guess I've wised up. I'm just not into being into things any more. I want out. I mean, like it's ...' He glanced apologetically at Tony. '... it's Cold-soupsville, Arizona. I wanna kick the habit, keep off the grass, know what I mean, man? Like I just don't know who I am.'

'I do,' said Mr Babbacombe. 'You're the warden.'

'I mean like I ... what?'

'You're the warden of Number Twenty-three,' said Mr Babbacombe.

David Harris-Jones looked round wildly. Prue smiled encouragingly.

'Oh, that creep,' said David. 'I saw him. Like I'm a dead ringer for him, know what I mean?'

'The only good ringer is a dead ringer,' said C.J.

'Where's the warden now?' said Mr Babbacombe.

'He's ... er ... he's ill,' said Reggie. 'He's got food poi ... no, not food poi ... er ... 'flu. That's it. 'Flu. He's got 'flu. He's definitely got 'flu.'

'He's the warden,' said Mr Babbacombe. He pointed at Doc Morrissey. 'He's the doctor. Neither of them are called Mrs Naylor. You're all staff.'

'Some of what you say is true,' said Reggie. 'To the extent that ... er ... he's the doctor ... er ... and he is the warden ... and ... er ... neither of them are called Mrs Naylor ... and we are all staff. Well done, you've come through the test with flying colours.'

'Test?'

'Spotting who are staff and who aren't. It's a little psychological test to ... er ... test your ... er ... ability to understand psychological tests.'

'Where are your guests?'

'You are.'

'What?'

'It's our first day, Mr Babbacombe, and you are our only guest.'

Reggie pleaded with Mr Babbacombe to give them another chance, and the little mortician was reluctantly persuaded.

They moved the chair around. There were now eleven chairs with their backs to the fireplace, and one chair facing it.

Mr Babbacombe sat facing the full complement of staff.

Reggie stood up.

'Good morning again,' he said. 'Now we hold these little group meetiings, Mr Babbacombe, so that we, the staff, can meet you, the ... Mr Babbacombe, and so that you, Mr Babbacombe, can meet us, the staff. We can help you and you can help ... er ... yourself, bringing up your problems, discussing them among ... er . .. yourself and ... er ... so let's get on with things, shall we? Now, who's going to start the ball rolling? Mr Babbacome?'

Mr Babbacombe stood up.

'We can stay as long as we like and at the end we pay according to what we feel we've got out of it, is that right?' he said.

'Exactly,' said Reggie. 'It seems the fairest way to me.'

'I think so too,' said Mr Babbacombe.

'Oh good. I am glad,' said Reggie.

'Goodbye,' said Mr Babbacombe.

When Mr Babbacombe had gone, Reggie turned to his staff.

'I'll be honest,' he said. 'This start has not been as auspicious as I had hoped. But, we must not panic. I have just one thing to say to you. Aaaaaaaaaaaaaaaaaagh!'

Even McBlane's excellent lunch and dinner couldn't raise morale.

And that evening the great chef himself came under the lash of disapproval. His ears would have burned, had they not been burning already, due to an attack of Pratt's Ear Itch.

The incident involving McBlane began when Linda entered the children's bedroom, to hear Tom saying, 'They're a famous Italian film director and an Irish air-line. Now go to sleep.'

'What are?' said Linda.

'Nothing,' said Tom.

It was eleven fifteen. The children had just sat exhausted and bored through a documentary on the life-cycle of the parasitic worm on BBC2. In the interests of personal freedom, Tom and Linda had not told them to go to bed. In the interests of personal pride, they had kept their red little eyelids open.

'Well, come on, Tom,' said Linda, when they had closed the children's door behind them. 'What are a famous Italian film director and an Irish air-line?'

'Jocasta said that she finds Uncle McBlane's stories boring,' said Tom, 'and Adam asked what fellatio and cunnilingus are.'

'Don't worry,' said Reggie, who happened to be passing on his way to bed. 'I'll deal with McBlane in the morning.'

Next morning Reggie tackled the unkempt Hibernian genius in his lair. Vegetables covered the kitchen table. Pots and pans lay ready on the Scandinavian-style traditional English fully-integrated natural pine and chrome work surfaces.

McBlane was crying. Reggie hoped it might be remorse, but it was only onions. McBlane swept the chopped onions imperiously into a large pan in which butter had been melted. One of his boil plasters was hanging loose.

'Morning, McBlane,' began Reggie.

McBlane grunted.

'McBlane, I must have a word with you,' said Reggie.

McBlane grunted again.

'I must speak to you frankly,' said Reggie. 'Er ... the salmon mousse yesterday was superb.'

McBlane proved a master at varying his grunts.

'But,' said Reggie. 'Life doesn't consist of salmon mousse alone. And ... er ... the navarin of lamb was also superb.'

McBlane barked an incomprehensible reply.

'On the other hand,' said Reggie, 'the duchesse potatoes were also superb. Incidentally, I understand you're telling stories to Adam and Jocasta. Thanks. It's much appreciated.'

'Flecking ma bloots wi' hae flaggis,' said McBlane.

'Quite,' said Reggie. 'Point taken. But ...'

McBlane swivelled round slowly from the stove, and looked Reggie straight in the face. He had a stye above his left eye.

'But,' said Reggie, 'I wouldn't like you to think that my praise of the potatoes implied any criticism of the choucroute à la hongroise.'

This time there was no mistaking McBlane's reply.

'Bloody foreign muck,' he said.

'Absolutely,' said Reggie.

McBlane glowered.

'I protest,' said Reggie. 'The choucroute à la hongroise was delicious.'

McBlane re-glowered.

'Well, fairly delicious,' said Reggie. 'Talking about the stories you're telling Adam and Jocasta ... er ... I hope you'll remember their age, as it were, and keep them ... er ... er if you see what I mean. Point taken?'

McBlane grunted.

'Jolly good,' said Reggie.

He walked briskly to the door. Then he turned and faced the dark chef fearlessly.

'Wonderful rhubarb crumble,' he said.

Later that day Reggie told Tom, 'I saw McBlane this morning. I gave him a piece of my mind.'

Reggie accepted much of the blame for the initial failure of his venture. He admitted that he had seriously underestimated the amount of advertising that would be needed. He had been reluctant to cash in on the name that he had made through Perrin Products and Grot. He was reluctant no longer. Soon adverts for Perrins began to appear in national and local newspapers, on underground stations, buses, and hoardings.

Some of the advertisements said, simply: 'Perrins'.

Others were more elaborate.

One read:

'Whatever happened to Reginald Perrin?
Remember Grot and its useless products?
Now Perrin rides again.
This time his product is USEFUL.
It's called HAPPINESS.
Visit PERRINS.
Stay as long as you like.
Pay as little as you like.'

Another read simply: 'Perrins—the only community for the middle-aged and middle-class.'

Others stated: 'Perrins—the In-place for Out-people', 'Perrins—where misfits fit', 'Are you a backward reader? Then come and be cured at Snirrep', 'Lost all faith in experts? Then come to Perrins. Guaranteed no experts in anything' and 'Want to drop-out but don't like drop-outs? At Perrins the drop-outs are just like you. They're more like drop-ins. Next time you feel like dropping-out, why not drop-in?'

The saturation coverage began on September the first.

The W288 carried the legend 'Perrins' past the front door.

McBlane wrapped the remnants of dinner in newspapers that all carried advertisements for Perrins, even though they were as divergent as the *Financial Times*, the *Daily Express*, and the *Botchley and Spraundon Press* (*Incorporating The Coxwell Gazette* and the remains of twelve lamb chops).

The saturation coverage took effect immediately.

On Monday, September the twelfth the staff swung into action once more.

And this time there wasn't just one client.

There were two.

Reggie decided to give all the clients an introductory interview before subjecting them to the rigours of a group meeting.

His new study was in Number Twenty-three, to the right of the front door. It had a brown carpet and buff walls. There were two upright chairs and a heavy oak desk. Two pictures of bygone Botchley adorned the walls.

It was a quiet September morning. Autumn was coming in modestly, as if bribed to conceal the ending of the summer that had never begun.

Reggie's first interviewee was Thruxton Appleby, the textiles tycoon. Thruxton Appleby was a large paunchy man with a domed shiny bald head. His nose was bulbous. His lips were thick and flecked with white foam. His enormous buttocks crashed down pitilessly on to the fragile chair provided. 'Call this furniture?' they seemed to cry. 'We eat chairs like this in Yorkshire.' Reggie quaked. His whole organisation seemed weak and fragile.

'I read your advert in *Mucklethwaite Morning Telegraph*,' said Thruxton Appleby. 'I liked its bare-faced cheek. I admire bare-faced cheek. Are you a Yorkshireman?'

'No,' said Reggie. 'A Londoner.'

'That's odd. You don't often find bare-faced cheek among namby-pamby Southerners.'

His paunch quivered over his private parts like junket in a gale.

'I'm a textiles tycoon,' he said. 'Everything I'm wearing is from my own mills. I don't usually bother with quacks, crack-pots and cranks, but I've tried everything. Head-shrinkers, health farms, religion. You're my last resort.'

'How flattering,' said Reggie. 'What is your problem?'

'I'm not likeable, Mr Perrin.'

Reggie drew a sheet of paper towards him and wrote, 'Thinks he isn't likeable. He's right.'

Thruxton Appleby leant forward, trying to read what Reggie had written.

'Professional secret,' said Reggie, shielding the paper with his hand.

'I'm not liked for myself, do you see?' continued Thruxton Appleby. 'I've made Mucklethwaite. I've fought a one-man battle against the depredations of Far East imports. You can go in the Thruxton Appleby Memorial Gardens, past the Thruxton Appleby Memorial Band-stand, and look out over whole of Mucklethwaite to Scrag End Fell, and what are you sat on? The Thruxton Appleby Memorial Seat.'

'Shouldn't memorials be for after you're dead?' said Reggie.

'What use is that?' said Thruxton Appleby. 'You're gone then.'

A blue tit was hanging under a branch on the bush outside the window. Thruxton Appleby's eyebrows rose scornfully. 'Call that a tit?' they seemed to say. 'In Yorkshire we call yon a speck of fluff.'

The blue tit flew away.

'I expect money to carry all before it,' said Thruxton Appleby. 'Cure me of that, and you can name your price.'

Reggie felt that he could do nothing for this man.

'My first impressions are unfavourable,' said Thruxton Appleby. 'Thruxton, I say to myself, tha's landed up in a tin-pot organisation, staffed by namby-pamby Southerners. I'll give it a go while Tuesday. So get on with it, Mr Perrin, and do it quickly. Time is money.'

Thruxton Appleby glanced at his watch, as if to see how rich he was. Reggie wondered what it said. Ten past six hundred thousand pounds?

Stop having silly thoughts, Reggie. Concentrate. Having silly thoughts and not concentrating are symptoms of lack of confidence.

How right you are.

Be confident. Be bold.

Look at him. He's all wind and piss. Already he's uneasy because you aren't speaking and it isn't what he expects. He's used to bullying. Bully him in return.

I think you're right.

Reggie smiled at Thruxton Appleby.

'Smoke?' he said.

'Please.'

'Filthy habit.'

96

He wrote 'smokes' on the piece of paper.

'I don't offer cigarettes,' he said. 'Do you like coffee?'

'Please.'

'Milk and sugar?'

'Please.'

'Takes coffee with milk and sugar,' Reggie muttered as he made another note. 'Caught you twice. Thick as well as nasty.'

Thruxton Appleby gasped.

'What did you say?' he said.

'Thick as well as nasty.'

'I'm not used to being spoken to like that.'

'Excellent. Why do you think you're so loathed?' said Reggie.

'Not loathed, Mr Perrin. Not even disliked. Just "not liked". I'm rich, you see.'

'I can easily cure you of that.'

Reggie shielded the piece of paper with his hand, wrote 'Nosey Bastard' on it, and left the room.

He talked briefly with C.J., asking him to interrupt in thirty seconds on a matter of no importance and be dismissive towards Thruxton Appleby.

He returned to the study. Thruxton Appleby didn't appear to have moved.

'I don't think I'm a nosey bastard,' he said.

Reggie laughed.

'Come in,' he said.

'Nobody knocked.'

'Give them time. Don't be so impatient. Come in.'

'Why do you keep saying "Come in"?'

'Third time lucky,' said Reggie. 'Come in.'

C.J. entered.

'Is this important?' said Reggie.

'No,' said C.J.

'Good. Take your time.'

'I just wondered if you'd heard the weather forecast.'

'I'll ring for it,' said Reggie, lifting the phone and dialling. 'Excuse me, Mr Dangleby, but this *is* a waste of time.'

He listened, then put the phone down.

'Yes, C.J., I have now heard the weather forecast,' he said.

'Oh good. I'll be on my way then,' said C.J.

'Oh, this is the chemicals tycoon, Throxton Dangleby,' said Reggie.

'Textiles,' said Thruxton Appleby.

'Nice to meet you, Mr Textiles,' said C.J.

'Appleby,' said Thruxton Appleby.

'You've probably heard of the Throxton Ingleby Memorial Hat-Stand,' said Reggie.

'Band-stand,' said Thruxton Appleby.

'Nice to meet you, Mr Dimbleby,' said C.J., and he closed the door gently behind him.

'Not very subtle tactics,' said the unlovely industrialist.

'For a not very subtle man,' said Reggie. 'Now. I can cure you, but it'll take time. Within a fortnight, you'll no longer be obnoxious. Irritating and mind-bogglingly boring, but not obnoxious. Within three weeks, you'll be tolerable in mixed company in medium-sized doses. Within a month, give or take a day or two either way, this is not an exact science, you'll be likeable.'

'Thank you,' said Thruxton Appleby hoarsely.

The bloated capitalist removed his unacceptable face from the study.

The second guest was known to Reggie already. He was Mr Pelham, owner of Pelham's Piggery, where Reggie had swilled out in the dark days before he had even thought of his first Grot shop.

'You've done well for yourself, old son,' said Mr Pelham.

'Not bad,' acknowledged Reggie.

Mr Pelham's honest, God-fearing, pig-loving face had a grey, uninhabited look. The chair, so puny under attack from Thruxton Appleby's buttocks, seemed ample now.

'I always liked you,' said Mr Pelham. 'You were different from the other hands. Chalk and cheese, Reg. Chalk and cheese, old son.'

'Thank you,' said Reggie.

'I shouldn't be talking to you like this,' said Mr Pelham. 'You're the guv'nor now.'

'Please,' said Reggie, waving a deprecatory hand.

'I read your advert for this place, I thought, "That's the self-same Perrin that swilled out my porkers".'

Reggie's heart sank. Why did anyone he knew have to come, and especially so soon? He could do nothing for Mr Pelham. Probably he could do nothing for anybody. He smiled, trying to look encouraging.

'Well, I am the self-same Perrin,' he said.

'You certainly are, old son,' said Mr Pelham. 'You certainly are. He's the man to go to with my problems, I thought.'

'Tell me about your problems,' said Reggie.

Mr Pelham told Reggie about his problems. He had diversified since the old days. He had bought the premises of his neighbours, the Climthorpe School of Riding and the old chicken farm that Reggie had called Stalag Hen 59. Pelham's Piggery had become Associated Meat Products Ltd. He sold pigs, chickens and calves. An abattoir in Bicester gave him group rates. His daughter never came near him. His son worked in a bank and had espoused vegetarianism. It was more than ten years since his wife had been knocked down by a bus outside Macfisheries. The shop wasn't even there any more. The nearest branch was at Staines.

'I'm alone in the world, Reg,' he said. 'And there's blood on my hands.'

'Aren't you exaggerating?' said Reggie.

'All those chickens in rows, Reg, living in the dark with their beaks cut back. All those calves, deliberately made anaemic so that people can eat white meat. How can people sleep in their beds with all that going on? How can I sleep in my bed?'

Reggie didn't know what to say, so he said nothing.

The blue tit returned to the bush outside the window. It clearly didn't see Mr Pelham as a threat to its security.

'I get dreams, Reg,' said Mr Pelham.

'Dreams?' repeated Reggie, writing 'Dreams' on his sheet of paper. 'What sort of dreams?'

'Dreams of Hell, old son,' said Mr Pelham. 'I dream about what'll happen to me when I get to Hell. And I will, don't you worry.'

'I will worry,' protested Reggie.

'I won't get a gander at those pearly gates, not if I live to be a thousand I won't.'

He dreamt of a Hell in which there were rows and rows of

Mr Pelhams, kept side by side in the dark, their innumerable cages soiled with the stains of centuries of Pelham faeces, their noses cut off, their diet unbalanced, the better to produce anaemia and white meat, while opposite them, lit by thousands of bare bulbs, hundreds of chefs turned thousands of Mr Pelhams on spits, and beyond, in a gigantic cavern, beneath vast crystal chandeliers that stretched to infinity, Satan and his thousands of sultry mistresses sat at long tables with velvet cloths, drinking dark wine out of pewter goblets and moistening their scarlet lips with spittle in anticipation of their finger-licking portions of Hades-fried Pelham.

'I'm in a cage among all the rows of me,' said Mr Pelham. 'And I get brought a portion of me, on a silver tray, with barbecue sauce. And I try to eat me. I'm not bad. I taste like pork. But I stick in my throat.'

'Has it ever occurred to you that maybe you're in the wrong line of business?' said Reggie.

'It's all I know,' said Mr Pelham.

Reggie wrote 'God knows what to do' on the sheet of paper. Mr Pelham tried to see what he had written, but he shielded the paper behind a pile of books.

'Professional secrets,' he said.

'Can you help me, Reg?' said Mr Pelham.

Reggie opened his mouth, convinced that no sound whatsoever would emerge, that it would open and shut like the mouth of a stranded grayling. Imagine his astonishment, then, when he heard confident and coherent sentences emerging.

'We can help you to make your personality whole,' he said. 'We can send you from here a kindly, nice, peaceful man, content with his personality, yet not complacent. This we *can* do. What we can't do is to solve the problems posed by your work. We can't increase society's awareness of the methods by which its food is produced or its willingness to pay the increased costs that more humane methods would entail. We can't tell you what you should do about your conscience. We can only send you off in the best possible frame of mind to deal with these problems. The rest is up to you.'

Mr Pelham smiled happily. It was as if a great burden had been taken from his shoulders. His trust was absolute.

'Thank you,' he said. 'I knew you could do it, old son.'

When Mr Pelham had gone, Reggie found that he was trembling.

He hadn't known that he could do it.

Three days after the arrival of the two clients, neither of them had left. It wasn't a triumph, but it was something. And one or two forward bookings were beginning to deflower the virgin sheets on the walls of the secretary's office.

The weather was discreetly unsettled.

It was not a busy time. When Jimmy applied to have Thursday lunchtime off, Reggie granted it without hesitation.

The purpose of his brief furlough was to visit Restaurant Italian Sorrentina La, Hill Notting, 12.30 hours, Horncastle Lettice Isobel, engagement for the breaking off of.

It had all been a dreadful mistake.

This time there would be no cowardly desertion in the face of a church. This time he would face Lettice bravely, across a restaurant table, and say, 'Sorry, old girl. Just not on. Still be friends, eh? Meet, time to time, meals, odd opera, that sort of crack? Be chums?'

Mustn't be frightened of a woman, he told himself, as the train sped with perverse punctuality towards Waterloo. Imagine her as Rommel. Come to think of it, she didn't look altogether unlike Rommel. A touch more masculine, perhaps. His face softened with affection. Poor, dear Lettice!

No! He hardened his heart. Eventually, warmed by four double whiskies, he made his way to La Sorrentina.

They sat at the same table. They were served by the same waiter. They ordered the same food. Only the two lady shoppers were missing.

Lettice was fiercely bronzed by the Hellenic sun. She showed him her snapshots of Greece. He gazed at blue skies and azure seas, at dazzling white hotels and cafés, at huge Horncastle thighs that began the holiday gleaming like freshly painted lighthouses and ended up like the charred trunks of oaks blackened in some forest fire.

'Who's the tall man with the beard?' he asked.

'Odd.'

'Odd?'

'That's his name. Odd.'

'Odd name, isn't it?'

'It's common in Sweden.'

'And was he?'

'What?'

'Odd.'

'Not that I know of.'

She showed him the next picture.

'Who's the blonde giant?'

'Bent.'

'Bent?'

'It's a common name in Denmark.'

'And was he?'

'What?'

'Bent.'

'No.'

'How do you know?'

'He didn't appear to be.'

She produced the next picture.

'This is Mikonos,' she said. 'Very touristy.'

'Odd and Bent all present and correct.'

'Are you jealous?'

'Course not.'

'Naxos,' she said, of the next snap. 'This was the hottest day. Thirty-four degrees Celsius.'

'Odd and Bent aren't absent on parade, I see.'

Lettice put her photos away. They had done their job.

Jimmy was jealous.

They decided to get married on Wednesday, December the twenty-first, and spend Christmas in Malta.

The money continued to drip out of the once-fat bank account of Reginald Iolanthe Perrin. The evenings drew in. The equinoctial gales began to blow.

On Sunday, September the eighteenth, a third client arrived. He was an insurance salesman who had lost his motivation.

'It's a dreadful thing to say,' he told Reggie at his first interview, 'but I couldn't care less if there are hundreds of people walking the streets of Mitcham seriously under-insured.'

To Reggie's incredulous relief, both Thruxton Appleby and Mr Pelham were showing definite signs of progress.

Under Linda's inexpert tutelage, Mr Pelham produced several paintings. Porkers were his favourite subjects, but sometimes, for a change, he would paint other kinds of pig.

Thruxton Appleby was making even more spectacular progress. On one of Jimmy's tactical exercises without troops, he helped a blind writer of Christmas card verses across Botchley High Street unbidden, and enjoyed the experience so much that he waited seven minutes to help him back again.

Joan reported few triumphs with her singing classes, but Prue was making steady progress, between the rain storms, with the thatching of the garden shed at Number Twenty-one.

One or two areas gave Reggie cause for concern.

Sporting activity was conspicuous by its absence, and culture was another area where progress was tardy.

Reggie found it necessary to speak to Tom and Tony about the slow progress of their departments.

On the afternoon of Thursday, September the twenty-second, he entered the garden of Number Seventeen. The beds around the surprisingly spacious lawn were given over predominantly to roses, and he noted with pleasure that C.J. had proved diligent in removing dead heads.

Reggie knocked on the door of the garden shed, alias the Sports Centre. Tom let him in reluctantly. On shelves all round the shed there were bottles. On the floor there were more bottles. Some of the bottles contained spirits, others contained liquids of strange and exotic hue. Still others were empty. In one corner a work table had been erected. On it were huge glass bottles connected together with drips and pipes. Under the table there were many trays of fruit. Reggie's heart sank.

'Do you remember that I used to make home-made wine?' said Tom.

'I seem to recall something of the kind,' said Reggie. 'You've started making them again, have you?'

'Oh no,' said Tom.

'Oh good,' said Reggie.

103

'I'm making spirits now.'

'Oh my God.'

'Sloe gin, prune brandy, raspberry whisky.'

'Oh my God! May I sit down?'

Reggie sat in the one chair provided. Tom looked at him earnestly.

'I'm afraid I've got a disappointment for you, Reggie,' said Tom.

'Oh dear. Well, tell me the worst. Let's get it over with.'

'None of them is ready to drink yet.'

'Oh dear, that is disappointing. Tom, I am prepared to accept against all the odds that these things will be delicious, but I have to ask you, are they sport?'

'I don't follow you, Reggie,' said Tom, taking his unlit pipe out of his mouth as if he thought that might help his concentration.

'You were put in charge of sport.'

'Oh that. I'm just not a sport person, Reggie.'

Reggie stood up, the better to assert his authority.

'I thought you accepted it as a challenge, Tom,' he said. 'And it got off to such a good start with that football.'

Tom gazed at Reggie like a walrus that has heard bad news.

'I've let you down,' he said. 'I've allowed myself to be discouraged by our early failures.'

Reggie patted him on the shoulder.

'There's still time, Tom,' he said. 'The community is young. Instigate some lively sports activity, and I'll let you carry on with the booze production. No promises, but I may even drink some myself.'

'Thanks,' said Tom. 'I won't let you down again, father-in-law.'

Reggie went straight round to the Culture Room which was situated in the garden shed of Number Twenty-five. This garden had been largely dug up and devoted to the production of greens. The door of the shed was painted yellow. On it hung a notice which read, 'Culture Room. Prop: T. Webster, Q.C.I.'

He knocked and entered.

The hut had been converted into a little living room with two

104

armchairs and a Calor Gas fire. All round the uneven wooden walls there were pin-ups of girls with naked breasts, taken from the tabloid newspapers.

Reggie gawped.

'Knock-out, eh?' said Tony, looking a little uneasy.

'What are they supposed to be?' said Reggie.

'Culture.'

'They aren't culture. They're boobs.'

'They're actresses,' said Tony. 'What are actresses if they aren't culture?'

'Actresses!'

'Read any one of the captions.'

Reggie approached the endless rows of breasts nervously, and read one of the captions that nestled timorously under the vast swellings.

'Vivacious Virginia's a radiologist's daughter,' he read. 'Her dad made some pretty startling developments in X-ray techniques, but you don't need an X-ray to see vibrant Virginia's startling developments. Volatile Virginia has plans to be a classical actress. Well, she might reveal some talents, but unfortunately she'd have to hide her biggest assets!'

'Culture,' said Tony.

Reggie peered at the equally well-developed female on Virginia's right.

'Curvaceous Caroline's a colonel's daughter,' he read. 'Dad might think she's improperly dressed for parade, but then she's fighting a different battle of the bulge from the one he got a D.S.O. for. Come to think of it we wouldn't mind giving Cock-A-Hoop Caroline a medal. We might even pin it on ourselves. Cultivated Caroline plans to become a Shakespearian actress. It's a case of "from the bared to the Bard!".'

'What did I tell you?' said Tony.

Reggie turned away from the multi-nippled walls of the garden shed and looked disgustedly at Tony.

'There are a hundred boobs in here,' said Tony. 'A ton of tits.'

'What does Q.C.I. stand for?'

'What?'

105

Reggie swung the door open. Daylight streamed into the little hut.

'Prop: T. Webster, Q.C.I.' said Reggie.

'Oh that,' said Tony. 'Qualified Culture Instructor.'

'I can't talk in there,' said Reggie. 'Come into the garden.'

They stood on the tiny lawn, surrounded by vast beds of autumn cabbages.

'Tony,' said Reggie. 'If a prospective client gets in touch with me, and says, "Do you have any cultural activities?" and I say, "Yes. We have a qualified culture instructor and he has a garden shed with a ton of tits", what do you think will happen?'

'He'll sign on.'

'Yes, well, very possibly. Forget that, then. But remove those boobs. And get some culture going. I'm not one for issuing threats, Tony. This community runs on love and trust. But if you let me down, I'm warning you, I will issue threats. And you know what they'll be threats of, don't you? Chucked out without a pennysville, Arizona.'

On Sunday, September the twenty-fifth, two more clients arrived.

The month expired quietly. There were no mourners.

October began gloomily. The weather was unremittingly wet. There was a race riot in Wednesbury. Four headless torsos were found in left-luggage cubicles at Temple Meads Station, Bristol. A survey showed that Britain came fifth in the venereal disease tables of the advanced nations. A Ugandan under-secretary was taken to a West London Hospital with suspected smallpox and claimed that it was impossible as he had diplomatic immunity. Third-form girls in a school in South London ter-rorised teachers after a drinks orgy.

But there was one bright spark amidst all this gloom. The fortunes of Perrins were looking up. Seven new clients arrived on Sunday, October the second, making the total twelve. And there were several forward bookings dotted around the wall charts in the secretary's office, including one from a fortune-teller who was going to have a nervous breakdown in April.

The twelve clients were Thruxton Appleby; Mr Pelham; the insurance salesman who had lost his motivation; an arc-welder from Ipswich named Arthur Noblet; Bernard Trilling, Head of Comedy at Anaemia Television; Hilary Meadows, a housewife from Tenterden; Diana Pilkington, an account executive from Manchester; a VAT inspector from Tring, who hated the fact that he liked his work; a probation officer from Peebles, who hated the fact that he hated his work; a director of a finance company that specialised in pyramid selling; an unemployed careers officer, and a middle manager in a multi-national plastics concern. The work of Perrins began in earnest.

The five suburban houses in Oslo Avenue, Botchley, were alive with activity.

Reggie wandered proudly around, watching the guests at their various activities.

In the Art Room he admired the work of Diana Pilkington, who painted as Monet would have painted if he'd been totally devoid of talent. The work of the VAT inspector from Tring was very different, however. He painted as Lowry would have painted if *he'd* been totally devoid of talent.

He listened with pleasure to the distortions of Gilbert and Sullivan that came from the Music Room.

'Keep it up,' he told the probation officer from Peebles. 'Any genius can sing like Tito Gobbi. It takes a real talent to persist when he sings like you.'

He attended group meetings, watched the progress of the thatching and went on expeditions with Jimmy. All the time he fought against a desire to take a more active part in things.

When he burst in unannounced upon Doc Morrissey, he fully intended to take a back seat.

Lying on the couch in the study of Number Nineteen was Bernard Trilling, Head of Comedy at Anaemia Television. Only the haunted expression in his eyes revealed the inner torment of the man.

Outside, the moisture hung from the trimmed privet hedge in the front garden, but the rain had stopped at last.

'Carry on,' said Reggie. 'My job is just to watch.'

'Let's try some simple word associations,' said Doc Morrissey. 'Mother.'

'Comedy,' said Bernard Trilling.

'Ah!' said Reggie.

107

'Please don't interrupt,' said Doc Morrissey. 'I want to go on and on, associating freely till we reach a totally uninhibited level of association. If we stop after each association, our future associations are affected by what we associate with the past associations.'

'I'm sorry,' said Reggie. 'I didn't mean to interrupt. It was just the way he came out with that mother/comedy association.'

'Yes, yes,' said Doc Morrissey impatiently. 'He resents his job and he resents his mother. Child's play.'

'I love my mother,' said Bernard Trilling.

'All right,' said Doc Morrissey. 'We may as well explore this area now. The thread's been broken.'

He glared at Reggie.

'Sorry,' said Reggie, moving his chair right back into a dark corner. 'Carry on. Behave as if I'm not here.'

'Why do you think you associated mother with comedy?' said Doc Morrissey.

Bernard Trilling was lying with his hands under his head. He glared at the ceiling.

'We're planning a situation comedy about a happy-go-lucky divorced mother who tries to bring up her three happy-go-lucky children by writing books,' he said gloomily. 'It's called "Mum's the Word".'

He turned his face to the wall and uttered a low groan.

'I started in documentaries,' he said. 'What went wrong?'

'Right. Let's start again,' said Doc Morrissey.

Reggie looked out of the window. A Harrods van drove past. He tried to let his mind go blank, in the hope that he would find some interesting association with the Harrods van.

It reminded him of Harrods.

Perhaps I'm imaginatively under-nourished, he thought.

He forced himself to concentrate on the events that were going on in the little room. He didn't want to miss anything.

Gradually he became aware that there was nothing to miss.

Nothing was going on in the little room.

Bernard Trilling lay hunched up on the couch.

Doc Morrissey was staring intently into space.

'Sorry,' said Doc Morrissey. 'My mind's going a blank. It's you, Reggie. You're unsettling me.'

'Please,' said Reggie. 'Take no notice of me. I'm not here.'

'But you are,' said Doc Morrissey.

'Make yourself believe I'm not,' said Reggie. 'Mind over matter. It's all psychological.'

'I know,' said Doc Morrissey glumly. 'Right. Here we go.'

There was silence for fully a minute.

'It's the enormity of the choice that's inhibiting me,' said Doc Morrissey.

'I don't want to interfere,' said Reggie. 'But shall I suggest one or two things, just to get you over your blockage?'

'All right,' said Doc Morrissey. 'But once you've started, don't stop.'

'Right,' said Reggie. 'Here we go. Farmhouse.'

'Comedy,' said Bernard Trilling.

'Egg-cup,' said Reggie.

'Comedy,' said Bernard Trilling.

'It's pointless if you're just going to say "comedy" all the time,' said Reggie.

Bernard Trilling sat up.

'It's all I ever think of,' he said. 'Every news item, every chance remark in the pub, I think, "Could we make a comedy series about that?" I'm on a treadmill. The nation must be kept laughing. I need just one successful series, and I'd be laughing. Well no, I wouldn't. I've no sense of humour.'

'You must try and think of other things or Doc Morrissey can't help you,' said Reggie.

'I'll try,' promised Bernard Trilling.

'Right,' said Reggie. 'Here we go again. Or would you rather do it, Doc?'

Doc Morrissey shrugged resignedly.

'Right,' said Reggie. 'Taxidermy.'

'Comedy,' said Bernard Trilling.

'Oh Bernard!' said Reggie.

'We're planning a new comedy series about a happy-go-lucky taxidermist,' said Bernard Trilling. 'It's called "Get Stuffed".'

The W288, grinding along Oslo Avenue on its slow progress towards Spraundon, sounded very loud in the ensuing silence.

'It . . . er . . . it sounds an unlikely subject,' said Reggie.

'It's what we in the trade call the underwater rabbi syndrome,' said Bernard Trilling.

'Ah!' said Doc Morrissey, with a flash of his former spirit. 'You dislike Jews?'

'It just means that in our desperation we're hunting for ever more unlikely subjects,' said Bernard Trilling. 'The unlikeliest we can think of is an underwater rabbi.'

'It needn't have been a rabbi, though,' said Doc Morrissey. 'It could have been an underwater Methodist minister. The fact that it's a rabbi suggests prejudice, albeit unconscious. It's what we call a psycho-semitic illness.'

Doc Morrissey smiled triumphantly, then frowned, as if vaguely aware that he had got it wrong.

'I've got nothing against Jews,' said Bernard Trilling. 'Some of my best friends are Jews. My parents are Jews.'

He blushed furiously.

An extremely noisy lorry drove by, carrying a heavily-laden skip.

'I was born Trillingstein,' admitted Bernard Trilling. 'I'm not ashamed of being Jewish. Very much the reverse. I just felt that if I was a big success people would ascribe it to my Jewishness. "Of course he's clever. He's a Jew." And I wanted them to say "Of course he's clever. He's Bernard Trilling." Some hope I should have that anyone should say I was clever.'

He smiled.

'I feel better already,' he said. 'I've kept that secret for fourteen years. And you've unlocked it. You're a wizard, Doc.'

'Me?' said Doc Morrissey. 'I did nothing.'

'Well it wasn't me,' said Reggie. 'I wasn't there.'

It was the same when he looked in on David Harris-Jones at the Sex Clinic, which was in yet another garden shed, at Number Nineteen. Outside, it appeared to be an ordinary, rather tumble-down wooden shed. Inside, there was a carpet, a desk and hard chair, and three armchairs. The wall and ceilings had been painted in restful pastel shades as recommended in Weissburger and Dulux's *Colour and Emotional Response*.

Reggie moved his armchair back, out of the limelight.

David sat behind his desk.

Hilary Meadows, the housewife from Tenterden, sat in the armchair. She was in her mid-forties, her face crinkled but attractive, her sturdy legs crossed.

'Now, Hilary,' said David, 'as I was saying, before Reggie ... er ...'

'Don't mind me,' said Reggie. 'I'm not here.'

'As I was saying there's no need to feel ... er ... er ...'

'Nervous,' said Reggie.

'Yes,' said David Harris-Jones. 'That's what I was going to ... er ... but I'm a little ... er ...'

'Nervous,' said Reggie.

'Yes. Maybe if you didn't ... er ...'

'Interrupt.'

'Yes.'

'Sorry. I won't interrupt any more. It's just that you go so ... how can I put it ... er ...'

'Infuriatingly slowly.'

'Yes.'

'I know. I just seem to sort of go to pieces when you're here, Reggie.'

'You'll have to get over that, David,' said Reggie, 'because I won't always be here to pick up the pieces.'

Hilary Meadows uncrossed her legs, and watched the two men with amusement.

'Carry on, David. I'll leave it all to you,' said Reggie.

David Harris-Jones fiddled with the papers on his desk.

'As I was saying, Hilary,' he said, 'there's no need to be nervous.'

'I'm not,' she said.

'I want you to feel completely ... er ... oh good, you're not. Super.'

He moved to the third armchair.

'No need to be formal,' he said. 'Now the subject I deal with, Hilary, is ... er ...'

'Sex,' said Hilary Meadows.

'Yes. As it were.'

As he talked, David Harris-Jones's eyes moved restlessly round his restful den.

'Lots of people ... er ...' he began. 'At times, anyway. After all, life's full of ... well not problems exactly. Difficulties. And ... er ... there's nothing to be ... er ... I mean ...'

'Oh for God's sake, David,' said Reggie. 'What David is trying to say, Hilary, and we must remember that he had an unusually sheltered upbringing in Haverfordwest and its environs, what David is trying to say, in his nervous, roundabout way, and he's probably going about it in a roundabout way because he's nervous, after all you are only the second woman that he's ever ... er ... talked to in this way, what as I say he's trying to say is ... well, I mean everybody at some time or other ... in some degree or other ... and there's no disgrace in that.'

'I have no sexual problems at all,' said Hilary Meadows.

'So if you ... er ... no se ... se ... oh good. Good.'

'Super.'

'My husband and I have it very happily at what I understand is roughly the national average.'

'Oh you do. Good. Good.'

'Super.'

Hilary Meadows crossed her legs.

'Well, that's got that off our chests,' said Reggie. 'That's got that out in the open.'

'Yes, but when we talk about ... er ... sex,' said David Harris-Jones, 'we don't just mean ... er ...'

'Sex,' said Hilary Meadows.

'Exactly. Modern ... er ... psychology, as you know ... I mean the gist of it is that ... er ... sex, and our attitude towards it, rears its ug ... let me put it another way. Much of our life is influenced by sex,' said David Harris-Jones.

'And much more of it isn't,' said Hilary Meadows. 'You poor unimaginative creatures. You can't imagine any problems except sexual ones. Let me tell you why I'm here. Because I'm bored out of my not so tiny mind. I'm bored with having my cooking taken for granted, not being listened to by my husband, not being helped and thanked by my children. Bored with not going out to work. Bored with cleaning the house so that the cleaning woman won't leave. Bored with slow check-out girls at unimaginative supermarkets and time-killing conversations at coffee mornings and playing golf with other women with thick

112

calves and thin white elderly legs and garish ankle socks. Bored, bored, bored.'

'Splendid,' said Reggie. 'Well, I think we can help you there.'

'I don't need help,' said Hilary Meadows. 'I've only come here for a change. I couldn't go to the Bahamas or my family wouldn't feel guilty. You poor men. You look so disappointed. No nice cure to do. No little toys to play with.'

'Well, I'll leave you two to it,' said Reggie. 'You're doing absolutely splendidly, David.'

Next day there was watery sunshine at last. Very slowly, the sodden gardens began to dry out.

At the long, crowded breakfast table, Reggie told C.J. that he'd like to see how his work on people's attitude to their work was progressing.

'Excellent,' said C.J. through a mouthful of McBlane's rich, creamy scrambled egg. 'We've got a pretty little role-playing session lined up for this morning. Arthur Noblet is applying to Thruxton Appleby for increased fringe benefits at the Hardcastle Handbag Company.'

'Excellent,' said Reggie. 'I'll just sit in and watch.'

'You have to play a role too,' said C.J. 'According to Doc Morrissey, everyone has to play a role.'

'It's against my policy,' said Reggie. 'I don't like to trespass on my staff's preserves.'

'Talking about trespassing on the staff's preserves, could I have the marmalade?' said the insurance salesman who had lost his motivation.

Reggie passed him the marmalade.

'You can be holding a watching brief for the industrial relations research council, Reggie,' said C.J.

'Wonderful,' said Reggie. 'What role will you be playing?'

'I'll be Thruxton Appleby's secretary,' said C.J.

Tony Webster choked in mid-toast.

'What'll I be called?' said Reggie.

'Perrin,' said C.J. 'I stick to the facts as far as possible.'

'What'll you be called then?' said Reggie.

C.J. glanced at Tony.

'Cynthia Jones,' he said.

113

Tony spluttered again.

'There's nothing ludicrous about it,' said C.J. 'It's a valuable exercise. But I couldn't expect you to see that. You know what they say. Small minds make idle chatter. How people change. It's hard to believe that you were once my golden boy at Sunshine Desserts.'

After breakfast they walked along Oslo Avenue in the pale sunshine.

At the gate of Number Seventeen, Reggie stopped.

'I don't want to interfere,' he said. 'But wouldn't this be a more valuable exercise if Arthur Noblet played the boss and Thruxton Appleby played the worker.'

'How come?' said C.J.

'Well,' said Reggie. 'They might learn something about the them and us situation which bedevils British industrial relations so tragically.'

'I didn't get where I am today by learning about the them and us situation which bedevils British industrial relations so tragically.'

'You certainly didn't, C.J. Maybe it's about time you did. But, as I say, it's entirely up to you.'

'Yes.'

'It might be more fun my way, though.'

'You have a point, Reggie.'

They entered Number Seventeen and went into the sun room extension which now formed C.J.'s office.

The room, built for suburban relaxation, was filled with office furniture. There were three desks, two typewriters, six chairs, green filing cabinets, two waste-paper baskets, and a hat-stand.

The watery sun streamed in.

Thruxton Appleby and Arthur Noblet were waiting. C.J. explained the revised scenario.

C.J. settled himself behind his typewriter and the other three went into the back garden.

Reggie knocked.

'Come in,' said C.J. in a mincing, pseudo-female voice.

Reggie entered.

'Can I help you?' minced C.J.

114

Reggie laughed.

'Reggie!' said C.J. 'This is an important social experiment, and all you can do is laugh. Immerse yourself in your role as I do. I become Cynthia Jones. C.J. is dead, long live Cynthia Jones. Now get out and come in.'

'Sorry, C.J.'

Reggie went back into the garden.

He re-entered the sun room.

'I meant, 'Sorry, Cynthia'' he said. 'Sorry, C.J.'

'Get out.'

Reggie went out and knocked on the door.

'Come in,' said C.J.

Reggie came in.

'Mr Noblet's office,' minced C.J. 'Can I help you?'

'The name's Perrin,' said Reggie. 'Industrial relations research council.'

'Ah, yes. Welcome to Hardcastle Handbags, Mr Perrin. Mr Noblet'll be in in a jiffy.'

There was a knock.

'Come in,' said C.J.

Arthur Noblet entered.

'No, no,' said Reggie. 'It's your office. No need to knock.'

'Sorry,' said Arthur Noblet.

'Sorry, I didn't mean to butt in,' said Reggie. 'But now that I have, may I make a point?'

'Go ahead,' said C.J.

'Come in with a bit of authority,' said Reggie. 'Make some remark about your journey. "Twelve minutes late. Traffic lights out of order at Hanger Lane." That sort of thing.'

'Excellent,' said C.J. 'First-class remark. Take an umbrella.'

Arthur Noblet took an umbrella.

'Go out and come in,' said C.J.

Arthur Noblet went into the garden, where Thruxton Appleby was examining the veins on a rose leaf.

He re-entered the sun room.

'Twelve minutes late,' he said, hanging his umbrella on the hat-stand. 'Traffic lights out of action at Hanger Lane.'

'This is Mr Perrin, Mr Noblet,' minced C.J. 'He's from the industrial relations research council.'

'I'm holding a watching brief,' said Reggie.

'Ready for dictation,' minced C.J., hitching up his trousers and crossing his legs.

There was a knock. Nobody answered.

'Oh, that'll be for me. It's my bleeding office,' said Arthur Noblet. 'Come in.'

Thruxton Appleby entered with massive authority.

'We want more fringe benefits, Noblet,' he thundered.

'O.K. You deserve them,' said Arthur Noblet.

'No, no, no!' said Reggie. 'Pathetic! Abysmal! Appleby, you wouldn't enter your office with massive authority if you were about to be interviewed by you. And Noblet, you mustn't give in like that. You must get inside each other's roles. Take your example from C.J., the Deborah Kerr of Botchley.'

C.J. waved the compliment aside modestly.

'Right,' said Reggie. 'We'll take it from Noblet's entrance.'

Arthur Noblet and Thruxton Appleby went out into the sun-filled garden, where they could be seen arguing about their roles.

'Nice morning, Miss Jones,' said Reggie.

'Very nice,' said C.J., crossing his legs.

'Have you planned your holiday yet, Miss Jones?' said Reggie.

'Well no, I haven't had time to draw breath yet, truth to tell, what with moving flats and my boy friend's promotion and that. I'm in a right tiswas,' said C.J.

Arthur Noblet burst into the sun room.

'Morning, Miss Jones,' he said, hanging his umbrella on the hat-stand. 'Sixteen minutes late. Jack-knifed juggernaut at Neasden. Have you typed the letter to Amalgamated Wallets?'

'I'm just doing it, Mr Noblet,' said C.J. 'This is Mr Perrin, of the industrial relations research council.'

'I'm extremely grateful to you, Mr Noblet,' said Reggie, 'both on behalf of myself and everyone at Research House, for letting me witness your arbitration procedures at ground roots level.'

'Don't mention it,' said Arthur Noblet.

There was a knock.

'Come!' roared C.J.

'No, no, no,' said Reggie.

Thruxton Appleby entered.

116

'Sorry,' said C.J. 'My fault that time. A case of the pot calling the kettle a silver lining, I'm afraid. Let's take it from Appleby's entrance. Appleby, go out and come in again.'

The massive textiles tycoon left the room meekly.

Almost immediately he knocked.

'Enter,' said Arthur Noblet, with a shy smile at his powers of verbal invention.

Thruxton Appleby entered. His demeanour was cowed, yet implicitly insolent.

'Sit down, Appleby,' said Arthur Noblet. 'This is Mr Perrin, of . . . er . . .'

'I.R.R.C.,' said Reggie. 'I'm holding a watching brief.'

'Now, what's this little spot of bovver, Appleby?' said Arthur Noblet.

'The chaps on the floor want more fringe benefits,' said Thruxton Appleby. 'Silly of them, the lazy good-for-nothings, but there it is.'

'What do you mean, silly of them?' said Arthur Noblet. 'How you blokes are expected to make ends meet when berks like me cop for twenty thousand a year defeats me.'

'No, no, no,' said Reggie. 'Useless. Oh, sorry, C.J. I didn't mean to get involved. Oh well, I've started now. Appleby, you really believe you deserve the fringe benefits. Noblet, you seriously believe you can't afford them. But you say the rest, C.J. This is your show.'

'Thank you, Reggie,' said C.J. through clenched teeth, 'Right, we'll take it from Appleby's entrance. We'll take your knock as read, Appleby.'

'I'd rather knock, if you don't mind,' said the burly West Riding chrome-dome.

'O.K., bloody well knock, then, but just get on with it,' snapped C.J.

Thruxton Appleby knocked, Arthur Noblet yelled 'Come!', Thruxton Appleby came, C.J. simpered flirtatiously at the typewriter, Reggie was introduced, and the negotiations began.

'The lads are a bit cheesed off,' said Thruxton Appleby. 'I know times have been hard, with the fluctuating of the yen, and we've had to announce a reduced dividend of seven and a half per cent, but the lads would like improved fringe benefits.'

117

'What kind of improved fringe benefits?' said Arthur Noblet.

Thruxton Appleby thought hard. He'd never taken much interest in workers' fringe benefits.

'Five weeks' holiday, automatic membership of the golf club, free investment advice, company cars, an increased share holding, and an improved dividend,' he said.

'Piss off,' said Arthur Noblet.

'No, no, no,' said Reggie. 'No, no, no, no, no. Mind you, that was better. I won't say another word, C.J. This is your show.'

'Well . . .' said C.J.

'Just an idea,' said Reggie. 'Supposing you and I demonstrate our idea of negotiation techniques?'

'Would that really have much value?' said C.J.

'With you as the powerful boss and me as the downtrodden worker,' said Reggie.

'It might be worth a try, I suppose,' said C.J. 'Hang it on the clothes line, see if the cat licks it up.'

And so Arthur Noblet became Cynthia Jones, Thruxton Appleby became the man from Research House, Reggie became the workman, and C.J. became C.J.

Arthur Noblet installed himself behind the typewriter, while the others went into the garden.

Arthur mimed a last glance in the mirror, Thruxton Appleby entered and was introduced, C.J. entered, hurled his umbrella at the hat-stand, missed, said, 'Twenty-two minutes late. Failure of de-icing equipment at Coulsdon,' and sat down, and Reggie knocked, was invited to enter, and did so.

'Now then, Perrin, what's the trouble?' said C.J.

'It's like this, guvnor,' said Reggie, sitting down facing C.J. 'We're falling be'ind as regards differentials and that.'

'Who's falling behind as regards differentials?'

'Everybody.'

C.J. looked pained.

'Everyone can't fall behind as regards differentials,' he said.

'No, what I mean is,' said Reggie, 'we're falling behind viz-à-viz workers in strictly comparable industries, i.e. purses, brief-cases, and real and simulated leather goods generally, like.'

'You had a rise eight months ago, in accordance with phase

three of stage eight,' said C.J. 'Or was it phase eight of stage three? Anyway, there's a world-wide handbag slump. Do you expect me to run at a loss?'

'Course not, guv,' said Reggie. 'Stone the crows, no. You're in it for the lolly, same as what we all are. You're forced to be. Forced to be. Course you are. You're forced to be forced to be. Course you are. We aren't arguing about the basic wage. Basically the basic wage is basically fair. It's the fringe benefits, innit?'

'What sort of fringe benefits?' said C.J.

'Areas where I could suggest amelioration of traditional benefits would include five weeks' 'oliday a year, rationalised shift bonuses, increased production incentives, longer tea breaks, coffee breaks brought up to the tea break level, a concessionary handbag for every year of service, and fifteen minutes un-penalised latitude for lateness due to previously notified genuine unforeseen circumstances.'

'I see,' said C.J. 'Well, Perrin, I might see my way to recommending the board to give a day's extra holiday and a seasonal shift bonus adjustment, and we might be able to work something out on incentives, and then report back to you.'

'Well,' said Reggie, 'I can put that to my members, and see if we can draft a resolution that the negotiations committee might be prepared to put to the steering committee, but I have a feeling my members will want something on the table now.'

'I'm afraid that may not be possible,' said C.J.

'We just want a fair share of the cake,' said Reggie.

'Ah, but can you have your fair share of the cake and eat it?' said C.J.

'We want deeds, not words,' said Reggie. 'Otherwise we're coming out.'

'I will not yield to threats motivated by political scum,' said C.J.

'I don't think my members will appreciate that nomenclature,' said Reggie.

'It's what they are, isn't it?' shouted C.J. 'Marxist scum. Reds under the handbags. I will flush them out.'

'Right. It's all out, then,' said Reggie quietly.

'You're all sacked,' said C.J.

119

'You bastard!' said Reggie.

There was a moment's silence.

'Yes, well, you get the general idea,' said Reggie. 'Seeing the other person's point of view, that's what it's all about.'

That evening Reggie and Elizabeth went to the George and Two Dragons after dinner. Several other members of the community were in evidence, both staff and guests. C.J. was drinking with Thruxton Appleby. Reggie was delighted when Arthur Noblet joined them. Tony Webster was chatting up Hilary Meadows, and getting nowhere expensively. The middle manager was talking to Mr Pelham. Subjects discussed included porkers and other kinds of pigs. McBlane popped in for a few minutes. He was on dry gingers as he'd found that alcohol played havoc with his psoriasis.

'I've just realised what's missing,' Reggie told Elizabeth. 'All these people shouldn't be down the pub every night. A community should have social evenings.'

Two days later, at the group meeting, Reggie made an announcement.

'Every evening, after dinner,' he said, 'there will be a social gathering. These gatherings will be totally voluntary. Obviously I hope everyone will attend, but there's no obligation.'

That evening, Reggie and Elizabeth sat in the living room of Number Twenty-one, waiting.

Nobody came.

At the next group meeting, Reggie spoke to them all again.

'I can't see how any guest who intends to get full value from the community wouldn't come to some at least of these gatherings, and I'd be very disappointed if members of staff didn't set an example by frequent attendance,' he said. 'Though of course I will emphasise once again that it is entirely voluntary.'

'You, you and you,' said Jimmy.

Reggie gave him a cool look.

'Sorry,' said Jimmy. 'Slipped out. Army volunteering. You, you and you. Wasn't suggesting that here. No need. Stampede.'

'You didn't exactly stampede last time,' said Reggie.

'Prior engagement,' said Jimmy. 'Wedding plans. All invited. Refusal *de rigueur*.'

'*De rigueur* means essential,' said Reggie.

'Exactly,' said Jimmy. 'Essential, all present, church parade, twenty-first December. Hope all be on parade tonight too. As I will, living room, twenty-thirty hours, delights social various for the enjoyment of.'

Jimmy was as good as his word. In fact he was the first to arrive that evening.

Others swiftly followed. Soon the living room was packed. Every available seat was occupied, and latecomers had to find a place on the floor.

The smokeless fuel glowed in the grate. The curtains were drawn on the cold October night.

Present were Reggie, Elizabeth, C.J., Doc Morrissey, Jimmy, Tom, Linda, Joan, David, Prue, Thruxton Appleby, Mr Pelham, the insurance agent who had lost his motivation, Diana Pilkington, Hilary Meadows, the VAT inspector from Tring, the probation officer from Peebles, the unemployed careers officer, the director of the finance company, and the middle manager.

Absent were Tony (down the George and Two Dragons), Arthur Noblet (down the Botchley Arms), and Bernard Trilling (watching TV).

The evening began stickily, but slowly began to develop its style. They shared cigarettes, passing them round after each puff.

'This is just as much fun as smoking pot,' said Reggie.

'I didn't get where I am today by smoking pot,' said C.J., who was sitting on the rug in front of the fire.

When the conversation flagged, Reggie asked if anybody had seen anything beautiful during the day.

'The sunset was beautiful,' volunteered Hilary Meadows.

'Yes, it was. I really noticed it,' said the unemployed careers officer. 'Too often I close my eyes to beautiful things like the sunsets.'

'We all do,' said Diana Pilkington from the settee. Her legs were crossed, revealing an expanse of slender, rather glacial thigh.

121

'I saw an old tramp in the High Street, and he picked up this sodden fag end and smoked it,' said Linda.

'I can't see anything beautiful in a sodden fag end,' said the insurance salesman who had lost his motivation.

'It was beautiful for the tramp,' said Tom. 'That's Linda's point.'

His eyes met Linda's and he smiled.

'It was a very beautiful thing, Linda darling,' he said, 'because it shows your understanding of people. I've said it before and I'll say it again. We're people people.'

Elizabeth, seated on the settee, put her hand on Reggie's shoulder. He stroked her leg. It made them happy to see Tom and Linda so happy.

'I'm still on the side of the sunset,' said Diana Pilkington.

'I'd like to talk to you about your social drives tomorrow, Di,' said Doc Morrissey, who was sitting between Elizabeth and Diana Pilkington on the settee.

'Any more beautiful experiences?' said Reggie.

'I saw a really beautiful missel thrush,' said the VAT inspector from Tring.

'Super,' chorused David and Prue Harris-Jones.

'It was eating a worm,' added the VAT inspector from Tring.

'Oh,' said David and Prue Harris-Jones.

'You wouldn't think it was beautiful if you were a worm,' said the middle manager in the multi-national plastics concern.

'I'm not a worm,' said the VAT inspector from Tring.

'Matter of opinion,' said Jimmy. 'Just joking,' he added hastily.

He looked round to see if Linda approved of his sally. She smiled at him, and mouthed the single word 'Lettice'. He nodded, his nod saying 'Oh, quite. Engaged. Eyes for one woman only. Looked at you out of affection. Favourite niece, that sort of crack. Other thing, past history, water under bridge. Self-abuse, ditto. New man. New leaf.'

'I saw a beautiful thing,' said David Harris-Jones. 'Well, perhaps it wasn't all that beautiful.'

'Tell us,' said Reggie. 'Let us decide.'

'I saw the driver of the W288 pull up between two stops to let an elderly woman on,' said David Harris-Jones.

'Yes, that is beautiful,' said the probation officer from Peebles.

'It's a miracle,' said Reggie.

'I wish you'd told me about the bus driver,' said Prue.

'Why?' said David.

'It's interesting,' said Prue.

'It isn't that interesting,' said David.

'Its interesting because you saw it, darling,' said Prue.

Elizabeth waited for Reggie to explode. He beamed.

'Any other beautiful sights?' he said.

'Yes. I saw Tony's private parts,' said Joan.

'Come come,' said C.J. 'Really!'

'They're beautiful,' said Joan.

'Yes, they are,' said Reggie. 'I mean I assume they are. I haven't seen them myself. But I mean surely if Joan thinks they're beautiful she should be able to say so. And surely the human body is beautiful?'

'I don't think so,' said Diana Pilkington.

'I think we might touch on that tomorrow, too, Di,' said Doc Morrissey.

C.J. shifted uncomfortably on the floor.

'Sorry,' he said. 'Not used to squatting on floors. Neither Mrs C.J. nor I has ever been used to squatting on floors.'

'Give C.J. your seat, Tom,' said Linda.

'I'm not a sitting on floors person either,' said Tom.

'Now's the time to start, then,' said Reggie.

'You're right,' said Tom. 'I've got to become less rigid in my attitudes.'

Tom snuggled up against Linda on the floor, and C.J. took the armchair he had vacated.

More beautiful experiences were related. More cigarettes were shared. The probation officer shyly produced a guitar. Joan sang a protest song. Mr Pelham sang a pig song. Thruxton Appleby sang a textiles song. The insurance salesman sang an insurance song. The middle manager tore up a fiver and threw it on the fire. They examined his motives. Linda kissed Tom. Not to be outdone, Prue kissed David.

'Touch,' said Doc Morrissey suddenly.

Everyone looked at him in astonishment.

'We should touch each other,' he said. 'We should make

123

physical contact. It's the outward expression of inward togetherness.'

He put his hand on Diana Pilkington's knee.

'Touching is good,' he said.

He slid his hand along her leg.

'Feeling is beautiful,' he said.

He pushed his hand right up inside her skirt, between her thighs.

She gave his arm a karate chop that numbed it completely.

'Smacking is good,' she said.

Doc Morrissey held his injured arm tenderly.

'Twelve karate lessons in Chorlton-cum-Hardy are beautiful,' said Diana Pilkington.

'I was only giving the outward expression of inward together-ness,' said Doc Morrissey. 'I only touched you because I was sitting next to you. I'd have done the same thing if I'd been sitting next to Reggie.'

'Thank God you weren't,' said Reggie.

'No, but touching each other is beautiful,' said David and Prue Harris-Jones, entwining their fingers with intense tenderness.

Reggie walked up to the VAT inspector from Tring, and put his hand in his.

'Foreign countries do it all the time,' he said. 'It's natural. You don't mind, do you, Mr VAT inspector from Tring?'

'Not at all,' said the VAT inspector from Tring. 'I rather like it.'

'Oh,' said Reggie.

He removed his hand.

'Not in that way,' said the VAT inspector from Tring. 'Just as friendliness.'

'Ah!' said Reggie.

He clasped the hand of the VAT inspector from Tring once more.

'Come on. Everybody touch everybody,' he said.

'I didn't get where I am today by touching everybody,' said C.J.

'I'm game,' proffered the probation officer from Peebles.

'Me too,' put in the unemployed careers officer.

'So am I,' agreed Tom. 'It's about time I broke the barriers of habit that have enslaved me.'

Everyone began to wander round the room, touching each other. At first there were a few giggles. Somebody said, 'We're groping towards success,' and there was laughter.

Soon, however, the giggles and laughter died down, and there was only the quiet, rather solemn ritual of touching.

The middle manager kissed the director of the finance company. Tom kissed Reggie. His beard tickled. All over the room people held hands, kissed, touched, regardless of age, sex and occupation.

'It's the new Jerusalem,' said Doc Morrissey.

Arthur Noblet entered, slightly unsteady after his evening at the Botchley Arms, took one look at the New Jerusalem, said, 'Bloody Hell' and lurched out.

'It went off very well,' said Elizabeth that night in bed.

'Too well,' said Reggie.

Elizabeth kissed the lobe of his ear. Her face wore a charming admixture of affection, amusement and exasperation.

'Will you never be content?' she said.

'Seriously, darling,' said Reggie. 'We're getting a bit of a problem. Nobody's leaving. That means nobody's giving us any money.'

The following day an incident occurred which delayed the likely departure of Thruxton Appleby, the wealthiest of Reggie's guests.

Reggie was accompanying Jimmy on one of his expeditions. A small group stood on the front porch of Number Twenty-one, in the pale golden sunlight, and Jimmy briefed them.

'Object of exercise,' he said, 'litter clearance. Done some major work already. Cleared Threadwell's Pond, flushed out old bedsteads in Mappin Woods. Today, mopping-up operations, isolated pockets of litter throughout borough. Place your litter in the king bin liners provided.'

They moved off down Oslo Avenue, their king bin liners in their hands, and turned left into Bonn Close, where Mr Pelham dealt summarily with a 'Seven-up' tin.

When they turned left into Addis Ababa Avenue, Reggie saw the unmistakable domed head of Thruxton Appleby in the phone box at the junction with Canberra Rise.

'Walk back the other way,' he said, and Jimmy led his team back down Bonn Close with the instinctive obedience of a military man.

Reggie tackled Thruxton Appleby, who admitted that he had been phoning his office and tearing them off a strip.

'You're the sort of person who pays a fortune to a health farm and then sneaks out to gorge himself on cream cakes,' said Reggie.

'You don't understand. Bilton's cocked up the forward orders,' said Thruxton Appleby.

'How many phone calls have you made?' said Reggie.

'Three,' said Thruxton Appleby. 'I just can't trust them a minute.'

A vein was throbbing ominously around his temple. Reggie thought of all Thruxton Appleby's money and sighed.

'One more phone call and you leave,' he said.

'If I promise not to make any more calls...?'

'You can stay.'

'I promise,' said Thruxton Appleby.

He glanced at his watch.

'They're open,' he said. 'Do you fancy a drink?'

They walked down Nairobi Drive to the High Street, and entered the saloon bar of the George and Two Dragons. Thruxton Appleby stood back politely to let Reggie get to the bar and his wallet first. They were the first customers. Hoovering was in progress, and there was a strong smell of furniture polish. The old dragon served them.

'What are you having?' said Reggie.

'Whisky and soda,' said Thruxton Appleby.

Reggie ordered a whisky and soda and a pint of bitter.

'No, by God, I'll have a beer too,' said Thruxton Appleby. 'And I'm paying.'

They sat in a window alcove.

'I'm getting almost likeable, aren't I?' said Thruxton Appleby.

'You're on the verge, Thruxton.'

'I might have done it by now if it hadn't been for those phone calls.'

'They've set you back, I'll not deny it.'

'We've got a word for people like me, where I come from,' said Thruxton Appleby. 'Am I to tell you what it is?'

'Please.'

'Thrifty. Canny. Cautious. In a word, mean as arseholes. But when I leave, Mr Perrin, I'm not going to be mean. I'll give you a goodly whack.'

'Well, thank you,' said Reggie. 'Cheers.'

'I'll be staying quite a while yet, though.'

'Oh. Well . . . good . . . splendid.'

'You'll have to take my generosity on trust.'

'Yes . . . well . . . splendid.'

'I might stay for ever, you never know.'

'Huh huh. Huh huh huh. Splendid.'

That Friday afternoon, however, the departures began at last. The first to call in at Reggie's study in Number Twenty-three was Mr Pelham. He entered shyly.

'Afternoon, Reg,' he said. 'May I sit down?'

'Of course,' said Reggie.

Mr Pelham's enquiry had not been an academic one. Informed that he might sit, he did so.

'I've come to the end of the road, old son,' he said.

Reggie's heart began to beat faster than he would have wished.

'Is this an admission of success or defeat?' he asked.

If he'd hoped for a simple answer, he didn't get it.

'Who knows?' said Mr Pelham. 'I came here, with blood on my hands, hoping for a miracle. What have I learnt? I'm a bloody awful painter, I can't thatch for toffee, and I sing like a pregnant yak.'

'Oh dear.'

'Sex clinic? Damp squib. My sex life finished years ago, old son. Analysis? My subconscious is as dull as my conscious.'

'Oh dear, oh dear.'

Mr Pelham looked out at the passing W288 to Spraundon much as a docker might watch the luxury liner whose hawsers he had handled slipping away to glamorous foreign parts.

'This is dreadful,' said Reggie.

'Don't get me wrong, Reg,' said Mr Pelham. 'I've enjoyed myself. Good food, new people. I haven't said much, but I've soaked it all up. I expected I don't know what. I know now that there isn't any don't know what. There's only what there is, old son. And I know now who I am.'

'Er . . . who are you?'

'I'm the meat man. When I go in the pub, the landlord says "Morning, meat man". When I meet the assistant bank manager in the street, he says, "And what sort of a weekend did the meat man have?" that's who I am, Reg. Not Leonardo da Vinci. Not Kim Novak. Not a tramp. Not the Headmistress of Roedean. The manager of the Abbey National Building Society doesn't say, "Hello, Mr P, can I enter our Sandra for your school?" The milkman doesn't say, "Saw the old Mona Lisa last week. Nice one, Leonardo. Stick at it." And so, I build up a dossier of my identity. I'm the meat man.'

'I don't know what to say,' said Reggie.

Mr Pelham got out his cheque book.

'I've been thinking while I've been here, Reg,' he said. 'And that's good. I'm returning to my chosen career which I do well. If the world wants my meat, they can have it. I'm not happy and I'm not miserable. You haven't succeeded and you haven't failed. I'm giving you a cheque for five hundred pounds.'

'Well, I . . . er . . .' began Reggie.

'You aren't going to turn it down, are you?' said Mr Pelham.

'No, actually I'm not,' said Reggie.

They shook hands.

'Goodbye, old son,' said Mr Pelham.

'Goodbye, Mr P,' said Reggie. 'And Mr P?'

Mr Pelham turned to face Reggie.

'Yeah?'

'Give my love to the pigs.'

The next person to call in at the drab, dark study was the insurance salesman who had lost his motivation.

'I'm very grateful. I'd give you more if I was richer,' he said, handing Reggie two hundred pounds in cash.

Reggie unlocked a drawer in his desk, put the bundles of notes in, and locked the drawer.

'You've done wonders for me,' said the insurance salesman who had lost his motivation.

'You realise that it doesn't matter that you've lost your motivation,' said Reggie. 'Splendid.'

'No, no. Much better than that. I've found my motivation again.'

'Oh. Well that really wasn't what I . . .'

'Large amounts of cash lying in drawers all weekend. Have you thought of increasing your protection against burglary?' said the insurance salesman who had found his motivation again.

The mellow weather continued. Arrivals outpaced departures, and the advance booking charts were dotted with names.

McBlane discovered that dry ginger inflamed his dermatitis and reverted to Newcastle Brown. The food remained as delicious as ever.

The social evenings became a permanent and valued feature of life.

One day, Tom announced that he had developed a new concept in sporting non-competition.

'Solo ball games,' he explained. 'You play squash and tennis on your own.'

Squash on one's own proved tolerable, though tiring. Solo tennis was much less enthusiastically received. Frequent changes of end were necessary to retrieve the balls.

When this complaint was voiced, Tom solved it almost immediately.

'A load of balls,' he told the group meeting excitedly.

But even with an adequate supply of balls, the drawbacks of solo tennis proved too great. Each rally consisted of only one stroke. It was a service-dominated sport, and when the weather broke it was abandoned without regret.

Hilary Meadows returned home to the bosom of a family who would no longer take her for granted.

'My husband'll send you a cheque,' she told Reggie. 'I'll

tell him to send whatever he thinks my happiness and sanity are worth. You'll get more that way. I hope.'

Reggie came across Bernard Trilling, Head of Comedy at Anaemia Television, putting the finishing touches to a splendid basket that he had woven.

'So, I've woven a basket already,' he said, no longer hiding his Jewishness under a bushel. 'If I could weave a television series, I'd be all right maybe.'

And he laughed.

'My wife's often said that she could knit funnier series than some you put on,' said Reggie.

'I know,' said Bernard Trilling. 'Some of our comedy series are a joke.'

He laughed again.

'Is this hysteria, I ask myself,' he said. 'I'd better leave before I answer.'

He gave Reggie a cheque for five hundred pounds, and two tickets for the pilot show of 'Mum's the Word'.

On the last day of October, Thruxton Appleby discharged himself reluctantly. He still appeared far too large for the little chair in Reggie's office, but this time his vast buttocks seemed gentle, apologetic giants.

Two blue tits flitted without fear from branch to branch of the bush outside the window.

The rain poured down. The brief summer was over.

'This is the moment of truth,' said Thruxton Appleby, getting his cheque book out slowly. 'Now, how much?'

'It's up to you,' said Reggie.

'Well,' said Thruxton Appleby, 'you've certainly succeeded. I'm likeable, aren't I?'

'Thoroughly likeable.'

'Lovable?'

'Perhaps not loveable yet. On the way, though. And the more you can get over your natural meanness and learn the pleasures of generosity, the quicker you'll be lovable.'

'So I ought to give you a fat sum?'

'For your own sake,' said Reggie, 'I think you should.'

Thruxton Appleby roared with laughter.

'I like your bare-faced cheek,' he said. 'I admire bare-faced cheek.'

And he made out a cheque for a thousand pounds.

'It's worth every penny,' he said. 'I'm a new man. All I've thought about for years is money and business. Money and business.'

Reggie slipped the cheque into the safe that had been installed the previous day.

'Please don't start worrying that it's too much,' said Thruxton Appleby. 'It's tax deductible.'

That night, the wind rattled the double-glazed windows of the surprisingly spacious master bedroom in Number Twenty-one. Reggie sighed. Once more Elizabeth put her book down and gave her husband a searching look over the top of her glasses.

'Still not fully content, darling?' she asked.

'Oh yes,' said Reggie. 'The money's pouring in. Cures are being made. New people are arriving. I really am fully content at last.'

He sighed.

'Then why are you sighing?' said Elizabeth.

'Contentment worries me,' said Reggie.

November took a dismal grip on Great Britain. Fierce winds destroyed three seaside piers, twelve scout huts, and the thatched roof of the garden shed at Number Twenty-one, Oslo Avenue, Botchley. For four days pantechnicons were unable to cross the Severn Bridge. Fieldfares and redwings reached Norfolk from Scandinavia in record numbers, to collapse exhausted on cold, sodden meadows and wonder why they had bothered. A survey showed that Britain had sunk to fifteenth place in the world nutmeg consumption league, behind Bali and Portugal. There were strikes by petrol tanker drivers, draymen at four breweries, and dustmen from eight counties. Twelve-year-old girls were found to be offering themselves to old men for money behind a comprehensive school in Nottinghamshire. Seven hundred and twenty-nine hamsters arrived dead at Stansted Airport from Cyprus, and a Rumanian tourist died after being

131

caught between rival gangs of Chelsea and Leeds fans in West London.

But at Numbers Seventeen to Twenty-five, Oslo Avenue, Botchley, things were far from gloomy. Guests were arriving in steadily increasing numbers. The majority of guests who departed were in expansive mood and gave generously. The engagement between Jimmy and Lettice was proceeding placidly. The marriages of Reggie and Elizabeth, David and Prue, and Tom and Linda were going smoothly. Young Reggie Harris-Jones was proving a model child, and the behaviour of Adam and Jocasta had improved beyond the expectations of the most sanguine idealist.

Not everything was perfect, of course. The first of Tom's sloe gin and raspberry whisky was ready for drinking, and the behaviour of Tony Webster still gave cause for concern.

One day, Reggie called unexpectedly at the Culture Room, in the garden shed of Number Twenty-five. The dreary, functional garden was dank and lifeless in the raw November mist. The notice 'Culture Room: Prop T. Webster, Q.C.I.' still adorned the yellow door.

There was a delay before Tony opened the door.

His hair was tousled.

He led Reggie into the Culture Room. The naked breasts had been removed, and the walls were bare.

Diana Pilkington sat in one of the armchairs.

Her face was flushed.

'We've been rehearsing *Romeo and Juliet*, Act Two, Scene Two,' said Tony.

And indeed, two copies of *French's Acting Edition* lay open on the floor.

'Excellent,' said Reggie.

'I know what you're thinking,' said Tony.

'I wasn't thinking anything of the kind,' said Reggie.

'I haven't told you what I know you're thinking,' said Tony.

'I know what you think I'm thinking,' said Reggie.

'Touché Town, Arizona,' said Tony.

Reggie flinched, and Diana Pilkington smiled, revealing small white teeth.

' I know,' she said. 'Doesn't he use *the* most dreadful phrases?

You'd have thought a bit of Shakespeare would have rubbed off on him by now. No such luck.'

'Come on, Di,' said Tony. 'Let's really hit Capulet's Garden.' And indeed they did give a spirited rendition.

'Well done, Di,' said Tony when they had finished. 'You're beginning to let it all hang out.'

That evening Reggie went to the George and Two Dragons in search of Tony. He found him chatting up the buxom barmaid, under the jealous glare of the young dragon. It was George's night off.

Tony bought Reggie a drink.

'I know what you're thinking,' he said, when they were settled in the corner beyond the food counter. 'And you're right. Di's a frigid lady, Reggie. She's got this computer programmer from Alderley Edge sniffing around her, and I'm just warming her up. It's a hell of a bore, but you've got to take your responsibilities to the community seriously, haven't you?'

'It's Joan I'm thinking of, Tony,' said Reggie.

'It's Joany's idea,' said Tony.

'What?'

'I'm a changed man, Reggie. I have a wonderful wife. Extramarital activity is Outsville, Arizona with a capital O. Joany trusts me. So, I'm the obvious man to warm up our cold career lady. No sweat.'

The young dragon cleared their table noisily and wiped it with a smelly rag.

'You never come to our communal evenings,' said Reggie. 'You're never with Joan.'

'Each in his own way, Reggie. Faith and trust. I'd have left Di to Tom or David, but they couldn't warm up a plate of custard. And I tell you what, Reggie. It'll be dynamite when it's warmed up. Its computer programmer won't know what's hit him.'

Four under-age drinkers from the fifth form debating society of Botchley Hill Comprehensive entered the bar. The young dragon listened to their order. Then, because it wasn't expensive enough to be worth the risk, she refused to serve them.

'May I venture a brief word of criticism of your linguistic habits, Tony?' said Reggie.

133

'Sure,' said Tony. 'Feel free. Shoot.'

'Doc Morrissey would no doubt suggest that you're compensating for the ageing process which you refuse to admit by larding your language increasingly with what you take to be the argot of the young,' said Reggie.

'I know what you mean,' said Tony. 'And I think you'll see a dramatic improvement pretty soon.'

'Oh good. That is encouraging. Any particular reason?'

'Yeah. O.K., I made out I was into culture, but I wasn't. I'm really into it now, Reggie. Know what changed my attitude?'

'No,' confessed Reggie.

'Shakespeare. He's a real laid-back bard.'

Soon there were only forty-four basket-weaving days to Christmas.

Tom told a group meeting, 'I've got an idea for a whole new concept of non-aggressive football. Playing with no opposition hasn't been the answer. We've had the occasional good result, like last week's 32–0 win, but basically it's boring. So now we'll play in two teams, but we're only allowed to score for the other side. That should get rid of the worst effects of aggression and partisanship.'

'Super,' said David and Prue Harris-Jones.

Soon there were only thirty-nine rethatching days to Christmas.

For the first time there wasn't a single empty bed. Extra accommodation would have to be found. Reggie and Elizabeth faced the problem fair and square.

'We can get one extra room by teaming up C.J. and Doc Morrissey,' said Reggie in bed that night. 'It'll mean rejigging the wardenships, but it's worth it. Every little helps.'

They'll never agree,' said Elizabeth.

'I'll use psychology,' said Reggie. 'And you'll be with me, so that they can't get too angry.'

The next morning Reggie asked C.J. and Doc Morrissey to come to the secretary's office. Elizabeth sat behind her desk, and Reggie sat in front of it, with the wall charts behind him.

C.J. came first.

'These wall charts reveal the expanding state of our business,' said Reggie.

'I always knew it would succeed,' said C.J. 'Out of the mouths of babes and little children.'

'We're going to need more accommodation,' said Reggie. 'Everyone is going to have to make sacrifices.'

'I'm glad to hear it,' said C.J.

'You'll have to share a room with McBlane.'

C.J.'s mouth opened and shut several times, but no sound emerged. At last, he managed a hoarse, piteous croak.

'I think I know what you're trying to say,' said Reggie. 'You didn't get where you are today by sleeping with pox-ridden Caledonian chefs.'

C.J. nodded.

'I didn't realise you'd feel so strongly,' said Reggie. 'All right. You can share a room with Doc Morrissey instead.'

'Thanks,' said C.J. 'Thanks very much, Reggie.'

When C.J. had gone, Reggie smiled triumphantly at Elizabeth.

'If you'd asked him to share with Doc Morrissey straight off, he'd have gone berserk,' she said.

'Exactly. But now he agrees eagerly, in gratitude at being spared the odiferous Scot. Thrill to my shrewdness now, as I try the same trick on Doc Morrissey.'

Doc Morrissey was soon installed in the chair that C.J. had so recently warmed.

'Psychological side of things still going well?' said Reggie.

'Damned well,' said Doc Morrissey, courteously including Elizabeth in his beaming smile. 'It's having a good effect on me, too.'

'Physician heal thyself.'

'Quite. Think I could take anything on the chin now.'

'Oh good. I want you to share a bedroom with McBlane.'

'What?'

'We're getting very crowded, due to our success. I want you to share your bedroom with McBlane.'

Doc Morrissey laughed. Then he smiled at Elizabeth.

'He had me going for a moment there,' he said.

Elizabeth smiled nervously.

'It isn't a joke,' she said. 'We really are awfully crowded.'

'Well, I know, but . . . McBlane!'

'He's a superb cook,' said Reggie.

'Red Rum's a fine horse, but I have no intention of sharing a bedroom with him,' said Doc Morrissey.

Reggie could hardly conceal his smugness as he made his master stroke.

'All right, then,' he said. 'I'll tell you what I'll do. You can share a bedroom with C.J. instead.'

Doc Morrissey fainted.

Two days later, Reggie called a staff meeting in the living room of Number Seventeen, to outline his plans for increasing the accommodation. Making C.J. and Doc Morrissey share a bedroom no longer featured in those plans. Assorted chairs, from large sagging armchairs to scruffy kitchen chairs, hugged the walls. A row of mugs hung on hooks at either side of the fireplace. Each mug bore the name of a member of the staff.

Reggie outlined their plans. Folding beds would be installed in the staff bedrooms, so that the various activities could be staged in them during the day. Reggie's office would move to the sun-room of Number Twenty-one and C.J.'s office would be in London, enabling work activities to take place within the context of commuting.

Eight bedrooms, four dining rooms, two studies, two sun-rooms, four kitchens and four garden sheds would be available as double bedrooms for guests. The unusual nature of the accommodation and the sharing of rooms would become an integral part of the exciting social journey on which the guests had embarked.

David Harris-Jones's hand shot up. Then he realised that he didn't really want to say what he had been going to say. He lowered his arm as unobtrusively as he could.

Not unobtrusively enough.

'You wanted to say something,' said Reggie.

'No,' said David Harris-Jones. 'Just . . . er . . . just a touch of lumbago. Exercise does it good.'

He raised and lowered his hand twice more.

'That's better,' he said.

136

'You were going to say something,' said Reggie. 'Don't be afraid!'

'David was going to say that you and Elizabeth still have your bedroom, and both your offices,' said Prue.

'Well, I was sort of going to say something along those ... er ...' said David Harris-Jones.

'Fair enough,' said Reggie. 'I'm glad you mentioned it.'

'... lines,' said David Harris-Jones.

'We'd like to give up our use of three rooms,' said Reggie. 'Sacrificing one's comforts in the interests of the community is a real pleasure, but it's one that we'll have to sacrifice. I have to command authority and respect. I have to inspire confidence. It's regrettable, but there it is.'

He told them that he would be opening other branches. There would be great chains of Perrins, from Land's End to John O'Groats. The great work had only just begun. These other communities would need managers. The jobs would command high salaries and great prestige, and Reggie would be looking for people experienced in this kind of work.

'It would be invidious to mention names,' he said. 'But I think it would be super and a knock-out if I could find some of these people among my own staff, because I'm a loyalty person. I didn't get where I am today without knowing that you can have a cock-up on the staffing front if you aren't a loyalty person.'

There were no more complaints.

Work began on the alterations. Elizabeth was a frequent visitor to the Botchley Slumber Centre, and barely a day passed without the arrival of new beds at one or other of the five houses. The bank accounts, briefly swollen by generous donations, began to dip alarmingly. Soon it would all pay off.

Perrins was a success.

All the time, they were growing more experienced and more confident.

All the time, life in the community was improving.

Reggie witnessed an eloquent example of this improvement when he entered Adam and Jocasta's bedroom on the very last day of that November.

The ecological wallpaper contained thirty-eight of the most threatened species in the world. Adam had some sheets of paper in his hand. Jocasta was sitting peacefully on the floor. Snodgrass was purring on Jocasta's bed. The room was tidy.

'I'm reading Jocasta a story, Uncle Reggie,' said Adam. 'I read better than her, but only because I'm older.'

'What's the story?' said Reggie.

'Uncle C.J. wrote it for us,' said Adam. 'It's all about ants. It's frightfully good.'

'I like Uncle C.J.,' said Jocasta.

December was a quiet month. Fewer people came to Perrins, although forward bookings remained good.

The alterations proceeded steadily.

The weather remained wet and windy.

The great days of Perrins lay ahead.

V

Christmas

CHRISTMAS REALLY BEGAN on the morning of Saturday, December the seventeenth.

That was when the snow came.

And the letter.

The letter was curiously brief.

'Dear Mother and Father,' it read. 'This will come as a complete surprise, I'm in Paris on my way back to England. I got your address from one of your adverts. My news can wait until I see you. I'll arrive on Friday, December 23rd. I'm looking forward to seeing you all. Your loving son, Mark.'

The snow began at half past ten. It wasn't heavy, but it caused the cancellation of eleven football matches.

Their festive plans received a further boost that morning. C.J. announced that he was going to spend Christmas with Mrs C.J. in Luxembourg.

Doc Morrissey would also be absent. He had committed himself to an Indian Christmas in Southall. He would miss the festivities at Perrins, but he couldn't let his old friends down.

The majority of the guests would be going home.

'It's going to be more a family Christmas than a community Christmas,' said Elizabeth in bed that night, snuggling against Reggie's chest.

'The community is a family,' said Reggie.

'I enjoy being secretary,' said Elizabeth. 'But I want to be a wife over Christmas.'

'So you will be, darling.'

'There's a fly in the ointment.'

'Fly? What fly?'

'McBlane.'

'I realise he needs a lot of ointment. I didn't know he was a fly in it.'

139

'Reggie!'

A carload of revellers squished homeward through the soft snow that carpeted Oslo Avenue.

'I want to cook the Christmas dinner myself,' said Elizabeth.

'No problem,' said Reggie. 'I imagine McBlane will be going home to his family.'

'Has he got a family?'

'Yes. He told me all about them the other day. I think. It was either that or the history of Partick Thistle.'

'He frightens me sometimes.'

'Nonsense, darling. I'll go and see McBlane tomorrow, and tell him that he's having Christmas off. No problem.'

Next day Reggie's predictions proved partly true and partly false.

He did go and see McBlane. There was a problem.

It was four o'clock on a Saturday afternoon, and the slim, dark culinary wizard was slumped on a wooden chair at the kitchen table. There was a pint bottle of Newcastle Brown in his hand, and his vest was stained with fat, oil and sweat. He had a rash on both arms.

'Good afternoon, McBlane,' said Reggie. 'I just called in to say that we ... er ... the ... er ... carbonnades of beef were wonderful today.'

'Bloody foreign muck,' said McBlane.

'Well, everyone is entitled to his opinion. At the risk of upsetting you, McBlane, I have to admit that we found them delicious. Now, the thing is, McBlane, the thing is is that we ... er ... my wife and I ... would like it if ... if we could have the carbonnades again some time.'

McBlane grunted.

'Oh. Good. That's settled then.'

McBlane took a long swig of beer.

'Oh yes. There is one other thing,' said Reggie. 'Not long till Christmas now.'

'Ee flecking wae teemee hasn't oot frae grippet ma drae wee blagnolds,' said McBlane.

'Well of course it is a bit over-commercialised,' said Reggie. 'But I expect you're looking forward to seeing your family.'

140

'Och nee I nivver flecking wanna same baskards ee flecking baskards ee immeee lafe wathee dunter mice stirring baskard done baskard firm baskard ling wasna flecking low dove haggan brasknards.'

'Well, no family's perfect, of course, McBlane. You'll go and stay with friends in Scotland, will you?'

'Willy fleck in ell? Wazz cottle andun firm ee? Eh? Fock loo her. Fock loo her. Banly sniffle baskards. Albie Stainer.'

'You'll spend Christmas with Albie Stainer! Absolutely splendid. Where does he live?'

'Albie Stainer. Albie Stainer.'

'You'll be staying here! Ah! Oh, what a relief. Oh, good, you'll be able to . . . er . . . cook the Christmas dinner then. That is splendid news.'

Reggie hastened from the kitchen, and McBlane tossed off the remains of his Newcastle Brown. A smile hovered around his sensitive, powerful lips. He had a cold sore coming.

The wedding between James Gordonstoun Anderson and Lettice Isobel Horncastle was scheduled for two thirty on Wednesday, December the twenty-first. The venue was St Peter's Church in Bagwell Heath, the very church at which, more than twenty months ago, Jimmy had failed to arrive. Once again the weather was wintry. Overnight there had been four inches of snow, and more snow fell intermittently throughout the morning. The same organist gave the same spirited rendition of the same old favourites. The same heating system accompanied him with a slightly increased cacophony of squeaks and gurgles.

It was an unevenly balanced congregation that had gathered in the spacious fifteenth-century church, with its famous Gothic font cover.

On the left of the aisle there sat just one person. Lettice's mother was a formidable lady in her late sixties, with a large square face. She wore her moustache defiantly, as if relishing the displeasure that the world felt in looking at it.

On the right were the friends and relatives of the groom. There were Tom and Linda, with Adam and Jocasta, C.J., Doc Morrissey, the Websters, and the Harris-Joneses. There were the same old army colleagues, their noses even redder from liquid indulgence, and the same assorted cousins with their even more assorted wives, and thirty-six past and present guests of Perrins had made the wintry journey to Bagwell Heath to pay homage to the leader of their expeditionary forces.

Altogether there were seventy-one people on the right-hand side of the church, yet it was Lettice's mother who looked proud, and the seventy-one who looked sheepish.

Lettice's mother's isolation seemed to say, 'We could have filled our pews twice over for a suitable groom.'

The massed ranks of Jimmy's friends and relations seemed to say, 'We felt we had to come, in case he doesn't.'

Outside, the snow fell steadily, carpeting Bagwell Heath in silence.

Elizabeth stood by the handsome lych-gate, sheltering from the snow under a smart, red umbrella.

The bride and her father sat in an upstairs room at the Coach and Horses, from which a fine view of the church could be obtained. They had large brandies in their hands. The be-ribboned car was parked in the pub car-park, whence it would not stir until the groom had put in his appearance.

The vicar turned to his wife, said, 'Oh, well, may as well be hung for a sheep as a lamb', and set off through the snow in his Wellington boots. He carried his shoes in a Waitrose carrier bag.

Reggie's be-ribboned car slowly approached the churchyard, with the groom sitting petrified in the passenger seat beside his best man.

It was twenty-seven minutes past two.

The car skidded on a patch of ice concealed beneath the fresh snow, and struck a lamp-post. Jimmy, who had forgotten to do up his safety belt, was jerked forward and cut his nose against the windscreen.

Blood gushed out.

'Oh my God,' said Reggie.

'Bit of blood, no harm,' said Jimmy, attempting to staunch the flow with his demob handkerchief. All to no avail.

'Lie down,' said Reggie.

'No time,' said Jimmy. 'Think I'm not turning up again.'

'I can't drive on till you're bandaged,' said Reggie,' or you'll be having your reception at the blood transfusion centre.'

He ripped the ribbons off the bonnet, and managed to produce a make-shift bandage.

It was two thirty-four.

The vicar changed his shoes. Lettice and her father sipped their brandies and watched. Elizabeth stood at the lych-gate and waited. The organist returned to the beginning of his meagre repertoire, but he played it more slowly this time.

Uneasiness grew, inside the church and out.

'It's flooded,' said Reggie. 'And there's no juice left in the battery.'

'Done for,' said Jimmy, slumping in his seat.

They set off to walk to the church, trudging frantically through the snow.

A car came towards them. They thumbed it. Reggie pointed at Jimmy, whose face was criss-crossed with yards of ribbon, and tried frantically to mime a wedding. He mimed church bells, standing at the altar, putting on the ring, eating and drinking at the reception. When he got to the honeymoon night, the driver accelerated, lost control of his vehicle, and crashed into a lamp-post on the other side of the road.

'We've got to see if he's all right,' said Reggie.

'Absolutely. First things first,' said Jimmy stoutly, public-spirited even in his greatest crisis.

They approached the motorist.

'Are you all right?' said Reggie.

'Go away, you bloody lunatics,' said the motorist. 'Get back to your bloody asylum.'

'He seems all right,' said Reggie.

They struggled on desperately through the snow. An AA break-down truck approached. They hailed it and it stopped.

'Wedding. Two-thirty. Bagwell Heath. Cock-up on car front,' said Jimmy.

'That your car back there?' said the driver.

'Yes,' said Reggie. 'Never mind the car.'

'Are you AA members?' said the driver.

Jimmy produced his membership card.

'Fair enough,' said the driver.

143

It was two forty-six.

Inside the church, Lettice's mother rose majestically to her feet, turned scornfully towards Jimmy's seventy-one friends and relations, and strode off up the aisle, like a footballer who has been sent off for a foul that he hasn't committed. She strode out of the church just as the AA van pulled up at the lych-gate. She watched Jimmy step gingerly out, the ribbons heavily stained with red.

'You're bleeding,' she said accusingly.

'A mere bagatelle,' he countered bravely.

He marched proudly up the aisle. Lettice's mother slunk in behind him.

The vicar entered, and smiled with grim astonishment at Jimmy.

Reggie took his place beside the wounded groom, and Elizabeth slid unobtrusively into her seat from the side-aisle.

It was two fifty-one.

At last they had a groom, but they still had no bride. Lettice was arguing with her father in the car-park of the Coach and Horses.

'I want to arrive by car,' she said.

'There's no time,' expostulated her parent. 'We'd have to go right round the new experimental one-way system.'

'Whose life is this the greatest day of, yours or mine?' said Lettice. 'I've waited twenty-one months. Jimmy can wait five minutes.'

Lettice's father's mistake was to try and knock a minute off that estimated time. At the furthest point from the church, the car slid across the snow into the hedge.

The desperate organist began his repertoire for the third time.

Jimmy whispered, 'Serves me right. Biter bit. Shove off?' to Reggie.

'Give her five minutes,' whispered Reggie.

Lettice's mother didn't know whether to smirk or have a nervous breakdown.

It was two minutes past three.

Lettice and her father limped exhaustedly through the drifts.

Behind them, two tearful little bridesmaids tried unavailingly to hold the train out of the snow.

The procession hobbled into the church at seven minutes past three.

The organist, in his incredulous relief, made a horrible mess of the first bars of the wedding march.

It was twenty-four minutes past three before Jimmy mouthed the first sentence of the day that even he was unable to shorten.

'I do,' he said.

'I really feel festive now,' said Elizabeth, as they lay in bed on the morning of Friday, December the twenty-third. 'Mark's arriving, C.J.'s leaving, and we're going to have a white Christmas.'

Mark did arrive, C.J. did leave, but they didn't have a white Christmas. All day it thawed, slowly at first, then faster, mistily, steamily, nastily. The snow was already losing its sparkle by the time the postman arrived. One of the cards which he delivered contained the heart-warming message 'Dynamite. Thanks. The computer programmer from Alderley Edge.' The W288 was churning up waves of brown slush by the time C.J. set off for Luxembourg. By the time Mark arrived there were great pools of water lying on the snow.

Mark looked well. Africa hadn't heightened him. He was still five foot seven, but he had filled out and looked even more disconcertingly like a smaller and younger version of Reggie. He kissed Linda affectionately, and was even polite to Tom. That was the trouble. He was too polite. As the evening went gently on its way, it was as if he wasn't really there at all. Reggie tried hard to venture no criticism of his way of life, and to avoid those awkward phrases like 'old prune' which he had always found himself using to his son. They told him about the Perrins set-up. He seemed interested, but not unduly impressed.

Reggie discovered that he desperately wanted him to be impressed.

They told him about 'Grot', and the departure in disguise of Reggie and Elizabeth. He seemed interested, but not unduly surprised.

Reggie discovered that he desperately wanted him to be surprised.

McBlane laid on a good dinner. Reggie felt proud of it.

145

Mark ate well, but made no comment.

Afterwards, the family held a private gathering in Tom and Linda's bedroom. The new double bed had been folded away, and comfortable armchairs had been moved in for the evening. Tom provided the drinks. There was apple gin, raspberry whisky and fig vodka. Mark praised the drinks politely. Linda took the bull by the horns, and said, 'Now then, shorthouse, what was all that theatre business in Africa?'

But Mark was not to be drawn on the subject of the group of freelance theatrical mercenaries, dedicated to the incitement of revolutionary fervour through the plays of J. M. Barrie, freely adapted by Idi 'Post-Imperialist Impression' Okombe.

Nor did he call Linda 'fatso', as in days of yore.

'Let's just say it was a phase I went through,' he said. 'Everyone's got to go through their wanting-to-overthrow-the-established-order phase. Anyway, it's over and done with. I don't really want to talk about it.'

'Supposing we do want to talk about it, old prune?' said Reggie.

Damn! Damn! Damn!

Mark shrugged.

'Well, this is nice. All together again,' said Elizabeth too hastily.

'Another drink, anyone?' said Reggie. 'More fig vodka, Mark, or would you prefer to enjoy yourself?'

Mark held out his glass, and Reggie poured a goodly measure of fig vodka. It was an extremely pale green.

'It doesn't matter if we get a bit olivered tonight,' he said.

'Olivered?' said Mark.

'Oliver Twist. Pissed,' said Reggie. 'You were always coming out with rhyming slang in the old days.'

'Was I?' said Mark. 'I think I must have been going through a solidarity-with-the-working-classes phase. Everybody has to go through their solidarity-with-the-working-classes phase.'

'Unless they're working class,' said Linda.

'I never did,' said Tom, pouring himself some of his raspberry whisky as if it was gold dust. 'I know the working classes are the salt of the earth, but the fact remains, I don't like them. I'm just not a working class person.'

'You still haven't told us what you were doing in Paris,' said Elizabeth.

'No,' said Mark.

'Oh come on, shorthouse, don't be infuriating,' said Linda.

'I met this film director in Africa,' said Mark, 'and he wanted me to make a couple of films in Paris.'

'How exciting,' said Elizabeth. 'When will we see them?'

'Never, I hope,' said Mark. 'They're blue films. I think I'm going through a reaction-against-my-political-period phase.'

When it was time to go to bed, Elizabeth said that she hoped Mark could stay a long time.

'Fraid not,' he said. 'I've got to go to Stockholm on the twenty-seventh. I'm making a film there.'

'Are you still in your blue period?' said Reggie.

'Fraid so,' said Mark. 'It's about a randy financier. It's called "Swedish loss adjustor on the job".'

In the morning, all traces of the snow had gone.

Christmas day was grey, still and silent, as if the weather had gone to spend the holidays with its family.

Elizabeth had to agree that McBlane's dinner was a good one. As he himself put it, if she understood him aright, 'There's none of that foreign muck today'. The turkey was moist and tasty, the home-made cranberry sauce was a poem, and even the humble bread sauce was raised to the level of art by the scabrous Caledonian maestro. If there was any criticism, it was perhaps of a certain native meanness with regard to the monetary contents of the Christmas pudding.

The wine flowed smoothly, the smokeless fuel glowed smokelessly, Mark passed cruets and sauce bowls with unaccustomed assiduousness, David Harris-Jones got hiccups, Linda found a pfennig in her pudding, Prue Harris-Jones got hiccups, Joan told Prue that her togetherness was slipping because her hiccups were out of phase with David's, Tom informed them that some people were hiccup people and other people were burp people and he was a burp person, Jocasta didn't cry when she found a shirt button in her pudding, Reggie asked McBlane to join them for the port and stilton, and received an incomprehensible reply, the four guests joined in as best they could, Tony

147

proposed a toast to Absentfriendsville, Arizona, there was speculation about the honeymooning activities of Jimmy and Lettice, some of it ribald and the rest of it obscene, everyone agreed that the jokes in the crackers were the worst ever, the candles flickered, the grey light of afternoon faded, and the very last, somewhat drunken toast was to the future of Perrins.

And what of those absent friends?

Doc Morrissey was sitting beside a gas fire in a much smaller room in Southall. He was surrounded by his friends. He had consumed a large meal of turkey musalla, with chipolata dhansak, korma bread sauce, sprout gosht and Bombay potatoes, followed by Christmas pudding fritters. His Indian friends were hanging on his every word, and he basked in the glory of their respect and adulation as he told them of his magnificent work at Botchley. He realised that they had journeyed to a far land in order to learn the mystical secrets of life. On that grey afternoon, Southall was Shangri-La, the mysterious occident, and Doc Morrissey was the guru who would reveal to them the transcendental secrets of metaphysics.

It was some minutes since he'd spoken, and they began their eager questioning again.

The guru was asleep.

C.J. and Mrs C.J. walked peacefully among the Luxembourgeoisie in the grey, still afternoon.

Clearly the weather hadn't gone to Luxembourg for yuletide.

C.J. held his hands behind his back. Mrs C.J. tried to link arms and failed.

'Don't you love me any more, C.J.?' she said.

'Of course I do, darling,' he said.

They walked slowly over the bridge which spans the ravine in Luxembourg City.

C.J. allowed Mrs C.J. to link arms.

'You're happy in Luxembourg, aren't you?' he said.

'Of course I am,' said Mrs C.J.

'Your friends are nice.'

'Delightful. But I miss you, C.J.'

'You seemed happy enough to come here.'

148

'Maybe I was, but I've grown to miss you.'

They stood, looking out over the ravine.

'Nice ravine, eh?' said C.J. 'I didn't get where I am today without knowing a nice ravine when I see one.'

'Don't change the subject,' said Mrs C.J.

'There isn't any subject,' said C.J. 'So how can I change it? We're walking in Luxembourg City. We come from a large country, and this is a small country, but I don't think we should be patronising on that account. I don't think we should just barge through, willy-nilly, wrapped up in our problems, ignoring nice ravines. Nice ravines don't grow on trees, you know. I mean, if we get back to England, and I say, "Nice ravine, that ravine in Luxembourg" and you say, "Which ravine?" and I say, "You know. That nice ravine" and you say, "I don't remember any ravine", I'm going to look pretty silly. Women don't always understand the rightness of time and place, my dear, and the time and place to talk about a nice ravine is when you're looking at it. That's what marriage is all about. Sharing things. And that includes ravines.'

C.J. gazed at the ravine. The light was fading slowly.

'That's the whole point,' said Mrs C.J. 'When *am* I going to get back to England? When *am* I going to share you? You don't want me there, do you? There's somebody else.'

'There isn't anybody else.'

'Why don't you want me there then?'

'Darling, it's Christmas. Hardly the time to be arguing.'

'Perhaps it's the time to be loving, C.J.'

C.J. drew his eyes away from the ravine and smiled earnestly at Mrs C.J.

'I want to come to Botchley and share your work,' she said.

'Botchley's dull. Suburban.'

'No ravines?'

'You're laughing at me.'

'I'm trying to get through to you. I'm lonely.'

C.J. put his arm round his wife, and hugged her. Slowly, they began to retrace their steps.

'We lead a monastic life at Perrins,' said C.J. 'Celibacy is the order of the day.'

Mrs C.J. looked at him in amazement.

'But Reggie,' she said. 'Tom. David. Tony. I thought they all had their wives with them.'

'Their wives are there,' said C.J., 'but they lead segregated lives. We sleep in dormitories. It's a strict community. They can stand it. I just couldn't stand being near you and yet not fully with you. Frustration is the thief of time, and that's all there is to it.'

Mrs C.J. kissed him.

'Oh, C.J.,' she said.

'Oh, Mrs C.J.,' he said.

Jimmy and Lettice had wakened to the growl of thunder and the drumming of heavy rain. Then had come gusty warm winds from the south, driving away the clouds. The wind had fallen away, and there had been hot sun. Now a cool breeze was setting in from the north.

Clearly, all the weather had gone to Malta for its holidays.

Jimmy and Lettice looked out over the ruffled, dark blue surface of the Mediterranean, from the terrace of their hotel restaurant.

'Happy?' said Jimmy.

'Happy.'

'Stout girl. Bus ride tomorrow?'

'We had a bus ride yesterday.'

'Aren't rationed. Different bus, different ride.'

'I don't know if I'll feel like a bus ride tomorrow.'

'Fair enough. Nice bus ride yesterday?'

'Yes.'

'Interesting ticket system they have.'

'It seemed much like ticket systems everywhere.'

'To the uninitiated. Top hole hotel?'

'Lovely.'

'A.1. grub?'

'Yes.'

'Everything up to expectation in marital rights department?'

'Lovely. Don't worry, Jimmy!'

'Bus ride Tuesday?'

'Must we make plans, Jimmy?'

'No. Course not. Honeymoon. Liberty Hall. You're right. Good scout. Bus ride not out of the question, then?'

'This interest in buses has come as a bit of a surprise, Jimmy.'

'Always been a bit of a bus wallah on the Q.T. If not Tuesday, maybe Wednesday.'

'Maybe.'

'You don't like bus rides, do you?'

'I just don't want to make plans.'

'Wonder if there'll be normal schedules tomorrow. Don't know if Maltese have Boxing Day as we know it. Ask at desk.'

'Does it matter?'

'Interesting. Little titbits, foreign ways. Nervous, Lettice. Know why?'

'No.'

'Happy. Admit it, cold feet. Probably guessed it, not turning up at church. One failed marriage. Don't want another. So happy now. Insecure. Don't want to lose it.'

'Oh, Jimmy.'

'See that kraut, table in corner, big conk. At bus station Friday morning.'

'I didn't know you went to the bus station on Friday morning.'

'Just popped in. Asked the cove there if they have any equivalent of a Red Rover. Didn't understand what I was on about.'

Mark left on Boxing Day as he had things to do before he went to Stockholm.

In bed that night, Reggie and Elizabeth were in pensive vein.

'I wonder how Jimmy and Lettice have got on,' said Elizabeth.

'Very well,' said Reggie. 'Jimmy's so much more relaxed since we started the community.'

'I wonder how C.J. and Mrs C.J. have got on.'

'Very well. C.J.'s so much kinder since we started the community.'

Elizabeth pressed the soles of her feet against the top of Reggie's feet.

'Poor Mark,' she said.

'Yes.'

151

'We seem to have lost him in a way.'

'I know.'

'He's gone away from us.'

'Maybe it's we who've gone away from him. The community's our whole life now, my darling. Christmas has just been an interlude, that's all. Our life has been suspended.'

'Is that bad?'

'No. But it's just as well the community's such a success.'

'Is it really such a success, Reggie?'

'Of course it is, darling. A tremendous success. What's happened so far is just a start. The best days lie ahead.'

VI

The Best Days

JANUARY BEGAN QUIETLY. Winter flirted with Botchley. There was snow that didn't settle, rain that didn't last, sun that didn't warm. The number of guests at Perrins increased steadily. There was an article about the community in a national newspaper. It was inevitable, since journalists read each other's papers, that the article would be followed by others. It was inevitable, since the bulk of television's magazine programmes are made up of ideas taken from the newspapers, that Reggie should appear on television. It was inevitable, given the nature of Reggie Perrin's life, that the interviewer should be Colin Pillock.

Reggie was nervous.

When he had been interviewed by Colin Pillock about Grot, he had not been nervous, because he had been bent on self-destruction.

The researchers made wary, desultory conversation with him over drinks and sandwiches in the spartan, green hospitality room. The researchers wolfed all the sandwiches. Colin Pillock entered, surveyed the large plates covered only in wrecked cress, and told the researchers, who already knew, 'You've wolfed all the sandwiches, you bastards.'

'They always wolf all the sandwiches, the bastards,' he told Reggie.

Reggie sympathised.

Colin Pillock gave Reggie a run-down of the questions he would ask.

When they got on the air, he asked totally different questions.

They went down to the ground floor in the goods lift and walked across the studio floor, past the huge hanging sign that said, simply, 'Pillock Talk'.

They were made up so that they'd look unmade-up under the lights.

153

Reggie felt increasingly nervous.

They sat in elegant armchairs, with a small circular table between them.

It was all very cool.

Reggie was not cool. If he made a fool of himself now, all would be destroyed.

When he'd been bent on self-destruction, he had failed dismally.

Would he fail equally dismally now, when he was bent on success?

They tested him for level.

The opening music began. His heart thumped. The four cameras stared at him impassively. The cameramen were calm and moderately bored.

'Good evening,' said Colin Pillock. 'My first guest this evening is a man whom I've had on the programme before, when he was head of the amazing "Grot" chain, Reginald Perrin.'

Reggie tried to smile, but his mouth felt as if it was set in concrete.

'Good evening,' he said.

'I didn't do too well with Reginald Perrin on that occasion,' said Colin Pillock. 'But I must be either a brave man or a fool.'

'Or both,' said Reggie.

No, no, no.

'I still can't get over your name,' said Reggie. 'Pillock.'

No, no, no.

No, no, no, no, no.

Take a grip on yourself.

Confine yourself to minimal answers till you're settled in.

'You're now running a community called Perrins, Mr Perrin?'

'Yes.'

'People come to your community for as little or as long as they like, and at the end they pay as little or as much as they like.'

'Yes.'

'Perrins has been described as part community, part therapy centre, part mental health farm. Would you say that was a fair description?'

'Yes.'

'It's been described as a community for the middle-class and the middle-aged, set in what used to be Middlesex.'

'Yes.'

Colin Pillock twitched.

Many people had had cause to regret the onset of Colin Pillock's twitch. Would Reggie be one of them?

'Do you intend to confine yourself entirely to this mono-syllabic agreement?' said Colin Pillock.

'No.'

'Oh, good, because our viewers might feel it was rather a waste of time for you to come here and say nothing but "yes".'

'Yes.'

No! No, no, no, no, no!

'Mr Perrin, are you genuinely doing all this for the good of humanity, or is it basically a money-making venture, or is it a giant con, or is it simply a joke? What's your honest answer?'

'Yes.'

'Mr Perrin!'

'I'm serious. It's all of them. That's the beauty of it.'

That stopped him in his tracks. That made him think.

'Well?' said Colin Pillock.

Reggie realised that he had been asked a question, and he had no idea what it was.

'Sorry,' he said. 'I was just thinking very carefully about my answer.'

'Which is?' said Colin Pillock, smiling encouragingly.

'My answer is . . . would you mind repeating the question?'

Panic flitted across Colin Pillock's eyes. He smiled desperately.

'What kind of people come to your community?'

'Well, perhaps it would be helpful if I told you who we have at this moment?'

'Fine.'

'We've got a stockbroker, a pub landlord, a time and motion man, the owner of a small firm that makes supermarket trolleys, a systems analyst, a businessman who answers to the name of Edwards, and a housewife who wishes that she didn't answer to the name of Ethel Merman.'

'I see. And . . .'

155

'An overworked doctor, a disillusioned imports manager, an even more disillusioned exports manager, an extremely shy vet, a sacked football manager, an overstressed car salesman and a pre-stressed concrete salesman.'

'Splendid. And . . .'

'A housewife who longs to be a career woman, a career woman who longs to be a housewife, a schoolteacher who's desperate because he can't get a job and another schoolteacher who's even more desperate because he has got a job.'

Colin Pillock smiled uneasily.

'So work is a major problem that causes people to come to you, would you say?' he asked.

'They have a wide variety of problems. Some have sexual problems, some have social problems, some have professional problems, some have identity problems. Some have sexual, social, professional and identity problems. There are women who are exhausted by the strain of trying to be equal with men, and men who are exhausted by the strain of trying to remain more than equal with women. There are people who live above their garages and their incomes, in little boxes they can't afford on prestige estates they don't understand, where families are two-car, two-tone and two-faced, money has replaced sex as a driving force, death has replaced sex as a taboo, sex has replaced bridge as a social event for mixed foursomes, and large deep-freezes are empty save for twelve packets of sausages. They come to Perrins in the hope that here at last they'll find a place where they won't be ridiculed as petty snobs, scorned as easy targets, and derided by sophisticated playwrights, but treated as human beings who are bewildered by the complexity of social development, castrated by the conformities of the century of mass production, and dwarfed by the speed and immensity of technological progress that has advanced more in fifty years than in millions of years of human existence before it, so that when they take their first steps into an adult society shaped by humans but not for humans, their personalities shrivel up like private parts in an April sea.'

'I . . . er . . . I see,' said Colin Pillock.'

'Not *too* monosyllabic for you, I hope,' said Reggie.

* * *

On Thursday, January the nineteenth, Reggie had a visit from Mr Dent, a planning officer from Botchley Borough Council. The weather was cold. Ominous clouds were moving in from the east. Oslo Avenue was lined with cars, and Mr Dent had to park in Washington Road. On his way towards Number Twenty-one, he passed Tom and a group of footballers dressed in the Botchley Albion strip.

They were about to instigate a new system of playing football. Scoring goals for the opponents hadn't worked. As each team played entirely for the opponents, they became the opponents, who became them. The result was two teams playing against each other in an absolutely conventional way. So now they were going to play as two normal teams, but with goals not permitted. If you scored, the opponents got a penalty. If they scored from it, you got a penalty. Etcetera etcetera.

Mr Dent knew none of this, as he walked resolutely up the front path towards Number Twenty-one. He was a short man with thinning dark hair, a small mouth, a receding chin and large ears. He would have passed unnoticed in a crowd and might even have passed unnoticed on his own.

Reggie led him into the sun-room and established him in an uninteresting chair.

'I'll come straight to the point,' said Mr Dent.

'Good,' said Reggie. 'I welcome that.'

'We've had complaints about the parking of cars in Oslo Avenue, Mr Perrin,' he said.

'They never block entrances,' said Reggie, 'and there's no noise or unseemly behaviour.'

'The cars themselves aren't my pigeon,' said Mr Dent. 'They come under the Highways Department. My worry is that you're conducting a business in private premises. We'd have been on to you long ago, but there's been a work to rule and an epidemic. Then, when we saw you on the other BBC . . .'

'The other BBC?'

'We call Botchley Borough Council the BBC.'

'Ah!'

'Because of its initials being BBC.'

'Quite.'

'We call the people over in the new extension in Crown Rise

BBC 2. Not a hilarious crack, but it causes mild amusement in the town hall canteen.'

'I can believe it.'

'Anyway, we felt that matters were getting out of hand. Now . . .'

'I'm not conducting a business,' said Reggie.

'You place adverts in the newspapers. Clients arrive. They receive treatment, They pay. Is that or is it not a commercial venture?'

'No,' said Reggie.

Mr Dent sighed.

'I'm a busy man, Mr Perrin,' he said. 'I don't particularly enjoy my job. My life is spent examining trivia, and I have a boss who invariably leaves me to do the dirty jobs.'

'I see,' said Reggie. 'I'm one of the dirty jobs, am I?'

The little council official looked round the immaculate sun-room, at the large gleaming picture windows, the tidy desk, the new filing cabinets.

'Not dirty,' he said. 'Awkward. Unusual. My boss shrinks from the unknown.'

'I invite people to come here, as my guests,' said Reggie. 'If at the end they want to give me something, fine. It would be heartless to refuse it.'

'But you advertise?'

'Suppose I advertised, "Party every night. All welcome. Presents not refused". Would that be a commercial undertaking?'

'We're splitting hairs now.'

'In my houses . . .'

'Houses?'

'I own Numbers Seventeen to Twenty-five.'

'I thought Numbers Nineteen and Twenty-three were purchased by non-white gentlemen?'

'Good friends of mine,' said Reggie. 'If they believe in me so much that they buy houses for me, who am I to say them nay?'

He spread his hands in a gesture of helplessness.

'I'm a remarkable man,' he said.

Mr Dent's eyes met his, and he had the impression that the Planning Officer would have smiled, if he had dared.

'What exactly are you aiming to provide in these houses of yours, Mr Perrin?' he asked.

'The universal panacea for all mankind,' said Reggie. 'Would you like some coffee?'

'No, thank you,' said Mr Dent. 'This business of the change of use becomes rather more important if we're dealing with five adjoining houses. I shudder to think what Mr Winstanley will say.'

'Mr Winstanley?'

'My boss.'

'You think he'd ruin an attempt to save mankind from suicide simply because of an infringement of council planning regulations regarding five detached houses in Oslo Avenue, Botchley?'

'Definitely,' said Mr Dent.

'A petty streak in his character, is there?'

'Most definitely.'

'But you're a man of a different kidney?'

'I'd like to think so, Mr Perrin.'

'So would I, Mr Dent. So would I. Are you sure you won't have some coffee?'

'Well, perhaps a small cup.'

Reggie left the sun-room, soon to return with a tray, decorated with a picture of Ullswater. On the tray were two cups of coffee and a plate of ginger nuts. Mr Dent was looking out over the garden.

'Looks like snow,' he said, regaining his seat.

Reggie handed him the coffee.

'Don't get me wrong,' said Mr Dent 'I'm in favour of your universal panacea for all mankind. It might do a bit of good.'

'Thank you.'

'M'm. Delicious ginger nut.'

'Thank you.'

'But my job is to make sure that there are no unauthorised changes of use,' said Mr Dent, through a mouthful of crumbs.

'I've made no structural changes,' said Reggie. 'Another ginger nut?'

'May I? They're tasty. Structural changes aren't the be all and end all, Mr Perrin.'

159

'I realise that,' said Reggie.

'M'm. Nice ginger nut,' said Mr Dent. 'Quite as nice as the first.'

'Thank you,' said Reggie.

'You're welcome,' said Mr Dent.

'You're a shrewd judge of a biscuit,' said Reggie.

'Are you trying to soft soap me?' said Mr Dent.

'It wouldn't work,' said Reggie. You're a man of too much moral fibre.'

'Thank you,' said Mr Dent. 'So you've made no structural changes?'

'None,' said Reggie. 'It's true that I'm using kitchens and garden sheds as bedrooms, but they could return to their former use at the drop of a hat. Where does it end? If the Jack Russell does big jobs in the dining room, is it on that account a downstairs toilet?'

Mr Dent stood up, and dumped his empty cup in the middle of Ullswater. He put his hands on Reggie's desk and leant forward till his face was close to Reggie's.

'I could get you,' he said, with greater mildness than the gesture had led Reggie to expect. 'I could get you on inadequate air vents. I can get anybody on inadequate air vents. Though I say it myself, as shouldn't, I'm mustard on inadequate air vents.'

Mr Dent sat down, and gave a shuddering sigh.

'What a pathetic boast,' he said. 'I'm mustard on inadequate air vents. What an abysmal claim. What a dismal piece of human flotsam I am.'

'Nonsense,' said Reggie stoutly, walking over to put his arm on Mr Dent's chair. 'I like you. Look, don't go straight on to your next dreary task. Watch us at work. Sit in on one of Doc Morrissey's group sessions.'

Doc Morrissey's group session was held in the spacious living room of Number Twenty-five. Thick yellow cloud, pregnant with snow, hung over the pocked lawns and heavy vegetable beds. A Calor Gas fire stood in front of the empty fireplace. It was turned to maximum and provided a steady heat. In front of it slumbered Snodgrass.

Reggie introduced Mr Dent to Doc Morrissey, and Doc Morrissey introduced him to the six guests who were present. They were the systems analyst, the stockbroker, the businessman who answered to the name of Edwards, the owner of the small firm that made supermarket trolleys, the extremely shy vet, and Ethel Merman.

'Who's going to set the ball rolling by talking about their problems?' said Doc Morrissey, who was seated in an old wooden chair with curved arms, at the centre of the group.

He beamed at them encouragingly.

Nobody spoke.

'Splendid,' said Doc Morrissey. 'Has anyone got anything to add?'

Again, nobody spoke.

'Does anybody feel they're over-aggressive?' said Doc Morrissey. 'Does anybody feel a need to dominate any group they're in?'

Nobody spoke.

'Obviously not,' said Doc Morrissey.

'I don't feel that I'm a dominating person at all,' said the systems analyst, flicking ash gently off the end of his cigarette into the shell-shaped ashtray on the table beside his chair. 'I'm cool, controlled, systematic, analytical, as befits a systems analyst.'

He looked round the group and gave a cool, controlled, systematic smile.

Reggie nodded encouragingly at Mr Dent, as if to say, 'We've started at last.'

'But underneath I'm a bubbling cauldron,' continued the systems analyst. 'I get aggressive in two areas really. Driving and ... er ...'

'Ah!' said the stockbroker. 'That's probably your sex drive. The car represents a woman.'

'Auto-suggestion!!' said Doc Morrissey.

Again there flitted across his face a look of professional satisfaction, almost immediately followed by the dawning of self-doubt.

'Maybe,' said the systems analyst. 'Because the second area is ... er ...'

161

The yellow gloom outside grew thicker. There was the distant roar of a pneumatic drill in Lisbon Crescent.

'The second area?' prompted Doc Morrissey gently.

The systems analyst looked shiftily at Ethel Merman.

'Lately I've developed an almost irresistible desire to . . . to . . .'

'To?'

'To punch pregnant women in the stomach.'

Ethel Merman drew in her breath sharply.

'You must have given this some thought,' said Doc Morrissey. 'Have you any idea why you want to . . . er . . .?'

He swung his arms in imitation of a vaguely aggressive gesture, but couldn't bring himself to say the words.

'I think I must hate women,' said the systems analyst. 'I see that complacent swelling, that maternal arrogance, that sheen of self-absorbed pregnancy, and I want to go . . . whoomf! whoomf!'

He punched an imaginary mother-to-be. His face was transformed by hatred.

Ethel Merman flinched.

'Oh, I've never done it,' said the systems analyst. 'I very much doubt if I ever will. I've too much to lose. Friends, acquaintances, work, insurance policies, credit rating. I'll never do it, but . . . wanting to's just as bad.'

The extremely shy vet looked at him sadly. Ethel Merman edged to the far side of her chair.

Reggie nodded towards Mr Dent, as if to say, 'You don't get that sort of stuff in the town hall canteen, do you?'

'You find that shocking, naturally?' said the systems analyst to Ethel Merman.

'I wouldn't be a woman if I didn't, would I?' she said.

She glanced round the wide circle of chairs nervously. The extremely shy vet smiled extremely shyly at her.

'I'm Ethel Merman,' she said, defiantly.

'Not the legendary Ethel Merman?' said the stockbroker.

'No, the unlegendary Ethel Merman,' she replied.

Reggie produced another of his meaningful smiles for Mr Dent. 'Life is such a rich tapestry,' this one seemed to say.

Ethel Merman fixed him with a baleful stare.

'It's no laughing matter,' she said. 'It's bugged my life. It's

162

brought home to me just how dreary Erith is. It's the same with my friend.'

She paused. She was still looking at Reggie, and he felt drawn into a reply.

'Your friend?'

'Mrs Clark. I said to her the other day, "Pet," I said, "Who'd have thought it? The two of us in the one street, with the names of famous international artistes, and nobody has ever heard of either of us. It's not fair." I said the same thing to her at the corner shop. "It's not fair, Shirley," I said.'

Reggie felt as if he was taking part in a double act of which only his partner knew the script.

'Shirley Bassey?' he heard himself saying.

'No. Shirley McNab. Shirley Bassey's the singer,' said Ethel Merman.

Reggie nodded resignedly. He *had* been taking part in a double act of which only his partner knew the script.

'Still,' said Ethel Merman. 'We all have our cross to bear.'

'I certainly do,' said the owner of the small firm that made supermarket trolleys. 'I'm a homosexual.'

The little gathering was stunned, less by the revelation itself than by the fact that it was this particular man who was making it. He spoke with an accent inappropriate for such admissions. Under the western edge of the Pennines the voices are flatter than anywhere else in Britain. In the Eastern Potteries there are still traces of the Midland drawl, mingling with the purity that finds its peak of flatness in the cotton towns of East Lancashire. In his case this complex Staffordshire accent had been diluted but not destroyed by his transition into the managerial classes. It had geography and social history in it, failure and success. It seemed strange that it should be used, bluntly, flatly, to say, 'I'm a raving pouf.'

'It's no disgrace these days,' said the businessman who answered to the name of Edwards.

It began, gently at first, to snow.

'Not in certain circles, I'll grant you. It's practically a badge of office in some quarters, I've heard tell. But it's not expected in a self-made secondary school lad who started out in a bicycle shop in Leek, saw the way the wind was blowing, got out before

163

the virtual demise of that mode of transport, shrewdly antici-
pated the growth of the supermarket and ended up with his own
firm making trolleys and wire baskets.'

'It's nothing to be ashamed of,' said the systems analyst.
'Not nearly as bad as wanting to punch pregnant women.'

'I agree. Why should I be ashamed, just because I have an
unusual distribution of my comatose? But it's bad for trade
if you're widely known as a jessie. It's tantamount to extinction.
"You don't get your trolleys from that bloody Jessie, do you?",
as if the very trolleys themselves were contaminated. And so I
lead a double life. By day, the solid local businessman. By
night, a shadowy figure in the gay clubs of the Five Towns.
And it's bad for your morale and self-respect, is leading a
double life.'

The snow began to fall in earnest, settling on lawns, flower
beds, paths and roofs alike, turning the drab garden into a
wonderland. They all watched in silence for a while, hypnotised
by the big, gentle, creamy flakes. Reggie was aware of the
aggression inside himself. He wanted the snow to go on and on,
plunging the mundane world into chaos, cutting off towns and
villages, blocking main roads, teasing the Southern Region of
British Rail to despair.

'I lead a double life as well,' said the stockbroker. 'I'm an
ant on the floor of the stock exchange and a king in armour.'

'I don't understand,' said Doc Morrissey.

'I go to a place in Marylebone once a fortnight. There's all
kinds of equipment there, for sexual pleasure. I wear armour,
and a crown, and I'm suspended in irons.'

There was a pause.

'How long can you keep it up?' said Doc Morrissey.

'All the time I'm hanging there.'

'No, I meant, how long do you hang there?'

'Oh. Two hours. It's ten pounds an hour. Rather steep, but
beggars can't be choosers.'

'Splendid,' said Reggie. 'Excellent. Oh, I don't mean it's
excellent that you ... er ... have to be ... er ... in order to ...
er ... what I mean is, it's splendid that, as you do have to be
... er ... in order to ... er ... you've had the courage to tell us
about your ... er ...'

164

'Kink.'

'Kink. No, I wouldn't say kink. Preference.'

It was eerily yellow now as the fierce snow storm swirled around Botchley. The blue-white flame of the gas fire glowed brightly, and Snodgrass stirred to the rhythm of a distant dream.

'I'm trying to give it up, as a matter of principle,' said the stockbroker.

'Well done,' said Doc Morrissey.

'The mistake you're making,' said the stockbroker, 'is in thinking that I'm giving it up for moral reasons. I have no feelings of guilt about it. It is totally absurd, and rather inconvenient, that I should find sexual gratification in this way, but I don't see it as wrong. Nobody else is involved. I don't mess about with small children.'

'Or men,' said the owner of the small firm that made supermarket trolleys. 'It's all right for you, the city smoothie, with your sophisticated bloody perversion. I'm the yokel, the simple straightforward jessie. Talk about the unjust society. Not even equality of perversions.'

'I honestly am sorry that you should take it so personally,' said the stockbroker. 'I'm not a happy figure that you should envy. I'm miserable. The mistake you make is in thinking that I'm miserable because of the two hours in Marylebone. I'm happy there. I make jokes. "You have heavy overheads," I comment as the mechanism is lowered to receive me. "This is the stockbroker belt" I say as I strap myself in. I'm miserable because the other three hundred-odd hours in every fortnight are so empty and sterile. I'm a hollow man, envying you your bicycle shop in Leek and your wire basket factory.'

There was almost an inch of level snow in the garden already. The pneumatic drill had stopped. The workmen had knocked off.

'Why do you intend to give it up on principle, then?' said Reggie.

'They're going to charge VAT,' said the stockbroker. 'And I'm convinced that a business like that wouldn't be VAT registered.'

He smiled. There was no warmth or coldness in his smile.

He smiled because he had learnt from experience that a smile was the appropriate facial arrangement for such an occasion.

'I may like being strapped up,' he said, 'but I don't intend to be taken for a ride.'

Doc Morrissey looked towards the extremely shy vet, who shook his head and sank deeper into the threadbare old recliner in which he was sitting.

'Oh well. I suppose I'd better have a go,' said the businessman who answered to the name of Edwards.

He had dark hair and a thin sallow face, and he was wearing fawn trousers and a blue blazer with gold buttons.

'As you, know, I answer to the name of Edwards,' he said.

'Yes,' agreed Reggie.

'What you don't know is that I also answer to the name of Jennings. And Levingham. And Brakespeare. Not to mention Phipps-Partington.'

Everyone looked at him in astonishment.

'I'm a con man,' he explained. 'Sometimes it's convenient to cover one's tracks, you see. Each of us has a different personality. Phipps-Partington is a gentleman down on his luck. Levingham's an out-and-out bastard who separates old ladies from their savings. Brakespeare's a likeable rogue who sets up rather wild, florid schemes, like collecting for a fund to build a replica of the Menai Bridge in Wisconsin, and have a corner of the U.S.A. that is for ever Welsh. You'd be surprised how many hard-bitten rugby players give to that with tears in their eyes on a Saturday night.'

'What made you decide to come here?' said Reggie.

The con man looked round the dark, warm living room, at the respectably dressed people in their assorted armchairs.

'I want to find out who I am,' he said. 'But there are thirteen people in this room, and five of them are me.'

'Thank you for telling us, all of you,' said Doc Morrissey.

He looked at the shy vet hopefully. The vet shook his head.

'I can only talk to animals,' he mumbled.

To Reggie's surprise, Mr Dent began to speak.

'I know perfectly well who I am,' he said. 'I'm a friendly genial, delightful man, not physically brave, but lit up from within by a generosity of spirit, an eagerness to love the human race. It's just that it never seems to come out that way. I do a rather dull, tiring, nit-picking sort of job, I don't have enough money to live with any style, I have a lot of administrative problems, all getting steadily worse with the financial cut-backs, and somehow, what with one thing and another, well, the real me doesn't stand a chance. Maybe here it will. Oh yes, I'll stay, Mr Perrin. Sod the council.'

He stood up and grinned down at the little gathering in the darkened room.

'Sod the air vents,' he said.

The meeting dispersed. The snow had almost stopped. The sky was lightening.

Reggie walked back along the white pavement to Number Twenty-one, for lunch. At his side was Mr Dent.

'Thank you,' said Reggie.

'Thank *you*,' said Mr Dent.

They stood in the hall, taking off their coats and stamping the snow off their shoes, bringing life back to numbed feet.

'I look at life, going on around me,' said Reggie. 'Ordinary, mundane. I look at the crowds in the streets or on the floor of the stock exchange, or streaming over London Bridge. The crowds on trains and buses. The crowds at football and cricket matches. Ordinary people, mundane. Then I read the papers. Court reports, sex offences, spying cases, fantasies, illusions, deceits, mistakes. Chaos. Rich, incredible chaos. Human absurdity. And I just can't reconcile the two. The ordinary crowds. The amazing secrets. This morning, in that room, they were reconciled.'

His face was alight with triumph. He banged his right fist into his left palm.

Tom, passing through the hall on his way to lunch, stood stockstill and stared at him.

'Eureka,' he said.

The whiteness of sun on snow flooded in through the frosted glass window in the front door, illuminating the stained glass of its central pane. As they went in to lunch, the sun shone brilliantly on the virgin snow. Within three hours, all traces of snow had gone. Botchley was grey and dark once more.

*   *   *

167

The explanation of Tom's excited cry of 'Eureka' didn't come until lunchtime the following day. Tom sat at Reggie's left hand, Tony Webster on Reggie's right. The guests all congregated towards the middle of the table, as if for protection.

'You remember when I said "Eureka" yesterday,' said Tom.

'I do indeed,' said Reggie.

'I had a brainwave, but decided to sleep on it. It's a new idea to take the aggression out of sport.'

He took a large mouthful of succulent roast pork and chewed it thirty-two times. At last he'd finished.

'Boxing,' he said.

'Once again, events have moved too fast for you,' said Reggie. 'The thing's been invented, I fear.'

'Non-aggressive boxing,' said Tom, taking a mouthful of McBlane's exquisite red cabbage.

'Boxing's the most aggressive sport there is,' said Tony Webster.

Tom chewed his red cabbage impassively. At last he had finished.

'It was your gesture that suggested it, Reggie,' he said. 'When you hit your palm with your fist.'

'Suggested what?' groaned Reggie.

'Each person hits himself instead of his opponent,' said Tom.

Reggie and Tony stared at him.

'That's a very interesting idea, Tom,' said Reggie.

'Knock-out,' said Tony.

'That's exactly what it won't be,' said Reggie. 'Well done, Tom.'

The following Wednesday afternoon, Reggie had another visitor from Botchley Borough Council. He was Mr Winstanley, Mr Dent's boss.

The weather was bright and breezy. Reggie was relaxed after his lamb cutlets with rosemary. Mr Winstanley was resentful after his cottage pie and chips. Reggie escorted him into the sun-room.

Mr Winstanley was a shambling, untidy, shiny man, with a paunch like a vast tumour. He could have looked like a gentleman who had fallen on hard times, if he hadn't let himself go.

'Did our Mr Dent come to see you last week?' he asked in a hoarsely resonant voice.

'He did indeed,' said Reggie. 'He sat in that very chair, and spoke kindly of my ginger nuts. Would you like some coffee and biscuits?'

Mr Winstanley shook his head and stifled a burp.

'You're getting too much starch and grease,' Reggie informed him.

'Mr Dent has disappeared,' said Mr Winstanley.

'That's odd,' said Reggie. 'I saw him at lunch.'

'At lunch? Where?'

'Here, of course.'

'Here?'

'Mr Dent has joined our community. Didn't he tell you?'

Mr Winstanley's eyes bulged.

'He most certainly did not,' he said. 'He has a secretive streak.'

'I didn't realise that,' said Reggie.

'He plays it very close to the chest.'

'It probably comes of having to keep things private at public enquiries,' said Reggie.

'Possibly,' said Mr Winstanley. 'But if you ask me he's a bit of a loner. Take my advice, Mr Perrin. Beware of loners.'

'Thank you, Mr Winstanley. I'll remember that.'

'Mr Dent is a bit too fond of stealing the plums from under my nose. Anything with a touch of novelty. A hint of the unusual. Off he trots. Doesn't put it in the diary. A good man, mind, if he wasn't so secretive.'

Snodgrass appeared at the window of the sun-room, miaowing to be let in.

'Cats exacerbate my asthmatic condition, I'm afraid,' said Mr Winstanley. 'Yes, Mr Dent telephoned us to say that he had the 'flu, which didn't surprise me, as he's not as robust as some of us. No resistance at all. Anyway, I didn't think twice about it.'

'You wouldn't. It's so boring.'

'Well, exactly. Then yesterday it came to light that he'd phoned Mrs Dent to say that he'd been sent off to a town planning conference in Harrogate. Of all the flimsy excuses!

169

We've tried to trace him through his diary, which was inadequately entered up.'

'The secretive streak.'

'Precisely. Eventually our Mr Pennell remembered that he'd said something about checking up on you.'

'Which you would have loved to do yourself as I've made totally unauthorised changes of use and am running a business from five adjoining residential houses with overloaded drains and inadequate air vents, and which I purchased in a most irregular way involving the impersonation of non-whites.'

Mr Winstanley's air was one of mystification, rather than gratification.

'It rather spoils the fun, doesn't it, when I admit it all like this?' said Reggie. 'It offends the hunter and the sportsman in you. Because unless I'm very much mistaken, Mr Winstanley, you are a sportsman.'

'You wouldn't be trying to flatter me, would you, Mr Perrin?' said Mr Winstanley.

'Of course not. You're far too shrewd,' said Reggie.

'Thank you,' said Mr Winstanley. 'We can go into the matter of the houses later. What are we going to do about Mr Dent, that's the pressing question.'

Snodgrass miaowed pitifully at the window.

'It's our sports afternoon. He'll be taking part in a boxing match. He's immensely game,' said Reggie.

Mr Winstanley's eyes bulged again.

'Mr Dent's taking part in a boxing match?'

'Yes.'

'Mr Dent, of Botchley Borough Council?'

'Yes.'

'Little shorthouse with big ears?'

'Yes.'

Suddenly, Mr Winstanley smiled. His face was miraculously transformed.

'This I must see,' he said.

A small ring, hurriedly ordered from the Botchley Sports Centre, had been erected in the centre of the living room of Number Twenty-five. There was barely room for the single row of hard chairs which had been placed round the walls for the spectators. Reggie entrusted Mr Winstanley to Doc Morrissey's care. They took their seats. There were some twenty spectators, staff and guests.

'This is a very exciting experiment,' Doc Morrissey told Mr Winstanley. 'Turning aggression upon oneself in order to come to terms with it.'

'I don't understand,' said Mr Winstanley.

There was a red sash on the ropes behind one of the boxers' chairs, and a blue behind the other. The two seconds entered with their towels and bowls, and took up their stations behind the chairs. The second in the red corner was the disillusioned imports manager. The second in the blue corner was the even more disillusioned export manager.

Mr Dent and the pub landlord stepped into the ring, discarded their dressing gowns and limbered up.

Mr Dent, in the red corner, was five foot four and thin, his matchstick legs gleaming white beneath the shorts that Elizabeth had bought for him at Lionel of Botchley.

The landlord was six foot three and broad-shouldered.

'It's not fair,' said Mr Winstanley, his resentment of his deputy's secretive ways temporarily forgotten. 'He should fight someone his own size.'

'He is,' said Doc Morrissey.

Mr Dent caught sight of Mr Winstanley and waved. Reggie stepped into the ring and called the ill-assorted fighters together. He inspected their gloves.

'And now, ladies and gentlemen,' he boomed. 'We come to the first bout of the afternoon. This is a three-round heavy-weight and fly-weight contest between, in the red corner, Mr George Dent, of Botchley and himself, and in the blue corner, Mr Cedric Wilkins, of Epsom, versus himself. May neither man win.'

Mr Winstanley looked at Doc Morrissey in bewilderment. The grand old man of the couch beamed. The bell rang. Both pugilists leapt from their chairs and the first round began.

The styles of the two men were as contrasting as their physiques.

Mr Dent put up a determined if somewhat over-cautious

defence which his determined if somewhat over-cautious attack was totally unable to penetrate.

Mr Wilkins' defence was somewhat wild and uncoordinated, so that, although his blows were somewhat wild and unco-ordinated, he was able to get in some pretty effective punches, pinning himself against the ropes for long stretches.

At the end of the round both seconds were enthusiastic about their man's chances.

'You're seeing yourself off,' Mr Dent's second told him, fanning the little council official's face with his towel. 'You've got yourself so you just don't know where to turn.'

'You're laying yourself wide open,' Mr Wilkins' second told him encouragingly, as the burly publican spat heartily into the bowl. 'Now go in there and finish yourself off.'

The bell went for the second round.

The landlord soon knocked himself down. He got up after a count of eight, knocked himself down again, struggled up bravely after a count of nine, and knocked himself senseless.

They carried mine unconscious host out of the ring, and he soon revived.

The third and last round was a distinct anti-climax. Mr Dent continued to duck, weave, feint, side-step and hold. Occasionally he managed to hit one hand with the other, but he didn't succeed in getting in one decent blow during the whole three minutes.

The crowd gave him the bird.

As Mr Dent left the ring to renewed booing he waved once more to Mr Winstanley. He seemed unperturbed by his reception.

The second bout began sensationally. The businessman who answered to the name of Edwards rushed into the middle of the ring, hit himself violently in the balls, cried 'Below the belt, you swine', and collapsed in a groaning heap.

'A victory for that congenital bastard Levingham over that congenial loser Phipps-Partington, you see,' he told Reggie, when he had recovered sufficiently to speak.

Later that afternoon, Reggie saw Mr Winstanley again. Once more, the venue was the sun-room at Number Twenty-one.

'That boxing was ridiculous,' said the paunchy official.

'Thank you.'

'Absolutely ludicrous.'

'You're too kind.'

'Everybody reacted as though it was the most normal thing in the world.'

'We ask them to join in. They enjoy it. Children enjoy the ridiculous and what are adults but older children? Unfortunately, adults tend to feel it destroys their dignity to enjoy the ridiculous.'

'I think it's ridiculous to enjoy things as ridiculous as that.'

'Thank you again. As you're so enthusiastic, why not stay and have a look at us? We have wonderful food.'

'So Mr Dent says.'

'I don't really expect you to stay, Mr Winstanley. You have all your work to do. With Mr Dent away you must be snowed under. Irregularities with air vents are rife in Botchley, I hear, and sun-room extensions are the rule rather than the exception. You don't want to have to sit with a lot of strangers over our lovely food when you could be indulging in merry banter with your fellow officials over the meat pies in the town hall canteen.'

'How can I stay?' said Mr Winstanley. 'What could I tell people?'

'Tell your office you've got 'flu, and tell your wife you've got to go to a town planning conference in Harrogate.'

'That's not a bad idea.'

January gave way to February. Snow gave way to rain, and rain gave way again to snow, as the winter continued to tease.

Jimmy and Lettice got the photos of their honeymoon back, and everyone admired them.

'There seems to be a bus in every picture,' Reggie commented.

'Damned hard to get a picture in Malta without a bus in it. Nature of the terrain,' said Jimmy. 'Nice old buses, aren't they?' Lovely shade of green.'

The granite of Lettice's face was touched by sunlight as love and amused exasperation played upon her features.

'Interesting ticket system. Tell you about it some time,' said Jimmy.

173

'I can't wait,' said Reggie.

'Tell you now, then,' said Jimmy.

'No. Anticipation is such sweet pleasure,' said Reggie.

'No equivalent of our Red Rover, as such, though,' said Jimmy.

Lettice spent her time helping Jimmy with his expeditionary activities, but it was understood that she could be used as reinforcements to plug any holes that might develop in the community.

'Stout girl,' was Jimmy's comment. 'Trouble-shooter. Feather in your cap.'

For the moment, however, there was no trouble to shoot.

There were no holes to plug.

Guests continued to pour in. Some had strange tales and quirks to relate.

There was the hotelier who owned a chain of small hotels and restaurants which bore famous names, but with the first letter missing. He owned the Avoy, Orchester and Itz in London, Affles in Singapore, Axim's in Paris, the Lgonquin in New York. The idea was that people would mistake them for their renowned equivalents. What actually happened was that some people said, 'Look. The first letter's dropped off the Dorchester. It must be going downhill,.' while the others said, 'Oh, look, some silly berk's trying to pretend that's the Ritz'. The final straw to his collapsing empire came when he stayed at the Avoy and found that its first letter had dropped off, so that the neon sign outside the grubby frontage read: 'VOY HOTEL'.

There was the research chemist whose sexual proclivity was for women who had glandular fever. Since all the women to whom he was attracted refused to go out with him because they were ill with glandular fever, his problem was one of loneliness and frustration.

Then there was the young homosexual who made supermarket trolleys and wire baskets at a small firm near the Potteries. Reggie excitedly informed him that his boss was also present, but the meeting between them was not a success. As the boss explained to Reggie, 'It wouldn't do for me to have an intimate relationship with a lad on the shop floor. We may both be one

174

of them, but there's a worker boss situation to be taken into account as well. A them and us situation. I'm one of them who's one of us, and he's one of them who's one of them.'

Reggie decided to convert the five garages into double bedrooms, to provide more accommodation.

The work was supervised by Mr Dent, with Mr Winstanley as his assistant. Both men enjoyed the reversal of their roles, but they got even greater pleasure out of the unauthorised change of use which they were helping to perpetrate. When Mr Pennell called round on the trail of his colleagues, he joined in the alterations with relish.

Another man to arrive at this time was Paul Pewsey, the photographer. He sat in the sun-room, confident, pale, superficially effeminate.

'I can only relate to, you know, things,' he said. 'I just can't relate to, you know, people. I'm in a not relating to people situation.'

Suddenly, to his own surprise, Reggie began to speak.

'This is because you see people as things,' he said, smiling hastily to take the sting out of his involuntary words. 'You see people as things which ought to relate to you. I think you've taken up photography not because you want to look at the world through your camera but because you want the world to look at you looking at it. Every photograph you take is really a photograph of yourself taking a photograph. You look like a homosexual but like to be seen in the company of attractive women. That way, you are an object of speculation and mystery. In fact, you are almost asexual, since you are more interested in being admired than in admiring. You want to be both the butterfly and the album. You're from a working class background and have joined the classless society, which as you know forms a very small and rather conspicuous class. I think that that is all I think and that you will be sorry that I've stopped talking about you.'

Paul Pewsey stared at Reggie in astonishment.

So did Reggie.

'Go on,' said Paul Pewsey. 'I love it.'

The arrival of Paul Pewsey was quickly followed by that of Clarissa Spindle, the designer, Loopy Jones-Rigswell, the playboy,

Venetia Devenport, the model, and Byron 'Two break-downs a year' Broadsword, the *avant-garde* impresario.

In the wake of the newspaper articles and the television appearance, Perrins was becoming fashionable.

Hastily, Reggie widened the scope of his adverts. He inserted an advertisement in the programmes of twenty football league clubs. It concluded with the words, 'Yobbos accepted. Party rates for mindless louts'.

In the *Daily Gleaner* he proudly announced, 'Nig-nogs welcome'.

In the *Daily Gunge* he declared, 'Illiterate pigs warmly invited. Get someone who can write to apply to 21, Oslo Avenue, Botchley'.

Confidence was high at this time.

Even C.J. was throwing himself into the spirit of things. In the evenings, it was true, he preferred to remain in his room, but by day he had become a fount of strength.

One day Reggie accompanied him on his commuting trip to London with a small band of guests.

'I have an idea,' Reggie said, as they assembled in the surprisingly spacious Genuine Hall of Number Twenty-one. 'You will never know, and need never see again, the other people in the compartment. So it's ridiculous to worry what they're thinking of you. Self-consciousness is the truly British disease, not bronchitis, homosexuality or tea breaks. Today we will overcome this self-consciousness. The conversation on the train will be utterly ridiculous. But I won't say any more. This is your show, C.J.'

'Thank you, Reggie,' said C.J. 'Our bodies are enclosed in conventional clothes. We carry conventional briefcases and umbrellas. But our minds are as free as air. They can swoop on ideas like swallows on flies. They can soar to flights of invention like a buzzard over the mountains.'

'Well put, C.J.,' said Reggie.

They set off down Oslo Avenue, six conventional commuters. The wind was razor sharp. They turned left into Bonn Close. They turned right into Ankara Grove. They walked down the snicket to Botchley Station. They waited for the eight fifty-two.

'May I suggest a simple device today, to get it off the ground?' said C.J.

'Please do,' said Reggie.

'We put urgle on the ends of words,' said C.J.

'Good thinking,' said Reggie.

'Thank yurgle,' said C.J.

Reggie couldn't hide his look of astonishment. C.J. smiled in return, acknowledging how extraordinary his transformation had become. Was this transformation genuine, or was C.J. playing a game, or simply earning his salary? Or all of these things? There was no clue on his face.

At three minutes past nine, the long dirty blue snake that was the eight fifty-two slid noisily into Platform One. The train was crowded, and they all had to stand.

The conversation began.

'Eleven minutes lurgle.'

'Typicurgle.'

'Blurgle Southern regurgle.'

'Derailed rolling sturgle at Wimbledurgle, I belurgle.'

'Not a bad mornurgle.'

'Nurgle.'

'Not at all burgle.'

'Bit curgle.'

'Yurgle.'

'Looks like rurgle.'

'Or even snurgle.'

'I didn't gurgle where I am todurgle withurgle recognurgle a mornurgle that lurgle like snurgle.'

'Did it make you feel better?' Reggie asked at Waterloo.

'Definurgle,' came the chorus.

'You can stop now, for God's sake,' said Reggie.

Every morning after that, C.J. led his clients down Oslo Avenue.

Every morning, they turned left into Bonn Close.

Every morning, they turned right into Ankara Grove.

Every morning, they went down the snicket to Botchley Station.

Every morning, they caught the eight fifty-two.

Every morning it was eleven minutes late.

Every morning, C.J. and the clients were dressed exactly like all the other commuters.

Every morning, they held absolutely ridiculous conversations, and proved that in spirit they had freed themselves from convention and conformity.

Every morning they all got seats.

Towards the end of February the coquettish snow storms gave way to the real thing. A fierce depression in the North Sea pulled the cold winds from the steppes. The winds roared far to the North of Britain, and were sucked back by the deepening cyclone. On the biting north-westerlies came the snow.

A faint sun was still shining over Botchley when the first reports of blocked roads came through on McBlane's radio, blaring away in the steaming kitchen as he scraped Belgian salsify with fierce disdain.

Soon the first flakes were falling in Oslo Avenue. By now there were so many road works reports that there was hardly time for any records at all, but in other ways the snow was harmful. By morning there were sixteen inches of level snow, and drifts up to seven feet at the exposed end of Lisbon Crescent. No trains ran from Botchley Station. No further council officials came to enquire into the strange goings-on at Perrins. The guests' cars were hidden beneath the drifts.

Jimmy speedily arranged snow-clearing sorties. Systematic checks were made in the poorer parts of Botchley for old people freezing slowly to death in badly-heated houses. Doctors were informed and proved not to be interested.

A survey printed in newspapers that were never delivered because of the drifts showed that Britain came seventeenth in the world snow-clearing league, behind Yugoslavia and Peru. There was ice in Ramsgate Harbour. Trains were stranded in the Highlands of Scotland and in Devon. All down the stern backbone of England, early lambs froze to death, and vets both shy and extrovert were stranded. Charms of goldfinches starved within sight of the oast houses of Kent.

But in Numbers Seventeen to Twenty-Five, Oslo Avenue, everything was cosy. People poured out their problems to Doc Morrissey. They tried to tell David Harris-Jones about their

178

sex lives. They formed barber shop quartets with Joan, boxed against themselves with Tom, enacted the great love scenes of literature with Tony, weaved baskets with Prue, and made snowmen with Linda.

'Pure art!' said Byron 'Two breakdowns a year' Broadsword, shaping his snowman excitedly, 'because totally ephemeral.'

In the evenings they helped McBlane prepare his superb food, they ate McBlane's superb food, they helped to wash up McBlane's superb food. And then they sat and talked as the smokeless fuel crackled. They shared cigarettes and bowls of Tom's loganberry brandy and prune rum. Every now and then, as if moved by some spontaneous force, they would all touch and embrace each other. Occasionally someone would strum a guitar, and a middle management shanty, or an import/export protest song would shake the rafters. From time to time a couple would drift off, make love and drift back in again. Yarns were exchanged, beautiful experiences related.

Slowly, the thaw came. A few guests left, to return to the outside world stronger and better than when they had come. Sincere were the thanks and generous the cheques. Typical of the tributes was one paid by a leading light in the Confederation of British Industry.

'When I came here, Perrin, I was dying,' he said. 'I was dying of a serious social disease. Complacency, Perrin. Terminal complacency.'

He puffed long and gently on his pipe as he made out his generous cheque.

'I'm not complacent any more,' he said. 'I'm a wiser, better, kinder, happier man. I'm honest with myself at last.'

These were the good times.

The centre of the little town was pulsating with life.

The light was fading, and the street lamps were on.

Shop windows were ablaze with light.

Reggie walked slowly down the long main street, lined with cheery buildings from many centuries.

A butcher handed an old age pensioner a lamb chop and refused payment.

A kindly young property developer trudged happily from

179

house to house, seeking the views of the residents on what they would like to see done to the pretty little town of which they were so proud.

Six youths in the colours of Chelsea Football Club ran down the main street, chanting, 'Be fair to the Somalis. Bring peace to the Ogaden.'

The dignified man sitting outside the Bull and Flag smiled at them. They smiled back.

Strapped to the dignified man's chest was a board, on which was written, in a strong, elegant hand, 'Successful merchant banker. Please take generously'.

In front of the merchant banker was a bowler hat. It was half full of coins.

Every now and then a poorer member of the community bent down and took a coin. The merchant banker smiled.

Down the street in the opposite direction from the Chelsea fans came a swarm of Tottenham supporters. They were cleaning the windows of all the shops as they passed.

'What was the score, young man?' called out the merchant banker to the leading youngster.

'We lost six-five, didn't we, old timer,' said the Tottenham supporter, and a cheer rose from the whole ragged assembly.

Reggie opened his eyes and found Elizabeth watching him with interest.

'You had a smile like a Cheshire cat,' she said.

'I was dreaming,' he said.

He stretched and yawned.

'Monday morning,' he said. 'Another week's work.'

He leapt out of bed and pulled back the curtains.

It was not yet quite sunrise, and the garden looked bare in the cold light of dawn.

Yet Reggie didn't feel cold.

The last of the snow had gone, and the first snowdrops were out. Soon the crocuses would come, then the daffodils. Spring was on the way.

Reality looked as beautiful as Reggie's dream.

Five guests began that Monday morning. They included the first yobbo, the first nig-nog, and a man who had crossed the path of Reginald Iolanthe Perrin before.

The first guest had a wet mouth and spoke very fast.

'I'm a philosopher,' he told Reggie, sitting on his chair so lightly that he gave the impression of balancing just above it. 'I believe that the art of philosophy is vital for mankind's survival. Politicians are finished,' he said. 'Such battles as they were ever equipped to fight have been won, even if the victories have been Pyrrhic.'

He laughed, and crossed his legs so violently that he almost fell off the chair.

'The relationship of politicians to the nation has become as that of top management to an industrial concern,' he said. 'They deal largely with economic management, not political principle. It's as inappropriate to elect politicians as to elect the top management of I.C.I.'

He flung his arms in the air with such force that his chair almost toppled backwards.

'The questions asked in the political arena today are "how" questions—"How do we manage our society?", not "what" questions—"What kind of society do we want?",' he continued. ' "How do we achieve continued growth?" rather than "Is continued growth desirable?" I believe, incidentally, that it is not, since the world's resources are finite, but it can't be abandoned without a fundamental change in our philosophy. So, I believe we must ask "what" questions instead of "how" questions. But how? Aha! Yes?'

'Yes.'

'One suggestion. Have philosophical elections instead of political elections.'

Reggie smiled.

'There now follows a party philosophical broadcast on behalf of the logical positivist party,' he said. 'This programme is also being broadcast on BBC 2 and ITV.'

'Precisely. Totally unrealistic, of course, like everything worth striving for, because once you have something, by definition you can't strive for it. "I plan an expedition to Samarkand." "This is Samarkand." "Blast, that's scuppered that, then." '

'It's better to travel hopefully than to arrive,' said Reggie.

181

The philosopher looked at Reggie as if seeing him for the first time.

'Yes! Awfully well put, if I may say so,' he said.

'Thank you.'

Suddenly the philosopher slumped dejectedly. All the energy went out of him.

'I've arrived,' he said.

'What at?' said Reggie, concerned at the abrupt change in his guest's manner.

'Everything,' said the philosopher mournfully. 'I've solved all the problems of ethics, mathematics, logic and linguistics, all of them.'

'The whole lot?'

'The whole bang shoot. It's no use pretending I haven't. It'd be like crying, "Eureka, but mum's the word".'

'Or "I won't climb Everest, because it isn't there",' said Reggie.

'No, that's different,' said the philosopher.

'Just testing,' said Reggie. 'What are your solutions?'

'I can't reveal a word of it,' said the philosopher. He lowered his voice. 'I've had threats.'

'Threats?'

'The existentialist mob. The linguistic boys. The logical positivist mafia. I've been getting anonymous letters, heavy arguing on the phone, pseudo-jocular messages.'

He handed a sheet of writing paper to Reggie. A message had been glued on to it in letters of assorted sizes. 'I think, therefore I am going to duff you up,' it said.

The philosopher nodded.

'I wouldn't have told anyone,' he said. 'I couldn't. It would have put every other philosopher out of work. It would have taken away the purpose of life. In finding the purpose of life, one destroys it. They didn't need to threaten me.'

Was this man genuine? Was he a phoney? Was he mad? Could his tale possibly be true?

There was no way of telling.

He wanted to say something brilliant.

'Well, well!' he said.

'Help me, Mr Perrin,' said the philosopher.

The yobbo entered the room awkwardly, shyly, nervously, arrogantly, defiantly, and plonked his eloquent body on the chair.

'Bleeding sub-human cunt, aren't I?' he said.

'Are you,' said Reggie. 'Well ... er ... hello.'

'Glenn Higgins. I'm a yobbo.'

'Are you?'

'Course I am. I'm a bleeding mindless lout. That bloke you've just had in here. Naffing philosopher, right?'

'Yes.'

'Philosophers don't stab the bleeding opposition with knives and break all the windows in their coaches, do they?'

'No.'

'Know why? Because they aren't sub-human cunts. Listen. The way I look at it is this. Right? When his naffing lordship bleeding philosopher and I were kids, we were both in prams wetting our bleeding nappies and crapping all over the bloody place, right?'

'Right.'

'Now he's a philosopher and I'm a football hooligan, right?'

'Right.'

'They have philosophy conferences and that, all expenses paid, white-haired geezers giving these talks and that, right?'

'Right.'

'They don't have conferences of elderly football hooligans, all expenses paid, right?'

'Right.'

'When we're fighting, we reckon we're proving a point, know what I mean?'

'You're showing society that you don't give a damn for the established order of things, right?'

'Right. But it isn't society that's the bleeding loser, right?'

'Right.'

'I reckon it's a mug's game, being a sub-human cunt. Help me, Mr Perrin.'

The third guest to face Reggie across the sun-room desk shook hands briskly, flashed his white teeth, and said, 'I'm the nig-nog'.

'I'm sorry about that advert,' said Reggie. 'But I wanted it to stand out. I really do want to get some coloured people in. It's in danger of becoming a kind of therapeutic Cotswolds. Your name?'

'Clyde Everton Frank Johnson.'

'Ah!' said Reggie. 'Named after the three Ws, eh? Walcott, Weekes and Worrell. What a team that was. Stollmeyer, Rae . . .'

'I hate cricket,' said Clyde Everton Frank Johnson. 'I hate the way you talk to us about it all the time, as if that's the only contact we can make. As if we're children. Black people are lovable when they're children. Cricketers and jazz singers remain so. Shit.'

'I couldn't agree more,' said Reggie.

Snodgrass scrabbled at the window with her paws, uttering plaintive supplementary miaows.

'What a lovely non-white cat,' said Clyde Everton Frank Johnson.

Reggie let Snodgrass in. She leapt on to Reggie's chair and he had to tip her off before he could sit down. She gave an injured squawk and settled down on the floor by the filing cabinets.

'You know why you all think we're lovable as cricketers, don't you?' said Clyde Everton Frank Johnson.

'Tell me,' said Reggie.

'Because cricketers wear white flannels,' said Clyde Everton Frank Johnson. 'Garbage. Do you know what I do for a living, Mr Perrin?'

'How could I?'

'Guess.'

'Well . . . bus conductor?'

'Schoolmaster.'

'Oh, I'm sorry,' said Reggie. 'It's just that . . .'

'Many of us have to do jobs which are below the level of our intellectual attainments?'

'Well, yes.'

'The joke is this, Mr Perrin. I'm doing a job which is above

184

my level of intellectual attainment. I ought to be sacked. But I'm not. You know why?'

'I imagine it's difficult to sack a teacher,' said Reggie.

'It's because I'm black. They'd have asked me to leave long ago if I was white. Man, I'm really bugged with all this prejudice. Hasn't a black man even got the right to be sacked in this damned country?'

Reggie drummed on his desk with his fingers.

'What do you want me to do?' he said.

'Teach me not to hate,' said Clyde Everton Frank Johnson. 'Help me, Mr Perrin.'

'Have you heard of the Fraternity of Universal Love?' asked Mrs Enid Patton, from Trowbridge.

'No,' admitted Reggie.

Her lips worked even when no words emerged. Her hair sagged listlessly under the crushing burden of life.

'Two months ago I was expelled,' she said, 'for inviting into my kitchen a woman who wasn't a member of the Fraternity of Universal Love.'

A roar shattered the silence of that blustery morning in early March. A pneumatic drill was probing the surface of Oslo Avenue.

'You were expelled for that?' said Reggie.

'My family aren't allowed to speak to me. They're still members, you see,' said Enid Patton.

'After what happened to you?'

'The community's their life, Mr Perrin. My husband's a Regional Reaper. The elder boy's a Group Leader and the younger boy's an Elder.'

Reggie walked over to her, and put an arm on her shoulder. She had begun to sob.

'I understand,' he said. 'You've lost your family and your faith. I can't help you with the family, but I will say this about the faith. I believe that every virtue praised by religion, with the single exception of worship itself, is just as valid in the name of humanity if there's no God and no purpose in life.'

Mrs Patton turned a tear-stained face towards him.

'You shouldn't say such wicked things,' she said. 'May God have mercy upon you.'

'You mean you . . . you still . . . er . . .' said Reggie.

'God's road has many turnings,' sobbed Mrs Patton. 'Help me, Mr Perrin.'

Last of the five came the man who had crossed his path before.

It was none other than Clive 'Lofty' Anstruther, best man at the wedding that never was, Jimmy's partner in staccato speech and his secret army, who had vamoosed with all the weapons and money.

Reggie greeted him neutrally. He felt that it would be a betrayal of Jimmy to show friendliness and a betrayal of Perrins to show hostility.

Clive 'Lofty' Anstruther was tall and sinewy. No irony attended his nickname. He lit a cigar which, like him, was long, thin, brown and showing signs of age.

'Permission to smoke?' he said, after taking a luxurious puff.

'Certainly,' said Reggie.

'Well done,' said Clive 'Lofty' Anstruther.

'Why are you here?' said Reggie.

'Remorse. Fear of death. Conscience. All that palaver,' said Clive 'Lofty' Anstruther.

He sighed.

'Like to pay poor old Jimmy back,' he said. 'Hoping I might run into him some time.'

'That shouldn't be too difficult,' said Reggie. 'He's here.'

Clive 'Lofty' Anstruther seemed as near to turning pale as he would ever be.

'Here?'

'Yes.'

'Working here, for you?'

'Yes.'

'Splendid. Well done.'

'Yes, isn't it?'

'Help me, Mr Perrin.'

Jimmy was out all that day, on an expedition that involved the use of no less than six bus routes, so it wasn't until evening that the touching reunion took place.

Reggie invited both men to the Botchley Arms for a pre-prandial snifter.

The saloon bar was awash with furniture. Chairs and tables abounded. The walls had erupted with swords, plates and horse brasses. Shelves were covered with Toby jugs. The carpet was fiercely patterned. The only thing that could be said in its favour was that it was the best bar in Botchley.

Reggie sat in a corner, underneath a mauve wall lamp, a tank full of mouldy goldfish, and a warming pan of no distinction. He sipped his Guinness nervously. This was the ultimate test of his community. If Jimmy could make his peace with the man who had so grievously wronged him, there was no limit to what Perrins could achieve.

He had asked Jimmy to arrive fifteen minutes before Clive 'Lofty' Anstruther, in order to prepare him.

At last he arrived.

'Sorry I'm late,' he said. 'Cock-up on the back collar stud front.'

Reggie bought him a large whisky and reflected on the old-fashioned nature of the old soldier's attire. Where other men simply slipped on a shirt and tie, Jimmy had two collar studs, two cuff-links and a tie-pin to contend with each evening. He changed for dinner every night, out of one shirt with frayed cuffs into another shirt with frayed cuffs. Reggie suspected that he also had a shoe-horn, shoe-trees and his personal pumice stone, but this wasn't the time to ask. There were bigger fish to fry.

'I've got you here to meet someone,' said Reggie, when they were both seated. 'I hope you're in no hurry.'

'No. Lettice is making herself beautiful. Be an hour at least.'

'Yes.'

'No slur intended, Reggie.'

'Jimmy, would you describe yourself as a charitable and forgiving man?' said Reggie.

'Other cheek, mote and beam, that sort of crack?'

'Yes.'

'Goodwill to all mankind, that kind of caper?'

187

'Yes.'

'Yes, I would, Reggie. Every time.'

'Would that include Tim "Curly" Beamish?'

Jimmy's mouth dropped open. His left eye twitched.

'Ah! That bastard. Ah well, that's different,' he said.

'It's goodwill to all mankind except Tim "Curly" Beamish?'

'Could put it that way. Johnny did me down, Reggie.'

A thought struck Jimmy, an event so unusual that it caused his hand to lurch and his whisky to spill.

'Not here to meet Tim "Curly" Beamish, am I?' he asked.

Reggie shook his head, and Jimmy relaxed.

'No,' said Reggie. 'Clive "Lofty" Anstruther.'

More whisky sloshed on to the table. In the tank, a fish abandoned life's uphill struggle. The other fish ate it. Jimmy gazed at the scene as if it was tenderness itself, compared to the emotions that he was feeling.

'He arrived this morning, to join our community,' said Reggie. 'He's had a change of heart. He wants to pay you back.'

'Think so, too,' said Jimmy.

Reggie put his hand on Jimmy's arm.

'I expect the highest standards,' he said. 'This is your supreme test. This is Australia at Lord's. This is Everest. This is your Rubicon.'

Jimmy breathed deeply, and forced a ghastly parody of a smile.

'Message received and understood,' he whispered faintly.

He downed the remainder of his whisky in one gulp, before he had a chance to spill any more.

Clive 'Lofty' Anstruther stepped anxiously into the bar. His face was tense. He approached them. He too tried to force a smile.

'Hello, Jimmy,' he said, holding out his hand.

There was a perceptible hesitation before Jimmy clasped the proffered extremity.

'Anstruther,' he said hoarsely.

'What are you having?' said Clive 'Lofty' Anstruther.

'Large whisky, please, Anstruther,' said Jimmy.

'Well done,' said Clive 'Lofty' Anstruther.

188

The former con man towered over the other customers at the bar. Reggie smiled at Jimmy.

'Well done,' he said.

'Just don't expect me to call him Lofty, that's all,' said Jimmy.

Clive 'Lofty' Anstruther returned with the drinks.

'Cheers,' he said.

'Cheers,' said Reggie.

'Cheers,' said Jimmy, after another slight hesitation.

'Long time, no see,' said Clive 'Lofty' Anstruther.

'Not surprising,' said Jimmy.

Clive 'Lofty' Anstruther cleared his throat.

'Jimmy?' he began.

'Yes?'

'Bastard business, that thing. Rotten show. Rifles and so forth."

Jimmy swallowed hard and looked at Reggie.

Reggie nodded encouragingly. 'Everest,' he mouthed.

'Oh well,' said Jimmy. 'Water under bridge, Anstruther.'

'Never in army,' said Clive 'Lofty' Anstruther.

'Can't all be,' said Jimmy. 'Funny old world if everyone in army.'

'Pack of lies from start to finish.'

'Oh well.'

'What happened to all the ... er ...?' asked Reggie.

'Weapons? Sold them. Dribs and drabs. Not a fighter. Yellow streak,' said Clive 'Lofty' Anstruther.

'Bad luck,' said Jimmy.

'Rotten through and through,' said Clive 'Lofty' Anstruther.

'Drew a lousy hand, that's all,' said Jimmy. 'All the other babies, two hearts, three no trumps, that sort of crack. You, no bid. Rotten luck.'

'Thanks.'

'Drink?'

'Thanks.'

Jimmy bought three large whiskies.

'Cheers.'

'Cheers.'

'Cheers.'

'Pay you back,' said Clive 'Lofty' Anstruther. 'Weekly instalments.'

He hunted in his pockets, found two grubby notes, and handed them to Jimmy. Jimmy stared at them.

'Harbour?' he said. 'Castle? What are these?'

'Guernsey notes,' said Clive 'Lofty' Anstruther. 'Legal tender.'

Jimmy put them in his wallet very carefully, as if he didn't trust them not to disintegrate.

'Remember the wedding you didn't turn up at?' said Clive 'Lofty' Anstruther.

'Yes,' said Jimmy. 'Bad business, that.'

'Don't blame you,' said Clive 'Lofty' Anstruther. 'She looked like the back end of a bus.'

'Married her just before Christmas,' said Jimmy.

'My God, is that the time?' said Reggie.

'Oh my God. Awfully sorry,' said Clive 'Lofty' Anstruther.

'Don't worry, Lofty,' said Jimmy. 'I like buses.'

They walked back up Bonn Close, and turned left into Oslo Avenue. Reggie felt a warm glow in his heart. The world was wending its way to his door, and saying, 'Help me, Mr Perrin.'

Many of their problems were difficult, but if he could reconcile Jimmy and Clive 'Lofty' Anstruther, he could solve them all.

Yes, these were the good times.

There would never be such good times again.

VII

The Difficult Days

THE CROCUSES APPEARED. So did a petty thief.

His existence came to light at a sex symposium presided over by David Harris-Jones in the sex clinic, alias his bedroom.

The double bed had been folded against the wall, and ten people sat round in a circle. Apart from David Harris-Jones, there were eight guests and Reggie, who was holding a watching brief.

The eight guests were Mr Winstanley; a depressed police Superintendent; the extremely shy vet, who appeared to be too shy to leave the community; a scientist who believed that scientific progress would eventually destroy mankind; an automation consultant, who believed that mankind would have succeeded in rendering itself surplus to requirements long before it was destroyed; a football hooligan from Sheffield who felt that, with United and Wednesday both down the plughole, being a football hooligan in Sheffield was a declining industry; a Highways Officer from Botchley Borough Council; and a British Rail traffic manager, who arrived seventeen minutes late, due to alarm clock failure.

The symposium began with a game of 'Sexual Just A Minute'. The guests had to talk for one minute on any subject connected with sex. They must not hesitate or repeat themselves or deviate from the subject. The aim of the exercise was to break down inhibitions.

The scientist described his favourite sexual activity. After eleven seconds he was buzzed for deviation.

The football hooligan spoke for one minute about a knee trembler in a back alley in Tinsley.

'Super,' said David Harris-Jones, when he had finished.

The automation consultant described a night he had spent

191

with a lady electronics expert in Geneva. After fourteen seconds he was buzzed for repetition.

The Superintendent spoke for a minute about the prostitutes of Trudworth New Town.

'Super, Super,' said David Harris-Jones, when he had finished.

The extremely shy vet was buzzed after one second for hesitation.

Mr Winstanley spoke of Mrs Winstanley's uncanny resemblance to Kim Novak. He illustrated this with a snapshot and was very upset when he was buzzed for inaccuracy. He grabbed the photo and shoved it back in his wallet.

Suddenly he began to examine the contents of the wallet very carefully.

'I've been robbed,' he said. 'I had thirty pounds. Fifteen's gone.'

'Are you sure?' said Reggie. 'I can't believe anybody here would take money.'

The extremely shy vet spoke, so softly that only dogs could have heard him.

'What was that?' said Reggie.

'I lost ten pounds last Friday,' he said.

'Why didn't you say?' said Reggie.

'I did, but nobody heard me.'

'You ought to send for the police,' said the Superintendent.

'Two cases isn't much,' said Reggie. 'Leave it for a bit, eh?'

The Highways Officer talked about his obsession for Andrea Bovington of Accounts. Reggie didn't listen. He knew that, if the thefts continued, they could destroy the delicate balance of faith and trust that had been created in the community.

He tossed and turned long into the silent Botchley night.

'What's wrong?' Elizabeth murmured sleepily, shortly after three o'clock.

'It's those thefts,' said Reggie. 'It's like a rape in a nunnery.'

'Stop exaggerating, Reggie,' said Elizabeth.

'This is supposed to be a place of trust and faith, darling,' said Reggie.

Elizabeth switched the light on.

'Men!' she said. 'Everything goes well for several months, then you get two puny little thefts, and you start panicking.'

'You're right, darling,' said Reggie. 'I'm sorry.'

'This is a test of *your* trust and faith,' said Elizabeth. 'You've got to have faith in the thief's conscience. Trust him to see the error of his ways.'

'You're right, darling.'

'You expect everything to go well all the time. It's impossible. It's through set-backs that you prove your strength.'

'You're absolutely right, darling.'

'Don't just agree with everything I say, Reggie. It's extremely irritating.'

'You're abso ... lu ... go to sleep, darling. It's gone three.'

He kissed her and turned over to go to sleep. She was right. Faith and trust. Everything would be all right. Quite soon he was asleep.

He woke to find that she was no longer in the bed. She was over at the dressing table, hunting through her handbag.

'What are you doing?' he asked her sleepily.

'You made me wide awake with all your not sleeping, and then you went straight to sleep.'

'I'm sorry, darling.'

'I came for one of my pills. I've got cramp.'

'I'm sorry, darling.'

She put her handbag down on the dressing table.

'My purse has been stolen,' she said.

'Are you sure?' said Reggie, wide awake now.

'Of course I'm sure. You're going to have to take some firm action over that thief, Reggie.'

'You're absolutely right, darling.'

He tossed and turned until dawn.

That morning Reggie called everyone together in the living room of Number Twenty-one.

The room was packed. There were seventy people present, including all the staff, all the guests, and McBlane.

'Ladies and gentlemen,' said Reggie, standing on a chair so that he could be seen by everyone. 'I'll be blunt. We have a petty thief in our midst. Three cases have been reported.'

'Four,' said the Deputy Borough Engineer of Botchley Council. 'I lost ten pounds last night.'

'All right,' said Reggie. 'Four cases of . . .'

'Five,' said Clive 'Lofty' Anstruther. 'I've lost twenty pounds and my watch.'

'Are we to put at risk everything we've built up so painstakingly,' said Reggie,' because we've lost seventy-five pounds and a watch?'

'Digital,' said Clive 'Lofty' Anstruther.

'We mustn't let ourselves be eaten away by suspicion,' said Reggie. 'I regard these lapses as relics of a past, mis-spent life, committed by somebody who hasn't been here long enough to come fully under the spell of our community. I say to this person : Cease your crimes, and free your conscience, by handing back the seventy-five pounds.'

'And the digital watch,' said Clive 'Lofty' Anstruther.

In the morning there were two more cases of theft, and none of the money had been handed back. Reggie called another emergency meeting. Once again he stood on a chair and addressed the crowd packed into the living room.

'We have not yet been successful in reclaiming the soul of our erring brother,' he said. 'I don't believe that this thief is evil or greedy. I believe that he's bored. The conventional channels have failed to provide the challenge that he craves. It's the risk, not the money that is the motivation here. I ask you therefore to eliminate that element of risk, and at the same time put this criminal to private shame, by a supreme act of faith. Leave your valuables lying around the house tonight.'

'Asking for trouble,' said Clive 'Lofty' Anstruther. 'I know the criminal mind.'

'Sometimes we have to ask for trouble,' said Reggie,' in order to overcome it.'

That night three hundred and eighty-two pounds, four watches, two rings and a bracelet were stolen.

Reggie held his third emergency meeting in the crowded living room.

'Help me nail the sod,' he said.

The Superintendent was about to depart on one of Jimmy's expeditions when Reggie asked him to lead the enquiries into the thefts.

'It's what I've come here to avoid,' he groaned, following Reggie into the sun-room.

The March sun was streaming in through the wide windows. In a gap between the houses in Lisbon Crescent a street lamp glowed a faint orange. There was a fault in the timing device.

'Please!' said Reggie.

The Superintendent sighed.

'How can I refuse you when you ask me so nicely?' he said.

There was a knock on the door. It was the automation consultant. He wanted to leave. He was disturbed by the petty thefts.

'Do you mind if the Superintendent asks you a few questions? Purely routine, of course,' said Reggie.

'Not at all,' said the automation consultant.

The Superintendent cleared his throat.

'Did you commit those thefts?' he asked.

'No,' said the automation consultant.

'Thank you,' said the Superintendent.

When the automation consultant had gone, Reggie remonstrated with the burly policeman.

'Why didn't you ask him any more?' he said. 'It wasn't exactly a searching enquiry, was it?'

'No point,' said the Superintendent. 'He isn't the type.'

'You shouldn't look at people that way,' said Reggie. 'That's stereotyped thinking.'

The Superintendent set off to pursue his enquiries, but not before Reggie had emphasised the importance of being discreet.

There was a faint knock on the door of the sun-room. Reggie had to call 'Come in' three times before the extremely shy vet entered.

'I'm leaving,' he mumbled.

'It's the thefts, isn't it?' said Reggie.

'It's burst the bubble,' mumbled the vet, 'but I would have had to have gone sooner or later.'

195

'You aren't conquering your shyness as quickly as you'd hoped.'

The extremely shy vet nodded.

Could he be the thief? Anybody could be. Even the Superintendent.

'Do you mind if I ask you a few questions?' said Reggie.

'No,' said the extremely shy vet.

'Did you commit those thefts?' he asked.

'No,' said the extremely shy vet.

'Thank you,' said Reggie. 'No further questions.'

Reggie knew that he hadn't made a conspicuous success of his first police enquiry, but he consoled himself with the thought that the extremely shy vet wasn't the type.

That afternoon both the football hooligans departed in high dudgeon, after their rooms had been searched. Before they left they punctured the tyres of every car in Oslo Avenue. Reggie was angry with the Superintendent.

'I suppose you searched their rooms first of anybody,' he said, as they reviewed the day's events in the sun-room that evening.

'They're the types,' said the Superintendent.

'I wish you hadn't done that,' said Reggie. 'You didn't find anything, I suppose?'

'No, but it was one of them. You run a nice, middle-class place. No crime. You bring yobbos in. Crimes begin. What they did to those tyres proves what they are.'

'They did that because you searched their rooms,' said Reggie. 'You force people into the roles you want them to play.'

'God save me from idealists,' said the Superintendent. 'That's the one good thing about Trudworth New Town. No idealists.'

The Superintendent handed Reggie fifty pounds.

'What's that for?' said Reggie.

'I'm leaving,' said the Superintendent. 'This place has failed me.'

At the door he turned.

'You won't get any more thefts,' he said.

There were no thefts that night, nor the next night.

The exodus continued. The trendies decided that Perrins

was no longer fashionable and proved mean with their money.

Mr Linklater, from the Town Clerk's Department of Botchley Borough Council, was ushered into the sun-room on the following day. He was a neat, concise man, who looked as if he was trying to cram his body tight into an invisible box. He sat very upright, holding his hands firmly into his sides.

'You have eleven of my staff here, Mr Perrin,' he said.

'Twelve, including you,' said Reggie.

'I won't be staying, though,' said Mr Linklater.

'They all said that,' said Reggie. 'A cup of my coffee, a couple of my ginger nuts, a quick gander at my community, and they're hooked. Would you like coffee and biscuits?'

'No, thank you,' said Mr Linklater firmly. 'The decimation of our staff cannot continue.'

'I didn't force them to stay,' said Reggie. 'It isn't my fault if working for the council is boring, the offices are dreary, the corridors are dusty, and the food in the canteen is vile.'

'May I see my staff?' said Mr Linklater.

'Certainly,' said Reggie. 'Let me show you around.'

They set off along Oslo Avenue. The bright sun was deceptive, for the air was still quite sharp.

'What a strange walk you have, Mr Linklater,' said Reggie. 'The way you bounce up and down, and hold your backside in so tightly, as if you're walking through Portsmouth on a dark night.'

That afternoon Mr Dent called on Reggie and told him that the Botchley council contingent were all leaving.

'I'll be sorry to see you all go,' said Reggie.

'We'll all be sorry to see us all go,' said Mr Dent.

'Is it the thefts?' said Reggie.

'I suppose they've brought it on,' said Mr Dent. 'That and Mr Linklater explaining about our benefits and back pay and how we wouldn't lose any if we came back now.'

Mr Dent remained standing, by the door.

'Sit down,' Reggie urged him.

'No thank you,' he said. 'You'd be offering me your ginger nuts next and then where would we be? Back at square one. We couldn't stay for ever, Mr Perrin.'

'I hope we've had an effect,' said Reggie. 'I hope you won't forget that real you that you spoke of. That friendly, genial, delightful man.'

'Don't you worry,' said Mr Dent, smiling. 'He's here to stay.'

He looked embarrassed.

'We . . . er . . . I'm collecting a sum of money from everyone. We've agreed how much we'll all pay, according to how long we've stayed. I've . . . er . . . I've done a cheque for us all.'

Mr Dent removed the cheque from his wallet and looked it over carefully.

'It's not a lot,' he said. 'You aren't millionaires if you work for the BBC.'

He handed Reggie the cheque. It came out at more per head than the amount donated by the trendies.

'Thank you very much,' said Reggie.

'May I ask you a question?' said Mr Dent.

'Of course.'

'What did you say to Mr Linklater this morning?'

Reggie told him.

'Out of my own pocket,' said Mr Dent, handing him two five pound notes.

That evening Clive 'Lofty' Anstruther's room-mate handed Reggie an envelope.

It contained two hundred pounds and a note.

The note read: 'Dear Mr Perrin. Couldn't face you. Sorry. Yellow streak. Had to leave. Place destroyed for me by thefts. Peace of mind gone. Mankind rotten through and through. Please find £100 for you, £100 for Jimmy. More follows. Lofty.'

Five days later, Reggie received a letter, second-class, post-marked London.

'A thousand pounds gone from your safe,' it read. 'Sorry. Rotten through and through. Fact of life. Don't want anyone else to be suspected. Not vicious. Don't try and find me. Waste of time. Love to Jimmy. Lofty.'

Reggie hadn't even known that there were a thousand pounds gone from his safe. He had failed the two yobbos. He had lost nineteen of his fifty-two guests. He called a meeting of his staff, in the living room of Number Seventeen.

They sat around the walls in the wildly assorted chairs, and

198

drank coffee out of the brown mugs, each of which bore its owner's name.

In a gesture of solidarity, they never drank out of their own mug. The names were on the mugs merely to remind them of other, less fortunate organisations, where a less happy spirit prevailed.

Reggie was smoking an opulent cigar.

'The petty thefts have knocked Perrins, but they haven't destroyed it,' he said. 'Things were too easy. We'll be all the stronger for the experience. It may even be a blessing in disguise as new guests will soon take up the slack, and will probably prove better payers than the trendies or the council officials. We've all got to work a little harder, but don't worry. We shall succeed. Any questions?'

'Yes,' said Tom. 'Why are you smoking a large cigar?'

'It's a psychological ploy,' said Reggie. 'It'll give me an air of authority and opulence which will help to re-establish an aura of confidence and well-being.'

He drew on the cigar luxuriantly, and sighed contentedly.

'I hate the bloody things,' he said. 'But it's a sacrifice I'm prepared to make, for the sake of the community.'

Buds began to appear on the trees, daffodils bloomed in the gardens, and all over Botchley men oiled their lawn-mowers.

The clock went forward, providing an extra hour of daylight in the evenings.

The March winds grew angry at mankind's presumptuousness. We'll show them whether winter's over, they howled. They hurled themselves against roofs, rattled upon double-glazing, sported with carrier bags and old newspapers, and sent daffodils reeling.

A container ship carrying thousands of tons of Worcester sauce from Immingham to Nagasaki crashed on to the jagged rocks off the west coast of Guernsey and was severely holed. Spicy brown tides roared up the holiday beaches. The rocks from Pleinmont to L'Ancresse were awash with vinegar, molasses, sugar, shallots, anchovies, tamarinds, garlic, salt, spices and natural flavouring. It was the worst Worcester sauce slick in modern mercantile history.

Six novelists began books about the incident. Five of the books were called *Worcester Sauce Galore* and the sixth was called *The Fall and Rise of Lea and Perrins.*

Deborah Swaffham arrived at the community.

Jimmy continued the endless task of clearing Botchley of litter all over again. It was an ecological Forth Bridge. He removed a sodden copy of the *Botchley and Spraundon Press* (*Incorporating The Coxwell Gazette*) from the bars of a gate in Rejkyavik View, where it had been flapping in impotent anger. He began to read it, for other people's newspapers are always more interesting than one's own. His eye alighted on an article by 'The Gourmet'. 'In the gastronomic treasure house that is War Memorial Parade,' the article began, 'no jewel shines more brightly than the wittily named Oven D'Or.'

Jimmy had just reached: 'My companion plumped for the prawn cocktail and pronounced it as delicious as it was ample,' when a bloodcurdling yell came from round the corner.

He abandoned his reading, and led his expeditionary force into action for the first time.

Three youths were attacking a smaller youth in Lima Crescent.

Jimmy's six-man force rushed in, with the exception of the philosopher, who hung back as much as he dared.

Jimmy tore into the midst of the fray, grabbed two of the youths, and banged their heads together before they knew what was happening.

'Take that, you bastards,' he shouted, bringing his knee up into the larger one's groin.

Four members of the expeditionary force were not far behind him, while the philosopher faffed around ineffectually on the edge of the fight.

The three youths were soon overcome.

'Love and peace, you bloody louts,' Jimmy shouted at them, as they limped sullenly off along Lima Crescent. 'Love and peace, do you hear? Reckoned without Major James Anderson, didn't you?'

One of the youths turned, and intimated, though not in those exact words, that retribution might be expected.

Jimmy turned to the rescued youth.

'On your way, lad,' he said.

The rescued youth set off equally sullenly in the opposite direction, without a word of thanks.

'Ungrateful sod,' said Jimmy.

The middle-aged expeditionary force stood panting in the road, regaining its corporate wind.

'Right,' said Jimmy, the glint dying reluctantly from his eyes. 'Back to clearing litter.'

'Leloipe,' cried the philosopher. 'My God! My God!'

'Know what you're thinking,' said Jimmy.

'I very much doubt that,' said the philosopher.

'Can't all be men of action,' said Jimmy, putting a consoling arm round the philosopher. 'Rum bag of tricks if we were.'

'No, no, no,' said the philosopher irritably. 'When you fought, I was thinking that here we have war and history in microcosm.'

'Microcosm, eh?' said Jimmy blankly.

'Violence to stop violence. A peace-keeping force is a contradiction in terms. Fighting for peace is as absurd as making love for virginity. And suddenly that led me on and I saw a fatal flaw in my solution. I'm wrong. All my life's work—wrong!'

'Bad luck,' said Jimmy.

'It's wonderful, you fool,' said the philosopher. 'I've lost everything.'

'Leloipe,' he cried again, and the wind hurled his triumphant cry of failure along Lima Crescent towards the Arctic.

Later that afternoon, as the winds spent themselves slowly, the philosopher saw Reggie in the sun-room.

His face was exultant.

'I haven't solved all the problems of ethics, mathematics, logic and linguistics after all,' he said. 'In fact I haven't solved any of them. Isn't it wonderful news? Aren't you happy for me?'

'Delirious,' said Reggie.

'My quest can begin again,' said the philosopher. 'The long search resumes. Please accept a cheque for four hundred pounds. I wish it could be more, but philosophers aren't millionaires.'

'I haven't earned it,' protested Reggie.

'You've flung me back into the exquisite cauldrons of doubt and speculation,' said the philosopher gratefully.

On her first day, Deborah Swaffham had been upstaged by Jimmy's little fracas.

On the Tuesday, she was upstaged by the petition. It was delivered at three thirty in the afternoon by Mrs E Blythe-Erpingham, of Windyways, Number Eighteen, Bonn Close. It had been signed by one thousand two hundred and seventy-six residents.

The purport of the petition was that the presence of Perrins in the midst of Mrs E Blythe-Erpingham and her friends was 'inconsistent with the character of this predominantly residential area'.

Reggie greeted Mrs Blythe-Erpingham courteously, and studied the petition carefully.

'Photostats have been sent to the leader of the council, our M.P., and to the *Botchley and Spraundon Press*,' she said.

'*Incorporating The Coxwell Gazette,*' said Reggie. 'I do apologise for interrupting, but I think we should remember our friends in Coxwell. We're all brothers and sisters under the skin, are we not, Lady Blythe-Erpingham?'

'*Mrs* Blythe-Erpingham,' said Mrs Blythe-Erpingham.

'Lady Blythe-Erpingham to me,' said Reggie.

Mrs Blythe-Erpingham simpered.

'I thought it would be courteous to bring you a photostat,' she said. 'And I would like to assure you, Mr Perrin, that this is only because of the parking, the punctures, the publicity, and the undesirable types that your excellent project attracts. There is nothing personal in this whatsoever.'

'I'm glad to hear it,' said Reggie. 'There's nothing personal in *this* either.'

He tore the petition into little pieces and dropped them over Mrs Blythe-Erpingham's head like snow.

In the early evening, in the late sunshine, Reggie strolled around the streets of Botchley, marshalling his thoughts.

Why did I tear the petition up?

Why was I rude to Mr Linklater?

I can't afford these gestures. They can destroy my work.

I shouldn't want these petty triumphs.

He entered the Botchley Arms and ordered a pint of bitter. The landlord had a long, gaunt face and a long, pointed nose beneath which a brown moustache bristled acidly.

'These fine evenings are bad for trade,' he said. 'People pop out to the country, when they see a bit of sun.'

Reggie felt an impulse to make a thoroughly rude reply.

No, no, no.

'I daresay it's as long as it's broad,' he said.

'That's exactly the way I look at it,' said the landlord. 'You've got to in this trade.'

On the Wednesday, it was the financial problems of Perrins that occupied Reggie, and enabled those posed by Deborah Swaffham to remain undetected. Elizabeth asked him to come and see her in the secretary's office. She was wearing a pair of severe horn-rimmed glasses which she affected when she wished to look businesslike rather than wifely. Her eyebrows rose at his large cigar, but she made no comment. Instead she gave a concise summary of their financial position.

'Our expenses have been enormous and have used up almost all our capital,' she said. 'During January and February we were full, and still only just exceeded our costs. We are now not full. We can't guarantee to be full all the time. We must therefore make economies.'

'I think those are long-tailed tits at the bottom of the garden,' said Reggie.

'Reggie!'

'Sorry, darling, I missed some of what you said. I missed that bit about the finances.'

'Reality won't go away because you don't look at it, you know.'

'You're absolutely right, darling, but those tits are lovely.'

Concentrate, Reggie.

Elizabeth repeated her pithy summary of their financial position.

Reggie puffed his cigar thoughtfully.

'We'll have to make economies,' he said.

'Those cigars can go for a start,' said Elizabeth.

'But not short-sighted economies,' he said. 'I mustn't lose my authority, darling, much as I might wish to. What are our major expenses?'

'Salaries and food. Salaries you can't cut down on. McBlane is extravagant.'

'You're suggesting that I go and see McBlane and tell him that we must make economies?'

'Frankly, yes.'

'Man to man, straight from the shoulder?'

'Frankly, yes.'

'Are you absolutely certain we need to economise?'

'Frankly, yes. Are you frightened of McBlane, darling?'

'Frankly, yes.'

Reggie walked slowly through the living room, bracing himself for his confrontation with McBlane.

The kitchen was filled with the pleasant aroma of prawns provençale. The pustular wizard of the pots was seated at the kitchen table pouring white powder over his left foot.

'Morning, McBlane,' said Reggie. 'Prawns provençale. Yum yum.'

McBlane grunted.

'Keeping the old feet in good condition, eh?' said Reggie. 'Splendid.'

McBlane replied. For all Reggie knew, he might have said anything from, 'Yes, I'm a bit of a stickler for pedicure', to 'Mind your own business, you Sassenach snob'.

'Splendid,' said Reggie, taking a calculated risk, for if McBlane had said, 'I have an incurable dose of McAllister's Pedal Gunge and will be bed-ridden 'ere Michaelmas', Reggie's reply of 'Splendid' would have been distinctly inflammatory.

'Splendid food all week,' said Reggie, as McBlane drew a thick woollen sock over his powdered foot. 'So good, McBlane, that a thought occurs to me. A chef of your calibre doesn't need expensive ingredients all the time. Any chef can make a delicious meal of parma ham with melon, crayfish thermidor, and syllabub. Only a genius like you could make a delicious meal of, shall we say, leek and potato soup and scrag end of

204

lamb. In other words, McBlane, were I to say to you that a degree of economy was needed, just a degree, you understand, then a chef of your brilliance and subtlety might see that as a challenge. Point taken, McBlane?'

'Guidy aud airseblekkt ooter her whee himsel obstrofulate pocking blae ruitsmon.'

'Jolly good. We'll say no more about it, then, McBlane.'

On the Thursday afternoon, in the Culture Room, alias the Websters' bedroom, Tony was instructing Deborah Swaffham in the dramatic arts. More precisely, they were studying *Antony and Cleopatra*, with particular reference to the relationship between the eponymous duo. Tony was taking the part of Antony while it was Miss Swaffham's task to portray the sultry temptress of the Nile.

Tony was feeling a certain lassitude, possibly as a result of his superb lunch of Parma ham with melon, crayfish thermidor, and syllabub.

Deborah Swaffham had long blonde hair, full lips with a suspicion of a pout, a good figure and long legs covered in a golden down. All Tony's lassitude disappeared when she said, 'How do you think Cleopatra would have kissed?'

'I really don't know,' said Tony. 'I've never given it much thought.'

'I think she probably used lots of tongue and things, rather slowly and thoughtfully,' said Deborah Swaffham.

'Perhaps you'd better show me,' said Tony.

And so, Deborah Swaffham and Tony sat in an armchair in the Culture Room on that quiet afternoon at the end of March in Oslo Avenue, Botchley, and were transported back through two thousand years of history.

After Deborah Swaffham had shown Tony how Cleopatra would have kissed, Tony showed her what he thought Antony's attitude to breast fondling would have been.

When Tony put his tongue in Deborah Swaffham's mouth, she gave it a little bite, like the remnants of natural aggression in a sleepy domestic cat.

'I couldn't do this as myself. It's only because I'm Cleopatra,' she said.

'I find that hard to believe,' said Tony.

'Honestly, Tony. I'm very inhibited as me. If you came to my room and things, when I was me, I wouldn't be like this. But then you wouldn't want to come.'

'How do you know?'

'I'm unattractive to men. I have this frigid element which turns them off.'

'Rubbish.'

Deborah Swaffham looked into Tony's eyes.

He held her gaze.

'If you came to my bedroom in Number Seventeen, I'm lucky, I've got a proper bedroom and no room-mate, if you came there during dinner, because food is pretty draggy, isn't it?'

'Food is Dullsville, Arizona.'

'If you came this evening, would you still be able to feel attracted enough to me to try and help me get over my inhibitions and things?'

'I could try,' said Tony.

That evening Tony complained of indigestion—'probably the crayfish, I've never really been into crayfish'—and told Joan that he'd miss dinner. As soon as she'd gone to eat, he sped along the road to Number Seventeen. He was awash with greedy waves of desire.

Outside Deborah Swaffham's bedroom, he paused to tidy his hair. Then he knocked and strode in, masterfully, without waiting for a reply.

The room was empty.

'Those meals were very expensive today,' said Elizabeth in bed that night. 'McBlane can't have understood what you said.'

'He understood all right. He's mocking us,' Reggie said. 'Tomorrow I'm going to sort McBlane out. Don't worry.'

Elizabeth took her reading glasses off and placed them on her bedside table. Then she turned towards Reggie.

'I'm worried,' she said.

'Everything's going to be all right,' he said. 'You'll see.'

Friday dawned cold and stormy. Patches of steely blue sky appeared only briefly between the angry clouds. Reggie walked slowly towards the kitchen and what might well be his final showdown with McBlane.

Adam and Jocasta burst from the kitchen, full of energy and high spirits on the first day of the school holidays.

'Been to see Uncle McBlane?' said Reggie, glad of an excuse for delay.

'He's been telling us a story,' said Jocasta.

'That's very kind of him, isn't it?' said Reggie.

'Yes,' said Jocasta doubtfully.

'Tell me,' said Reggie, 'can you understand what Uncle McBlane is saying?'

'Of course,' said Adam. 'We're big.'

'You can understand every word?'

'Of course,' said Adam.

'Just checking,' said Reggie.

'Except words we don't know,' said Adam. 'Like syphilitic.'

'Yes, quite.'

Adam lowered his voice, confiding in Reggie, man to man.

'Uncle McBlane's stories aren't as nice as Uncle C.J.'s stories about ants,' he said. 'Uncle McBlane's stories are boring.'

'Fucking boring,' said Jocasta.

'Yes, you can understand every word Uncle McBlane's saying,' said Reggie.

He entered the kitchen purposefully. If the pimply genius of the herbs hadn't had a meat cleaver in his hand, Reggie's task might have been easier.

'Hello again,' he said. 'Superb meals yesterday, McBlane. Superb. Not perhaps quite as economical as I'd have wished . . .'

McBlane raised the cleaver.

'. . . but, as I say, superb.'

McBlane grunted, and brought the meat cleaver down savagely upon the hare that he was preparing.

'But,' said Reggie, 'and this implies no criticism, McBlane, but, and it is a big but . . .'

McBlane raised the cleaver once more.

'. . . well not that big a but. A medium-sized, almost a small but. But still a but. Well, almost a but.'

McBlane hacked another portion off the splendid creature so cruelly denied the opportunity to display its seasonal mania.

Hailstones rattled against the window panes. The sky was a bruised magenta. A breeze swept through the kitchen, stirring the loose ends of McBlane's boil plasters.

'I gather you're still telling stories to Adam and Jocasta,' said Reggie. 'Splendid. I wonder if for their age some of the stories are a little spicy, like your wonderful seafood pilaff.'

McBlane held the cleaver poised in his right hand. His poisoned thumb was encased in a sling, stained red with the blood of hares.

'Not too spicy, I hasten to add,' said Reggie. 'Far from it.'

The cleaver thudded into the hare.

'But perhaps spice, so brilliant in your seafood pilaff, is a little less appropriate in your stories.'

'Baskard brock wee reeling brawly doon awa' wouldna cleng a flortwingle.'

'Come off it, McBlane,' said Reggie. 'Stop playing games with me, you mobile bandage emporium. You can make yourself understood when you want to, you pock-marked Caledonian loon. You're all right when you tell your dirty stories, corrupting the children's minds, you diseased thistle from Partick. You stand there, like a demonstration model for a lecture on skin diseases, a walking ABC of ailments from acne to yellow-fever, ruining us with your extravagances, laughing at us, mocking us. Well, rather like you, McBlane, it just won't wash.'

Reggie stopped.

So did the hailstones.

The silence was deafening.

McBlane walked slowly towards him, the meat cleaver clasped in his right hand.

The hairs on the back of Reggie's neck stood on end.

McBlane walked straight past him and picked another hare from a huge plate which was lying on the Scandinavian-style traditional English fully-integrated natural pine and chrome work surface.

He was poker-faced, and spoke quietly.

He might have said, 'I applaud the spirit if not the justice of your rebukes', or, 'I'll endeavour to mend my ways in future', or even, 'You'll pay for this, you long streak of Sassenach piss'.

Reggie would never know.

Later that afternoon, a longer, fiercer hailstorm clattered down on Botchley. Some of the hailstones were the size of exceptionally large hailstones. They caused the abandonment of Tom's latest football experiment. Having failed with no opponents, trying to score for the opposition, and goals being illegal, Tom hoped that at last he'd solved the problem of removing the aggression from football. There were now two teams of equal numbers, each trying to score in the opponents' goal. There were rules, and breaches of the rules were marked by free kicks and penalties. Players who committed serious or repeated fouls were sent off.

When he was told that this was exactly how football was played, and that the system was not notably successful, he replied, 'Oh well, I always told you I wasn't a sports person'.

On the way home it seemed natural that Tom should find himself walking beside Deborah Swaffham. She looked extremely attractive in her Botchley strip, her cheeks and legs reddened by the stinging hail, and Tom felt acutely conscious of the flabby whiteness of his nether limbs.

The storm abated as they crossed into Addis Abbaba Avenue. Deborah Swaffham swayed towards Tom. She clutched him for support.

'Sorry,' she said. 'I thought I was going to fall.'

She kept her arm round his waist. When they turned into Washington Road, he grew visibly nervous. He lifted her arm and removed it from his waist.

'Sorry,' she said. 'I know I'm not the sort of person who turns men on and things.'

'You are,' protested Tom.

'It wouldn't worry me so much if I was ugly,' said Deborah Swaffham as they turned into Oslo Avenue. 'It's knowing that I've got full, firm breasts and a flat, taut stomach and rounded hips, and long shapely legs, and things, and still I have this distancing effect which shrivels the male libido.'

Tom's voice came out in a ghastly, strangulated croak.

'I assure you my libido isn't shrivelled,' he said.

'You could come to my bedroom during dinner,' said Deborah

209

Swaffham throatily. 'Unless of course I'm not exciting enough for you to miss your food.'

Tom looked round furtively, to see if any of the other footballers had heard. Nobody was near them.

'I'll be there,' he croaked. 'I'm not a food person.'

'I'm not hungry,' Tom told Linda that evening.

'Not hungry?' she said. 'Are you ill?'

'Yes. Ill. That's it. Ill,' said Tom. 'I need to go to bed.'

As soon as Linda had gone to dinner, Tom dressed rapidly and hurried to Number Seventeen.

He paused briefly outside the door to tidy his hair. Then he knocked, and plunged in, masterfully, without waiting for a reply.

The room was empty.

Tom went back to bed and lay there, deflated, angry and ravenous.

'I thought of bringing you some cheese and biscuits,' said Linda on her return. 'But I thought I'd better not, if you're ill.'

'Quite right,' said Tom. 'Well, what masterpiece did I miss?'

'Cold meats,' said Linda. 'McBlane has disappeared.'

The policeman arrived at midnight. Reggie went downstairs in his dressing gown, and talked to him by the remnants of the living-room fire.

Elizabeth waited anxiously. At last she heard the front door go, and Reggie came upstairs.

'It's McBlane,' he told her. 'He's broken an arm.'

'Oh my God,' said Elizabeth. 'Well, I'll have to do the cooking, that's all.'

'McBlane can cook,' said Reggie.

'You can't cook with a broken arm.'

'I'll go bail for him.'

'Bail?'

Reggie climbed into bed and kissed her.

'It wasn't his arm he broke,' he said. 'Apparently he went into that big pub by the roundabout on the by-pass.'

'The Tolbooth.'

'Yes. And he attacked a Salvation Army lady with his meat cleaver when she tried to sell him the *War Cry*.'

'Oh my God.'

'I imagine that's what she cried. Unavailingly.'

Reggie switched off the light at his side of the bed.

'I think I may have gone a bit far in what I said to him this morning,' he said.

'What did you say?'

Reggie told her. She looked at him in considerable alarm.

'Why did you say all that?' she asked.

He shrugged.

'People are saying you tore up a petition over Mrs Smythe-Erpingham's head.'

'Yes.'

'Did you?'

'Yes.'

'Apparently you were insulting to Mr Linklater from the Town Clerk's Department.'

'Yes.'

'Oh Reggie.'

'Yes.'

'You destroyed yourself at Sunshine Desserts, Reggie.'

'Yes.'

'You destroyed yourself at Grot.'

'Yes.'

'You're not trying to destroy yourself again, are you?'

'Of course not. I couldn't stand Sunshine Desserts and I didn't mean Grot seriously. This is my life's work. Why should I destroy it?'

Elizabeth hugged him tightly.

'I couldn't bear it if everything was destroyed all over again,' she said.

Reggie squeezed her hand tightly and pressed his body against hers.

They made love.

Afterwards, just before he drifted off to sleep, Reggie said, 'Everything'll be all right, darling. You'll see.'

Elizabeth kissed him on the forehead.

'You'll see,' he said.

By a stroke of ill-luck, the Tolbooth was the local of a reporter from Reuters and the arrest of the chef of Perrins, the community of faith and trust and love and peace, on a charge of assaulting a Salvation Army lady with a meat cleaver made good reading in several papers.

'McBlane's just an employee,' complained Elizabeth. 'But they make it sound as if all our ideals are in ruins.'

McBlane returned to work, but an atmosphere of gloom hung over Perrins.

Reggie took to drinking champagne. Rarely was a glass absent from his hand.

'It's a gesture,' he told Elizabeth. 'A touch of style. I have to re-establish confidence all over again. You know I don't like the stuff. It's far too gassy. It's like the cigars. But what are my lungs and my digestion, compared to the future of Perrins?'

He topped up his glass.

On Sunday evening, Reggie called an emergency staff meeting. The demoralised group sat around, in the varied old armchairs, drinking coffee listlessly out of each other's mugs. A small baize-topped card table had been set up for Reggie, opposite the fireplace. On the table was a pad of writing paper, a supply of pencils, and an auctioneer's gavel which Elizabeth had picked up cheap at an auction of the belongings of a deceased Spraundon auctioneer. It would come in handy for keeping fractious meetings in order. So far there had been no fractious meetings, but the gavel's brief hour of glory was at hand.

Reggie entered two minutes late. He had a fat cigar in his mouth and a glass of champagne in his hand. He sat at the table and waited for the conversation, such as it was, to cease.

'Ladies and gentlemen,' he said. 'Morale has declined and these things must be nipped in the bud. This meeting is to discuss which buds, and how they should be nipped, and in what. I'd like one firm suggestion for improving morale from each of you. Who'll be first?'

He met in turn the eyes of Elizabeth, Tom, Linda, David,

Prue, C.J., Jimmy, Lettice, Tony, Joan and Doc Morrissey. Did any man ever have such a staff?

'Get rid of Deborah Swaffham,' said C.J.

All eyes turned towards C.J., seated in a relatively smart sofa, facing the window.

'Is she the one with the ...' said Reggie.

'Yes,' said C.J.

'Expelling people looks to me like an admission of defeat,' said Reggie. 'However, if you insist on that suggestion, I'll make a note of it.'

'I do,' said C.J.

'Perhaps you could give us your reasons,' said Reggie.

'Certainly,' said C.J. 'When I do a job, I do it properly. I have never in my life spoilt a ship for a ha'porth of spilt milk, and I don't propose to start now. So, when Miss Swaffham, during our role-playing session earlier this week, proposed a further extra-mural session one evening, I heard the trumpet call of duty. I abandoned the story I was writing for Adam and Jocasta, and she came to my room. We ... er ... we had a role-playing session.'

'What roles did you play?'

'It was her idea.'

'What roles did you play?'

'Doctor and patient.'

C.J. looked at Elizabeth, appealing for moral support as his reward for having left her alone throughout the community's life. She tried to smile encouragingly.

'I felt out of my element,' he said. 'I didn't get where I am today by playing doctors and patients with Deborah Swaffham.'

Reggie took his cigar from his mouth and gazed steadily at C.J.

'Did the role playing involve ...?' he began.

'An examination? Yes,' said C.J. 'She was the patient, by the way.'

'Ah!'

'It was her idea. She took off her clothes ...'

He shuddered at the memory.

'I didn't know whether I was coming or going,' he continued. 'I ... I forgot myself, Reggie.'

213

'Forgot yourself, C.J.?'

'It's been a long time. I think everyone knows how much I miss Mrs C.J.'

'It's a *sine qua non*, C.J.'

'Is it really? Well, there you are. Anyway, I forgot myself. She hit me. She hit me, Reggie.'

C.J. flinched as he remembered the experience.

'We got dressed in angry silence,' said C.J.

'Oh, I see,' said Reggie. 'You'd got undressed as well.'

'She was shy of undressing. Said she had an unsexy body. I said, "You haven't seen mine". She said it might help her if she did. Oh God.'

'Thank you, C.J.,' said Reggie. 'It was brave of you to tell us that. It only goes to show that we should leave medical matters to the Doc.'

'No,' said Doc Morrissey.

All eyes turned to Doc Morrissey. He was sitting on a hard chair, pushed back slightly out of the circle to Reggie's right.

'She got up on the couch,' he said. 'She seemed very tense and vulnerable. I just put my arm round her.'

'Where were you?'

'Oh. I was on the couch as well. I didn't want to be in an analyst patient situation, with the inequality that that entails. I thought she would feel better, professionally, in an analyst analyst situation, or patient situation, whichever you like. Let's call it a person person situation, if you prefer.'

It seemed that Jimmy didn't prefer, for he let out a thunderous snore from the depths of his shabby armchair. Lettice kicked him gently from the adjoining chair, whose springs hung down like a prolapsed uterus. He jerked to life with a moan.

'Sorry,' he said. 'Must have nodded off.'

'He's not been sleeping since that business with Clive "Lofty" Anstruther,' said Lettice.

'Sorry,' said Jimmy. 'Morale shot to ribbons. Bad show. What's meeting all about? Rather missed that bit.'

'It's about low morale,' said Reggie.

'Ah! Treacherous chap, low morale. Depressing sort of cove.'

Reggie banged on the card table with his gavel.

214

'Order,' he said. 'Finish your story, Doc, and then maybe we can move on from this woman.'

'She told me she had sexual problems,' said Doc Morrissey. 'I'm afraid I . . . I forgot myself as well. She flung me off the couch. I practically broke my . . . er . . . well anyway it's still pretty painful.'

'Were you able to make an assessment of her character?' said Reggie.

'Yes,' said Doc Morrissey. 'She's a cow.'

'My community psychologist, and that is your considered opinion. She's a cow. I despair,' said Reggie. 'Anyway, Doc, enough of all this nonsense. Do you have any suggestion for improving morale?'

'Yes, I do,' said Doc Morrissey. 'Get rid of Deborah Swaffham.'

Reggie groaned.

'Right,' he said. 'I want a woman's view next. Maybe then we'll begin to get some sense. Any ideas, Joan?'

'Get rid of Deborah Swaffham,' said Joan.

'Oh my God,' said Reggie. 'Joan! You haven't been taking your clothes off with Deborah Swaffham as well, have you?'

'No, but Tony has.'

'Is this true, Tony?'

'No.'

'He's doing *Antony and Cleopatra* with her,' said Joan. 'She suggests going back to her room. What does my faithful husband say? "O'oh! Knock-out!" He's really into Deborah Swaffham. She's where it's at.'

'But she isn't,' said Tony. 'That's the whole point.'

'Children!' said Reggie. 'Why can't you be like David and Prue?'

'Please. Leave us out of it,' said David and Prue Harris-Jones.

They were sitting in identical armchairs, holding hands. They were wearing brown trousers and navy-blue sweaters.

'Self-satisfied prigs,' said Joan.

'Please,' said Reggie, banging his gavel. 'Can't we do anything except squabble and talk about Deborah Swaffham and fall asleep?'

'Jimmy can't help it,' said Lettice. 'He's worked his heart

215

out for you, and he's taken this Clive 'Lofty' Anstruther business very hard. Haven't you, darling?'

Jimmy launched himself into a fierce snore. Lettice kicked him with gentle affection.

Jimmy looked round the room in puzzled surprise.

'Some sort of meeting, is it?' he said.

'We're discussing the fact that you keep falling asleep,' said Reggie.

'Sorry. Missed that bit. Must have dropped off,' said Jimmy. Reggie buried his head in his hands and groaned.

'Please. Let's move on, away from Deborah Swaffham,' he said.

'Hear hear,' said Tony. 'It's Prick Tease City, Arizona, that one. O.K., so I did go back to its room. The cow wasn't even there.'

'No, I'm not ... er ... I'm not ... er ... not sure what I was going to say,' said Tom. 'Sorry. Carry on.'

'Tony would have,' said Joan. 'Pretending he was ill and not wanting any dinner. As if that would fool anyone.'

A vivid flush spread over the few bits of Tom's face that weren't covered by his beard.

'Tom!' said Linda. 'Oh my God. So that's why you said you were ill.'

'Oh my God,' said Reggie. 'Not you too! Perrins? Sodom and Gomorrah, more like.'

'She ... er ... she played football the other day,' said Tom. 'She's not a bad little striker actually. Pretty good distribution. She put through some fairly shrewd ...'

'Balls!' said Linda.

'Exactly,' said Tom. 'I went to her bedroom to discuss tactics before the hailstorm. That's all. No, Poggle chops, nothing happened.'

'No, she wasn't there, you poor sap.'

Reggie banged the gavel down on the table. It broke.

'Wonderful,' he said. 'Even the bloody gavel doesn't work.'

He hurled it across the room. It struck the mug marked 'Reggie', breaking it.

'A symbolic moment,' he said. 'Perrins is finished.'

Elizabeth stood up.

'I'm disgusted with you all,' she said. 'Haven't we better things to do than insult each other?'

'Exactly,' said C.J. 'Out of the mouths of babes and little children.'

'What the hell does that mean?' said Elizabeth.

'It's obvious,' said C.J.

'It's meaningless, you stupid fool,' said Elizabeth.

'Darling!' said Reggie.

Elizabeth stood in the middle of the room, and glared at them all in turn.

'You're behaving like fools,' she said. 'We've had a run of bad luck, that's all. A few petty thefts. One act of violence from our chef. And a cow who makes a fool of you. So are we to expel her because she's awkward? This nation is full of doctors who refuse to have patients on their lists because they're sick or old. It's full of homes for difficult children which refuse to take children because they might be difficult. Is it asking too much to hope that here we have somewhere which can actually cope with the people for whom it's intended? I suggest that tomorrow Deborah Swaffham goes to the sex clinic. It's what it's there for. I suggest that we fight all the harder for the success of this project we believe in, and reveal these set-backs for what they are. Pin-pricks. And now, could we at last have some sensible suggestions?'

She sat down. Reggie smiled proudly at her.

There was a moment's silence. It was broken at last by Jimmy.

'Well, why don't you have Red Rovers, you stupid Maltese bugger?' he said. 'Oh. Sorry. Dreaming.'

In the morning, Mr Cosgrove of the Highways Department called round.

'You're using a residential street to park cars for business purposes,' he said. 'The police could get you on obstruction. This is a bus route, Mr Perrin, and the magistrates are very protective towards bus routes. A purge on bald tyres also suggests itself. We only have to give the word.'

Reggie spread his arms in a gesture of helplessness.

'I know very little about these things,' he said. 'We're very unworldly here.'

'People have been laying off you,' said Mr Cosgrove. 'You've friends in the Town Hall. But your friends may not be able to help you much longer. The vultures are gathering over Oslo Avenue.'

The bed had been folded away. David Harris-Jones sat on a hard chair, behind a desk, and Deborah Swaffham curled foetus-like on the settee with her long legs tucked under her.

'I'm off-putting to men,' she said.

'Maybe it's because when they visit you, your room is empty,' said David Harris-Jones.

'That's awful of me, isn't it?' she said. 'But when I was inviting those men back to my room and things, I didn't intend to get all frightened and leave the room empty. It's just they give off this aura of sexual aggression. I bet people like Tony had hundreds of pre-marital conquests before they were married. And there's something a bit sinister in the way those older men go about it, Doc and D.J. and things.'

'C.J.'

'I'm hopeless with names. Oh God, what a mess.'

Deborah Swaffham began to cry. Real salty tears trickled from her grey-green eyes.

David Harris-Jones didn't intend to walk across to the settee and sit beside her. He didn't intend to put his arm round her. And he certainly didn't intend that the limb in question should fondle her consolingly.

Yet all these things happened.

Deborah Swaffham tried to smile. David Harris-Jones handed her a tissue and she blew her nose.

'I don't think I'd be frightened with you,' she said.

David Harris-Jones closed his eyes and felt himself sinking.

'You don't give off an aura of sexual aggression.'

'Oh, thank you. Thank you very much.'

'I bet you had hardly any pre-marital conquests before you were married.'

'Hardly any,' he agreed. 'It wasn't easy to be a Casanova in Haverfordwest.'

'I bet you get premature ejaculation and dementia praecox and things.'

'Well, I . . . er . . . thank you very much. Super.'

'Come to my room at lunchtime, David, and teach me not to be frightened.'

'Well, I . . . er . . . thank you very much. Super.'

David Harris-Jones went round to her room at lunchtime.

It was empty.

He stalked out angrily and found Prue standing grimly by the garden gate.

'Goodbye,' she said.

'Well, I . . . er . . . oh God. Oh God.'

At lunch Reggie noticed the absence of David and Prue Harris-Jones. He knew that Deborah Swaffham, at that moment chatting animatedly to a newly arrived yobbo, had seen David that morning.

He hurried round to Number Twenty-three.

He met them coming down the stairs. Prue was carrying a suitcase and little Reggie.

'We're splitting up,' said David and Prue Harris-Jones.

Reggie felt as if he'd been hit by a sandbag filled with lumps of old iron.

A taxi drew up, and Prue stepped into it, taking young Reggie with her. Nothing Reggie or David Harris-Jones said could persuade her to change her mind. David stared after the disappearing taxi with vacant eyes.

'She's gone,' he said.

He began to whimper.

'Prue!' he said. 'Prue!'

He stared at the forsythia bush.

'Prue!' he said. 'Oh Prue!'

No miracle happened. The bush did not turn into his wife.

Reggie put his arm on David's shoulder, felt David's knees begin to buckle, and hastily removed his arm.

'How can I live without Reggie, Reggie?' said David Harris-Jones.

Reggie stalked the litter-free streets of Botchley angrily. Along

Oslo Avenue he went, and down Bonn Close to the High Street. The purpose of his walk was to control his anger and direct it towards its natural target. Deborah Swaffham.

It began to rain, a sharp shower on a merciless wind. Large spears of rain.

There was just time for a drink at the Botchley Arms before closing time. Reggie ordered a pint of bitter and a whisky chaser. There weren't many people in the bar, just a few businessmen angling for some after-hours drinks, and two housewives chatting animatedly over their toasted sandwiches. They looked at Reggie as at some monster from outer space. This was the fiend who'd torn up Mrs Blythe-Erpingham's petition.

Anger welled up in Reggie.

Anger at Deborah Swaffham.

Anger at his staff.

Anger at himself.

Anger at Botchley.

Anger at the nation.

Anger at the Northern Hemisphere.

Anger at the whole damned, stupid world.

But anger above all at Thomas Percival Crankshaft, licensed to sell beers, wines and spirits.

Because at that very moment the landlord pushed his long, gaunt face towards Reggie and said, 'These cold wet days are bad for trade. People have sandwiches in their offices, in the dry.'

'What a miserable, mean, boring, petty-minded prick you are,' said Reggie.

He hastened home to beard Deborah Swaffham in her den.

He must treat her as a human being and try to help her.

It wouldn't be easy.

At that time she ought to be taking part in one of the manifold activities which were still continuing, despite the traumas. Whenever she ought to be in her room, she wasn't. Perhaps now, when she oughtn't to be, she would be.

She was.

*   *   *

Reggie sat in an old wicker chair that Elizabeth had picked up in one of the leading antique shops in Botchley.

'Anyone can be frightened of men, Deborah,' he said.

Deborah Swaffham walked casually round the room. She glanced at the print of bygone Botchley. Suddenly she pounced on the door, and locked it. She removed the key.

'I'm not frightened of men,' she said. 'All that was a blind to get to see you. You're the man with the power and things round here, and power fascinates me.'

'Give me that key, Debbie,' said Reggie.

Deborah Swaffham dropped the key between her breasts.

'Come and get it,' she said.

'I will not come and I am not going to get it,' said Reggie.

Deborah Swaffham sat on the bed and began to unzip her dress.

'Please, Deborah!' implored Reggie.

'Call me Debbiekins, Reggie.'

Reggie closed his eyes and counted ten.

'I'm not going to call you Debbiekins, and you will please call me Mr Perrin, Miss Swaffham,' he said.

He opened his eyes.

She had removed her dress. Her legs were long and shapely.

'You can't help being what you are,' said Reggie. 'But you can help me to help you to become different from . . .'

'You don't find me attractive,' said Deborah Swaffham. 'Nobody does.'

She began to take off her tights. Reggie hurried over to the window.

'You are attractive,' he said. 'You're gorgeous.'

He undid the sash and tried to lift the lower half of the window. It had stuck. He pushed desperately and at last it opened.

He breathed in the bracing spring air, and looked down at the flower bed in the front garden below.

Deborah Swaffham advanced towards him.

'I put you off, don't I?' she said.

'You're lovely,' he said, shoving her backwards on to her bed as gently as he could.

He ran to the window and began to climb out.

221

'You just don't fancy me,' he heard her sob. 'You hate me.'
'I find you irresistible,' he cried as he jumped out of the window.

Jimmy and his expeditionary force, trudging home from an afternoon of carrying shopping bags for old ladies, were surprised to see the leader of their community leap out of a bedroom window yelling, 'I find you irresistible'.

Reggie would have crashed into the flower bed, if his fall had not been broken by several small rose bushes.

Jimmy sent the guests rushing off to look for Doc Morrissey.

'I can't move,' Reggie groaned.

Doc Morrissey arrived with a makeshift stretcher.

'I need a doctor,' said Reggie.

'I am a doctor,' said Doc Morrissey.

There was a film of sweat on Reggie's brow.

'I mean . . .' he began feebly.

'Faith and trust, Reggie,' said Doc Morrissey.

Reggie nodded resignedly.

They put him on the stretcher, and carried him to Doc Morrissey's room. Doc Morrissey examined him carefully.

'Is anything broken?' said Reggie.

Doc Morrissey stood up with difficulty. His back creaked like unoiled rowlocks.

'You need a doctor,' he said.

Miraculously, nothing was broken. A sprained ankle, a twisted knee, a strained back, severe bruising and widespread abrasions —these things can be lived with.

Three guests left, declaring the place to be a shambles.

Reggie decided that he had no alternative but to ask Deborah Swaffham to leave. It was either the community or her.

He hobbled along the street to Number Seventeen. His face was covered with pieces of elastoplast. Painfully, a step at a time, he hobbled up the stairs. He limped along the corridor, knocked on her bedroom door, and hobbled in without waiting for a reply.

The room was empty.

222

None of them ever saw Deborah Swaffham again.

The April weather remained changeable, but the fortunes of Perrins were not. People crossed the road to avoid speaking to anyone connected with the community. They were banned from every pub in Botchley. Youths jeered at Jimmy's expeditionary force. Among them Jimmy noticed the three who had attacked the smaller youth in Lima Crescent. And the smaller youth.

Mr Dent paid them a visit.

'I've come to check your air vents,' he said awkwardly.

Reggie nodded slowly.

'Rats don't desert sinking ships any more,' he said. 'They condemn them for having irregularly spaced portholes and the wrong kind of hinges on the companionways.'

'I can't blame you for casting me as Judas,' said Mr Dent.

Reggie accompanied him on his inspection. He was still hobbling, but the little municipal official didn't seem to mind their slow progress.

'You still have friends in the Town Hall,' he said, peering at the bricks of Number Twenty-five. 'We're being as slow as we can, but the wolves are closing in on Oslo Avenue.'

'Thank you for warning me, anyway,' said Reggie.

When the inspection was over, they shook hands.

'That other Mr Dent you spoke of?' said Reggie. 'What happened to him?'

'He can't really cope with life. He's keeping a low profile, but he's there. A faint flicker of your work lives on in me. All is not lost, Mr Perrin.'

All is not lost.

Reggie took the farewell words of the likeable little official as his text for those difficult days.

He continued to keep up appearances, enduring his cigars and his regular doses of champagne. As soon as he was sufficiently recovered, he went to London and bought himself a whole new wardrobe of clothes including a velvet jacket which suited him to perfection.

'You know how I'm never happier than when I'm pottering

around in old trousers and pullovers,' he told his staff. 'Well, that's one more thing I've had to give up for the cause.'

All the activities continued. Paintings were painted, baskets were woven, roofs were thatched, songs were sung, sexual problems were mulled over, good deeds were done, ridiculous conversations were held on trains, and in the evenings they relished their bowls of apple gin and pear vodka, their protest songs and their acts of physical solidarity all the more for the fact that they were banned from every pub in Botchley.

It began to seem as if the community could gain new strength from its vicissitudes and new solidarity from its isolation.

All was not lost.

Not yet.

VIII

The Final Days

ONE DAY IN the middle of April, Reggie's bank manager sent for him. He had good news and bad news. The good news was that Reggie wasn't in the red. The bad news was that the level of his reserves was ninepence.

Reggie spoke eloquently about the ideals behind Perrins. He reminded the anxious financier about the amazing success of Grot, and opined that a similar success could shortly attend Perrins.

The bank manager lent him ten thousand pounds.

'It's a lifeline,' said Reggie in bed that night, as Elizabeth struggled to find the place in her book. 'It's a reprieve. Nothing more.'

'We mustn't waste a penny of it, Reggie,' said Elizabeth.

'I agree. Not a penny. Tomorrow we'll get a lawyer for McBlane.'

Elizabeth lost her place in her book just as she had at last found it.

'Don't be silly, Reggie,' she said. 'McBlane is blatantly guilty.'

'I agree' said Reggie. 'He's obviously blatantly guilty. But the press are going to be gunning for us. Peace Community Chef in Sally Ally *War Cry* Drunken Meat Cleaver Assault Scandal. We simply must put up some good mitigating circumstances, so that we don't look too ridiculous in the eyes of future guests.'

Reggie slid his arm under Elizabeth's back and kissed her nose.

'I have a plan,' he said.

She groaned.

*   *   *

The little public gallery at Botchley Magistrates' Court was crowded. So were the press seats.

The court had been built four years ago. It was panelled in light woods which had been stained to give an appearance of age and tradition. In the centre of the ceiling there was a sky-light, with a dome of frosted glass. There were three lay magistrates, two men and a woman. They looked decent enough to realise how absurd it was that they would hold the scales of justice in their unqualified hands.

At ten past eleven McBlane entered the court room. He looked gaunt and long-suffering. He was wearing a suit, and had left his boil plasters off in the interests of respectability, yet he still looked like a threat to a civilised community.

He took the book in his right hand, and repeated certain words after the clerk of the court. It is to be presumed that they were the oath, but they could equally well have been extracts from the timetable of the Trans-Siberian Railway.

He was asked if he was Kenny McBlane, chef, thirty-four, of Twenty-one, Oslo Avenue, Botchley.

His nods led the court to understand that he was.

Mr Hulme, a confident young man in a striped blue shirt with separate white collar, announced that his client was pleading guilty to the charge of committing grievous bodily harm upon Ethel Henrietta Lowndes, spinster, in the Tolbooth Hotel, Botchley, between nine and ten p.m. on the evening of Friday, March the thirty-first.

He also pleaded guilty to the charge of possessing an offensive weapon, to wit a meat cleaver.

He pleaded not guilty to the charge of using abusive language.

The case for the prosecution was brief and clear. Mr Hulme questioned P.C. Harris only about the abusive language.

'You say he used abusive language?' he said. 'What did he say?'

P.C. Harris consulted his notebook.

'This is a note I made at the time,' he said. 'I said to him, "What exactly has been going on here, then?" He replied, "Ye steckle hoo flecking clumpthree twinkoff".'

'Would you repeat that, please, officer?' said Mr Hulme.

'He said, "Ye steckle hoo flecking clumpthree twinkoff".'

226

'The court will draw their own conclusions from that,' said Mr Hulme. 'Now, did any further conversation ensue?'

'Yes, sir. Further conversation ensued,' said P.C. Harris. 'I said, "Lor, luv a duck, you're going to have to repeat that". He said, "Ye steckle hoo flecking clumpthree twinkoff".' I said, "Never mind that, my good man. What are you doing with that offensive weapon, to wit a meat cleaver?" He replied, "Flecking sassen achenpunk schlit yer clunge". I said, "I don't advise you to employ language like that to me", and he said, "Schpluff".'

'And this is his abusive language?'

'Yes.'

'But you don't know what it means?'

'No.'

'Then how do you know it was abusive?'

'It sounded abusive.'

'It sounded abusive. It seems to me, officer, that he used elusive language.'

'Yes, sir.'

'Are you aware that using elusive language is not an offence in English law?'

'Yes, sir.'

'No further questions.'

Miss Ethel Henrietta Lowndes was small and lined like an old tea cosy. Her left arm was in plaster. She had an extremely unfortunate effect on the magistrates. The effect was of hostility towards McBlane.

Mr Hulme only asked two questions.

'Did the accused speak to you?'

'Yes.'

'What did he say?'

'I don't know.'

After the prosecution's case had been completed, Mr Hulme called upon McBlane to take the stand.

'Would you please give the court your version of what transpired in the Tolbooth Hotel on the evening of Friday, March the thirty-first?' said Mr Hulme.

The magistrates leant forward, and McBlane began to speak. He spoke fast and incomprehensibly.

'Would you speak more slowly?' said Mr Hulme.

McBlane spoke slowly and incomprehensibly. The magistrates leant further forward.

'What's he saying?' asked the chairman.

'I don't know,' confessed the young lawyer.

An impasse!

'It seems to me that we're up a cleft palate with no paddle,' said the chairman of the magistrates.

'Absolutely!' murmured C.J. in the public gallery.

'There is one possibility,' said Mr Hulme. 'There's a man in this court who does understand my client. It's his boss, Reginald Perrin.'

'That is correct, sir,' said Reggie, standing up. 'I'm familiar with his speech, and furthermore I was evacuated to Glasgow during the war, to avoid the bombing. Awa hoo frae broch acha blonstroom doon the crangle wi' muckle a flangebot awa the wee braw schlapdoodles.'

'I don't understand,' said the chairman.

'No, but I do,' said Reggie.

The magistrates decided that they had no alternative. Reggie was warned of the dangers of perjury, and sworn in as interpreter.

McBlane began his version of events anew.

'He says he'd been drinking quite heavily, and his speech was becoming slurred,' said Reggie.

McBlane continued.

'The lady from the Salvation Army approached him,' said Reggie.

McBlane resumed his narrative, at considerable length.

'She asked him to buy the *War Cry*,' said Reggie. 'He told her how much he admired the publication's splendid mixture of information and entertainment. He said he'd buy the lot and then she could go home and put her feet up. She didn't understand a word of what he was saying.'

McBlane spoke earnestly.

'When he reached to take the pile of *War Crys*, she thought he was trying to steal them,' continued Reggie. 'In the ensuing misunderstanding, they were scattered. He reached for his wallet, but drew out the meat cleaver instead. In his semi-alcoholic confusion he didn't realise this.'

'What were you doing with the meat cleaver?' interpolated Mr Hulme.

McBlane looked round the crowded room for a moment before launching into his reply.

'The meat cleaver was blunt,' said Reggie. 'He was taking it to a friend who sharpens meat cleavers. He was expecting to meet this friend in the Tolbooth, but he didn't turn up.'

McBlane continued his narrative.

'McBlane saw that the lady, whose cause he had been attempting to help, was terrified and regarded him as a violent criminal,' said Reggie. 'For one brief moment all the frustrations of his misunderstood life welled up. He made one angry blow which unfortunately broke the lady's arm. He bitterly regrets it.'

McBlane nodded vigorously.

He was fined fifty pounds on the charge of grievous bodily harm, and fifteen pounds for being in possession of an offensive weapon.

The charge of using abusive language was dismissed.

There was widespread press coverage of the case of the lady from the Salvation Army and the mad Scottish chef with the meat cleaver. In spite of, or possibly because of, Reggie's intervention, much controversy was stirred up.

It was suggested in some quarters that Reggie's interpretation had been a pack of lies. The Salvation Army were not pleased. The vexed question of the lay magistracy was fiercely argued. Reggie was besieged by reporters. Several guests left, and many forward bookings were cancelled.

Reggie plucked up his courage and sacked McBlane. He told him that the community couldn't be associated with violence in any shape or form. He gave him a week's notice and a golden handshake of fifteen hundred pounds.

McBlane promptly disappeared.

In the morning, the papers carried widespread coverage of his sacking.

'They preach faith and love,' he was reported as saying, 'yet they sacked me for one offence, after I'd promised never to do it again.'

The journalists appeared to have no difficulty in understanding McBlane.

Reggie made a handsome donation to the Salvation Army, and informed the newspapers that he was willing to reinstate McBlane.

McBlane returned and resumed his duties, striking superb gastronomic form immediately.

Reggie went into the kitchen and welcomed him back with a firm handshake.

'Talking of handshakes,' said Reggie, 'obviously now you will return your golden handshake.'

McBlane examined his poultry knife, to see if its sharpness still met his exacting standards.

'Or then again it might be simpler to regard it as an advance on your salary,' said Reggie.

McBlane raised the knife in his right hand.

'Another possibility occurs to me,' said Reggie. 'Perhaps we could regard it as a bonus for your truly splendid cooking.'

McBlane, apparently satisfied with the sharpness of the knife, replaced it in its drawer.

'McBlane?' said Reggie.

McBlane turned and faced him.

'You can make yourself understood when you want to,' said Reggie. 'I know you don't like us and you feel that society has given you a raw deal, but I didn't choose to be born English and middle-class. And I did support you in court, whatever my motives. Please, McBlane. Talk to me so that I can understand.'

'Ye flickle mucken slampnach nae blichtig fleckwingle,' said McBlane.

Reggie wagged his finger sternly.

'A bit more of your jugged hare wouldn't come amiss,' he said.

Four clients departed. Seven forward bookings were cancelled. Four thousand pounds of Reggie's loan had gone.

Every hour of need throws up a hero, and this one was no exception.

The hero was Doc Morrissey.

The ageing medico called on Reggie in his sun-room, on the afternoon following McBlane's return, and plonked a milk bottle full of colourless liquid on his desk with an air of suppressed triumph.

'Taste it,' he said.

Reggie poured a minute measure, sipped it cautiously, then spat it out.

'It doesn't taste of anything,' he said.

Doc Morrissey sat back in his chair and stretched his legs like a somnolent dog.

'Precisely,' he said.

'Well, thank you very much,' said Reggie. 'It's just what I wanted.'

'Your sarcasm isn't lost on me, Reggie,' said Doc Morrissey.

He leapt slowly to his feet, and began to give an impression of a brilliant scientist, pacing around the sun-room like a tethered greyhound on heat.

'It can control entirely our supplies of insulin and adrenalin, our sugar level, and blood pressure,' he said. 'It can cure us of all our aggressions and neuroses. It can keep our bodies in a state of perfect chemical equilibrium. It can do everything you're trying to do here.'

Reggie lifted the bottle to the light and examined the liquid. It was absolutely clear and totally lifeless.

'Why have I never heard of this?' he said.

'It's a new invention,' said Doc Morrissey.

Reggie turned the bottle round and round slowly.

'British invention?' he asked.

'I invented it,' said Doc Morrissey.

Reggie handed the bottle back to its creator.

'You invented it?' he said at last.

'My antennae have become pretty sensitive to nuances since I started looking into this psychology lark,' said Doc Morrissey. 'I detect a lack of confidence in your attitude, Reggie, and it pains me.'

Reggie went to the window and looked out, drinking in the

231

white blossom on the apple trees and the delicate pink of the almond.

Four clients jogged by on the gravel path, followed by a breathless Tom.

Faith and trust.

'Are you prepared to stake your reputation on this working?' said Reggie.

'Without hesitation,' said Doc Morrissey. 'I bring it to you, Reggie, in your hour of need.'

Before dinner that evening, Reggie called a staff meeting. They drank coffee out of each other's mugs. It was six fifteen on a cool spring evening, and one section of the Calor Gas fire was on.

Reggie sat gavel-less at his card table and explained about Doc Morrissey's wonder drug. A milk bottle full of the stuff stood on the card table in front of him.

Doc Morrissey addressed them, his face touched with a becoming modesty. He said that the drug was made up of many ingredients with long names which would be meaningless to laymen. He proposed that the staff and guests should take regular doses of his cure-all.

'I'm sorry,' began Tom.

'So am I,' said Linda.

'I haven't said what I'm sorry about yet.'

'I'm sorry you're about to pontificate.'

'Well I'm sorry that you're sorry, Linda,' said Tom, 'but pompous Patterson is about to pontificate. Is it ethically desirable that we should expose people to this drug? Surely the real benefit that people get out of the place is the feeling that they have been involved in helping to create the improvements that have taken place in their mental adjustment to the environment as a consequence of the manifold activities that we provide?'

'We don't need to let them know they're taking it,' said Tony.

'That would disturb my sense of moral rectitude,' said Tom.

'We can't afford to look a gift horse in the mouth, or we may go down with a sinking ship,' said C.J. 'I didn't get where

232

I am today by looking gift horses in the mouth and going down with sinking ships.'

Jimmy patted Lettice's hand. The gesture was an admission that he also thought the ship was sinking, to join the flotilla of his past disasters. More ships had sunk under Jimmy than were afloat under the Royal Navy.

'Army put bromide in men's tea, subdue sexual feelings,' he said. 'Heat of battle, erotic fantasies dangerous. Chaps falling in love with their bayonet frogs, that sort of crack. Ends justify means. I'm for old thingummy's wonder whatsit.'

'Me too,' said Lettice.

'Good girl,' said Jimmy.

Reggie smiled.

'What are you smiling at?' said Elizabeth.

'Do you remember the English versions on Cretan menus?' said Reggie. 'Some of them had lamp chops, some had lamb shops, but we never actually found one that said lamp shops. Well, I was just thinking the same thing about Jimmy. He refers to Lettice as "good scout", "stout girl", and "good girl", but he never, well so far as I know he doesn't, and I can only go by what I've heard, never uses the fourth possible combination "stout scout".'

There was a stunned silence.

'Reggie!' said Elizabeth.

'Sorry,' said Reggie. 'It's a bit of a red herring at this important time, but you did ask me.'

He began to sweat.

Concentrate, Reggie. This is no good.

Elizabeth gave him a worried look and he smiled reassuringly.

'Yes, well,' said Doc Morrissey, somewhat needled by the red herring. 'Are there any further views on my wonder drug?'

'Is it really going to work?' said Tony. 'Because I've had the pineapple whisky syndrome up to here and I don't feel like scoring any more revolting drinks unless it's going to be Results City, Arizona.'

'We've never had pineapple whisky,' said Tom.

'Children,' said Reggie. 'Please! Tony does have a right to

ask if it's going to work, though. I mean, has it been tested at all?'

'A bit,' said Doc Morrissey.

'Ah! Good!' said Reggie. 'What on?'

Doc Morrissey glanced round the company uneasily.

'Pencils,' he said.

'Pencils?' said Jimmy incredulously.

'Pencils,' affirmed Doc Morrissey.

'What sort of pencils?' said C.J.

'H.B., C.J.,' said Doc Morrissey.

'I didn't get where I am today by drinking liquids that have only been tested on pencils,' said C.J.

'Did the pencils show a marked lack of aggression?' said Tony.

'Come come,' said Reggie. 'It's all too easy to be sarcastic. It's a failing that I've slipped into myself once or twice, but it really is terribly negative. I'm sure Doc Morrissey had his reasons. Tell us, Doc, what's the point in testing the liquid on pencils?'

'Not much,' said Doc Morissey. 'I didn't have any animals, though.'

'I'm glad,' said Tom. 'I'm against testing animals on principle.'

'Pencils are all right, though, are they?' said Linda. 'What about the poor old Royal Society for the Prevention of Cruelty to Pencils?'

'I think vivisection of Paper-mates is shocking,' said Joan.

'I was outraged to read about the propelling pencil that was trained to turn round and propel itself up its own sharpener,' said Tony.

'Please!' said Lettice.

She rose from her armchair and stared fiercely at the assembly. She had a kind of beauty at that moment, as the Grampian Mountains sometimes do, when touched by the evening sun.

'I think it's pathetic to listen to you all being sarcastic about pencils when Doc Morrissey has stuck his head on the block for the sake of the community,' she said. 'I'm happy to take a dose of the medicine now.'

She sat down, and there was an abashed silence, broken only

234

by the twanging of a spring deep in the tattered bowels of her chair.

'Stout scout,' said Jimmy, patting her hand with proprietary pride. 'Count me in too.'

Reggie banged on the table with his fist.

'Hands up all those prepared to test Doc Morrissey's magic potion.'

The hands of Doc Morrissey, Jimmy, Lettice, Linda and Elizabeth shot up.

'I may as well,' said David Harris-Jones. 'What does it matter if it kills me?'

'Oh get off your self-pitying backside and go and drag Prue back,' said Reggie.

'I happen to believe that she was justified,' said David Harris-Jones. 'I succumbed to craven weakness. It's Dolly Lewellyn from Pembroke Dock all over again.'

'Dolly Lewellyn from Pembroke Dock?' said Reggie. 'Who's she?'

'I don't really want to go into her, if you don't mind,' said David Harris-Jones. 'I didn't much want to at the time. One isolated lapse in a lay-by on the A1076 and I had to make thirteen visits to the outpatients department at Haverford-west General. I knew then that I wasn't destined to be a Casanova. I didn't have another woman from that day till I met Prue, and now I do this. Men are such fools. I . . .'

David Harris-Jones suddenly seemed to realise that he was talking to the collected staff of Perrins.

He blushed.

'Sorry,' he said. 'I . . . I didn't . . . er . . . realise. Sorry. Tragedy must have loosened my . . . er . . .'

'Go and find her, wherever she is,' said Reggie.

'. . . tongue,' said David Harris-Jones. 'I will. I'll go to her mother's and find her, wherever she is. Tomorrow. But first, I'll take Doc Morrissey's potion.'

'Thank you,' said Doc Morrissey, whose lone hand was still raised in a gesture of long-suffering patience. 'I wondered when we were going to get back to that.'

David Harris-Jones raised his hand. So did Elizabeth, Jimmy, Lettice and Linda.

Linda looked at Tom.

'I still have moral qualms,' said Tom.

'If Doc Morrissey's drug had been given to Jack the Ripper, his victims wouldn't have died,' said Reggie. 'Do you think they'd have had qualms?'

Tom raised his arm slowly.

'It was probably just the qualm before the storm,' he said. 'Joke. Joke over.'

Joan looked at Tony. Tony looked at Joan.

'Oh come on,' said Joan. 'It's May As Well Be Hung For A Sheep As Lambsville, Arizona.'

Joan and Tony raised their arms.

'Oh well,' said C.J. 'Never let it be said that I was the one ugly duckling that prevented the goose from laying the golden egg.'

'I promise you I'll never let that be said,' said Reggie.

C.J. raised his arm.

'And you?' said Elizabeth.

'Oh no,' said Reggie. 'Somebody has to remain totally un-affected in order to observe the results scientifically.'

Slowly, one at a time, all the hands were lowered.

'And what more natural than that that somebody should be McBlane?' said Reggie.

'Perhaps you'd like to be the first to drink,' said Doc Morrissey.

'Splendid,' said Reggie. 'Absolutely splendid.'

Trust and faith. He poured himself an inch of the potion.

'The dose is half a glass,' said Doc Morrissey.

'I want to leave enough for the others,' said Reggie.

'My resources are to all intents and purposes infinite,' said Doc Morrissey.

'Oh good,' said Reggie. 'Splendid.'

He drank his dose swiftly, and to his surprise he didn't fall down dead.

All the staff took their doses.

Reggie called a special meeting of the staff and the eighteen remaining guests. Doc Morrissey spoke about the drug. The staff took their second dose, and Reggie asked the guests for volunteers.

236

All eighteen volunteered.

Afterwards, they shared cigarettes and swapped yarns. A squash player with a drink problem sang Cherokee love songs. A time and motion man who'd investigated his own firm and been declared redundant as a result sang his own compositions, bitter-sweet laments for a less ruthless age. An overworked builder, known throughout his home town as Mañana Constructions, told an interminable story about the amazing prescience of his cat Tiddles. The manager of a dry-cleaner's in Northamptonshire went into the garden and made love to a lady computer programmer from Essex. Snodgrass was quite shocked when she came upon them, shivering from cold and ecstasy, naked and dewy under the suburban stars.

In the morning David Harris-Jones set off for Prue's mother's place in Exeter.

McBlane prepared twenty-nine portions of chicken paprika, and C.J. felt slightly queasy at breakfast.

Shortly after breakfast, both Tony and Joan felt slightly ill.

By half past ten, all three of them, plus Linda, had retired to bed with stomach trouble.

By twenty to eleven, stomach trouble was already a euphemism.

News of the outbreak spread rapidly. So did the outbreak. Was Doc Morrissey's potion to blame?

At five past eleven, Reggie confronted the inventive ex-medico in his upstairs room at Number Nineteen.

'Five members of my staff are ill,' he said. 'Three guests are feeling queasy.'

'Four,' said Doc Morissey. 'One just left me in a hurry.'

'Your potion's responsible,' said Reggie.

'It can't be,' said Doc Morrissey adamantly.

'How can you be so certain?' said Reggie. 'Tell me just what *was* in that liquid.'

A strange smile played on Doc Morrissey's lips.

'It was water,' he said.

'Water?'

'Plain simple water. You don't really think I'm skilful enough to create a drug that does all I claimed for it?'

237

'Well, I did wonder,' said Reggie.

'Oh you did, did you? I shall take that as a personal insult,' said Doc Morrissey.

Reggie sat on the couch.

'May I ask why you presented us with a wonder drug which was in reality water?' he asked grimly.

'Faith and trust. It was a psychological, not a medical experiment, Reggie, but I didn't want you to know it was psychological.'

'You concealed it for psychological reasons?'

'Exactly. But I didn't want you to know that the reasons were psychological. Psychology, Reggie. I wanted you to think that I was concealing the ingredients because I couldn't remember their medical names. When in fact I was concealing them because there weren't any. Pretty good, eh?'

'Excellent.'

'It was all lies, Reggie. Even the bit about the pencils. I just tossed that in to add authenticity.'

'It wasn't a conspicuous success.'

'I felt that. I wanted you all to gain confidence because you believed you'd taken a wonder drug.'

'I see. Then why is everybody ill?'

'I've no idea.'

Reggie looked Doc Morrissey straight in the eyes.

'I don't know how to put this without being mildly rude,' he began.

'Be mildly rude, Reggie. I can take it,' said Doc Morrissey, smiling the cheerily mournful smile of a man reconciled to his pessimism.

'Your medical reputation at Sunshine Desserts wasn't high. You weren't known as the Pasteur of the Puddings. This reputation wasn't enhanced when you were sacked from the British Medical Association for gross professional incompetence. It is possible that, far from inspiring us to confidence, your mystery panacea has provoked us to fear, that my staff are persuading themselves into illness. The obverse of the mind over matter syndrome, Doc. The dark side of the psychological moon.'

Doc Morrissey looked stricken.

'Mass auto-indigestion!' he said. 'It's possible.'

He clutched his stomach and groaned.

'Excuse me,' he said, and he hurried from the room.

The epidemic continued to spread

An accident prevention officer swooned on his way to the toilet, fell downstairs and broke his leg.

Reggie sent for a doctor. He arrived at twelve twenty-three. Eight members of the staff and nine guests were by this time ill.

'It's mass hysteria,' he told Reggie at the conclusion of his visit. 'I've known similar things in girls' schools, and what is this place but a girls' school where the pupils happen to be adult and predominantly male?'

'I see no similarity,' said Reggie.

'I only mean,' said the doctor, 'that the emotional soil is favourable to hysteria. Hysterical dysentery. Fascinating.'

'And what do you propose to do about it?' said Reggie.

'Ah, that,' said the doctor, as if treatment was an afterthought of little consequence.

He prescribed medicine for people on the National Health and a better medicine for the private patients.

'Thank you,' he said, as he set off down the garden path in a burst of tactless sunshine.

'Thank you,' he repeated, for all the world as if the epidemic was a charade laid on for his delectation.

The symptoms of dysentery are widely known and it is best to draw a veil over them. Suffice it to say that at one o'clock fifteen people were sitting down, and in only seven cases was it for lunch.

The seven lunchers tackled McBlane's hare terrine in circumstances that were far from propitious.

'Tidworth all over again,' muttered Jimmy cryptically.

All five attempted to make cheerful conversation over the chicken paprika.

'Worse than Tidworth,' declared Jimmy, still in gnomic vein.

It was a deflated trio that struggled with McBlane's superb lemon meringue pie.

Both men accepted coffee.

'Far worse than Tidworth,' asserted the gallant old soldier, rushing out to meet his Waterloo.

And so, when McBlane entered to collect the pudding plates,

he found Reggie in solitary state, defiant to the last, alone on the bridge of continence as his ship was scuppered about him.

'Thank you, McBlane,' said Reggie bravely to the pock-marked Pict. 'A superb luncheon.'

The bad luck that had assailed Perrins seemed determined to continue to the last.

It was bad luck that the doctor should have a drinking acquaintance who was a stringer for several national newspapers, so that Reggie spent much of the afternoon fending off the queries from the gentlemen of the press.

It was bad luck that it should be on this of all days that the environmental health officer came to review the sanitation arrangements. At first, all went well. He began with an examination of the kitchen. As luck would have it, McBlane was preparing a marinade for boeuf bouguignonne, and not powdering one of his extremities or recycling his boil plasters.

McBlane appeared to be, albeit unconsciously, an advocate of Cartesian dualism. I, McBlane, can be monumentally filthy, inventively scabrous and permanently itching. You, the kitchen, must be clean and gleaming at all times. In truth, however, it was emotion and not logic which created this spectacular dichotomy. McBlane loved his kitchen. Nay, more. He was in love with it. Romeo and Juliet, Antony and Cleopatra, McBlane and his kitchen, three great love stories, passionate, vibrant, ultimately tragic.

Violent death parted Romeo and Juliet. Violent death parted Antony and Cleopatra. The tragedy of McBlane's great love was different.

His passion was unrequited.

Why did the tough scion of Caledonia love his kitchen? Because he didn't dare give his love to a woman. Women would spurn him. He had too many skin diseases.

While the kitchen didn't love him, it didn't spurn him. It didn't know that he was covered in spots. McBlane, ever a realist, had settled for the kitchen.

The Environmental Health Officer didn't know any of this.

'Only one health hazard there,' he told Reggie. 'The chef.'

Their examination of the toilets was hampered by the fact that they were constantly occupied. The presence of people standing in agonised poses waiting to enter the toilets was explained away by Reggie as art therapy.

'They're representing the agony of the human struggle in modern dance,' he said.

'They look as if they're waiting to go to the toilet,' said the philistine official.

'You see what you're capable of seeing,' said Reggie.

The Environmental Health Officer told Reggie that he'd be turning in a very unfavourable report.

'What do you have to say to that?' he said.

'Excuse me,' said Reggie.

He spent three days in bed with hysterical dysentery.

The newspaper headlines included 'Hysteria Bug Hits Jinx Community', 'The Squatters of Botchley' and 'Perrin Tummy K.O.'s Commune'.

Undoubtedly, the hysterical dysentery would have caused many of the guests to leave, if they hadn't been too ill with hysterical dysentery.

Gradually, the staff and guests recovered. Four guests did leave.

A post-dysentery evening was planned, in which they would drink from communal bowls of Andrews Liver Salts and Bisodol.

Reggie let himself out of the side door and then remembered that he was banned from every pub in Botchley.

He walked down Oslo Avenue, and turned left into Bonn Close, a sinister figure with the collar of his raincoat turned up against the penetrating drizzle of early May.

He turned right into Ankara Grove, went down the snicket to the station, and took the narrow pedestrian tunnel under the tracks. It dripped with moisture and smelt of urine.

He plunged into the streets of the council estate, on the wrong side of the tracks. Here the houses were poor and badly maintained. Every possible corner had been cut, in the interests of persuading the inhabitants that they were inferior, so that they would accept their role in society and commit the vandalism that was expected of them, thus confirming the people on the right side of the tracks in their belief that they were right to stick these people in council estates on the wrong side of the

241

tracks. Thus mused Reggie bitterly as he slipped through the dark, inhospitable streets.

Beyond the housing estates came the damp backside of Botchley, a rump as pitted and pocked as McBlane's. The street lamps were widely spaced and feeble, dim as a Toc H cabaret, their faint yellow glow deepening the darkness of the night around them. Here the streets were like teeth—old, stained, badly maintained, and full of gaps. It was the sort of area that film companies use for their blitz sequences. Even the potatoes on the tumble-down, refuse-ridden allotments were suffering from planning blight.

At the far end of these streets lay the Dun Cow.

Reggie entered the public bar, a tiny, ill-lit, raucous place, where the beer tasted as if several elderly dogs had moulted in it.

But it had one great advantage. He wasn't known here, and so the ban would not be imposed. He ordered a pint and prepared to assault it.

'Holy God, it's Mr Perrin himself,' said a familiar Irish voice.

Reggie turned to find himself gazing into the agreeable features of Seamus Finnegan, the former navvy whom he had plucked from obscurity to become Admin Officer at Grot.

'Seamus Finnegan!' said Reggie.

'If it isn't, some bastard's standing in my body,' replied that worthy.

'Terrible beer,' said Reggie.

'It is that,' said Seamus Finnegan. 'Undrinkable.'

'Have another?'

'Thank you, sir.'

They sat in a corner, watching two youths in filthy jeans throwing inaccurate darts at a puffy travesty of a board.

'It's good to see you, Seamus,' said Reggie.

'Thank you, sir,' said Seamus.

'Come on, Seamus. We're friends. Less of the "sir".'

'Thank you, sir, but your insistence that I don't call you sir is based on a false premise.'

'What premise is that?' said Reggie.

He closed his eyes, shut his nose, and forced a sizeable draught of beer down his throat.

'You're thinking "Poor Seamus. I brought him out from the obscurity of the Climthorpe Slip Relief Feeder Road, a simple tongue-tied Irishman from the land of the bogs and the little people, I rescued him from the swollen underbelly of that fat old sow that is urban deprivation, I made him Admin Officer in the hope that his simple Irish idiocy would send the whole Grot empire tumbling about our ears, but with the true contrariness of Erin he proved to be a genius, and then I disbanded Grot, leaving poor old Seamus to return to the drunken monosyllabic slime of the road works, his only companions simple oafs, and the occasional inarticulate driver of an articulated lorry, back in the gloomy underbelly of the aforementioned sow of urban deprivation from which I had so irresponsibly rescued him",' said Seamus Finnegan.

Reggie gave a sickly grin.

'Well, yes, I suppose I was thinking something along those lines, if not in so many words,' he said. 'I'm terribly sorry, Seamus. It was a dreadful thing to do.'

'I own eight companies,' said Seamus Finnegan.

'I . . . Well, that's marvellous, Seamus. That's marvellous. So . . . er . . .'

'What am I doing drinking in this dismal hell-hole?'

'Well . . . yes.'

'It would be facile to suggest that success has not changed Seamus Finnegan. Success, sir, he's a feller that changes everything. But it doesn't mean that I don't have time to slip away from my spiritual Athenaeum and while away an idle hour with the mates of my erstwhile existence. To me, sir, class distinction is a horse of dubious character, a non-runner, a late withdrawal, as the actress said to the Catholic bishop.'

'Quite.'

'Same again, sir?'

'I'd rather a whisky, Seamus.'

'Yes indeed. A noxious brew.'

Seamus went to the bar, passed a few brief words with the mates of his erstwhile existence, and returned with two large whiskies.

'Seeing you here, Mr Perrin,' said Seamus Finnegan, as they clinked glasses, 'did not lead me to believe that you had fallen

243

upon evil days. I don't judge a man from his surroundings. His innate character, he's the feller I look for. The old essential nature of the unique and individual homo sapiens, he's the man for me.'

'I am justly rebuked,' said Reggie with a wry grin.

One of the darts players farted. There was loud laughter. Life went on. So did Seamus Finnegan.

'However,' he said, 'curiosity is a frisky nag. She's liable to sweat up in the paddock, that one. And, sir, curiosity rather than social stereotype compels me, in my turn, to ask of you, "What are *you* doing drinking in this dismal hell-hole?".'

Reggie described Perrins and its situation as best he could. Seamus Finnegan's amiable ruddy face expressed shock and alarm, but when asked why, his garrulity vanished, and he displayed all the characteristics of an unusually introverted clam.

Next morning, at ten past nine, Seamus Finnegan called at Number Twenty-one, Oslo Avenue.

'Hello!' said Reggie. 'To what do I owe this pleasure?'

'Dark deeds,' said Seamus Finnegan.

Reggie led him into the sun-room. Seamus produced a briar pipe of great age, filled it with foul tobacco at his leisure, lit it, took a cautious puff, seemed pleased and spoke.

'You remember my colleagues of last night?' he said.

'The mates of your erstwhile existence?'

'Them's the fellers. They're right villians, them lot. Well, they've been having enquiries from some yobbos and ruffians with a view to duffing up a certain community that has aroused resentment.'

Reggie's eyes met Seamus's, and a cold fear stabbed him. 'Perrins?'

'Yes.'

'When?'

'Saturday night. It's only rumour, but that's one horse you can never write off.'

'Thank you for warning me, Seamus.'

*   *   *

Reggie called a staff meeting for six thirty that evening.

At half past three, David Harris-Jones arrived back, without Prue. He was starving, and Reggie led him into the kitchen.

McBlane was upstairs, taking a rare opportunity to put his athlete's feet up, but Reggie managed to rustle up some left-overs.

'I got as far as Paddington, and nemesis overtook me,' said David Harris-Jones, between mouthfuls. 'I spent twenty-nine hours in one of the toilet cubicles. Can you imagine spending twenty-nine hours in the cubicle of a Western Region toilet?'

'The plight is horrific, the region immaterial,' said Reggie.

'Every graffitus is etched on my memory,' said David Harris-Jones, shuddering at the enormity of the obscenities.

'It was hysterical dysentery,' said Reggie. 'It's odd that you should get it in isolation like that.'

'The seeds of hysteria were sown before I left.'

When David had almost seen off another mouthful, Reggie asked him how things stood with Prue.

'She didn't believe me,' he said. 'She said I'd been visiting. . . that woman. I quoted the graffiti as proof. They seemed to make matters worse.'

Reggie nodded understandingly.

'Would you ... er ... would it be asking too much, Reggie? Yes, of course it would,' said David Harris-Jones.

'What?'

'Would you ... no, it's stupid to even ... but what can I do?'

'David!'

'Would you ring Prue and tell her it's all true, and I'm feeling absolutely ... er ...'

'All right,' said Reggie.

'... suicidal. Oh, thank you, Reggie,' said David Harris-Jones.

Reggie told Prue the full story of the hysterical dysentery.

'Well?' said David Harris-Jones, who had been hovering near the phone like an injured peewit. 'What did she say?'

'Very encouraging,' said Reggie. 'She said I must think she's a complete fool and rang off.'

David Harris-Jones groaned.

'What's encouraging about that?' he said

245

'It wasn't what she said,' explained Reggie. 'It was the way she said it! She was icily cold.'

David Harris-Jones looked at Reggie in dismay.

'Let's go back in the kitchen and have a beer,' said Reggie.

David followed him less out of enthusiasm than out of an inability to formulate an alternative plan. Reggie got two beers out of the fridge.

'Don't you recognise Prue's anger for what it is?' he said. 'Cheers.'

'No. Cheers. What it is?'

'Love.'

'Love?'

'Fool that she is, she loves you.'

'I never want to set eyes on her again.'

'You see. You love her too.'

David Harris-Jones sipped his lager angrily. His concept of his own uniqueness was insulted by this revelation of how true the most dismal clichés of love are.

'A lesson in love from old Uncle Perrin,' said Reggie. 'You make too much of your quarrels because you quarrel too little. Tony and Joan make too little of theirs because they quarrel too much. There are six marriages in this place. Four will survive. Two may not. Gaze at Uncle Reggie's crystal ball.'

David Harris-Jones managed a faint smile. Reggie's lecture across the kitchen table continued.

'Your marriage will survive because you love each other,' he said. 'Tony and Joan's will survive because they don't. Elizabeth and I will survive because we've survived so much already. Jimmy and Lettice will survive because there's no alternative. McBlane and his kitchen may not survive . . .'

'McBlane and his kitchen?'

'A great if one-sided love. There's a strain of desperation in McBlane, David, and one day he'll seek a response from his kitchen—it may be this kitchen, it may be another—which it's unable to give. All that talent, and no chance of happiness, David.'

'And the sixth marriage?'

'Tom and Linda. I fear that won't survive, because Linda will expect more than Tom can give, and Tom will expect less than Linda can give. Bear one thing in mind about my predictions, David.'

'What?'

'Nobody can safely predict anything about anyone. Now, to more serious matters.'

'More serious matters! It wouldn't be more serious to me if this place was going to be razed to the ground by hordes of Vandals and Visigoths.'

'It is.'

Once again, the staff gathered and drank out of each other's mugs.

Reggie explained the threat.

It was decided that they had three alternatives.

They could fight.

They could give in.

They could go to the police.

They soon decided—possibly against the wishes of David Harris-Jones and Tom—that they couldn't give in.

There was widespread reluctance to get involved with the police even if it would have been of any use on the hearsay of one eccentric Irishman.

Resistance was declared to be the order of the day.

Adam and Jocasta would be sent to the Perrymans' for the night, and McBlane wouldn't be included in the action, as it was doubtful whether killing eight yobbos with a meat cleaver would come into the category of justified self-defence.

Jimmy appeared to regret this decision.

The next question to be decided was the selection of a leader of the defence.

'You, of course,' said Tom.

'No,' said Reggie. 'This is a specific task. It calls for a natural leader. A man who seeps authority from every pore. Need I say more?'

'I don't think so,' said C.J.

'I refer, of course, to Jimmy,' said Reggie.

'Me?' said Jimmy. 'Good God.'

'Hear hear,' said Doc Morrissey.

'Was that "hear hear" to the appointment of Jimmy, or "hear hear" to "Good God"?' asked Reggie.

'I don't honestly know,' said Doc Morrissey. 'I just thought it was about time I spoke.'

Jimmy was elected defence supremo by ten votes to one.

'Elected unanimously,' declared Reggie.

'Hardly unanimously,' said C.J.

'Jimmy voted against himself,' said Reggie. 'A mere formality.'

'Didn't actually,' admitted Jimmy. 'Couldn't. Frankly, between you, me, gatepost, goodwill expeditions, fish out of water. Defence of H.Q., repulsion of loutish elements, bingo, message received, can do, wilco, roger and out.'

'Splendid,' said Reggie. 'So one person voted against Jimmy. I wonder who that was, don't you, C.J.?'

'I certainly do,' said C.J.

'Now,' said Reggie. 'If anyone wants to leave, we must let them. Does anyone?'

Linda gave Tom a meaningful glance. He looked straight ahead, resolutely.

'I don't want to leave,' said David Harris-Jones. 'Heaven forbid. Leave you in the . . . er . . .'

'Lurch.'

'Exactly. My word, no. But . . .'

'Ah!' said Reggie.

'No,' said David Harris-Jones. 'Wait. It's . . . well . . . Prue. I think I . . . er . . . ought to . . . er . . .'

'Go and bring her back in time to join the defences, because we need everyone we can get. Good thinking, David. Like your style,' said Reggie.

'Yes, well . . . er . . . yes,' said David Harris-Jones.

'Right,' said Reggie. 'It's now Wednesday. We have just three days. We'll have another meeting tomorrow night. I trust that by then Jimmy will have come up with a plan.'

'What about the guests?' said Elizabeth.

There was a lengthy silence. Everyone had forgotten all about the guests.

Later that evening, Reggie told the fourteen remaining guests of the threat to the community. They had three alternatives.

248

They could stay, they could leave, or they could leave for the weekend and return when the threat was over.

Three voted to leave, three to stay and eight to go away for the weekend.

When they discovered that the other eleven guests would be leaving, the last three decided to go away as well.

At half past six the following evening, the staff met in the living room of Number Seventeen for the last time.

They didn't know it was the last time.

They drank out of each other's mugs for the last time.

Some of them may have suspected that it was the last time.

For the first time, it was warm enough not to light the Calor Gas fire.

Perrins had survived one autumn, one winter and one spring. It would die just as its first summer began.

This time there were only ten members of staff present, as David Harris-Jones had gone to Exeter.

This time it was Jimmy who conducted the meeting. Reggie sat at his right hand.

At Jimmy's request, the chairs of the other eight had been rearranged in three rows, like an armchair rugby scrum, facing Jimmy, who stood behind the card table with a baton in his hand, even though there was no plan at which he could point it.

If Jimmy felt any dismay as he looked down at his puny forces, he didn't show it.

'Good evening,' he began. 'Purpose of exercise, repulsion of yobbo invaders. Tell you my thought processes.'

'That should be good for fifteen seconds,' whispered Tony, from the second row of the armchair scrum.

Lettice, who was in the hooker's position, turned round furiously, and hissed, 'Sssssh!'

'Element of surprise essential,' said Jimmy. 'Must assume Finnegan has kept mouth shut. Enemy doesn't know we know they're attacking. Where will enemy expect us to be?'

'Inside,' said Elizabeth from the loose head position.

'Exactly,' said Jimmy. 'So where will we be?'

'Outside,' said Doc Morrissey from the middle of the back row.

249

'Precisely. In garden.'

'They'll see us if we're in the garden,' said Tony.

'Disguised,' said Jimmy.

'Ah!' said C.J.

'Precisely,' said Jimmy.

'What as?' said Joan.

'Exactly,' said Jimmy.

They looked at him expectantly. He didn't fail them.

'First thought, molehills,' he said.

'Disguised as molehills?' said Reggie.

'Yes.'

'Molehills aren't big enough.'

'Precisely,' said Jimmy triumphantly, as if their agreement over the unsuitability of molehills would clinch his military reputation for posterity. 'Exactly what I thought. Next thought. Compost heaps. Ten of us. Heap in each garden. Two bods in each heap.'

Jimmy's ragged army stared up at him in astonishment.

'I'm told that I keep saying, "I didn't get where I am today by whatever it might be",' said C.J. 'Well, I'm sorry. I'll endeavour not to use the phrase in future. However, if I didn't get where I am today by any one thing above all other things that I didn't get where I am today by, it must be by being disguised as half a compost heap.'

'Compost heap, pros and cons,' said Jimmy, as if he hadn't heard a word that C.J. had said. 'Credit side, big enough, nice and warm, element of surprise when attacked by compost heap considerable. Debit side. Smelly, bad for morale, normally in back gardens, field of vision limited, delay in getting out of compost heap considerable. Careful consideration, but, on balance, thumbs down.'

Nobody demurred.

'Better idea, trees,' said Jimmy. 'Let them approach house, take them in rear, terrify them, nail the sods.'

If the staff had looked towards Reggie to nip the idea of being disguised as trees in the bud, they were disappointed. His attitude seemed to be that, having appointed his master supremo, he would stand by any plan that he might make.

On reflection, Jimmy's mention of compost heaps had been

250

a master stroke, for it made being disguised as trees seem almost sensible by comparison.

Friday morning was spent preparing themselves as trees. Lettice was i/c tree making.

Shortly after lunch Reggie answered the door to find Mrs C.J. with two suitcases.

'I want to be with him,' she said. 'You can't understand that, can you?'

'With difficulty,' said Reggie. 'I wouldn't want to, but I'm not his wife.'

He put the cases down in the hall, and escorted Mrs C.J. into the living room.

'I simply don't care about the monastic restrictions,' said Mrs C.J.

'Monastic restrictions?' said Reggie.

'The celibacy. The dormitories. The sexual segregation.'

Mrs C.J. sat on the settee, with a sigh.

'I'm pooped,' she said.

Reggie stood facing her, in some perplexity.

'C.J. told me at Christmas,' said Mrs C.J.

'Ah!' said Reggie. 'Good for him. Very wise. What exactly did he tell you at Christmas?'

'About the monastic restrictions.'

'Ah! Let me get this right. C.J. told you at Christmas that we live in segregated dormitories and lead a life of celibacy?'

'Yes. You do, don't you?'

'What? Oh yes. Yes. Of course we do. Or rather did. Yes. We gave it up on Wednesday. Because of the attack. No doubt C.J. was going to write to you, after the attack.'

Reggie slumped into a chair.

'What attack?' said Mrs C.J.

Jimmy entered, disguised as an aspen.

'This is Mrs C.J.,' said Reggie. 'Mrs C.J., Jimmy.'

'Hello,' said Jimmy. 'Can't shake hands. I'm an aspen. Not bad, eh Reggie?'

'Excellent,' said Reggie. 'You're a dead ringer for a slightly mangy aspen.'

It was Mrs C.J.'s turn to look perplexed.

251

'Could you ask C.J. to come in?' said Reggie. 'Don't tell him why. Let it be a lovely surprise.'

'Will do,' said Jimmy.

Jimmy shuffled out of the room, shedding twigs on the carpet as he went. Reggie explained to Mrs C.J. about the attack, and Jimmy's master plan.

Soon C.J. entered. He went white when he saw Mrs C.J., and stood rooted to the spot, as if he was already an aspen.

'Good God,' he said. 'I mean, "Wonderful to see you, darling".'

He embraced his wife.

'You looked horrified, C.J.,' she said.

'I am slightly,' said C.J. 'There's a nasty business happening on Saturday.'

'I've told her,' said Reggie.

C.J. sat beside Mrs C.J. on the settee.

'That was the only reason I looked horrified,' he said.

'C.J. doesn't want you mixed up in our arboreal deception,' said Reggie.

'Precisely, Reggie,' said C.J.

Mrs C.J. melted sufficiently to let C.J. put an arm round her.

'I presume you were going to write after the attack to tell me that the monastic restrictions had been lifted.'

'Monastic restrictions?' said C.J. 'What monastic restrictions?'

'The monastic restrictions of our community, that you told Mrs C.J. about at Christmas,' said Reggie. 'How until Wednesday we lived a strictly celibate life in segregated dormitories.'

'Oh, *those* monastic restrictions,' said C.J.

Jimmy re-entered, minus his costume, plus Lettice.

'Top-hole aspen my clever Lettice rustled up, what?' said Jimmy.

'A.1.,' said Reggie.

'You're being fitted for your box hedge at five, C.J.,' said Lettice.

'I know,' said C.J. glumly.

Lettice was introduced to Mrs C.J.

'How did you cope with the monastic restrictions?' said Mrs C.J.

'Monastic restrictions?' said Lettice.

252

Mrs C.J. burst into tears.

Reggie ushered Jimmy and Lettice out of the room.

When they were alone, Mrs C.J. hit C.J. across the cheek.

He stood up, holding his nose in his hands.

There was no blood.

'You lied to me,' said Mrs C.J. 'You hate me.'

'I love you,' said C.J., standing at the french windows, looking over the bursting verdure of the garden. 'I lied to you because I didn't want you to come here till I'd finished my masterpiece.'

'Masterpiece?' said Mrs C.J. scornfully. 'What pack of lies is this?'

'Every evening, when the day's work is done, I retire to my room and write,' said C.J. 'My book will do for ants what *Watership Down* did for rabbits.'

He returned to the settee, and turned to face his wife.

'It's the only reason I didn't send for you,' he said. 'I could never have done my masterpiece and been with you. It would have been the last straw that broke the camel's hump.'

'What's this masterpiece of yours called?' said Mrs C.J.

'I've tried everything,' said C.J. '*Watership Ant, Watership Hill, Charley's Ant, Lord of the Ants, Ant of the Lords, Ant of the Flies, Ant of the Rings, No Sex please we're Ants, No Ants please we're British.*'

'Show me your masterpiece,' said Mrs C.J.

'You still don't believe me, do you?' said C.J.

He took Mrs C.J. to his room and showed her his masterpiece.

The fateful day dawned warm and sunny, innocent and smiling. They all felt foolish, as they prepared their disguises under Lettice's supervision. It wasn't the sort of day on which it was easy to believe in attacks by bands of marauding yobbos. Mrs C.J. was determined to stay at her husband's side, and it was decided that they should both be part of the same box hedge.

Shortly after lunch, David Harris-Jones arrived with Prue.

'We're reconciled,' they said. 'We've come back to help in the defence of our community. Little Reggie's safe in Exeter.'

Prue looked radiant. David's radiance was tempered by fear.

'Unfortunately you haven't time to disguise yourselves as trees,' Reggie told them.

'Trees?' said David and Prue Harris-Jones.

Reggie explained the plan, and it was decided that they should stay in the house and act as reserves, in case any invaders broke through the leafy cordon.

By the time Linda drove Adam and Jocasta to the Perrymans', the sunshine had gone and there were menacing clouds.

It became much easier to believe in the threatened attack.

Jimmy had gambled on the invaders not attacking before dusk. For, while Lettice had done extremely well in the short time available, it has to be admitted that the deception would not have been effective in daylight.

As dusk gathered, and the rain began, Jimmy armed his band with clubs disguised as branches.

'I hope we don't intend to be violent,' said Tom.

'Of course not,' said Jimmy. 'But these people are louts. They're the dregs. It's the only language they understand.'

'We're supposed to be a community of peace and love,' said Tom.

'That's why we've got to nail the bastards,' said Jimmy.

He led his band of trees, shrubs and hedges to their stations.

Afforestation took place. The night began. The rain grew heavier.

Every twenty minutes a W288 slid past, a pool of golden light in the murk.

Ten o'clock, and not a yobbo in sight. A flock of starlings tried to roost in Joan. Somewhere, a larch sneezed.

The evening grew colder. The rain grew harder. They weren't coming.

They might come after the pubs closed.

They didn't.

At twenty to twelve, the ridiculous, freezing, sodden, pointless vigil was rudely interrupted. Splitting the silence of the night came a screeching of brakes. A crashing of metal. A scream.

Reggie began to run.

'Phone for an ambulance, David,' he yelled into the house.

'Stay in your places,' called Jimmy. 'It's a diversion.'

'It's an accident,' said Reggie.

People converged on the junction of Oslo Avenue and Bonn Close.

So did trees, shrubs and a box hedge.

Both cars had horribly mangled bodies.

Reggie bent down to talk to the driver of one of the cars.

'It's all right,' he said. 'The ambulance is on its way.'

The driver opened his eyes, saw a length of box hedge scurrying down the road, overtaken by a hawthorn yelling, 'Let me through. Let me through. I'm a doctor', and fainted.

Later that night, they all sat in the living room and shared a communal bowl of prune whisky. The smokeless fuel roared brightly in the hearth.

Miraculously, nobody had been seriously hurt. They had returned home, feeling foolish. Defoliation had occurred.

Now the feeling of foolishness had given way to a sense of relief. They were dry and warm and united by strong bonds of shared experience. Many of their relationships were informed with true affection, and the others with a very adequate facsimile.

Joan sang excerpts from Gilbert and Sullivan, and everybody joined in the choruses.

To everyone's astonishment, Tony blushed. Nobody could recall his blushing before.

'Would you like me to hit *Richard the Second*, Act Two, Scene One, and score the old John of Groat speech?' he asked.

'Please,' came the chorus.

'It's John of Gaunt actually,' said Tom.

'Same difference,' said Tony, and he launched himself into it.

He declaimed with rare fervour, and only made one small verbal slip, when he said:

'This blessed plot, this earth, this realm, this England,

This knock-out, teeming womb of royal kings.'

Everyone agreed that his rendition was splendid. 'Top-hole' was Jimmy's chosen epithet, and a man would have had to have been a veritable churl to have quarrelled with the old warrior's assessment.

'To try and follow that would be a case of the morning after the Lord Mayor's show before,' said C.J., 'but ... er ... well ...'

He glanced at Mrs C.J. She nodded eagerly.

'I wondered if you'd like to hear a short extract from my book on ants,' he said.

'Book!' exclaimed Elizabeth.

'On ants!' cried her equally surprised partner.

C.J. smiled at them all benevolently.

'I know what you're going to say,' he said.

'You didn't get where you are today by writing books about ants,' they thundered in unison.

'True,' said C.J. 'But on the other hand it's never too late for a leopard to change horses in mid-stream.'

He went to fetch his manuscript. Soon he returned, clutching a large sheaf of papers.

He sat down. His audience adopted the cautious pose of self-conscious embarrassment that people have when listening to the literary efforts of their friends—a determination not to be patronising mixed with a conviction that it's going to be dreadful.

He coughed.

'Every evening, throughout the time of the year that is called Nith,' he read, 'which comes after Glugnith but before the festival of Prengegloth, the ants of the Hill of Considerable Fortitude sit around and tell stories. And listen to them too, because if nobody was listening it would be pretty silly to bother.'

C.J. paused to chuckle, then resumed his narrative.

' "Tell us a tale, Great Ant Ogbold," squeaked little Squilblench. "Tell us the one about the journey of Thrugwash Blunk."

' "Okey dokey, then," said Great Ant Ogbold, smiling like a Cheshire cheese. "After all, it is Nith, and if we can't let our hair down during Nith, then things have come to a pretty pass.

' "In the dark years before anybody believed in the Great Sludd," he began, "a little ant named Thrugwash Blunk went on a journey.

' "His daddy didn't want him to go.

' " 'Rolling stones butter no parsnips,' he warned him.

' "But Thrugwash Blunk went anyway, and got lost in the land of Threadnoddy, where there was a big fog, and he went round and round in eccentric circles.

' "Then he met a conceited owl, who thought he was the cat's whiskers and the bee's knees." '

C.J. chuckled again.

' " 'Help me, owl, for I don't know where I am,' said Thrugwash Blunk, 'and I didn't get where I am today by not knowing where I am.'

' " 'I'll tell you where you're at,' said the conceited owl. 'No sweat, baby.'

' " 'Oh, thank you, owl,' cried Thrugwash Blunk, and suddenly, without any warning . . ." '

The yobbos came.

There was the almost musical sound of breaking glass from several directions. Everybody leapt to their feet and stood irresolute, not knowing in which direction to turn.

Everywhere there was crashing and shouting.

The first yobbo burst in through the curtains, yelling fiercely like a demented apache.

Everyone looked to Jimmy for leadership. This was his greatest moment.

At first he looked lost, still in the world of ants. Then he pulled himself together and issued his orders. They were a model of succinctness, if not of precision.

'Get the bastards,' he roared.

All was confusion. Youths appeared from all directions. The staff scattered in all directions.

C.J. hurried towards the front door, clutching his masterpiece. He was too late. Two youths rushed in from the hall. One of them grabbed him and the other pulled the pages from his grasp. They had no idea what they were destroying. It was enough that he wanted it not to be destroyed.

The air was full of sheets of paper. Epic set pieces of ant life were ripped asunder, as C.J. and his assailants lurched around the living room.

David Harris-Jones ran from the dining room and up the stairs, chased by a youth with a knife. An older man followed, grappling with Reggie.

Elizabeth crept out of the kitchen, McBlane's pestle raised above her head, but just as she was about to bring it down on the head of the man who was grappling with Reggie, another

257

man pulled her off, twisted her arm, grabbed the pestle, and knocked her senseless.

Tony, Joan and Doc Morrissey were conducting a running battle upstairs, in and out of the bedrooms.

In the kitchen, Prue, Linda and Mrs C.J. were fighting off the invaders like cats.

On the settee, three men were trying to hold Lettice down. She was screaming and yelling, thrashing around like a dying whale.

A huge man with a twisted nose walked casually into the living room and felled C.J. with one casual blow. He lay prone among the ruins of his book.

David Harris-Jones ran downstairs and collided with Tom, who was running upstairs. They crashed down the stairs together and landed in a heap at the bottom, with Tom on top of David.

'Get off me,' hissed David Harris-Jones, but Tom was unconscious.

David Harris-Jones pretended to be unconscious as well.

A very tall young man kicked Tom casually, as he passed him on his way upstairs. Tom didn't stir.

He kicked David Harris-Jones, and David groaned. The young man kicked him until he passed out.

Reggie and the older man were wrestling ferociously on the floor of the living room.

Jimmy crawled over the carpet behind the heaving settee, a vase in his hands. He stood up, raised the vase, and aimed it at the biggest of Lettice's assailants. Lettice made one last titanic heave which propelled her to the top of the writhing heap. Jimmy brought the vase down on the back of her head. The vase shattered and she passed out. Jimmy looked down aghast at what he had done.

Upstairs, Joan locked herself in a cupboard. Doc Morrissey lay gasping for breath. Tony was the last to succumb.

The three wild women in the kitchen were finally tamed by the superior strength of their aggressors.

In the living room, the three men who had been freed from the attentions of Lettice turned on Reggie and Jimmy. The guiding spirit of the community and his defence supremo fought bravely, but age and numbers were against them. Reggie heard

Jimmy murmur one single word in his ear. It was 'Dunkirk'. Then Jimmy passed out.

Reggie was on his own now. Further resistance was useless. He continued to resist, wildly, flailing arms and legs, yelling, screaming, a last berserk defiance amid the ruins of his dream.

And then he was falling. He couldn't see. Darkness was all around him.

He felt a sharp blow in the small of the back, then a stabbing pain in the ribs. A fierce buzzing filled his head, and he could hardly breathe.

He was falling again. He had thought that he was lying on the floor, and yet he was still falling.

He tumbled far beyond the floor.

He tumbled far beyond Botchley.

He toppled over the edge of the universe into the blackness between our universe and all other universes.

At last he fell no more.

He grew dimly aware that somebody was becoming conscious.

But who?

It must be he, if he was conscious of it.

He remembered dying.

Was this Hell?

He tried to move. The display team of the Chinese Acupuncture Service, the famous Red Needles, were practising massed acupuncture upon his body.

He tried to swallow, but his mouth seemed to be full of sour carpet.

He became aware of voices, groans, low conversation.

The yobbos! They'd come back.

A hand grabbed his wrist. He froze, waiting for further blows.

'He's dead,' said a voice, and with joyous relief he recognised it as Doc Morrissey's.

He opened his eyes.

'Buggered if I am,' he said. 'You won't get rid of me that easily.'

He managed to struggle agonisedly to his feet.

He looked round the room. Nobody had died. The whole

259

staff were there, battered, bruised, but alive. Their faces were hideously distorted by contusions and black eyes.

A strange overwhelming pungency filled the air, and the carpet was covered in a fine multi-coloured dust. Pictures lay slashed on the floor, cushions and chairs had belched forth their innards, and there were torn sheets of paper everywhere. The curtains were billowing into the room as the wind tore through the gaping holes in the french windows. Reggie passed out.

There followed a sombre week.

Every chair in all five houses had been smashed, every window broken, every drawer pulled out and upturned.

On his arrival home at five fifteen a.m. McBlane discovered that his herb and spice racks had been destroyed. He wept. Luckily for him there were no witnesses.

The spicy pungency was explained. So was the fine dust on the living room floor. The whole house was covered in rosemary, thyme, sweet basil, tarragon, mace, dill, oregano, cayenne pepper, allspice, crushed chillies, paprika, coriander, nutmeg, turmeric, ground bay leaves, meat tenderiser, sage, ginger, cinnamon, cardomon, saffron, fennel and parmesan cheese. So were the remnants of C.J.'s manuscript.

Reggie put a consolatory arm on C.J.'s shoulder. C.J. winced, and Reggie speedily removed the consolatory arm.

'It was no good,' said C.J.

It was a damned good first effort,' said Reggie.

Other comments included 'super', 'knock-out', 'top-hole yarn', 'I liked it, and I'm not an ant person' and 'the most interesting story about ants I've ever heard'.

'I realised that it was no good as I was reading it,' said C.J. 'I console myself with the thought that it's a long lane that has no turning.'

The police arrived at nine fifteen in the morning. They didn't believe Reggie's story of a private fight that had got out of hand, and departed in bad humour.

The doctor did believe Reggie's story. After the hysterical dysentery, he was prepared to believe anything.

Several people needed bandaging, splinting and strapping at

260

Botchley General Hospital. Slowly, with agonising delays, this was done.

As they tried to get comfortable in bed that Sunday night, Elizabeth asked Reggie why he had lied to the police.

'I don't want to be bothered with it any more,' he said. 'It's all over.'

And so it proved. The guests who returned after the weekend took one look at the devastation and fled.

The newspaper reports of yet another chaotic event at the jinxed community caused the cancellation of all remaining future bookings.

Reggie arranged with an estate agent to put all five houses up for sale, as soon as essential repairs had been effected. He borrowed money from his bank manager, against the sale of the houses. He hired an overwhelmed glazier who almost cried with joy when he saw the extent of the damage. The glazier had a glass eye.

Reggie offered his staff three months' wages in compensation. C.J., Tony and McBlane accepted. Tom and Doc Morrissey accepted one month's salary. The rest refused to take anything.

It was time for farewells.

'Bye bye,' said Reggie. 'Back to Godalming, eh?'

'Yes, the old house is still there,' said Mrs C.J.

They were standing at the front gate of Number Twenty-one on a lovely May morning.

'What'll you do?' said Elizabeth.

'I may see my brother about a job,' said C.J. 'There comes a moment in everybody's life when he has to swallow his pride.'

C.J.'s brother ran a pub called the Dissipated Kipper on the Hog's Back in Surrey. Reggie couldn't imagine C.J. working in a pub, but he supposed that beggars couldn't be choosers.

C.J. extended his hand.

'Well, this is it,' he said.

'Yes,' said Reggie. 'This is it.'

Mrs C.J.'s handshake was limp.

'Never outstay your doodah,' said C.J.

'Absolutely,' said Reggie.

*   *   *

'Well, this is it,' said Jimmy.

'Yes.'

'Never forget Perrins,' said Jimmy. 'O.K., final analysis, flop, crying shame. Brought me something, though. Biggest thing in my life. Lettice.'

He kissed Lettice on the mouth and clasped her hand affectionately.

'What'll you do?' asked Elizabeth.

'This and that,' said Jimmy.

'Especially that,' said Lettice.

'Saucy girl,' said Jimmy. 'No, start small business, private bus company, foreign parts, that sort of crack. No cock-up this time. Buses on up and up. Buses are coming back everywhere, Reggie. Chap I know, offer of backing. Nigel "Ginger" Carstairs. Top drawer. All right, eh, Lettice?'

'Absolutely.'

'Stout scout. Suppose you haven't any food, big sister? Odd egg, crust, that sort of caper. Bit of a cock-up on the ... no, suppose you wouldn't have. Hard times, eh? Well well, chin chin.'

Jimmy and Lettice clambered into the remains of Jimmy's old car. Reggie and Elizabeth pushed, and at the corner of Oslo Avenue and Bonn Close it burst into a parody of life.

Our last sight of them is of two beefy hairy arms, waving frantically.

One of the arms was Jimmy's. The other was Lettice's.

Our last sound of them is of the car back-firing noisily, as if it shared its owner's military nostalgia.

'It failed in the end,' said Doc Morrissey, 'but nobody can say you didn't have a go.'

'Not a bad epitaph,' said Reggie. 'Here lies Reginald Iolanthe Perrin. Nobody can say he didn't have a go. Doc, we'll miss you.'

'Me too, Reggie. And Perrins didn't fail me. The discovery of my unsuspected talent for psychology has done wonders for my self-esteem.'

'Where will you go?' said Elizabeth.

'There is a corner of Southall that will be for ever English.

And there, one day in the not too distant future, Professor Morrissey, that old fraud, will teach his last English lesson, and die not desperately discontent.'

'Ciaou City, Arizona.'

'Absolutely. Keep him in order, Joan.'

'I will. No sweat.'

'No need. I'm a reformed character. And I owe it to you, Reggie. O.K., it was a shambles, ultimately, but you've shown me where it's at. It's at maturity, Reggie. I'm into responsibility. I don't have unrealistic dreams any more. I'm going to buckle down to the hard grind of hard work. I'll be a millionaire in ten years.'

'Goodbye, Reggie. Goodbye, Elizabeth,' said David and Prue Harris-Jones.

'Sorry you called him Reggie?' said Reggie.

'No fear,' said David and Prue Harris-Jones.

'What'll you do?' said Reggie and Elizabeth.

'There are jobs for both of us in the old family firm in Haverfordwest,' said David and Prue Harris-Jones. 'Our wandering days are over.'

'We'll see you one day, though,' said Reggie and Elizabeth.

'Oh yes, we must,' said David and Prue Harris-Jones.

'Super,' said Reggie and Elizabeth and David and Prue Harris-Jones.

'Well, we've got a nice day for it,' said Tom.

'Bye bye, dad,' said Linda. 'Bye bye, mum. See you soon.'

'Bye bye,' said Adam and Jocasta.

'It's had such a good effect on them,' said Linda, getting into the car. 'It hasn't all been in vain.'

'Nothing is,' said Reggie.

'I shall take up the reins of estate agency once again,' said Tom. 'But I regret not one minute of the events that have transpired. Frankly, I was becoming a bit of a bore. Without you, Reggie, and not forgetting you, mother-in-law, I would have gone on and on, slowly but steadily ossifying, and I would have ended as pomposity personified.'

Tom held out his hand.

'A dream is over, Reggie, but because of that dream, reality will never be quite the same again,' he said.

'I'm so glad you won't end up as pomposity personified,' said Reggie.

'Come on, Tom,' said Linda.

'Coming, Squigglycrutch. I won't say goodbye properly, Reggie, mother-in-law, because we'll be seeing each other, we're family, and I don't like goodbyes. I'm not a goodbye person.'

'Oh good. Well, goodbye,' said Reggie.

'Goodbye,' said Elizabeth.

'I fail to see the point of protracted goodbyes,' said Tom. 'I like to say goodbye and get it over with. It may be a fault, but that's the way I am. Well, goodbye.'

'Goodbye.'

'Goodbye.'

'Goodbye.'

'Goodbye.'

'Goodbye.'

Reggie and Elizabeth dined alone that night. They sat at either end of the long table that had so recently been vibrant with gossip and pregnant with metaphysical speculation. Savage cuts disfigured the table top.

It was McBlane's last night. He served them with deep disdain four courses of superb foreign muck—borscht, sole dieppoise, osso buco milanese, and sachertorte. Large and rich though the meal was, it was also light and subtle, and they did full justice to it.

Afterwards they sat in silence, savouring this wonderful experience that had come to them in the midst of ruin. McBlane entered with the last of the sunflower brandy.

'Thank you for a superb dinner, McBlane,' said Elizabeth.

'Thank you,' said Reggie.

McBlane's lips parted. His teeth appeared. His cheeks creased. He was smiling.

'Will you join us in a glass of sunflower brandy?' said Reggie.

'Eeflecking gaud loupin puir dibollolicking aud frangschlibble doon the brizzing gullet, ye skelk,' said McBlane.

The summer blazed. The refrigeration broke down in a cold store in Wapping, and twenty thousand pork pies were condemned. A survey showed that Britain had dropped to nineteenth in the world survey league, behind Malawi and Spain. Vandals smashed three osprey's eggs on Loch Garten. A Liberian tanker collided with an Albanian freighter off Northumberland, pouring oil on untroubled waters. Thirteen hundred guillemots died.

Numbers Seventeen to Twenty-five, Oslo Avenue, Botchley were sold.

There was just enough left, when all the debts had been paid, to enable Reggie to buy a modest house outright, which was lucky, as no self-respecting building society would have touched him now, and all building societies are self-respecting.

They could go anywhere. The Cotswolds, the Lake District, Spain, the Dordogne, Tierra Del Fuego.

They bought a three-bedroomed semi-detached villa in Goffley.

The address was Number Thirty-eight, Leibnitz Drive.

IX

The Aftermath

On their first evening in their new home, they had a
bottle of wine. They sat in the living room, on hard chairs, for
all the armchairs had been ruined beyond repair. The only other
furniture in the surprisingly unspacious room was the old card
table from Number Seventeen. It was laid for the evening meal.
The dining table from Number Twenty-one, though not quite
ruined beyond repair, was too big for Number Thirty-eight,
Leibnitz Drive.

The floorboards were bare. The main windows afforded a
view over a garden that was at once neglected and tame. The
lawn was mottled with bare patches and studded with tufts of
rank grass. In the middle was a small area of concrete, and
on it stood a swing, swaying rustily in the midsummer zephyrs,
in squeaking memory of the children who lived there no
longer.

Around the lawn there were flower beds which appeared to
have been planted with earth. Nothing green disturbed their
virgin slumber. The evening sun was slowly sinking towards
the roofs of the houses in Kierkegaard Crescent.

They drank their wine slowly, savouring every drop. It might
be a long while before they could afford wine again.

'Supper ready?' enquired Reggie.

'It isn't much to write home about,' said Elizabeth.

'That's lucky,' said Reggie, 'because I don't intend to write
home about it, since this is home. What is it?'

'Shin of beef casserole.'

'Shin of beef casserole. Yum yum.'

They ate with hearty relish, washing it down gently with the
wine. All too soon the last of the food and wine was gone.
Reggie sighed.

266

'Never mind, darling,' said Elizabeth. 'Something will turn up.'

Nothing turned up the next day.

Reggie went to the public library and scoured the newspapers for jobs. Elizabeth explored Goffley High Street, combing the shops for bargains. They met in the Bald Faced Stag, and allowed themselves one half of bitter each.

The pub was suffused with the aura of impending sausages.

'You managed to get something for supper, did you?' said Reggie.

'We're having goujons de coley.'

'Goujons de coley. Yum yum.'

Next day Reggie went to the public library and scoured the newspapers for jobs. Elizabeth explored Goffley High Street, combing the shops for bargains. They met in the Bald Faced Stag, and allowed themselves one half of bitter each. The pub throbbed with the threat of packet curry.

'How did you get on?' said Elizabeth.

'Absolutely splendidly,' said Reggie.

'Oh good.'

'Yes,' continued Reggie. 'The papers were full of adverts for people like me. "Amazing opening for washed-up executive. Geriatric Electronics requires unemployed post-menopausal loonie. Previous sackings an advantage. Bonuses for mock suicides. The successful candidate will have frayed trouser bottoms, anxious eyes and at least three major career cock-ups." '

Elizabeth patted his hand.

'Never mind,' she said. 'Something will turn up.'

That evening, black pudding ragout turned up.

'Black pudding ragout. Yum yum,' said Reggie, as Elizabeth dolloped lashings of the steaming dark mess on to his plate. Half way through the meal, Reggie let out a tremendous sigh.

'Is it that bad?' said Elizabeth.

'It isn't the food,' said Reggie. 'It's me.'

'Darling!'

'I've brought you such trouble.'

'Don't be silly.'

Elizabeth clasped his hand firmly across the card table.

'I regret nothing,' she said.

Reggie smiled faintly.

'The Edith Piaf of Goffley,' he said.

'Please don't be depressed, darling,' said Elizabeth. 'I've said it before . . .'

'I'll say it as well this time,' said Reggie. 'Maybe it'll help.'

'Something will turn up,' they said in unison.

Next day it did.

A letter.

'Listen to this, darling,' said Reggie. 'It's from the Personnel Manager of Amalgamated Aerosols. "Dear Mr Perrin. No doubt you have heard of us." No. "As you probably know, we are one of the fastest growing companies in the highly profitable growth industry of aerosols. We produce both the can and the contents." Wow! "We are known equally for industrial chemicals, insecticides, furniture polishes and hair lacquers, while our air fresheners and deodorants are experiencing the sweet smell of success." Ha ha! "As you can see, we are also not without a sense of humour." No! "We feel that the inspiration behind Grot and Perrins must have ideas to offer the world of aerosols." They must be mad. "Perhaps you would care to telephone my secretary to fix an appointment. Yours sincerely, James A. Fennel, Personnel Manager." I wonder how they heard of me.'

'They did. That's what matters,' said Elizabeth.

'Yes, but . . . aerosols! I'll phone them at eleven. I mustn't sound too eager.'

Father Time, the bearded tease, moved slowly towards that hour.

'My name's Perrin,' he told Mr Fennel's secretary.

'Ah. Yes. When would it be convenient for you to come and see Mr Fennel, Mr Perrin?' she asked, in a brisk but sexy voice.

'Let me see . . . just having a look through my diary . . . yes. Tuesday or Wednesday afternoons would suit me best, as late in the afternoon as possible, especially if it's the Wednesday.'

'Thursday week at nine thirty.'

'Splendid.'

At last the fateful Thursday dawned.

Elizabeth brushed Reggie's suit with the brush which she had bought for that very purpose the previous day at Timothy White's.

'Thank you, darling,' he said.

She handed him his umbrella.

'Thank you, darling,' he said.

He kissed her goodbye.

'Good luck, darling,' she said.

The hazy blue sky was teeming with insect life, and swallows and swifts darted joyously over Reggie's head as he walked down Leibnitz Drive. He turned right into Bertrand Russell Rise, then left into Schopenhauer Grove. This led him on to the main road which wound uphill past Goffley Station. He struggled up the hill, feeling his age. The day was warm, still, sticky. The haze was thickening, and Reggie felt that it might rain.

He followed the crowds along the subway to platform three. A fast train roared above their heads, frighteningly close. Nobody turned a receding hair.

Would he soon be doing this day after day, he wondered.

Did he want to do this day after day, he wondered.

What could he do, day after day, if he didn't do this, day after day, he wondered.

Would he wonder the same thing, day after day, he wondered.

Opposite him, on platform four, there was a poster advertising the French railways. The gleaming train was gliding past the blue sea of the Cote D'Azur like a sleek snake. An observation car bulged on the snake's back like an undigested rat.

The eight eleven wasn't like a sleek snake. It was like a grubby blue worm with a yellow clown's face. It was also fourteen minutes late.

Do you, Reginald Iolanthe Perrin, take British Rail, Southern Region, to be your awful dreaded life, for better for worse, for fuller for dirtier, in lateness and in cancellation, till retirement or phased redundancy do you part?

I do.

I have to.

Place the ring of dirt around your collar. It will be there every day.

The train arrived at Victoria twenty-two minutes late. The

269

loudspeaker announcement blamed passengers joining the train and alighting.

Reggie arrived at Amalgamated Aerosols at twenty-eight minutes past nine. It was a gleaming affair of glass and Portland stone. Two window cleaners were busy on cradles above the main entrance.

Reggie entered the foyer. It was all rubber plants and soft music. The receptionist had a soft, musical, rubbery voice. She told Reggie to go to the third floor, where Mr Fennel's secretary would meet the lift. Mr Fennel's secretary was twenty years older than her telephone voice, and no slouch where meeting lifts was concerned. She led Reggie along a central corridor. The walls were of glass from four foot upwards, affording a view of an open-plan rabbit warren where people worked and idled in full view of each other and everyone else

Mr Fennel's office was right at the end of the corridor. He stood up and smiled broadly at Reggie, extending a welcoming hand. He was almost tall, with receding fair hair and an anxious air. He was fifteen years older than his secretary's voice.

'Bonjour,' he said. 'Bienvenu à Londres.'

'Bonjour,' said Reggie, surprised.

'Asseyez-vous,' said Mr Fennel.

'Merci beaucoup,' said Reggie, feeling capable of playing this kind of executive game until the vaches came home.

Outside, beyond the wall-to-wall glass, a splendid, delicately elegant Wren church was dwarfed by massively inelegant prestige office developments.

'Est-ce que que vous fumez?' said Mr Fennel in execrable rather than executive French, holding out a silver cigarette case initialled J.A.F., and filled with Marlboros.

'Non, merci,' said Reggie.

'Seulement les gauloises, n'est-ce pas?' asked Mr Fennel.

'Non. Je ne fume pas,' said Reggie.

Mr Fennel lit a cigarette.

'Bon,' he said 'Maintentant. A les affaires. Le temps et les courants de la mer attendent pour personne.'

'I don't understand. Je ne comprends pas,' said Reggie.

'Time and tide wait for . . . you're English?'

'Yes.'

'Are you sure?'

'There's no possible doubt about it.'

'You aren't Monsieur Duvavier?'

'No.'

'Oh hell. Well who are you?'

'Reginald Perrin.'

'Oh hell.'

'Sorry.'

'Not your fault. Is it Friday?'

'No. Thursday.'

'Damn! I've got tomorrow's files. Why the hell did you answer in French?'

'I thought it was some kind of executive game.'

Mr Fennel laughed.

As soon as Reggie joined in, Mr Fennel's laughter died abruptly.

'Now, what exactly did you want to see me about?' said Mr Fennel.

'You wanted to see me.'

'What? Oh. Yes. Ah. Bit stymied without my files. Millie'll be back in a moment. I'm a bit lost here. We were on the second floor. Now, what do I want to see you about?'

'I don't know. I presumed from your letter you were planning to offer me a job.'

Mr Fennel looked out of the window, as if he expected a passing sky-writer to remind him. London shimmered in darkening haze.

'You must be the bod F.J. wants to see,' said Mr Fennel at last.

'F.J.?'

'Our managing director.'

'Your managing director's called F.J.?'

'Yes. Why?'

'Nothing.'

'Perrin! Grot?'

'Yes.'

'You *are* the bod F.J. wants to see. Why didn't you tell me?'

271

'I didn't know I was the bod F.J. wanted to see.'

Reggie tried to keep the irritation out of his voice. Mr Fennel had three pens in his breast pocket. Reggie didn't like men who had three pens in their breast pocket and he didn't much care for being called a bod.

'F.J. seems to think you're the kind of bod we want,' said Mr Fennel.

'Oh good,' said Reggie. 'I'd certainly like to work in a high-growth, rapid-yield, multi-facet industry like aerosols.'

'Save that guff for F.J.,' said Mr Fennel.

'Come!' called F.J.

Reggie entered F.J.'s office. It was huge, and had large picture windows. The glass was tinted brown.

F.J. advanced to meet him.

'Perrin!' he said. 'Welcome!'

F.J. pumped his hand vigorously.

'I believe you know my brother C.,' he said.

Reggie felt his head swimming.

'So you *are* C.J.'s brother,' he said. 'I did wonder. I . . . er . . . didn't know there was a third brother.'

F.J. sat down behind his vast desk. Its tinted-glass top matched the windows.

He looked rather like C.J., but a bit slighter. More tidy and self-contained.

'Oh yes,' he said. 'I didn't get where I am today without being C.J.'s brother.'

'Oh my God,' said Reggie. 'I mean . . . you say that too.'

F.J. laughed heartily.

'No,' he said. 'That was my little joke.'

'Oh. Thank God,' said Reggie.

'I'm very different from C.,' said F.J.

'Oh. Thank God,' said Reggie.

'Do sit down,' said F.J., indicating a low white leather chair shaped like a coracle.

Reggie sat down. The chair blew a raspberry.

F.J. roared.

'Good gimmick, eh?' he said. 'C. copied it. Didn't carry it through, though. My brother's too soft.'

272

'Soft?'

'All mouth and no trousers. You never let his manner fool you, I hope?'

'No! What? I should say not.'

'You weren't frightened of him?'

'Frightened of C.J.? Huh. Pull the other one.'

'Good. Now I am hard. Cigar?'

'Thank you.'

Reggie reached forward, but the chair was too far from the desk. He had to stand. He took a huge cigar from the large box on F.J.'s desk, and sat down.

The chair blew a raspberry.

F.J. laughed.

'Light?'

Reggie thrust himself out of the chair again, held his cigar to the flame offered by F.J., and sat down again.

The chair blew a raspberry.

F.J. laughed.

'Thoroughly discomfited, the hopeful employee quakes,' he said.

'Absolutely,' said Reggie.

'Do you fancy working here?' said F.J.

'I certainly do,' said Reggie. 'I'd like to work in a high-growth, rapid-yield, multi-facet industry like aerosols.'

'Save that guff for Fennel,' said F.J. 'He's the one who does the hiring and firing.'

'I've seen Fennel,' said Reggie.

'You've seen Fennel?'

'Yes.'

'Ah!'

F.J. leant forward and glared at Reggie through slitted eyes.

'Nozzles?' he said.

'Pardon?'

'Nozzles. Views on. Think on your feet.'

'Well, I...er...they're those things you press on aerosol cans, but you can't see the arrow properly, so you point it the wrong way and cover yourself with air freshener.'

'I like a man who can think on his feet,' said F.J.

He swivelled slowly round in his chair.

'Our laboratories in Boreham Wood are on the verge of a nozzle breakthrough that'll do for the aerosol canister what the apple did for gravity,' he said 'Whichever way you point the canister, the spray will always emerge pointing away from you.'

'That's fantastic.'

'Is it not?'

Large drops of rain began to spatter against the windows.

'You and your good lady must come to Leatherhead and have dinner one day, Perrin,' said F.J.

'Thank you, F.J.'

'My good lady cooks an amazing lobster thermostat.'

'Oh. Really? That sounds ... amazing.'

'You have to be very careful at what temperature you serve it. Hence the name.'

'Really?'

'No.'

'What?'

'There's no such thing as lobster thermostat. It's lobster thermidor.'

Reggie began to sweat.

'I know,' he said.

'Then why the hell didn't you say so?'

'Well, I ...'

'You thought I was a pretentious *nouveau riche* ignoramus who'd got it wrong.'

'Well, F.J., I ... er ...'

'And fell headlong into my executive trap.'

'I certainly did, F.J.'

'Huh huh huh.'

'Absolutely.'

'You're not just another yes man, are you?'

'No, F.J.'

The rain began in earnest. It was quite dark outside and the lights in all the tower blocks shone brightly.

'May I ask you a question, F.J.?' asked Reggie.

F.J. regarded him sadly.

'Why have I got these flaps at either side of my face?' he asked. 'To help me fly?'

'No, F.J.'

'Those are my ears, Perrin.'

'They certainly are, F.J.'

'They're for listening. So, if you have a question, ask it. Don't waste time asking if you can ask it.'

'Sorry, F.J. The question is, F.J., did C.J. recommend me to you?'

'Yes.'

'Good gr . . . oh good.'

F.J. lifted one of his phones.

'Get Fennel please, Ingeborg,' he said.

He put the phone down. Almost immediately it barked. He lifted it.

'Fennel?' he said. 'I have your chap Perrin here . . . You thought he was *my* chap? No, no. He's your chap, I assure you. What do you think of him? . . . Well, it's not up to me . . . Well, I happen to believe he has a flair for unusual invention and is just the man for us, but that's irrelevant . . . You agree? Well, I hope for your sake you're right. It's your decision, Fennel.'

F.J. replaced his telephone on its cradle lovingly.

'You start on Monday fortnight,' he said. 'You'll be working in our air freshener and deodorant division.'

The fine weather returned, and the days passed slowly.

Elizabeth took a secretarial job with a firm of solicitors in Goffley, to start the week after Reggie.

Every morning they called for a drink at the Bald Faced Stag. Often they'd accompany it with a ham sandwich or a portion of gala pie with pickle.

They visited the Goffley Carpet Centre and stared in bewilderment at rolls of hideously patterned material. Eventually they settled on a carpet for the living room. The price was astronomical.

They went for walks among the quiet yet subtly varied streets around their home. Often they walked down Sartre Rise and Wittgenstein View to the golf course. Between Wittgenstein View and Nietsche Grove an old windmill survived from the days when all this had been open farmland. It had no sails. It was called John Stuart Mill, in memory of John Stuart, a Goffley landowner of bygone days. It was sad to look at the windmill and dream of the days when these gentle hills had been open fields.

One afternoon, as they crossed the golf course on footpath number seventy-eight, which followed the Piffley Brook to East Franton, the wife of a quantity surveyor hooked her seventh at the short twelfth, and the ball struck Reggie on the backside before she had remembered what you were supposed to shout to warn people.

But for the most part they were quiet times.

The first day of employment began.

Elizabeth brushed Reggie's suit, removing a minuscule crumb of toast from the lumbar region in the process.

She handed him his new briefcase, engraved with his initials 'R.I.P.'.

'Thank you, darling,' he said.

She handed him his umbrella.

'Thank you, darling,' he said.

She kissed him goodbye.

'Thank you, darling,' he said.

'Have a good day at the office,' she said.

'I won't,' he said.

Was this pessimism premature? Only time would tell.

Reggie walked down Leibnitz Drive, turned right into Bertrand Russell Rise, then left into Schopenhauer Grove. High in the summer sky a commuting heron flapped lazily towards the Surrey ponds. Reggie walked up the punishing slope to Goffley Station, showed his new season ticket, and stood on platform three, opposite the poster for the French railways.

This is the life for you, he told himself. This is the life that you are destined to lead. Your dreams have been out of place. They have caused great suffering and chaos.

Now you have a job, a new challenge, a new adventure. You must be thankful.

He told himself.

But not too thankful. You mustn't be craven or afraid. You're an old hand, and you mustn't allow yourself to be used as a doormat by anybody. Life is too short.

He told himself.

The train reached Victoria twenty-three minutes late. The loudspeaker announcement blamed chain reaction to the effects of a landslip at Angmering. He reached the office fourteen minutes late, and willed himself not to hurry as he approached the gleaming edifice of glass and Portland stone.

It was called Aerosol House. You will be impressed, it said.

Will I hell, replied Reggie's nonchalant walk.

He entered the foyer. You will feel dwarfed by our air of impersonal affluence, it said.

Cobblers, said Reggie's demeanour as he walked across the slippery marble floor from the sliding doors to the reception desk.

He took it at a steady pace, moving with determined though not over-stated authority.

'Perrin (air fresheners and deodorants)' he announced, employing oral brackets with a dexterity born of long practice.

'I'm not sure if he's in,' said the receptionist.

'No, I am he,' said Reggie. 'I am Perrin (air fresheners and deodorants). I start work here today, and I wondered where my office was.'

The receptionist checked her list. He wasn't on it.

'What exactly is your job?' said the receptionist.

Oh my God.

'I don't know.'

'You don't know?'

'No.'

'You're working here and you don't know what your job is.'

'Yes.'

'Oh.'

She checked her special instructions. He wasn't on them. She telephoned Mr Fennel. He was on holiday. It took the combined efforts of Mr Cannon of Admin and Mr Stork of Communications to locate his office.

Reggie sat on a black leather settee, surrounded by rubber plants, fighting against feelings of guilt and insignificance. It's not your fault, he told himself. You've done your bit, in that

277

you've arrived successfully. It's Amalgamated Aerosols that should feel guilty.

And so he adopted a defiant, long-suffering look, until he realised that it might be interpreted as over-compensation for insecurity. And it was he who had talked of the dangers of excessive self-consciousness. Had he learned nothing?

At last his office was located. It was two one seven, on the second floor. Mr Cannon escorted him there.

'I'm sorry about this,' he said. 'There's been a big shift around, and Cakebread hasn't put the P139 through.'

They went up in the lift, and walked along a corridor lined with offices. They weren't open plan, and their doors bore names and titles. Perhaps he was about to find out what his job was.

No such luck. The legend on his door said simply 'Reginald I. Perrin'.

The windows overlooked the Wren church. The desk was of moderate size. There were green filing cabinets, and two phones, one red and one green. On top of a cupboard stood a mug and a bent wire coathanger. There was a communicating door to the offices on either side. The paint on the radiator was peeling, and the brown carpet was laid in strips that didn't quite meet.

'All right?' said Mr Cannon.

'Fine.'

'Jolly good,' said Mr Cannon. 'I'll leave you to your own devices, then.'

He was as good as his word.

But what are my own devices, thought Reggie.

He opened and shut three empty drawers.

There was a knock on the westerly connecting door.

'Come in,' he said.

A pert, self-confident young red-head entered.

'Mr Perrin?' she said.

'Yes.'

'I'm your secretary. I'm Iris Hoddle.'

They shook hands. Her smile was friendly.

'Coffee?' she said.

'Please.'

278

She returned shortly with a beverage that approximated vaguely to that description. Reggie explained the difficulty that he had experienced in finding his office.

'Mr Cakebread didn't put through the P139,' she said. 'This was Mr Main-Thompson's office, but he's gone to Canisters. There's been a big shift around. He's taken the in and out trays. He shouldn't have, they're like gold, but that's Mr Main-Thompson for you. Anyway, I've put through an F1765, so fingers crossed.'

'Thanks.'

He smiled at Iris Hoddle. She smiled back.

'They haven't exactly told me what you do,' she said.

'They haven't exactly told me what I do either.'

Iris Hoddle laughed.

'That figures,' she said. 'It's Fred Karno's Army, this place. Anyway, C.J.'d like to see you at ten thirty.'

Reggie spilt his coffee down his crutch, and stood up hurriedly. The hot liquid was burning his private parts.

'Damn!' he exclaimed.

He pulled his trousers and pants away from his skin. It was not an elegant way to stand before one's secretary on one's first morning.

'C.J.?' he said.

'Do you know him?' said Iris Hoddle.

'I have run into him,' said Reggie.

He's just started here too,' said Iris Hoddle. 'He's Head of the Department.'

'He's my boss?'

'Yes.'

C.J. entered Reggie's office through the easterly connecting door. He didn't knock.

'Morning, Reggie,' he said. His eyes flickered briefly over Iris. 'Morning, Iris.'

He held out his hand to Reggie. Reggie shook it.

'I'm next door,' he said. 'We can use the connecting door.'

'Ah! Splendid,' said Reggie.

He led Reggie into his office. It was twice the size of Reggie's and three times as plush. Reggie sat down gingerly. The chair didn't blow a raspberry. C.J. laughed.

'I leave all that to F.,' he said. 'These childish tricks seem to amuse him. Well, Reggie, we meet again.'

'We certainly do, C.J.'

'Adjoining offices, eh, Reggie?'

'Absolutely, C.J.'

'We can be in and out like lamb's tails.'

'Yes, C.J.'

'*But*, Reggie, not in each other's pockets.'

'Definitely not, C.J.'

'Neither Mrs C.J. nor I has ever believed in being in anybody's pockets.'

'A wise attitude, C.J.'

'We're settled again in Godalming.'

'Splendid, C.J.'

'It is not splendid, Reggie.'

'Sorry, C.J. One small question about my work, C.J.'

'I'm all ears, Reggie.'

'What is it?'

C.J. laughed.

'They didn't tell you?'

'No.'

'That figures. This is Fred Karno's Army. You're my right hand, Reggie.'

'I am?'

'You're my think tank. Cigar?'

'Thank you, C.J.'

Reggie took a large cigar. C.J. proffered his lighter and Reggie held his cigar to the tiny flame.

'I've stuck my neck out over you, Reggie. "F.," I said, "you've always said that if things go wrong there's a place for me at Aerosal House." "There certainly is, C.," he said. "I've preferred to make my own way," I said, "but I'd like a job now, F., on one condition." "What condition's that, C.?" he enquired. "I want Reggie Perrin as my number two," I replied.'

'Thank you, C.J.'

C.J. smiled.

'I'm your boss again, Reggie.'

'Yes, C.J.'

'Not that that's why I've asked for you.'

'No, C.J.'

'It's not in my nature to gloat.'

'I should think not, C.J.'

'I've asked for you because you're an ideas man.'

'Thank you, C.J.'

C.J. leant forward and glared at Reggie.

'Do you remember that exotic ices project at Sunshine Desserts, Reggie?' he said.

'How could I ever forget it?'

'I like your attitude, Reggie.'

C.J. lifted his phone.

'Jenny?' he said. 'C.J. on red. Send Muscroft and Rosewall in.'

C.J. put his phone down.

'You . . . er . . . want me to do the same for aerosols?' said Reggie.

'You're a shrewd one,' said C.J. 'The world of air fresheners is in the doldrums, Reggie. The horizons of the small men here are limited. Pine, lavender, heather. Slavish imitation of the big boys.'

'You want new smells, C.J. Raspberry, strawberry and lychee.'

'Exactly, Reggie. I like your thinking.'

There was a knock.

'Come!' said C.J.

Two tall men wearing keen suits and enthusiastic shoes hurled themselves dynamically into the plush executive womb. They were introduced as Muscroft and Rosewall.

'You take your instructions from Perrin,' said C.J.

'Marvellous,' said Muscroft.

'Terrific,' said Rosewall.

'We're going for exotic air fresheners,' said C.J. 'The world is our oyster. The spices of the orient, and the wild flowers of the Andes are your playthings. Between us we shall transform a mundane visit to the toilet into a sensual wonderland. This is a biggie.'

'Marvellous,' said Muscroft.

'Terrific,' said Rosewall.

'Every dog has its day,' said C.J.

'It certainly does,' said Muscroft, Rosewell and Reggie.

When Reggie's two assistants had left the room, C.J. looked at Reggie earnestly. He lowered his voice.

'I don't want any funny business, Reggie,' he said.

'Absolutely not, C.J.'

'You've been on a switchback of fate, Reggie. You were discontented. You believed that there is a greener hill far away with grass on the other side. You set off in search of it. You discovered that there is no greener hill far away with grass on the other side.'

'There certainly isn't, C.J.'

'I'm glad to hear you say it. You've returned, Reggie, a better and a wiser man, and that's an order.'

'Yes, C.J.'

'I want you to familiarise yourself with the current state of play, odour-wise. There's a smelling in Boreham Wood tomorrow.'

'A smelling in Boreham Wood!'

'I like your attitude, Reggie. Edrich from Nozzles can take you in his car.'

C.J. stood up, and Reggie was not tardy in following his example.

C.J. held out his hand. Reggie clasped it.

'I hope we've learnt something about human relations amidst all the twists and turns of our entangled fates Reggie,' he said.

'I hope so, C.J.,' said Reggie.

Reggie walked to the connecting door, and opened it.

'Reggie?' said C.J.

'Yes, C.J.?'

'We aren't one of those dreadful firms that would sack a man just because he always turns up fourteen minutes late. Goodbye, Reggie.'

He caught the six twelve home. It was nineteen minutes late, but he didn't let it upset him, because he was an older and a wiser man.

He walked down Schopenhauer Grove, turned right into Bertrand Russell Rise, then left into Leibnitz Drive. He felt exhausted, but he didn't let it depress him. He told Elizabeth that he had had a good day at the office. He relished his lamb cutlets and apple charlotte. He slept the troubled sleep of the exhausted. He ate a hearty breakfast. He walked down Leibnitz Drive, turned right into Bertrand Russell Rise, then left into Schopenhauer Grove.

He told himself that he was enjoying this routine, because he was an older and a wiser man. As he laboured up the punishing final straight to Goffley Station he consoled himself with the thought that, like life, it would be downhill in the evening.

Mind over matter, he told himself. All you have to do is convince yourself that your hobbies are tedium and exhaustion, and that decay and decline are the most exciting processes in the world.

On the spine-crunching, vein-throbbing, armpit-smelling journey to Victoria, he tried to inject a sense of mission into his work.

'Roll on deodorants,' he said.

'I beg your pardon?' said the man opposite him.

'Sorry,' said Reggie. 'I didn't mean it to come out loud. That's what people must have said in the bad old pre-aerosol days. "Roll on deodorants." Sorry.'

He began to sweat.

Careful. Mustn't arrive at the smelling smelling.

Oh God.

Edrich from Nozzles drove him to the smelling at Boreham Wood. The laboratory was an undistinguished two-storey building at the back end of a large industrial estate. Edrich led him to a room which was like a doctor's waiting room, bare with rows of hard chairs round the walls.

There were five doors in one wall. Each door had a small window, barred with a thick grille. Beyond the doors were the smell-proof booths. Reggie felt tired and crumpled. He had a thundery headache coming on.

Also present were Muscroft and Rosewall from Air Fresheners and Deodorants, Lee from Furniture Polishes and Hair Lacquers, Gryce from Communications, Price-Hetherington from Industrial Chemicals, Coggin from Admin, Taylor from

283

Transport, Holmes and Wensley from the lab, Miss Allardyce from the typing pool, Miss Hanwell from Packing, and representatives of the National Smell Research Council and the Campaign for Real Aerosols.

Ten smells were to be tested, two in each booth. They were each handed ten cards numbered one to ten. They had to mark each smell, out of ten, for strength, pleasantness, originality and commercial appeal. They also had to say what the smell reminded them of, and suggest a brand name for it.

Everyone filled in their cards most assiduously.

'Marvellous, isn't it?' said Muscroft.

'Terrific,' said Rosewall.

'Fascinating,' said Reggie. 'A pretty stodgy range of smells, though. I'm looking for something that packs far more wow for our exotic range.'

'Marvellous,' said Muscroft.

'Terrific,' said Rosewall.

C.J. popped in just before lunch.

'Well, Reggie, which way's the wind blowing?' he asked.

'I came, I smelt, I conquered,' said Reggie.

'I like your attitude,' said C.J.

On his way home Reggie began to regret his actions.

Why had he done it? What was the use?

Out here in the open air, walking down Schopenhauer Grove, what had seemed an amazingly apt gesture in the claustrophobic booth in Boreham Wood seemed utterly stupid. I'm a lucky man, he told himself as he turned right into Bertrand Russell Rise. I have a lovely wife and two lovely children, even if one of them has married a bearded prig and the other has disappeared into the huge vagina of the pornographic film industry. There are worse things in life than bearded prigs and pornographic film industries, he told himself as he turned left into Leibnitz Drive.

'Did you have a good day at the office?' Elizabeth asked.

'Very good,' he said.

He enjoyed his lemon sole meuniere and rhubarb crumble. He slept the troubled sleep of a condemned man. He ate a hearty breakfast.

Elizabeth handed him his brand new briefcase, engraved with his initials 'R.I.P.'.

'Thank you, darling,' he said.

She handed him his umbrella.

'Thank you, darling,' he said.

She kissed him goodbye.

'Thank you, darling,' he said.

'Have a good day at the office,' she said.

'I will,' he said.

Why did you do it, he asked himself as he walked down Leibnitz Drive.

You're a lucky man, he told himself as he turned right into Bertrand Russell Rise. You live in a peaceful country.

You're free to walk through pleasant residential streets, he told himself, as he turned left into Schopenhauer Grove.

You're walking up the hill to Goffley Station. Trains have been invented. You're not ill. You have a roof over your head, clothes on your back and food in your belly. It isn't raining. Your credit rating will improve with time. Here comes the train. It's only twenty minutes late. You have a seat. Your newspaper is not a lackey of the government. You earn a good salary. You're reasonably personable and can make friends without extreme difficulty. Iris Hoddle is pleasant and helpful. Muscroft and Rosewall are marvellous, terrific people. You're happy.

Why did you do it?

The wheels were saying, 'You can still get away with it. All is not lost.'

He believed the wheels, because he was an older and wiser man.

'Something rather extraordinary seems to have happened at the smelling,' said C.J.

'Really? How extraordinary,' said Reggie.

'Normally nothing extraordinary happens at them,' said C.J. 'But yesterday it did. Cigar?'

Reggie took a cigar.

C.J. handed him the lighter.

Reggie knew that C.J. was looking to see if his hand was shaking.

He fought hard to keep it steady. At last the cigar was lit.

'What sort of extraordinary thing, C.J.?' he asked.

'The computer has processed the results of the smelling,' said C.J.

'Ah!'

'Exactly. "Ah!", as you so rightly say. This is what smell number one reminded its smellers of, Reggie. Mountains, five people. Snow, three people. Fresh water, two people. Larch forests, two people. Scotland, one person. Camping, one person. Bolivian unicyclist's jockstrap, one person.'

'Good lord, C.J. That is extraordinary,' said Reggie.

'Smell number two,' said C.J. 'Herbs, eight people. One person each for rockery, lavender, thyme, marjoram, spice factory, heather and Bolivian unicyclist's jockstrap.'

'This is astonishing, C.J.,' said Reggie.

C.J. picked up the sheet of paper from which he had been reading, and waved it violently at Reggie.

'Smell number three,' he said. 'Roses, fourteen people. Bolivian unicyclist's jockstrap, one person.'

'I can hardly credit it,' said Reggie.

'The same sorry story occurs with regard to all ten smells, Reggie.'

'Oh dear, oh dear.'

'I didn't get where I am today by having everything smelling of Bolivian unicyclists' jockstraps, Reggie.'

'I can believe it, C.J.'

C.J. gave Reggie a long hard look.

'Can you suggest any explanation, Reggie,' he said.

'I certainly can, C.J.'

'Ah!'

'A fault in the computer.'

'It seems a strange fault for a computer, Reggie. It doesn't have an electronic ring about it.'

'I grant you that, C.J.'

'Do you have any other suggestions, Reggie?'

Reggie returned C.J.'s gaze levelly.

'It looks as if somebody's playing silly buggers,' he said.

'It looks that way to me too,' said C.J. 'Who could it be, do you think?'

'I've no idea, C.J.'

A shaft of sunlight broke through the morning cloud and lit up the narrow steeple of the Wren church.

'I don't like it,' said C.J. 'Neither Mrs C.J. nor I has ever played silly buggers.'

'Perish the thought, C.J.'

'I intend to find out, Reggie. There will be an investigation.'

'An excellent idea, C.J.'

'Who do you think will head that investigation?'

'I don't know, C.J.'

'I do, Reggie.'

'Who, C.J.?'

'You, Reggie.'

'Me, C.J.?'

'You, Reggie. Goodbye.'

Reggie walked slowly towards his connecting door.

'Be thorough, Reggie,' said C.J. 'Leave no worm unturned.'

'I'll get to the bottom of it, C.J.,' said Reggie.

'I like your attitude,' said C.J.

Reggie entered his mean little office and sank into his chair. Why did you do it, Reggie?

C.J. knows. C.J. knows that I know that he knows. I'm trapped.

I can still get away with it.

I don't want to get away with it.

He lifted the red phone.

'Perrin on red,' he said. 'Come in, Miss Hoddle, please.'

His heart began to thump.

His pulse began to race.

His ears began to buzz.

Damn it, he would not lie and evade the issue any more.

Miss Hoddle entered. He smiled at her.

'Sit down, Miss Kettle,' he said.

'Hoddle,' she said.

'I thought I'd call you Kettle for a change.'

Reggie!

'Take a saucepan, Miss Hoddle.'

Letter!

'Saucepan, Mr Perrin?'

287

'I meant letter, Miss Kettle.'

'Hoddle.'

I seem to be calling things by the names of household utensils. It's out of the frying pan into the colander.

Not colander. Fire.

Oh what the hell. May as well be hung for a sheep as a baking tin.

Miss Hoddle's looking at you, wondering. She's worried. She's a nice girl, and you're upsetting her.

Get it over with.

'To all present at the smelling yesterday,' he began. 'At the smelling yesterday somebody played silly buggers, and wrote that every single air freshener smelt of Bolivian unicyclists' jockstraps.'

Miss Hoddle stared at·him in astonishment.

'That somebody was me,' he continued. 'I did it, and I'm not ashamed. I want you all to know why I did it. I did it because I believe that the whole thing is absolutely fish slice. Not only that. It is also totally and utterly egg whisk.'

Silence filled the little office. Reggie smiled reassuringly at Iris Hoddle.

'Find out the times of trains to the Dorset coast. would you, please?' he said.